M.R. Mackenzie was born and live
at Glasgow University and has an
Studies.

In addition to writing, he works as a Blu-ray/DVD producer and has overseen releases of films by a number of acclaimed directors, among them Dario Argento, Joe Dante, Hideo Nakata and Jacques Tourneur. Writing as Michael Mackenzie, he has contributed chapters to books on cult cinema and regularly provides video essays and liner notes for new releases of celebrated films. He used to work in a library, before leaving to spend more time with books.

In 2019, his first novel, *In the Silence*, was shortlisted for the Bloody Scotland Scottish Crime Debut of the Year and longlisted for the McIlvanney Prize. His third novel, *The Library Murders*, was featured in Crime Time's Best of the Year 2020 list.

Praise for M.R. Mackenzie

'Brings a fresh new voice to the field of Tartan Noir.'
JAMES OSWALD

'Writes with precision and passion.' CARO RAMSAY

'Splendidly written stuff.' BARRY FORSHAW, *CRIME TIME*

'An immersive slow burn of a tale, peppered with
disquieting fire-crackers of revelation.' MORGAN CRY

'Mackenzie has come up with something that defies easy
definition and is truly original.'
PAUL BURKE, *NB MAGAZINE*

'Up there with the best contemporary authors working today.'
DAVID B. LYONS

Also by M.R. Mackenzie

The Anna Scavolini series
In the Silence
Cruel Summer
The Shadow Men
Women Who Kill

Other novels
The Library Murders
Bury Your Secrets

Box sets
The Anna Scavolini Mysteries – Volume One

M.R. MACKENZIE

Bury Your Secrets

MAD**HOUSE**

Copyright © 2022 M.R. Mackenzie

All rights reserved. No part of this book may be reproduced in any form or by any electronic or mechanical means, including information storage and retrieval systems, without written permission from the author, except in the case of a reviewer, who may quote brief passages embodied in critical articles or in a review.

This book is a work of fiction. Names, characters, places and incidents are either the product of the author's imagination or are used fictionally. Any resemblance to actual persons, living or dead, or to actual events or locales, is entirely coincidental.

Cover design by
Tim Barber / Dissect Designs

Typeset in 11pt Minion Pro

First published in 2022 by Mad House

ISBN: 978-1-9160948-5-7

Text version 1.02

www.mrmackenzieauthor.com
facebook.com/MRMackenzieAuthor
@landofwhimsy

He that has eyes to see and ears to hear may convince himself that no mortal can keep a secret. If his lips are silent, he chatters with his fingertips; betrayal oozes out of him at every pore.

           Sigmund Freud

The twin beams of car headlights glanced between the trunks of densely packed pine trees, their harsh glare causing the freshly fallen raindrops to glisten on the foliage. A fox, padding across a narrow dirt track running through the woods, stopped, turned in the direction of the approaching lights, started, then fled into the trees as a Land Rover pulled into view. It moved at a crawl, following the track as it wound its way between the trees, the driver exercising due caution to avoid colliding with the trees as they grew ever denser – or, perhaps, to avoid attracting unwanted attention.

Eventually, the track petered out into nothing, the trees ahead too tightly packed to proceed any further. The driver, a fair-haired woman in her early thirties, brought the Land Rover to a standstill.

'This'll do,' she said.

She opened the door and stepped out, followed by two other women of similar age. The first to emerge, from the front passenger seat, was short and dark-haired, the thickly gelled spikes of her undercut glistening in the moonlight. She was followed from the back seat by a tall, willow-thin woman, her upturned hood all but obscuring her face. She lingered by the side of the car, picking at the skin around her fingernails, as her two companions headed round to the boot. They returned moments later, each armed with a shovel.

'Come on,' said the fair-haired woman.

They set off, tramping through the woods, the fair-haired woman sweeping a torch in a wide arc in front of her to light their way. The tall woman trailed behind the others, dragging her feet in a way that suggested either exhaustion or deep, overpowering melancholy – or both.

After two hundred yards or so, they came to a small, secluded clearing. The fair-haired woman halted, tested the ground with her foot and turned to her short, dark-haired companion.

'What d'you reckon?'

The dark-haired woman tested the ground herself. 'Never thought I'd say this,' she said, her accent a heavy Australian drawl, 'but thank fuck for Scottish rain.'

They began to dig. They worked quietly and diligently, the only sounds escaping from their lips their grunts of exertion at each fresh thrust. The tall woman made no move to help them. She stood a little way off, seeming to pay less attention to them than to her surroundings. Every now and then, her head jerked sharply, recoiling at some night noise or other: the hoot of an owl, the scurrying of tiny woodland feet, the wind sighing in the branches overhead.

In the space of just over two hours, the two diggers succeeded in fashioning a pit, approximately six feet long and four feet deep. By then, both were stripped to their T-shirts, lashing with sweat and covered in dirt. However, they didn't stop to either catch their breath or contemplate their handiwork. Around them, the woods were growing lighter, the grey hour before dawn fast approaching. Downing their shovels, they set off back the way they'd come, their tall companion again following them like a reluctant shadow. They reached the Land Rover and made their way round to the back, where the fair-haired woman thrust open the door to the boot.

Standing side by side, they gazed down at the body lying inside, wrapped from top to tail in a white sheet, Egyptian mummy-style.

The fair-haired woman turned to her two companions with a look that bordered on impatience.

'Right, then,' she said, 'shall we get on with this?'

THEN

From: Hazel Knight (hazelknight1989@icloud.com)
To: Matthew Ellis (m.ellis@wtnaccountancy.org)
Subject: Us

Matthew,

I like to think, after everything we've been through together, after everything we've shared, that we can at least be honest with one another. Honest about our feelings, about our wants and needs, honest about the areas where each of us might be lacking.

I've been trying, for several hours now, to put into words how I feel about what I walked in on. Hurt, obviously. That goes without saying. Betrayed too. Again, that should be self-evident. And embarrassed. No, embarrassed isn't a strong enough word. I feel humiliated. Completely and utterly humiliated, more than I've ever felt in my life.

But mostly, I'm confused. Confused as to how things could have gone so wrong with us, how I could have been so blind to what was going on around me that I never once suspected you were

MESSAGE DELETED.

From: Hazel Knight (hazelknight1989@icloud.com)
To: Matthew Ellis (m.ellis@wtnaccountancy.org)
Subject: Why?

Help me to make sense of this, Matthew. I don't understand. In all the time we've been together I've never once so much as THOUGHT about anyone else, and I thought it was the same for you. How long has this been going on? Have you and her been

MESSAGE DELETED.

From: Hazel Knight (hazelknight1989@icloud.com)
To: Matthew Ellis (m.ellis@wtnaccountancy.org)
Subject: Is it me?

If there's something I haven't been giving you, something I haven't been doing for you, something you could only get from elsewhere, then I

MESSAGE DELETED.

From: Hazel Knight (hazelknight1989@icloud.com)
To: Matthew Ellis (m.ellis@wtnaccountancy.org)
Subject: Our bed??? Seriously?????

Could you not at least have gone to a bloody hotel like people normally do when they

MESSAGE DELETED.

From: Hazel Knight (hazelknight1989@icloud.com)
To: Matthew Ellis (m.ellis@wtnaccountancy.org)
Subject: (no subject)

FUCK YOU.

MESSAGE SENT.

1

Two weeks later

'Where *is* it?'

I spoke my question aloud, even though there was no one else within earshot and I was, in any event, the only person in a position to answer my own question. My camera – my trusty old Fujifilm Instax 500AF – was nowhere to be seen, and I was damned if I was going to leave without it. To make matters worse, it was almost twelve-thirty and I knew my ride would be here any minute.

As I stood in the bedroom doorway, eyes shut, attempting to visualise the last place I'd seen it, I heard the sound of a car pulling up outside, followed by the blast of a horn, strident and sustained enough to rouse the whole of Leith from its Saturday lunchtime torpor. I crossed over to the bedroom window in time to see Mickie – who I was confident was the one who'd sounded the horn – leaning her entire body out the passenger window of Claire's Land Rover, hollering at the top of her lungs:

'COME ON, HAZEL! MOVE YOUR FUCKING ARSE!'

That's what she said – though, in her South Queensland drawl, it came out sounding more like, *MEWV YAH FACKIN AAAAHS!* I couldn't actually see Claire – who doesn't allow swearing in her house, and presumably, by extension, her car – but I could picture her hunched over the wheel, grinding her teeth to dust.

I turned to find myself face to face with Matthew, standing just a few inches away from me, and all but jumped out of my skin.

'Your friends are here,' he said, seemingly unconcerned by the fact he'd almost given me a minor heart attack.

'I know,' I said, somehow managing to sound plausibly in control of myself. 'I can't find my camera.'

'Have you tried around your neck?'

Even before he'd finished speaking, I was aware of the familiar sensation of the leather strap digging into the exposed skin above the collar of my top, accompanied by the equally familiar weight of the camera itself against my chest. I felt my cheeks reddening in shame at my foolishness. As if to complete my humiliation, Matthew raised a solitary eyebrow as if to say, *Seriously?*

'Well,' I said, trying my best to cover my embarrassment, 'fancy that.'

'That you got everything you need, then?'

I glanced at my holdall, parked at the foot of the bed and ready to go. 'Seems so.'

'You'll call to let me know you've arrived safely?'

'Why? It's not as if we're jetting off into the wide blue yonder.'

That had been the original plan: a long weekend in Marbella, just the two of us. What better way to mark my thirtieth birthday than four days at a luxury resort in the Costa del Sol with the man I'd shared my life with for the past decade? Until, that is, I came home early from work two Fridays ago to discover him in bed – *our* bed – with a pneumatic blonde who was doing more moaning and writhing than you'd ever expect to encounter outside of a cheap porno . . . which, at the time, was what I felt like I'd stepped into.

'Still,' Matthew said. 'For peace of mind.'

Spoken in a tone that implied I was being utterly unreasonable – going out of my way to make things difficult out of pure stubbornness. As if peace of mind was something he was entitled to.

We continued to face one another, neither of us moving. I wondered if he was deliberately blocking my path or if it simply hadn't occurred to him that, in order to reach the door, I would actually have to pass through the space he currently occupied. Both seemed equally plausible.

Another blast from the car horn sounded outside. At this rate, I figured I had about thirty seconds before one or both of them came looking for me.

'Fine,' I muttered, conceding defeat. 'I'll call you.'

That seemed to do the trick. He gave a strained – and, to my mind, somewhat condescending – smile and moved aside, leaving me just enough space to get by. Again, I wondered if he'd done it deliberately – a ploy to make sure there would be some form of physical contact between us as I passed him. Well, two could play at that game. I hoisted my holdall onto my shoulder – the one closest to him – and strode towards the door, forcing him to step out of the way at the last minute to avoid his face taking the full impact of the heavy travel bag.

I made it as far as the landing before he spoke again.

'Haze.'

I stopped. Turned to look over my shoulder at him. 'What?'

He hesitated. For a moment, I wondered if this was going to be the big moment where he dropped to his knees and threw himself at my mercy, begging me to overlook his inadequacies and forgive him for giving into temptation, swearing that it would never, ever happen again. I'm not sure how I'd have reacted if he *had*. Not sure I could have trusted myself to remain resolute.

But, in the end, there was no great outpouring of contrition – just a small, rather strained smile and shrug of his shoulders.

'Happy birthday tomorrow.'

I couldn't muster even a smile in response. Instead, I turned my back on him and clomped down the stairs, grabbed my coat from the rack by the door and stepped out into the early May afternoon sun, just in time for the Land Rover's horn to sound yet again.

As I jogged down the garden path, I felt the eyes of Mrs Marchbanks glowering at me through the parting in the lace curtains of her next-door living room window, no doubt holding me personally responsible for this appalling breach of the peace. I slung my holdall into the Land Rover's back seat, then turned to face Mickie, still leaning halfway out the passenger window, preening at me like an annoyingly short, spiky-haired peacock.

'Don't know what you're looking so pleased with yourself about,' I said.

Mickie merely pouted even more shamelessly in response, her upper lip curved into the distinctive W-shape it always assumes when she makes that particular expression.

'Right.' Claire jerked her head. 'You know the drill. Into the back.'

Mickie turned to Claire with a pout. 'Aw, why?'

'You know why. Because you need less leg room, that's why.'

'So? S'not my fault she's built like a bloody heron.' She glanced briefly in my direction. 'Nae offence, wee hen.'

'Oh, none taken,' I said, totally unfazed by the all-too-familiar drama currently playing out in front of me.

''Sides, finders keepers, losers weepers.'

'Just give her the seat, Mickie,' Claire sighed.

For a couple of seconds, Mickie just sat there, eyeballing her insolently. Then, in a move so sudden I had to jump back to avoid being hit, she swung the door open and stepped out. Nose in the air, she strode past me and clambered into the back seat, shoving my holdall out of the way as if it had personally impugned her.

I slid into the passenger seat, copping an exasperated *kill me now* look from Claire as I shut the door. Mickie, meanwhile, squirmed behind me as she tried to get comfortable, kicking the back of my seat – and the small of my back – with a Doc Marten-clad foot.

'It's cramped as buggery back here,' she grumbled. '*And* it smells of wet dog.'

'She's been like this all the way here,' Claire told me, her Home Counties accent lending her words an appropriately haughty primness. 'Honestly, my nine-year-old shows more maturity.'

'What can I say?' said Mickie. 'You bring out my inner child.' She leaned forward, resting her elbows on the backs of our seats and poking her head between us. 'So,' she said, addressing me, 'what's the shitbag gonna be getting up to while you're away?'

'*Mickie* . . . ' began Claire, a warning edge to her voice.

'What? He *is* a shitbag. Did the dirty on my big cousin, so he did. Am I not allowed to be outraged on behalf of my own flesh and blood?'

'I'm just saying, there are more diplomatic ways of putting it.'

'More anal-retentive, more like. Says a lot about a person's morals when she's more upset by a spot of the old sailor talk than the actual deed being discussed.'

Claire laughed in contemptuous disbelief. 'Oh, I *hardly* think you're in a position to lecture me on morality.'

'Ladies, *please*!' I raised my voice above the fray before Mickie could hit back with another jibe. 'Can we not do this right now? Let's all just try and get along for the next few days, shall we? I mean, hello – injured party sitting right here.'

Neither Mickie nor Claire spoke. They just sat there, eyes downcast, both looking so utterly chastened I had to fight the urge to burst out laughing at the sight of them. Mickie's always known exactly how to push Claire's buttons, and Claire – well, she's more than capable of giving as good as she gets, and her tendency, when provoked, to accentuate the very aspects of her personality Mickie considers worthy of ridicule only serves to egg Mickie on to ever more incendiary heights. I just knew they'd have been winding one another up all the way here, chip-chip-chipping away at each other passive-aggressively till they were both coiled springs waiting to snap.

'Come on.' I looked imploringly at each of them in turn. 'Let's just put some miles between ourselves and the city. We'll all feel a whole lot less stressed out once we're on our way.'

Mickie replaced her look of contrition with a grin. 'Yeah, no kidding. Dunno about yous two, but work's been a complete ballache this week. Boss man's been riding me like a used bike for this, that and the other. Plus I've got the landlord from hell who for some reason thinks it's totes hilare to whack up the rent at a moment's notice.' She blew out a noisy breath. 'Man, I *need* this holiday . . . even if we are gonna spend it tramping through bog and briar, wringing swamp-water out of our scuffs.'

I glanced at Claire, who gave a rueful smile. 'I guess I *have* been feeling a bit highly strung lately,' she admitted.

'Well,' I said primly, 'for the next three days, no one inside this car is permitted to so much as *think* about work or rent or any of all that real-world unpleasantness. I forbid it!'

Mickie shot Claire a wolfish grin. 'Hear that? She still thinks she gets to set the agenda this weekend. Boy, is *she* in for a rude awakening!'

Claire's smile broadened, though she tried to hide it by affecting to scratch the side of her face.

Sensing victory, Mickie leaned forward, grinning at each of us in turn. 'So, ladies, are we ready?'

Claire and I both made noises to the affirmative.

'Are we set?'

More expressions of approval. This time, even Claire sounded halfway enthusiastic.

Mickie drummed her hands on the backs of our headrests and

gave a loud, celebratory whoop. 'Whoo-ee! Then let's get this show on the road!'

Claire turned the key in the ignition and pulled away from the kerb. I watched in the rearview mirror as the house I'd shared with Matthew for the last four and a half years receded into the distance before finally disappearing from view as we swung out of Hermitage Place and onto Duke Street, heading towards Newhaven, Granton and the road north. Four and a half years, plus, before that, another five doing what my late grandmother would have quaintly referred to as 'courting' – all turned to ash and dust in the blink of an eye. Like Mickie, I wondered what Matthew would find to do with himself in my absence. With the liquidation firm he worked for having gone into a rare company-wide shutdown for the bank holiday weekend, it wasn't hard to imagine him at a seriously loose end, deprived of his steady diet of meetings, phone calls and emails. As someone who ate, slept and breathed his work, he wasn't the sort of person who could readily lose himself in a good book or a film. It seemed only too likely that, stuck at home with only the television and the four walls for company, he'd give into temptation and pay a visit to the bit on the side he'd sworn to me had been a one-off.

In an effort to banish these thoughts from my mind, I switched on the car radio, channel-cycling till I came to one of those stations that played nineties rock hits all day long. I cranked up the volume and, by the time we'd left Leith behind us and were cruising along the Queensferry Road, all three of us had caught the bug and were singing along to the classic power ballads of our younger days, belting out half-remembered lyrics in a mixture of clashing rhythms, tempos and pitches. We cleared the Queensferry Crossing and hurtled up the M90, the country opening up before us like a children's pop-up book: wide, flat fields on either side, high mountains on the horizon ahead.

To hell with Matthew and his indiscretions. This was going to be A GREAT WEEKEND. In less than twenty-four hours, I would be turning thirty – an event that couldn't help but feel significant. The rational part of me knew there was no earthly reason why turning thirty should feel any more noteworthy than turning twenty-nine or thirty-one, or indeed any other age. And yet, for some reason, a ten-year milestone is always regarded as a moment of great importance: a staging post marking the end of one chapter and the beginning of another.

Either way, I was on my holidays with my favourite people, and come hell or high water, I was bloody well going to enjoy myself. I wound down the window, leaned my head out into the sharp, stinging wind, inhaled a deep breath and screamed as loud as I could, distilling all my pent-up frustrations into a single, sustained expulsion that went on and on until I ran out of air.

2

The trip had been the very definition of a last-minute bodge, our plans only coming to fruition the night before we set out. Once it was clear my romantic weekend in Marbella was off the agenda, Claire had immediately suggested going away somewhere together instead – just the two of us. I hummed and hawed for nearly a week, before finally agreeing on the condition that Mickie came too. Claire wasn't exactly over the moon about that, I could tell – though, to give her her due, she didn't actually try to talk me out of it. I was too preoccupied by Matthew's betrayal to give any thought to planning anything, so I left her to take care of the whole thing, stipulating only that I didn't want anything extravagant – which was true enough, not least because I knew she'd insist on paying for everything and I couldn't countenance her shelling out a fortune on my account – even if she *does* make more than twice what I do on her GP's salary.

In true Claire fashion, she set to work immediately, approaching the task with the same diligence she applies to everything she does – only to discover that, owing to it being the May bank holiday weekend, every holiday home from Gretna to John o' Groats was already booked. For a while, it looked like the plan was dead on arrival, until, late on Friday evening, she rang me in a flurry of breathless excitement, saying she had it all figured out. Her parents down in Stevenage had neighbours who owned a holiday cabin up on the Aberdeenshire coast. They visited the place two or three times a year at most, and, having heard we were struggling to find somewhere for our weekend getaway and eager to burnish their altruistic credentials, they'd offered us the use of it free of charge, on the condition that we left it in the same state we found it and replaced any perishables we consumed.

It wasn't exactly Marbella in the sun, and Mickie made some predictable noises about slumming it out in the boonies where folk got overly familiar with their own livestock, but, ultimately, we all agreed it was as good an offer as we could realistically hope to receive at such short notice. And so the die was cast.

Port Catrin lies approximately one hundred and twenty miles north of Edinburgh as the crow flies. On a good day, with a clear run and everything going according to plan, the journey should take just under two and a half hours. Today, though, the traffic on the A90 was nose to tail, the bulk of it heading north – fellow bank holiday weekenders, probably, who'd had much the same idea as us and were heading in the same general direction. It wasn't until we'd passed Dundee and were heading through Angus towards Aberdeenshire that things began to quieten down and you could actually put more than a cigarette paper between our car and the one in front.

A little after four, we left the A90 and took to the narrower, considerably windier roads through the seemingly endless fields that covered this wild and desolate part of the country. The North Sea loomed to our right, grey and choppy in the middle-distance, the squalling gulls that circled above it mere specks against the bruised and swollen sky. We met no other traffic, apart from a rickety old tractor which Claire actually had to swerve into a ditch to avoid. Only the electricity pylons that occasionally dotted the distant, heather-clad hills served as any indication that civilisation had ever made it this far north.

The radio failed us first, followed soon after by our phones. With no SatNav to guide us, we had to do things the old-fashioned way, pulling over and getting out the old AA map Claire keeps stowed in the glove compartment for emergencies. Mickie – who'd been looking for an excuse to have a proper barny for some time now – chose now to stick the boot in, demanding to know what sort of mental cases would choose to have a holiday home out here in the middle of Woop Woop where even your frigging *phone* didn't work properly. I could sense Claire gnashing her teeth at my side, so it came as a considerable relief when, having spent the last five minutes staring at the spaghetti tangle of highways and byways on the page, I had a sudden epiphany and it all snapped into focus.

'There!' I said, pointing. 'We took a wrong turn at the last junction. We want to be going *this* way.'

It was getting on for five when we finally trundled into Port Catrin. It was one of those quaint, picturesque little villages you find dotted all along the north-east coastline, filled with white pebbledash bungalows and streets so narrow there was barely room for people to walk two abreast, let alone two vehicles to pass each other. The port itself, which we skirted on our way into town, consisted of a beach and a single jetty with a couple of fishing boats moored nearby, bobbing up and down on the tide.

As we wound our way uphill through the village, we drew curious looks from the handful of locals who were out and about. Their expressions weren't malicious, just wary – and who could blame them? I got the distinct impression this was the sort of place where everyone knew every car, who owned it and whether they'd paid their road tax. The presence of an unfamiliar vehicle could well be the most noteworthy thing to have happened here all week. News of our arrival would no doubt have spread to every corner of the town by the time we reached our destination.

The cabin that was to be our billet for the weekend was at the top of the hill, a few hundred feet above the village and accessible only by an overgrown, winding gravel track that had clearly been designed with a much smaller car in mind – or no car at all. We reached the summit in one piece, and by the time we scrambled out of the Land Rover, flexing our stiff legs and arching our backs, we were positively grateful for the cold wind whipping at our hair and the light smattering of rain on our faces. The cabin in front of us was long, low and wood-panelled, with a gently sloping gable roof and a bolt-on tool shed off to the side. Claire made for the front door and, lifting the solitary stone slab lying next to the step, retrieved the key.

'Top marks for security,' Mickie quipped to me as Claire slid it into the lock.

I very much doubted security was something anyone around here was over-concerned with, though I said nothing for fear of being accused of stating the obvious and followed the other two inside, lugging my holdall.

We stepped into a wide, low-ceilinged living area with a polished mahogany floor. The centre of the room was dominated by a large steel chimney that put me in mind of an upside-down trumpet, suspended from the ceiling and hovering over a raised fireplace that some thoughtful soul had already piled high with logs. An assortment of sofas and armchairs, all tastefully upholstered and spotlessly clean, surrounded it in a loose semi-circle.

'Hey, free booze!'

I turned as Mickie made a beeline for the generously stocked drinks cabinet over by the far wall. She turned to us with a leering grin.

'I'll say one thing for these pals of yer folks,' she said to Claire. 'They obviously know how to bevvy.'

'You'll keep your greasy mitts off them,' retorted Claire. 'They're not yours. Besides, I've brought plenty of provisions to see us through the weekend.'

'Yeah, bread and water, most like,' Mickie retorted – though she did as she was told and left the cabinet alone. Instead, she prodded the hardwood floor with her toe, then kicked off first one boot, then the other.

'Yo, check it.'

With both of us watching, she skated across the floor in her socks, arms outstretched for balance. Reaching the other end, she spun round to face us, smirking triumphantly.

'Nancy Kerrigan eat your heart out,' said Claire, distinctly unimpressed. 'Stop messing and help me empty the car.'

'Yes, Mother,' said Mickie, and lined herself up to skate back over to us. She was halfway there when she lost her balance. For a Keystone Cops moment, she remained upright, arms flailing as she tried to right herself, then went tumbling down, landing hard on her backside.

'What did I just say?' said Claire, as I hurried over to help Mickie up.

'Hurts like a bastard,' Mickie grumbled, rubbing her tender rear end. Then, in an instant, her self-pity vanished as a fresh thought entered into her head. 'Oooh, dibs on the master bedroom!'

Her recent injury seemingly forgotten, she took off, haring towards the back of the house with me and Claire hot on her heels.

In the course of our exploration, it soon became apparent that what had looked like a bungalow from the outside was in fact a two-storey affair, albeit one that was arranged upside-down compared to most houses. The building was partially cut into the hill on the side facing away from the village, with the living room, kitchen and other dayrooms on the upper floor and the sleeping quarters down below. The same hardwood flooring we'd discovered upstairs extended to the long, narrow corridor at the foot of the steps and to the three bedrooms leading off it. Mickie's talk of bagging the master bedroom proved to have been premature: all three were of similarly modest size, tastefully furnished and comfortable enough, but geared more towards function than form.

I dumped my holdall on the floor and sat down on the bed, closing my eyes and inhaling deeply as I listened to the sounds of my two friends unpacking in their respective rooms, Mickie giving a noisy running commentary about the décor ('State of this gaff! Did no one ever tell these people lace doilies went out of fashion in 1975?') as she clattered about. I smiled softly to myself, oddly comforted by her lack of internal filter or social etiquette. You know where you are with Mickie. No airs and graces for her – she tells it how it is.

The moment passed. I opened my eyes, got to my feet and headed upstairs to see if there was anything still needing brought in from the car. It turned out that, between them, Claire and Mickie had made a pretty thorough job of it, so instead I went for a wander around, circling the house and sizing it up from various angles, before getting out my camera and crouching down to take some pictures of the various plants and flowers that sprouted on the hillside.

Folk are always ribbing me about the fact that I shoot on an old instant camera, and one that's seen better days at that. They think it's an affectation, like lensless glasses or those fake spines some people buy to fill their bookshelves, or else that I can't afford anything more up to date – both of which are seriously wide of the mark. It was a present from my dad, a couple of years before he died, so the sentimental aspect of it should be obvious. But beyond that, I genuinely love shooting on it. To me, it represents the best of both worlds. Just like with digital, you get the instant satisfaction of seeing what you've taken straight away (well, more or less), but because you're shooting on a physical medium and are limited by how much film you've brought with you, you're forced to be selective; to actually take care to compose your shots instead of just clicking the shutter willy-nilly. Matthew had offered on numerous occasions to buy me some all-singing, all-dancing digital model that'd do everything including measure my heart rate and track my ovulation cycle, but I'd always held firm. *If it ain't broke, don't fix it.*

Speaking of Matthew – and speaking of things that were broken – I'd promised I'd ring him to let him know I'd arrived. After what he'd done, I was honestly tempted to let him think we'd crashed or got lost on the way or been carried off by descendants of Sawney Bean – but I entertained the idea for less than five seconds before realising I couldn't do that to him. *Too considerate for my own good.* I got out my phone and spent a minute or so with it raised above my head, searching in vain for reception. Nothing materialised, but when I went into the settings I discovered an unsecured wi-fi network, helpfully labelled 'GUEST', with a couple of bars of signal strength. I connected to it and rang Matthew's mobile on the speed dial.

'Hi, this is Matthew Ellis. I'm not available to take your call, so please leave a message after the beep. Alternatively, if your enquiry is work-related, contact my office and I'll get back to you within normal business hours. The number is . . . '

So much for *let me know you've arrived safely*. He couldn't be *that* concerned about me if he wasn't even bothering to pick up. Unless, that is, he'd received a more appealing offer than sitting at home waiting for my call.

I realised his answerphone was patiently awaiting my message.

'Uh . . . hey, Matthew. It's me. Just ringing to let you know we've arrived. The reception's non-existent here so looks like I'll be pretty much incommunicado for the next couple of days. Um . . . '

I racked my brains, trying to think of something with which to fill the silence. We were so out of the habit of actually communicating with one another that it was like trying to make conversation with a stranger.

'Yeah, so the house is nice and the village looks really pretty. I dunno what you've got planned for this evening – whether it's a quiet one or . . . ' *Or if you're planning on having another session with Miss Platinum Blonde while the coast is clear.* 'But yeah, give me a call when you get this – or send a text or whatever. Either's good. OK, bye.'

I rang off, cursing my lack of imagination, or lack of bottle, or whatever else it was I lacked. I pressed the phone to my chin and stood there, lost in a cloud of doubt and self-recrimination, the cold, hard plastic digging into my flesh, leaving an indentation.

I sensed a presence behind me. Turning, I discovered Mickie standing in the doorway, leaning on the frame. Our eyes met and she grinned.

'There ya are! Thought mibby you'd done a runner on us. Listen, the pair of us are for getting some dinner, but I can't be arsed cooking and you know the doc – she'll only make a right old song and dance about it and we'll still be sitting with empty bellies two hours later while she fannies about in the kitchen. So whaddaya say we head doon the toon and see if we can rustle up some local scran?'

3

We set out, following the path downhill towards the lights twinkling below. The sun wasn't due to set in this part of the world for a few hours yet, but the sky was so heavy with black clouds you'd hardly have known the difference.

There was only one place in town that served food – a pub called The Anchorage. We stepped over the threshold, and I swear to you, it was like that scene from *An American Werewolf in London*. Every man in the place – and they *were* almost all men – instantly stopped talking and turned, glaring at us from their tables and barstools like we were something the cat had dragged in. For a few seconds, no one moved. Then one of the barflies gave a grunt that presumably amounted either to acceptance or indifference and swivelled back round to face his pint. That seemed to be the cue for the others to do likewise, and a moment later a low hubbub of conversation resumed.

We made our way over to a vacant table in the far corner – a semi-enclosed booth with a padded banquette piled with cushions. It seemed a little odd no one else had snagged it already, given its fairly incontestable status as the best seat in the house, but none of us had any intention of looking this particular gift horse in the mouth. Before long, we had our drinks in front of us and were tucking into our food. It was solid, unfussy fare – not the sort of cuisine that got you a glowing write-up in *The Good Pub Guide*, but none the worse for it and all the more satisfying after our long trip.

At first, all three of us were occupied primarily with the task of filling our bellies, but once we'd finished eating, the refills soon began to flow, and with them the conversation. I did my best to keep things light-hearted and inconsequential, but it was abundantly clear Mickie had something she wanted to get off her chest, and during an inopportune lull in the conversation, she finally came out and asked the question I'd been dreading all evening.

'So,' she said, turning to face me, arms folded, elbows resting on the tabletop, 'whatcha gonna do about the shitbag?'

I choked as the mouthful of rum and Coke I'd been swallowing went down the wrong way. 'What am I going to . . . ?'

'Yeah – I mean, it's plain as a pikestaff the two of yous can't carry on playing happy families, kidding on like ya didn't walk in and catch him *in flagrante* with the secretary or whetevs. So ya planning to kick him to the kerbside or what?'

It was, of course, the question I'd been wrestling with virtually non-stop for the last two weeks. And yet, for all my soul-searching, I was still no closer to an answer.

'Do we have to talk about this now?' I said weakly. 'Can't we just have a nice time and try to get through one night without making it all about *him*?'

Mickie shrugged. 'Hey, no time like the present. Way I see it, longer ya leave it, longer the odds are you'll actually *do* anything. I mean, if it'd been me, I'da grabbed 'em both by the lugs, dragged 'em outside in their birthday suits and tossed 'em in the gutter where they belong.'

When Mickie learned about Matthew's infidelity, she was all set to march round to our place then and there and knock his block off, or at the very least take a baseball bat to the windshield of his prized Porsche. It took all my powers of persuasion to talk her out of confronting him, and only when I practically got down on my knees and begged her did she relent, muttering ominously about not being able to control herself if she ran into him in a dark alley.

'Yes, well,' said Claire quietly, 'we're not all *you*, are we?' She turned to me as Mickie pulled a face. 'Let's all try to keep cool heads about this, OK? You don't want to go rushing headlong into something you'll only regret.'

'Just don't be dilly-dallying *too* long,' Mickie put in. 'Else next thing ya know, he'll have sweet-talked you into thinking it wasn't what it looked like or that it didnae mean anything. You're the only woman he's ever had eyes for, all that jazz. Then, 'fore ya know it, another ten years've sailed by and you're stuck in a loveless marriage with a snot-nosed brat and a Labrador tying ya down.' She glanced at Claire. 'No offence.'

'Oh, none taken, I assure you,' said Claire, her lips a thin, saccharine smile.

'And let's face it,' Mickie went on, 'now he's done it the once, sure as morning glory he'll do it again. Love rats are like serial killers: they never stop at just the one.'

Claire rolled her eyes, then, turning to me, laid a hand on my arm. 'I know right now it's tempting to throw in the towel. And I'm not saying you're wrong to feel that way. But before you do anything rash, think about what that would mean. You and Matthew have a decade's worth of shared history between you. That's a lot to untangle.'

'That's why ya gotta do it good and quick.' Mickie again, the veritable dog with a bone. 'Like ripping off a bandaid. Longer you leave it, the more it's gonna eat away atcha, like – I dunno, like gangrene or something. I say get it over and done with – short term pain for long term gain.'

Claire shot Mickie a withering look. Mickie held up her hands in mock apology and mimed zipping her lips shut.

Claire turned to me again. 'There's no reason to commit to a definitive course of action right this minute. You've been together this long – I'd say that's worth taking just a little bit longer to think things through, wouldn't you?'

'I guess,' I said, not sure how convinced I really was by this line of thought.

Claire smiled and squeezed my arm gently. 'You know I'll help you in any way I can. Just make sure, whatever you ultimately decide, it's what *you* want.'

I said nothing, but I let her words sink in. For as long as I've known her, Claire's been fighting my corner. Not in the aggressive, belligerent, in-your-face sense (that's more Mickie's department) but rather with a quiet, steely determination that makes me wonder what on earth I'd do without her. I know I can always rely on her to provide a sympathetic ear or serve as a sounding board – or, as was the case with our holiday, to knuckle down behind the scenes to salvage a thoroughly crummy situation into something halfway decent. We met while we were both at Edinburgh University. It was the end of my second week there studying architecture, I didn't know anyone, and, in an effort to forge some connections, I'd forced myself to go along to a freshers' party at the Lounge Bar, organised by the Students' Association. The whole thing was my idea of absolute hell – all that loud music, drinking and unfettered adolescent libidos – and within five minutes of arriving, I'd convinced myself I'd made a humongous mistake and was just about to make for the exit when another girl – not as tall as me but straight-backed and upstanding whereas I'd always had a tendency to slouch in order to compensate for my height – sidled up to me, glass in hand, smiled at me and said, 'Lovely to meet you. I'm Claire. OK if I hang out with you?'

I've always appreciated that that was her opening gambit – making it seem like *I* was the one doing *her* a favour, when in reality we both knew she was the one saving me from social death. For the rest of that evening, we were attached at the hip, laying claim to a couch in a quiet corner where we chatted non-stop and with such focused intensity that I completely forgot about the party carrying on around us. I discovered that, like me, she was a first-year, embarking on her medical training having arrived just a fortnight ago from the South-East of England – her first ever venture north of the border. I'd chosen to study in Edinburgh precisely because it was a known quantity: it was where I was born and had so far spent my entire life, and it meant I could get the bus in every day and not have to worry about student accommodation. I'd turned eighteen just four months earlier and was still as gauche as a girl scout; she was a year older but, with all the self-assurance and pragmatism she exuded, could have had decades on me. Looking back on it, I think I was ever so slightly in awe of her, not to mention flattered that someone so got-together was prepared to give me the time of day. I didn't realise how long we'd been talking until one of the staff came over and asked us if we could hurry up and finish our drinks because it was after two in the morning and they wanted to close up.

By the time the taxi dropped me home, I knew beyond a shadow of a doubt that I'd made a friend for life. Before the end of first year, we'd moved into halls together, and we continued to flat-share all through uni, even once I'd started going out with Matthew and Claire had met Rob, the man she went on to marry. More than just a friend, I'd found someone who'd always have my back no matter what – a constant companion and source of sound advice. In the last twelve years, every major decision I've made, I've run by her first. More than once, she's talked me out of doing something that would have ultimately proved disastrous, gently steering me back towards the straight and narrow with a well-placed *now, Hazel, I really don't think that's for you* . . . At times, it feels like she knows my mind better than I know it myself – aware that, above all else, what I crave is stability and predictability, even if I occasionally get a mad notion to throw caution to the wind and do something truly reckless.

'Well, while you're taking your sweet time deciding' – Mickie's voice brought me crashing back to the present – 'if you ask me, you oughta take a leaf out of yer other half's book, find some prize hunk of manflesh and embark on a massive shagathon with him.' She shrugged. 'Yer man's hardly gonna be in a position to cry foul.'

Claire scoffed. 'Yeah, because of course a spate of tit for tat is going to solve *everything*.'

'Who said anything about solving anything? Shagging's not about problem-solving – s'about satisfying an itch, and feeling a whole lot better 'bout yourself into the bargain. I mean, nae offence, H,' she added, turning to me, 'but ya do kinda look like you could use a good screw. You're awfy tightly wound these days. Ya never know – grass might turn out to be greener on the other side of the septic tank.' She raised herself up off the seat, craning her neck as her eyes swept the room.

'What are you *doing*?' I hissed.

'Looking for eligible specimens. Even a dive like this must have a suitable candidate or two on offer.'

'Would you sit *down*?' I hissed – partly out of fear that someone would hear and partly because I was worried she might actually be serious.

'Yeah, Mickie,' said Claire, fingering the little silver cross that hung around her neck. 'This is crass, even by your standards.'

'What?' Mickie turned to us, aggrieved. 'Turnabout's fair play. 'Sides, it's not even cheating if you're on your holidays. *Everyone* knows that.'

'Well, *I* don't,' said Claire, getting to her own feet and shoving

Mickie back into her seat. 'Just because *you* couldn't keep your knickers on if your life depended on it doesn't mean we all have to follow your example. Pay no attention to her, Hazel,' she went on, without pausing for breath. 'There really is no shame in being the bigger person in all of this.'

I realised both she and Mickie were looking at me, waiting for me to say something. Stalling for time, I reached for my glass and raised it to my lips, only to find it empty.

'I don't know about you, ladies,' I said, with forced levity, 'but I could do with a refill. Same again?'

4

As I weaved through the throng as gracefully as I could, Mickie's words continued to sting. *Tightly wound. In need of a good screw.* Was that really how folk saw me? That Matthew was the only man I'd ever been with was no great secret: shy, awkward girl goes to uni, meets her first serious boyfriend there, is still with him a decade later . . . it wasn't hard for people to fill in the blanks. Until now, I'd never felt I'd missed out on anything by virtue of not having sowed my oats far and wide, but now I wasn't so certain. Sure, it was Mickie who'd said it, and her mind does have a tendency to veer towards the gutter – but could it be that she was just giving voice to what everyone else thought but was too polite, too bound by social niceties, to actually say?

Somehow worse, though, were Claire's words. *There's no shame in being the bigger person.* Of course, it went without saying that I was expected to take what Matthew had done to me on the chin; to give no thought whatsoever to revenge, let alone my own personal gratification. Because everyone knows I'm sensible and even-tempered and accommodating, and that conflict and drama are anathema to me. Not that I actually *wanted* to go out and have sex with the first man I encountered . . . but just supposing I *did*? Would that somehow make me the lesser person in folk's eyes? I'd never really been one to thump the tub for women's lib, but I couldn't help feeling there was more than a whiff of double standards in all of this. Implicit in Claire's exhortation was the assumption that Matthew's actions, while wrong and deplorable and deserving of condemnation, were still, to an extent, expected and understandable, because he was a man and therefore hardwired to lust after anything with two X chromosomes. But me? I had to be whiter than white – Hazel Knight, pure as the driven snow. Don't stoop to his level, Hazel. Hold onto your dignity. *Be the bigger person.*

I continued on my way, feeling like I was battling against a relentless tide. No one seemed to be in any great rush to make way for me – a state of affairs which continued when I reached the bar and found every stool occupied, men sitting elbow to elbow, leaving not even the tiniest opening for me to squeeze through. My feeble *excuse-me*s went unacknowledged, drowned out by the clamour of conversation. Even when I found the courage to shove myself between the two nearest figures, leaning past them to deposit my empty glasses on the counter, the most I got in response was an annoyed grunt.

'Excuse me,' I called to the landlord, who was conversing with one of the locals a couple of feet away. 'Could I . . . ?'

The landlord glanced in my direction for the briefest of moments, then turned back to the customer and resumed his conversation as if I wasn't even there.

I felt my cheeks beginning to burn. '*Excuse* me,' I began again, my voice doing that whiny, self-righteous-sounding thing it always does when I'm on edge and which always makes me cringe when I hear it.

Once more, I was ignored by all and sundry. I was just about to hail him again when another voice, deep and rustic, piped up behind me.

'Now then, what seems to be the trouble?'

Whenever I look back on the events that would later transpire, this is the moment I always single out as where everything began to go wrong. It wasn't, in and of itself, the point of no return, but it *was* the one that irrevocably set me on the path which ultimately led to it.

I turned and found myself facing a man of about my own age or perhaps slightly younger. He was a big guy in every sense – not fat, but he took up a lot of space, with wide shoulders and a barrel chest. *Substantial* – that was the word. He had a friendly, open face – pleasant as opposed to conventionally handsome, with thick, unkempt brown hair and a short, slightly scruffy beard, both of which looked overdue for a trim. His clothes were clearly designed for comfort and protection from the elements: a chequered flannel shirt and weather-stained jeans, plus a pair of mud-spattered Caterpillar boots. He looked at me and gave an expectant, rather uncertain smile.

'I don't mean to butt in,' he went on, 'but you looked like you were having some difficulty.'

'I can't get anyone to serve me,' I explained, instantly cringing at how feeble I sounded.

'Oh,' he said, and for a moment he looked so genuinely concerned that I wondered if perhaps he'd misheard me and thought I'd said something much worse. 'Well, that's not very good, then, is it?'

His speech was slow and deliberate, all flat vowels and melodic, rising-and-falling intonation. It reminded me a bit of Treebeard and the Ents in *The Lord of the Rings*: unhurried, unflappable, gathering moss while the world around them continues to turn. *Do not let us be . . . hmmmm* – loooooong pause – *hasty.* I caught myself smiling reflexively and instantly checked myself.

'It's really not,' I agreed, before it crossed my mind that he might not take kindly to me criticising his local watering hole. 'I mean,' I added, 'it *is* hopping tonight. Perhaps—'

'We can't be having that, now, can we?' he said, shaking his head slowly and thoughtfully. Then, before I could stop him, he elbowed his way into the gap I'd occupied just moments before, put two fingers in his mouth and gave a piercing whistle.

'Ho! Can we get some service here?'

With a swiftness that caught me by surprise given his previous indifference, the landlord stopped yakking midstream and strode over.

'Yes?'

My would-be rescuer turned to me. It took a moment for my brain to kick into gear.

'Oh! Um . . . a G&T, a pint of stout and a rum and Coke.'

My new friend repeated all this to the landlord, reciting each item slowly and pausing afterwards to make sure the landlord was keeping up – or perhaps to double-check he had the order right in his own head. As the landlord gathered up my empty glasses and moved off, the big guy turned to me again with a vaguely conspiratorial smile.

'Thanks,' I said, just as he opened his mouth and began to say something himself. We both stopped. Looked at each other sheepishly.

I tried again. 'What's—' I began, just as he once more began to speak as well.

I giggled. 'Jinxed!'

He gave a slow, uncertain laugh, as if he wasn't quite getting the joke.

I straightened my face. 'Sorry. You go first.'

'That's all right. I was just going to say, Terry can be a bit of a crosspatch, but he's all right once you get to know him.' He paused. 'I'm Aidan, by the way.'

I smiled. 'Hazel.'

I held out my hand and he took it, his big, hairy-knuckled paw enveloping it completely. His palm was rough and calloused, but his grip was surprisingly gentle, as if he was aware of his own strength and going out of his way not to hurt me.

'Are you . . . new to the area?' he asked, once we'd let go of each other's hands.

'You could say that.' I caught him looking at me quizzically. 'Sorry. No.' It felt as if we were operating on different wavelengths, like two radios whose tuning was ever so slightly out of whack trying and not quite managing to communicate. 'I'm actually from Edinburgh,' I explained. 'I'm just here for a couple of days. I turn thirty tomorrow and came up to celebrate.'

'To *Port Catrin*?' said Aidan, unable to hide his incredulity.

I shrugged. 'Sure. Why not?'

'But you're from *Edinburgh*. The *capital*,' he added, as if to underscore his point. 'All those sights and sounds on your doorstep and you chose to come *here*?'

'Takes all sorts, I guess.'

'Of course. I didn't mean to criticise. It's just . . . ' He shrugged sheepishly. 'Well, round here, all the young things can't wait to up sticks and get as far away from the place as possible. I've never heard tell of anyone from the Big Smoke coming out *here* for a knees-up before. Not that there's anything wrong with that,' he added quickly. 'Don't be thinking you're not welcome here. We just don't get a lot of outsiders, is all.' He paused for a moment, then remembered something. 'Oh – happy birthday, by the by.'

'Thank you,' I said, sincerely.

He smiled again, and I caught my own lips upturning instinctively. I couldn't help myself. I'm not sure if it was his straightforward good-naturedness or his slow, almost sing-songy way of speaking or those deep brown eyes that I couldn't help but be drawn into, but I found it impossible not to like him.

'Er . . . you'll not be having these all to yourself, will you?' he said.

This time, it was *my* turn to be slow off the mark. For a moment,

I had no idea what he was getting at. Then I remembered: the drinks.

'Oh no!' I said. 'I'm sure my friends will lend a hand.'

Aidan looked puzzled for a moment, then laughed. 'Of course!' he said, though I could tell from the bemused look on his face that he was wondering why these friends were nowhere to be seen. I turned in the direction of our table, intending to point them out, but our view of it was blocked by the throng of bodies, which only seemed to have grown in number since we'd been talking.

We smiled at one another – both of us, I sensed, aware that this situation was awkward in some vague, indefinable way. We were saved from any fresh embarrassment by the landlord returning with my order, which he slammed down on the counter like it had done something to offend him.

'One G&T, one stout and a rum and Coke.'

I reached for my purse, but before I could get any further, a crumpled twenty was already in Aidan's hand.

'You don't have to—' I began.

But Aidan was sliding the money across the counter to the landlord – who, I noted, was only too quick to accept it despite his apparent reluctance to serve me.

'It's very kind of you,' I said, as Aidan gathered up the glasses and turned to me again.

'It's my absolute pleasure,' Aidan said, beaming broadly. ''Sides,' he went on, as he handed the first two glasses, 'between you and me, I'm flush with cash at the moment.'

'Oh?'

He nodded. 'Just finished up a big job this morning. Cash in hand. Sure it'd only be burning a hole in my pocket.'

'What is it you do?'

'Oh, this, that and the other. Whatever I can to keep my hand in. Place this size, you can't afford to be fussy.'

He didn't elaborate and I didn't ask. I got the sense that was how things worked around here: people eking out a living however they could, doing informal deals under the table so the tax man didn't swoop in and pocket his share. It was a different world out here from the one I was used to, and I was acutely aware I was in no position to judge.

An uneasy silence elapsed between us. I could tell neither of us was in any hurry for this moment to end, but, at the same time, we'd exhausted everything there was to say.

'Well,' I said, finally breaking the silence, 'this was really good of you. I'd better get back to my friends before they think I've been swept off my feet by a tall, dark stranger.'

He smiled uncertainly, clearly trying to work out whether I was referring to him.

Ugh, what possessed me to come out with that?

'Well, anyway,' I said, clearing my throat awkwardly, 'thanks again.'

Forestalling any fresh foot-in-mouth escapades, I took the remaining glass from him, flashed him my teeth to simultaneously convey my thanks and farewell, then turned and headed back the way I'd come, clutching the drinks to my chest in an awkward, hands-free hug.

As soon as our table came into view, I realised something was amiss. Four men in oilskins were standing uncomfortably close to Claire and Mickie, both of whom were on their feet, as if braced for a fight. I quickened my pace, though I wasn't sure what I was supposed to do to defuse the situation – especially not with three laden glasses to contend with.

'I really don't see what the big deal is,' Claire was saying. 'Surely one table's as good as another?'

'Who d'yous think yous are,' said one of the men – a short guy with a protruding bottom lip and eyes that seemed far too small for his head, 'coming intae *our* pub and telling us where we can and cannae sit?'

'All right, keep the heid, pal,' said Mickie. 'I didnae see your names on the sign ootside the windae.'

Something I haven't mentioned about Mickie – but which you've probably noticed by now anyway – is that, despite her accent being as Australian as they come, she has a tendency to pepper her speech with Scots words and phrases. When she first moved here a year and a half ago, she embraced her Scottish ancestry with almost cartoonish gusto, buying into all the tourist tat, soaking up the local mythology and adopting a smörgåsbord of (often thoroughly mangled) Scottishisms she'd picked up from various sources of dubious provenance, under the apparently sincere conviction that it allowed her to pass as a native. I've become so used to hearing them that, these days, I barely even notice them, but there was a time when I had to fight incredibly hard not to burst out laughing whenever she casually dropped the latest bit of vernacular she'd picked up into a conversation. I wasn't laughing now, though – and, more to the point, neither were the four men, who I immediately realised thought she was taking the piss out of them.

'Have you got a problem?' said the short guy – who, it seemed, was the group's designated spokesperson. Then, before Mickie could formulate a response, 'I said, *have you got a fuckin problem?*'

I figured now was as good a time as any to announce my presence. 'Look,' I said, sidling into view, still clutching my drinks, 'we really don't want any trouble.'

Short guy turned to face me. 'Shoulda thought about that before yous parked yourselves on our patch.'

'All right, now.' Claire raised her hands for calm, adopting the same tone of voice I've always imagined she uses to address wayward patients in her consulting room. 'Don't let's be silly about this.'

It was the wrong thing to say. Shorty turned to Claire with a face like thunder. 'Well, la-de-fuckin-da!' he crowed, doing a thoroughly unconvincing – but nonetheless deeply insulting – imitation of her cut-glass accent. 'You've got some fuckin nerve, you know that? Waltzing in here, laying claim tae our seats, telling me I'm stupid?'

Claire, I suspected, had inadvertently touched a decidedly raw nerve. It didn't require much imagination to conclude that this was a man who was used to people calling his intelligence into question.

'I never said—' began Claire, the Home Counties in her accent growing even more pronounced in her indignation.

'Can we all just calm down?' I pleaded.

'DON'T YOU FUCKIN TELL ME TO FUCKIN CALM DOWN!' Shorty bellowed, a glob of spittle flying from his mouth and hitting my cheek.

'Lads, lads, what's all this, now?'

And then, before I could even respond, Aidan was by my side, relieving me of my drinks with a deftness I hadn't expected from him. He set them down on the table, then turned to face the four oilskin-clad men.

'It's no very nice, is it?' he said. 'Four big bruisers like yourselves squaring up to three young lassies? What sort of an example is that to set? They're gonnae think this is how we do things round here.'

I heard footsteps behind me and turned to see the landlord approaching, dishcloth in hand, no doubt come to see what the commotion was about.

'It's OK,' Aidan said to him, holding up a hand in reassurance. 'I'm dealing with it.'

The landlord gave a surly grunt and backed off but continued to linger nearby.

'Now then, lads,' Aidan turned once more to address the men, 'the ladies have had a long drive to get here. They're tired and they're thirsty. Wouldnae be right to make them shift, now, would it? Not now they've got themselves settled.'

Surly, sullen looks from the four men. I couldn't tell whether there was genuine contrition behind their expressions or they simply resented being held to account like this.

'So here's how we're going to make this right,' Aidan went on. 'You're gonnae leave the ladies in peace and park yourselves at one of they tables over yonder. And see if you do that? For the rest of the night, drinks are on me.'

Shorty eyed Aidan suspiciously. 'For real? No bullshitting?'

'Word of honour. But only if you promise no to give the ladies any fresh hassle.'

For a moment, the men hesitated – torn, it seemed, between the promise of free booze and the inevitable loss of face they would incur by backing down. They glanced at one another. One of the men shrugged.

Decision seemingly made, Shorty turned to Aidan. 'All right,' he said. 'Deal.'

Aidan gave a big, jovial smile and clapped him heartily on the shoulder, as if they were the best of friends. 'That's the ticket. See – costs nothing to make folk feel welcome.'

Arm still draped across Shorty's shoulders, he led him away, flashing me a quick wink as he went. The other three hesitated for a moment, then began to follow.

As Claire, Mickie and I glanced at each other, our expressions rendering words unnecessary, the landlord made his way over.

'If you three know what's good for you,' he said, in a low voice that was hardly any less threatening than that of Shorty and his associates, 'you'll finish those drinks in record time and be on your way. I don't need this sort of aggro – not now, not anytime.'

He shot us a final dirty look and stalked off, the silence that lingered in the wake of his departure heavy and stifling.

'Know what?' said Mickie after a moment. 'The hell with this. We're obviously about as welcome here as a kiddie-fiddler in a Wendy house. I say fuck the drinks and let's skedaddle.'

'Right there with you,' said Claire quietly.

I didn't even feel the need to voice my agreement. As far as I was concerned, the matter was settled. We gathered out coats and headed for the door.

5

We emerged from The Anchorage, Mickie leading the way. It was properly dark now, a light drizzle spattering our faces. Claire and I halted in the middle of the narrow street, watching Mickie as she paced up and down in search of a target for her pent-up anger.

'Bunch of bloody wazzocks!' she yelled. 'Can't believe I've had to give up a perfectly good pint of Murphy's just cos some retarded drongo from Boggerbumfuckville gets his panties in a twist over someone sitting in his favourite seat.'

'You can't say "retarded", Mickie,' I said, though my heart wasn't really in it. 'It's offensive.'

'Oh.' Mickie halted in her tracks, momentarily chastened. 'Well . . . good. They deserve to be offended, the pricks.'

Claire exhaled a weary sigh. 'Come on – we may as well head back to base.'

'Heh, yeah.' Mickie gave a rueful grimace. 'Doubt there's much scope for a pub crawl in this one-horse town.'

Turning our faces to the rain, we began to make our way up the road. We hadn't gone more than a hundred yards, however, when we heard a shout behind us.

'Whoa there!'

We turned to see Aidan jogging up the street after us, a windcheater slung over his shoulder. He caught up with us and stood there for a moment, catching his breath.

'What is it?' I asked, more harshly than I'd intended. Like Mickie, I was still feeling raw about what had gone down inside the pub, and I didn't feel particularly inclined to look favourably on any of its patrons – even the one who'd just stopped things from turning a whole lot uglier.

'I just wanted to make sure you were all right, and . . . ' He shrugged. 'Well, I sort of wanted to apologise.'

'For what? You weren't the one threatening to start World War Three over a table.'

'No,' he conceded, 'but like I said before, we don't get a whole lot of visitors round here, and a welcome like the one Calum MacKintry and his mates gave you back there . . . well, it's not a good look for any of us.'

'Your civic-mindedness does you proud.'

Aidan gave a sideways smile. 'For what it's worth, that stuff I said about paying for them to drink themselves cross-eyed? That was just a ruse to get them off your backs. There'll be more than a few sair heads when Terry orders them to settle up.'

In spite of myself, I felt myself returning his smile. As we stood there, regarding one another in an oddly contented state of mutual silence, I became aware of Mickie by my side, arms folded, head tilted sideways as she studied Aidan quizzically.

'And who are you again?' she said.

'Oh, um . . . this is Aidan,' I said. For reasons I couldn't pin down, I suddenly found myself feeling decidedly flustered. 'He bought us those drinks we never got round to.'

'That right?' said Mickie. 'Last of the big spenders, huh?' Her tone, though still laced with sarcasm, had already thawed perceptibly. There are few ways more guaranteed of getting into Mickie's good books than the offer of free alcohol.

'That was very kind of you,' said Claire. Her tone, like Mickie's, was guarded, bordering on distrustful. 'And, erm . . . thanks for stepping in back there. I fear we were in danger of biting off rather more than we could chew.'

'Ah, sure you would've been grand. Actually, it's Calum and his mob I was more worried for. They've no much experience dealing with the ladies – 'specially not ones who use words you cannae find in a kiddies' picture book.'

This time, I wasn't the only one who smiled. Claire's lip curled mirthfully, while Mickie threw back her head and let out an approving cackle.

'Ah, you're all right, you are.' She stepped forward, extending her hand. 'Aidan, yeah? I'm Mickie. And that one there with the webbed feet and vestigial tail is Claire.'

'Ignore her,' said Claire. 'She suffers from an acute case of infantile regression. It's desperately sad.'

Aidan gave a bemused smile, the intricacies of our group dynamic – understandably – a mystery to him.

'So tell me, Aidan,' said Mickie, continuing to look him up and down, though with an appreciative edge to her gaze now, 'you make a habit of buying randos drinks, or just ones as delectable as my cousin here?'

Aidan rubbed the back of his neck, suddenly bashful. 'Ah, well now, the lady looked like she was in a spot of bother, and I couldn't very well—' He stopped short as the latter part of what Mickie had just said belatedly registered with him. 'Wait a minute. Cousins? The two of you are *cousins*?'

Mickie shrugged. 'What of it?'

Aidan smiled guilelessly, a part of him evidently wondering if this wasn't some bizarre prank. 'You don't look like cousins.'

'Observation of the century there, mate.'

'You don't *sound* like cousins either.'

'No flies on you, are there?' Mickie turned to me. 'Know what? I reckon this one's a keeper.'

I could hardly blame Aidan for his incredulity. Most people, when they find out Mickie and I are related, have a hard time reconciling that knowledge with what their eyes and ears are telling them. While I'm pale, gangly and Scottish, Mickie is short, olive-skinned and quintessentially Australian in everything from her accent to her complete unfamiliarity with the concept of tact. Technically we're second cousins, though even that caveat doesn't generally help people make much sense of it. As the story goes, my great-uncle moved out to Oz in search of warmth and wealth back in the early fifties, and Mickie was the result of a torrid fling between his daughter and a half-Australian, half-Indonesian trucker on a stopover in Brisbane. From there, the details become even more sketchy. In actual fact, I had no idea I even *had* an Australian branch to my family till she rucked up on my doorstep one morning less than eighteen months ago with all her worldly possessions on her back and announced, 'Hiya! I'm Mickie and I'm your wee cousin!'

I found out later that, much like me, she hadn't known she had family on the other side of the world until recently, the fact having only come to light during a soul-searching conversation with her grandfather shortly before he passed away. Despite knowing nothing about Scotland other than what she'd seen in films and on shortbread tins, she instantly fell in love with the idea that she had Celtic blood running through her veins and set about digging into her family history, ultimately tracking me down via the trail of digital breadcrumbs I'd left on various social media platforms (the implications of which, if I actually stop to think about them, are mildly unsettling). Concluding that there was nothing to keep her in Brisbane, she promptly sold everything that wouldn't fit in her rucksack and booked herself on the first flight leaving for Scotland. She touched down in Edinburgh twenty-four hours later, and from there it was only a hop, skip and a jump to my front door. We've been making up for lost time ever since.

Back in the present, Mickie was circling Aidan, putting me in mind of a wild animal toying with its prey. 'So, Aidan,' she mused, 'what's a big, strapping lad like yourself do round here for kicks, hmm?'

'Not much,' he said breezily – though I could tell, from the way he was trying to keep her in his sights while simultaneously holding his ground, that her hungry predator act was seriously throwing him off his game. 'There's not a whole lot goes on round here, to be honest.'

'You don't say,' said Mickie drily.

Aidan nodded, seemingly oblivious to her sarcasm. 'If it's the nightlife you're after, you'd be better off heading up to Aberdeen.'

'Oh, we're just here for a quiet getaway,' said Claire. 'We're not looking for anything too rowdy.'

'Speak for yourself,' muttered Mickie, loud enough for the rest of us to hear.

'Hazel was saying it's her birthday tomorrow?' Aidan ventured.

'That right?' Mickie raised an eyebrow. 'And just how in-depth a sharing session *did* you two crazy cats get up to while the drinks were getting poured?'

I felt myself blushing and looked hastily at my feet to avoid catching Aidan's eye. But then I thought, *Why not? What have I got to feel ashamed of?* It wasn't as if I'd *done* anything.

'We were just saying,' Mickie went on, ' – weren't we, girls? – that we were planning on carrying on the celebrations back at our billet. C'mon, big guy – whaddaya say? Care to join us?'

'Ah, love to,' said Aidan, rubbing the back of his neck again, 'but I'd really best be making tracks.'

'Off home to Mrs Aidan?' said Mickie, disappointment and, I sensed, a vague hint of disapproval in her voice.

Aidan laughed. 'Chance'd be a fine thing. There's no Mrs Aidan.'

'*Really*,' Mickie purred – the cogs of her mind already, it seemed, beginning to turn.

'He's right,' said Claire, stepping forward and adopting a tone not unlike the one I've heard her use when her daughter refuses to pick up her toys or finish eating her vegetables. 'It's probably for the best. We'll be wanting an early night ourselves if we're to be up bright and early tomorrow to make the most of the day.'

Very smooth, Claire. Could you try and make your cock-blocking any more *obvious?*

Yikes. I wasn't sure where that thought had come from, but the more I considered it, the more I concluded I wasn't entirely unjustified in feeling aggrieved. Not that I was the sort of person who went around flirting with random strangers and plotting torrid affairs with them, but after what I'd been through over the last couple of weeks, could she really hold it against me if I decided to do just that?

There's no shame in being the bigger person in all of this.

'Ah, come on,' I said, moving towards Aidan and taking hold of his arm. 'Just come back with us for one drink. We don't bite – not normally, anyway.'

I had my back to them, but somehow I could sense the other two staring at me in surprise – or perhaps it was just because I knew that would be a perfectly natural reaction to my decidedly uncharacteristic behaviour. For a moment, I thought about backtracking, passing it off as a slip of the tongue or something. Then I decided I quite liked this new, impulsive, flirtatious me.

'Just one drink,' I repeated, giving Aidan what I believe are what's known in the trade as bedroom eyes while continuing to clutch his arm.

For a moment, Aidan said nothing. Then he gave an easy shrug. 'Ah, sure, why not? I never did get to finish my pint.'

'All *right*!' whooped Mickie. 'Party at our place! Rock on!'

Seizing hold of Aidan's free hand, she dragged him away from me and set off up the road, tugging him after her. Looking utterly bemused by the whole affair, Aidan allowed himself to be led away, casting a brief, helpless glance over his shoulder in my direction as he went.

I was about to follow when I caught Claire's look. She didn't utter any actual words, but her expression said it all. *What are you* doing? it said. I met her gaze unblinkingly, gave a shrug that bordered on insolent and set off up the hill, following the foghorn sound of Mickie's voice as she prattled away unceasingly to Aidan, filling his ears with whatever nonsense came into her head. I didn't look back, but I knew, from the heavy clomp of her footsteps, that Claire was trudging behind me with a face like a wet weekend in . . . well, Port Catrin, I suppose.

6

We stepped into the cabin, Aidan pausing momentarily before crossing the threshold.

'So *this* is how the other half live,' he said.

'You kids make yourselves comfortable,' said Mickie. 'I'll get the bevvy.'

'That's not—' began Claire, as Mickie made a beeline for the drinks cabinet.

But Mickie wasn't paying the blindest bit of attention, and Claire, evidently deciding either that it wasn't worth it or that it would be unseemly to make a scene in front of a guest, swallowed a sigh and let the matter drop.

'Why don't you have a seat?' I suggested to Aidan.

Still gazing wide-eyed at his surroundings, Aidan draped his windcheater over the back of the nearest sofa and sat down. Claire hung up her own coat and laid claim to a low easy chair on the other side of the fireplace, her jaw set. Mickie, meanwhile, rummaged around inside the drinks cabinet with gleeful abandon, humming a little ditty, completely unaware of – or possibly just unfazed by – the simmering tension in the air.

I chanced a quick glance at my phone. There was nothing from Matthew: no missed calls, not even a text acknowledging my own message to him earlier. This left me feeling simultaneously infuriated and strangely triumphant. Of *course* he hadn't rung me back. He didn't care about me. He'd already moved on to a younger model – blonder, bustier and clearly able to satisfy him in ways I wasn't. And, as my gaze strayed once more to Aidan, perched on the sofa, looking bewildered and slightly overawed, the overriding thought running through my head was, *Screw him.*

I headed over and joined Aidan on the sofa, opting to perch directly beside him, even though it was a three-seater. He glanced across at me. I smiled at him and he smiled back – a little uncertainly, but seemingly buoyed by my show of solidarity.

He was about to say something when a burst of soulful, disco-infused jazz rang out. Mickie, it seemed, had discovered and activated the cabin's music system. Its speakers, whose reach seemed to extend to every corner of the room, were pumping out the strains of . . . was that *Marvin Gaye*? Waggling her backside in time to the beat, she sashayed over to us, clutching a bottle of Glenfiddich and an assortment of tumblers.

'Would sir care for a drrrram?' she enquired, in a cod-Miss Jean Brodie voice.

She proceeded to pour us each a glass, then turned to Claire, waggling the bottle in her direction. Claire gave a curt shake of her head and continued to look mutinous.

'Suit yourself,' Mickie smirked.

Turning to us, she pulled a face and mouthed something so profane I'm not going to *attempt* to repeat it here, before pouring herself an exceptionally generous measure and strutting off to crank up the volume while Aidan and I, both having caught the laughing bug, struggled to stifle our giggles. This seemed to be the final straw for Claire, who lurched to her feet and stormed off. She disappeared into the kitchen, slamming the door behind her. From behind it, we heard the sounds of cupboard doors opening and closing and crockery clattering as she engaged in what I could only assume was a spot of angry housekeeping – though what she had to be so worked up about, I couldn't imagine.

'Almost forgot.'

Mickie's voice snapped me out of my thoughts. I looked up as, standing before us once more, she took a tab of pills from her pocket.

'What's this?' I asked.

'A little something to set the mood.' She pressed a single round, white capsule into my hand. 'Call it an early birthday present.'

I gazed down at the pill. It had a little smiley face on it – a symbol that seemed almost perverse in its inappropriateness.

I looked up at Mickie. 'Are those *Es*?' I said, my voice dropping almost to a whisper.

'Might be. C'mon – live a little, H. Before you're *completely* over the hill.'

I'll have you know I'm not a *total* square. I sampled the odd spliff during my uni days, and I'm pretty sure I once ate some shrooms by accident on a camping trip in my teens. But this was something else altogether. I said nothing. All of a sudden, my mouth was painfully dry, so much so that even swallowing required considerable effort. In the background, Marvin continued to croon about coming straight to the point and not wasting time.

Evidently fed up waiting for me to piss or get off the pot, Mickie turned to Aidan, offering the pill to him instead. 'Howsabout you, big guy? You look like a man of the world, so you do.'

Aidan, looking every bit as uncertain as I felt, said nothing for a long moment, then turned in my direction. 'Are *you* having one?'

There's no shame in being the bigger person.

Know what? Fuck it. I was on my holidays, it was my birthday weekend, and after tonight I'd never be a twentysomething again. If ever there was a night for throwing caution to the wind, this was it.

'Tell you what,' I said. 'Let's go halfsies.'

I broke the pill in two and offered one half to him. For a moment he hesitated, looking at it uncertainly. Then, as if he feared I'd either rescind the offer or his own nerve would desert him, he snatched it from me, clutching it tight in his fist.

'We'll go together,' I said, holding up my half. 'On three, OK? One . . . two . . . three!'

In unison, we popped the pills into our mouths, then washed them down with a sloosh of Glenfiddich. With an unmistakeable look of triumph in her eyes, Mickie did likewise, then flung herself on the chair recently vacated by Claire and let out a sigh of contentment.

'What happens now?' I asked.

'Now,' said Mickie, 'we wait for the magic to happen.'

I'm not sure when it was that the Es actually began to kick in. At first, nothing appreciably changed, and I must confess to feeling ever so slightly disappointed. In my mind, I'd imagined something like the final scenes of *2001: A Space Odyssey* – a kaleidoscopic light-show as the universe expanded before my eyes – accompanied by a deep and profound sense of every living organism on Earth being connected to me. Instead, everything remained exactly the same as the three of us lounged about, drinking, talking and listening to music, with a heavy emphasis on the former. The notion of Aidan staying for just one drink quickly fell by the wayside as Mickie continued to serve him refills and Aidan – either possessing a taste for Glenfiddich I wouldn't have credited him with or simply too polite to say no – continued to knock 'em back.

There's not much point in recounting everything we talked about. Most of it was of no great importance or substance – the sort of disposable chit-chat everyone forgets before they've even finished speaking. I was, however, aware of Mickie becoming more and more peripheral to the conversation. I'm not sure whether it was by design on her part, but she seemed to increasingly fade into the background, the world shrinking until it encompassed only Aidan and me as we sat facing one another on the sofa, gazing into each other's eyes as we spoke.

'Is that a Polaroid?' he said suddenly, pointing to my camera, lying on the coffee table where I'd left it before we headed out for dinner, alongside the modest little pile of photos I'd taken earlier.

'Sort of,' I said. 'It's an Instax 500AF. Same concept, different make.'

He gestured to it. 'Can I . . . ?'

'Sure.'

'I never knew they still made these.'

He picked it up and turned it this way and that, studying it carefully – Clearly a man with a keen interest in the practical side of things.

'It's a bit of an acquired taste,' I said, already feeling sheepish in anticipation of the inevitable *why don't you just use an iPhone?* question that always seemed to follow. 'But it has . . . sentimental value.'

'Well, you cannae beat the classics. This one looks like it's seen good use, anyway.' Then, without warning, he put the viewfinder to his eye and pointed it in my direction. 'Smile.'

'Nooo!' I squealed, covering my face with both arms.

He lowered the camera. 'How no?'

'Cos I look a fright, that's how!'

I pictured myself in my holey old pullover, my hair wind-blown and untamed, my face scrubbed of makeup, every spot and pockmark captured onto celluloid for all eternity.

On the other side of the fireplace, Mickie, lying splayed in the easy chair with her head upturned towards the ceiling, gave a contemptuous snort. 'Ah, dinna be talkin' pish!' she slurred, the words running together in a continuous drawl. 'You're a peach. Any man in his right mind'd wanna grab a piece of that—' She trailed off into a thankfully incomprehensible mumble as she once more succumbed to the effects of the drug working its way through her system.

Aidan and I met each other's eyes momentarily before both looking away, embarrassed. For a moment, neither of us seemed to know what to say. Aidan glanced at the camera, then back at me, as if to say, *Shall we?*

I thought about objecting – about exercising my inalienable moral right to refuse consent for my likeness to be taken – but I couldn't think of a single valid reason other than my own squeamishness.

'Ah, go on, then,' I said.

I dutifully sat up straight, legs crossed, hands folded in my lap, my expression studiously neutral, as if I was having my passport mugshot taken. At the sight of me looking so deadly serious, Aidan almost creased up laughing, and it took all my willpower not to follow suit. Then, with what seemed to be a herculean effort, he straightened his face, raised the camera to his eye and snapped the shutter.

There was a flash, a whir and a click, and the camera coughed up its single square of photo paper. Aidan plucked it out and held it up, frowning.

'There's nothing on it,' he said, sounding almost aggrieved.

I laughed. 'You have to wait for it to develop.'

He continued to frown at the blank square, as if a part of him still thought this was some sort of a put-up job. 'Should I shake it or something?'

'That's just a myth. Patience is the watchword.'

I flashed him a wink. It was meant to be conspiratorial in nature, as if I was passing on trade secrets, but as soon as I'd done it, it occurred to me that it could easily have come across as either weirdly lecherous or just plain weird. To cover my own embarrassment, I cleared my throat noisily.

'My turn now.'

Seizing the camera from him, I angled it towards him, peering through the viewfinder as I lined up my shot.

'Smile and say, "smelly feet".'

He looked utterly bemused, but he did as he was told, dutifully parroting the inane phrase as I pressed the shutter, committing him to celluloid.

'There,' I said, setting the camera aside, 'that wasn't so bad, was it?'

Leaving the latest picture developing in the ejection slot, I picked up the one Aidan had taken of me earlier, which by now was starting to take shape. No one would mistake it for anything other than the work of a serious amateur. I was off-centre and tilted too much to the right, and my proximity to the flashbulb had blown out the highlights, giving my already pallid features an almost ghostly appearance.

I pursed my lips, pretending to examine it critically. 'Not bad for a first try. I see signs of promise.'

'Shame you're only here a couple of days. You could've shown me the ropes properly.'

I could tell he was disappointed by the result – so much so that I found myself gripped by an urgent need to toss him a bone of some sort. Leaning forward, I slipped the picture into the breast pocket of his shirt.

'There,' I smiled. 'A present to remember me by.'

Aidan's lips twitched with the inklings of a smile of reciprocation, but I sensed regret in him, as if he'd just been handed an underwhelming consolation prize. An awkward pause elapsed between us, during which I became aware that the music was no longer playing and that the only sound in the room was a rhythmic ticking of the clock on the mantelpiece.

Aidan's eyes flitted to and fro, as if in search of a distraction. They alighted on the pile of photos on the table. He reached over and picked them up.

'Did you do these?'

'Yes,' I said, resisting the urge to snatch them back. I've never been comfortable showing my work to others, thanks to a constant fear that they'll judge it to be subpar. I hadn't even had a chance to sift through these to decide which were worth keeping and which were only fit for the bin. I watched, skin prickling with embarrassment, as he flipped through them, peering at each in turn before lifting his head.

'These are good,' he said.

I felt my cheeks flushing and belatedly wondered whether I'd have felt less self-conscious if he'd dismissed my efforts out of hand rather than lavishing me with praise that felt undeserved.

'Thanks,' I said, unable to meet his eyes. 'Um . . . I mean, they're really not, but it's kind of you to say.'

He continued to flip through my pictures, seeming not to have heard me. 'Have you ever thought about selling these? Or, y'know, putting them in, like, an exhibition or something? I reckon you could make a packet.'

I rolled my eyes to cover my embarrassment. 'Oh, come on! Now you're just being silly.'

Aidan set the photos aside and looked at me with a frown of consternation. 'How come?'

I laughed, partly out of continued embarrassment and partly because of what I perceived as the utter absurdity of what he was suggesting. 'Because I'm not some undiscovered genius or something. I'm just a boring, regular person with a tatty old camera dabbling in something I know next to nothing about.'

Aidan shook his head slowly, brows pursed in concern. 'That's no good,' he said. 'No good at all. You oughtn't to put yourself down like that. You could be anything you wanted to be.'

In my present mental state, that seemed like just about the most profound thing anyone had ever said in the entire history of human consciousness. And sitting there within touching distance of him, I felt an overwhelming surge of affection towards him. *THANK you, I wanted to say. Thank you for expressing your unqualified, wholehearted belief in me, even if you really don't know me at all.* I realised suddenly that, in all the years we'd been together, I'd never known Matthew to convey anything even remotely close to these sentiments.

As we continued to sit, looking into each other's eyes and saying nothing, I had a sudden awareness of things having slowed almost to a standstill. It's hard to describe, but it was like the very nature of time had shifted in some indefinable way. The ticking of the clock sounded unnaturally loud, the silence separating each tick seeming to last an eternity. I could hear my own heart beating too; was hyper-aware both of it and of the rhythm of my breathing. The air seemed to be filled with static, a thousand tiny electric shocks sparking on my skin. I felt hot, flushed, slowly melting inside my pullover, so much so that I wanted to tear it off then and there.

Then, before I was even aware of having moved, I was lunging towards him and we were kissing, our lips locking together, our hands all over each other. I was on top of him, our harried breathing mingling together, thrumming in my ears, our bodies grinding against each other through our clothes. And then, in a sudden explosion of pent-up breath, we both came up for air at the same time. We lay there, staring into each other's eyes, our hearts, pressed together, seeming to have become a single, unitary organism beating in tandem. Every nerve cell in my body was crackling, and I knew beyond a shadow of a doubt that I didn't just want this – I *needed* this.

There's no shame in being the bigger person.

I became aware that we had an audience and turned to see Mickie grinning across at us from the easy chair.

'Get a room, you two,' she said.

I'd never heard a better suggestion in all my life. With a deftness that, in retrospect, is remarkable given the state I was in but which, at the time, seemed completely natural, I stood up, took Aidan's hand and hoisted him to his feet. Without a word, I led him towards the stairs.

7

As we descended to the lower level, the ground beneath my feet seemed to tilt and slant, as if we were going below deck in a ship at sea. I trailed my free hand against the wall for support as I led Aidan down the long corridor towards my room.

We stumbled in, barely able to control ourselves long enough for me to kick the door shut behind us before the kissing resumed with newfound fervour. I had no idea I'd had this much animal lust inside me. It was as if I was making up for years of self-imposed abstinence, trying to frantically soak up all the passion I'd been missing out on before the window of opportunity closed.

With our lips still locked together, Aidan lifted me up off the ground, sliding his hands under my buttocks as I curled my legs around his back. He carried me over to the bed and set me down, clambering onto the mattress after me as I shimmied backwards till I reached the headboard. I pushed myself up onto my elbows and gazed up at him as he loomed over me, huge and imposing, blotting out everything else from my field of vision. As he leaned in to kiss me again, a small silver pendant hanging from a chain round his neck collided with my forehead.

'Ow!' I winced, and we both laughed at our shared clumsiness.

Amid much fumbling and sheepish apologies, we managed, between us, to unloop the pendant from around his neck. He reached over and set it on the nightstand, then resumed his ministrations. In a brief, hurried interval between kisses, I raised my arms and he pulled my jumper and T-shirt over my head in a oner, leaving just my bra. I lay back and closed my eyes as he worked his way down my body, his hands cupping my hips while his tongue slicked the inside of my navel. My fingers gripped the mattress as he began to undo my jeans.

That was when my phone rang.

In truth, I hadn't given it a second thought since I'd shoved it back in my pocket after checking it for messages earlier. Now, however, the opening instrumental to 'Mud' by Tiger Feet rent the air, disconcertingly loud in the otherwise silent room. Aidan straightened up, a look of confusion etched into his features as he tried to work out where the jaunty beat was coming from. I fumbled to silence it, but my sweat-slick palm slipped on the smooth surface and it slid from my hand, landing out of reach on the floor.

'Whoops!' said Aidan, with a dopey laugh.

Then, before I had time to process what was happening, he leaned down and picked it up. He angled the screen towards his face, a clueless grin plastered on his features.

'Who's Matthew?'

My throat was dry. I couldn't speak.

The ringtone continued for a couple more seconds, then stopped.

'Gone to voicemail,' said Aidan, still grinning obliviously. 'Will we find out what he wants?'

Before I could stop him, he tapped the screen a couple of times, and Matthew's voice cut in mid-sentence.

'—just a word. One we say without thinking – say it so many times every day it loses all sense of meaning. But I *am* sorry. You've no idea *how* sorry. For what I did to you. For what I did to *us.*'

His voice sounded strange, almost alien. It was obviously Matthew, but at the same time it wasn't. Gone was his usual self-assurance, his precision with his words. His tone was maudlin, uncertain, and it was clear, from the slight slurring of his speech, that he'd been drinking.

'I made a mistake – a truly terrible mistake. I took you for granted, and that's the one thing I promised myself I'd never do. Because you're worth more than that. So much more.'

For a moment, there was silence, apart from a curious rasping noise, distorted by the phone's tinny speaker. For a moment, I had no idea what I was listening to. Then, with a sudden rush of understanding, I realised the unfamiliar sound was Matthew crying.

'Do you remember our first proper date?' he went on after a moment, his voice thick and phlegmy. 'We had dinner at the Witchery, and then we wandered round the Old Town for hours, not saying anything, just holding hands and looking into each other's eyes. Then, afterwards, we climbed to the top of Arthur's Seat, and I held you in my arms and we sat and watched the sun coming up over the Firth of Forth. That was the night I knew I wanted to spend the rest of my life with you.' He paused to clear his throat. 'I still feel that way. I just lost sight of what was important.'

A lengthy silence elapsed, during which I belatedly became aware once more of Aidan, kneeling on the bed in front of me, holding the phone, brows knitted together as he continued to stare uncomprehendingly at the screen.

'Anyway,' said Matthew, his tone resolute, as if he'd found a new sense of clarity, 'I'll understand if you just delete this message. I'll understand if you never want to see me again. But before you do anything rash, please think about what I've said. If you want to talk, or just . . . you know . . . I'm here. I love you, Haze. Always have.'

With that, he rang off. As silence descended once again, Aidan slowly lowered the phone, staring at me wordlessly.

I swallowed heavily. I felt my stomach contracting. There were few things I would have welcomed more right now than the ground opening up and devouring me whole. Suddenly acutely aware of my state of undress, I hugged my arms to my chest.

'Who was that?' said Aidan, in the sort of voice that told me he already knew he wasn't going to like the answer.

I licked my dry lips and swallowed again. 'My . . . my partner.'

'Your *what*?'

I didn't speak. My mind was racing, the entire situation turned on its head in the blink of an eye. I wasn't sure whether I was ready to forget everything and take Matthew back unquestioningly. I just knew I was no longer ready to cast him aside without a second thought in the way I had been moments earlier. And I definitely knew I wasn't ready to sleep with a man I'd just met purely out of some misplaced compulsion to get even.

'I don't understand,' said Aidan.

'I'm sorry,' I said – and really, I was. For myself, yes, but more than that, I was sorry for him, and the obvious hurt I'd done to him.

As we sat facing one another, a new, unfamiliar look came over Aidan. There was still confusion in his eyes, and disbelief, but those feelings were giving way to a growing sense of anger. It was slowly dawning on him that he'd been made to look like a mug.

'Did *they* put you up to it?' he said quietly.

'Sorry . . . what?'

'Those mates of yours. Was this some sort of a bet? See who could seduce the local bumpkin first?'

'No!' I cried, horrified by the very idea. 'It wasn't . . . I mean, I never set out to . . . I mean . . . ' I trailed off helplessly.

Aidan didn't seem to hear. Eyes lowered, jaw set, he shook his head firmly. 'It's no right,' he said, seemingly to himself, 'doing that sort of thing. No right at all.'

'Aidan, please, just give me the phone,' I said, holding out my hand for it while still trying to cover myself with my other arm.

Once more, he didn't seem to hear me. 'No right,' he muttered, and began to stab at the phone's screen with a blunt finger.

I looked at him in horror. 'What are you *doing*?'

He was too focused on his task to look up. 'Calling him back,' he said, as if it was obvious. 'Gonnae tell him just what sort of woman his girlfriend is.'

Panic seized me. Matthew couldn't find out – not now, not like this. I lurched forward, grabbing for the phone. He jerked it away, but I lunged at him again, and this time managed to get both hands round it.

What I remember most about that brief struggle is how eerily quiet it was. No shouting, no laboured breathing, just silence as we both tugged the phone this way and that, each trying to dislodge it from the other's grip. Aidan had the advantage of his superior weight and strength behind him, but my desperation had lit a fire under me and I was able to match him – or perhaps he was holding back out of some misplaced sense of chivalry. Back and forth we struggled, both of us hellbent on the contested prize. Then, without warning, Aidan gave a short, sharp tug, and I felt myself being pulled forward, my grip on the phone slipping.

In that same instant, I experienced the closest thing I've ever had to what I imagine an out-of-body experience must be like. I saw myself and Aidan with total clarity, from the perspective of a third party floating high above us. We seemed to be frozen in a state of limbo, as if the normal rules of time and space had ceased to apply. I seemed to know what I was going to do long before I did it, though in reality only a fraction of a second can have passed between Aidan tugging the phone towards him and me releasing my grip on it, powerless to stop what I was setting in motion.

For a moment, he remained upright, a look of surprise mingled with triumph on his face. Then gravity kicked in, the momentum carrying him backwards with the same force he'd applied to the phone. He tumbled off the bed and disappeared from view. I heard a soft crunch, then nothing.

For almost a full minute, I didn't move. I remained on the bed, my back against the headboard, knees drawn up to my chin, trying not to make a sound even though I felt a desperate need to gulp down as much air as possible. Then, slowly, my entire body shaking with trepidation, I crawled to the foot of the bed and peered over the edge.

Aidan lay on his back on the hardwood floor, one arm bent upwards in an 'L' shape, the other limp by his side. His bloodshot eyes stared up at me – wide, unseeing, unblinking. Blood trickled from his nostrils and ears, pooling beneath his head. No movement came from him. No rise and fall of his chest. No sound of breathing.

That was when I began to scream.

8

When I finally became aware of my surroundings again, I found myself curled up at the top of the bed, a blanket draped over my shoulders. Either Claire or Mickie must have put it there. I'd been dimly conscious of them arriving – summoned, no doubt, by my screams. Of Claire bending down to check for a pulse. But everything since then had been a blur. I had no grasp of how much time had passed. The two of them were on opposite sides of the room, and I could tell, from the direction of their respective gazes, exactly what they were looking at. I was grateful not to be able to see it from my position. Once had been more than enough.

'Maybe we could just say we found him here,' said Mickie, breaking the stifling silence.

She didn't sound overly convinced by this idea herself, and Claire's prompt scoff and eye-roll made *her* thoughts on the matter abundantly clear.

Mickie's eyes flared in her direction. 'You got any better ideas, then, Charlie Church? I mean, I suppose we could always pray for divine intervention.'

'You're not helping.'

'After all, Jesus is meant to have brought that Lazawhatsit guy back from the dead, isn't he? What's the difference here?'

'I'm warning you—'

'Why? Gonna strike me down with holy vengeance?'

'STOP IT!!!'

I hadn't meant for it to come out so loud or so shrill, but it did the trick. The pair of them both clammed up instantly and spun round to face me.

'You're absolutely, one hundred percent sure he's dead,' I said carefully, a part of me still clinging to a faint and distant hope, despite what the rational part of my brain was telling me.

Claire sighed unhappily. 'His skull's fractured. He has major compression to the occipital and lower parietal bones. He'd have suffered a massive bleed on the brain. He has no pulse or heartbeat.' She offered me a strained, apologetic smile. 'Yes, I'm sure.'

I felt my chest tightening, my own heart rate ramping up. As panic ballooned inside me and I struggled to catch my breath, I was aware of Claire perching on the side of the bed next to me, forcing my head down between my shoulder-blades, telling me to focus on slowing down my breathing.

'See?' she said encouragingly, as the spots stopped dancing before my eyes and I found I could get my breath once more. 'You're all right.'

As she spoke, Mickie made a gagging noise and contorted her entire body in disgust. 'Jesus Christ on a Christmas cracker! What is that *smell*?'

I realised I could smell it too – that, on some subconscious level, I'd been aware of it for some time. And I knew the answer even as Claire got to her feet and moved over to inspect the body.

'His muscles would have relaxed at the moment of death,' she said, sounding quite detached and matter-of-fact about it. 'That would have included his sphincter, which would have caused his bowels and bladder to empty.'

I felt my stomach pitching. 'I need to get out of here,' I mumbled, lurching to my feet, the blanket falling from my shoulders.

Claire hurried over to me. She put an arm round my shoulders and took my hand in hers, shepherding me towards the door as if I was a little old lady. Gently but firmly, she steered me in a wide arc round the body. I tried not to look, forcing my eyes to go blurry as we skirted the ever-expanding pool of blood, but that heavy, dark shape nonetheless loomed large on the periphery of my vision.

Claire got me up the stairs to the living room and settled me on the sofa. Mickie, bringing up the rear, handed me a hoodie she'd brought with her from the bedroom.

'Here ya go, wee hen,' she said, as I felt the soft fabric in my limp hands. 'Don't want ya catching hypothermia on top of everything else.'

It was only then that I realised that, apart from my bra, I had nothing on above the waist, and that I was shaking as much from cold as from shock. I struggled into the hoodie with numb, trembling fingers and sat, legs curled under me, gazing up at Mickie and Claire, their faces as grave and drawn as I'd ever seen them.

'What am I going to . . . ' I began, then stopped. I couldn't say it.

Claire, her face awash with compassion and concern, knelt before me, taking my hand in hers and squeezing it.

'*We*,' she said. '*We* are going to get through this, OK? We're all in this together.' She glanced up at Mickie. 'Right?'

I sensed Mickie hesitating for a beat, before giving a curt nod. 'Right.'

Claire continued to squeeze my hand. 'We'll fix this, I promise.'

'All for one and one for all,' said Mickie, with little enthusiasm.

'OK,' said Claire, pacing back and forth in front of the sofa, 'we need to think things through logically.' She stopped and turned to face me. 'Take us through *exactly* what happened.'

Some time had passed, and I was calmer now – no longer struggling to force enough oxygen into my lungs, no longer failing to form a single coherent thought. I told the story as succinctly as possible, from the moment Claire disappeared into the kitchen to the struggle in the bedroom. The whole evening had a hazy, indeterminate sort of feel to it, like a waking dream – one in which both the precise order of events and the passage of time were difficult to pin down. The E I'd taken must have got to work inside my system far sooner than I'd realised.

When I'd finished, silence descended on the room. Mickie was sitting at the other end of the sofa, knees drawn up to her chin, arms wrapped round her lower legs. Claire was still on her feet, standing before me, arms folded, weight placed on one leg, the other curled slightly behind her, like a dancer in a resting pose. Both looked to be deep in thought.

It was Mickie who broke the silence. 'So,' she said, looking around and shrugging expectantly, 'what we gonna do?'

'Well,' said Claire, after a moment, 'as I see it, we have three options. The first is *your* suggestion.'

'Remind me?'

'We leave the body where it is and do nothing.'

'I wish you wouldn't call him that,' I said.

Claire turned to me with a frown. 'What?'

'"The body". He's not an "it". He has a name. Aidan.'

'*Had* a name, H,' said Mickie softly. '*Had* a name.'

I said nothing. I had no idea why I was so wrapped up in the semantics of it all. However we chose to describe him, and whether we referred to him in the present tense or the past, weren't going to change the situation in which I now found myself.

'Well,' said Claire, 'whichever pronouns we're using, I think I can safely speak for all of us when I say that leaving him where he is – then presumably acting surprised in a couple of weeks' time when the cleaning lady stumbles across him and raises the entire village – is the non-starter to end all non-starters.' She gave Mickie a vaguely condescending look. 'No offence.'

Mickie looked sullen but said nothing.

'Option two is, we pick up the phone and call the police without any further delay.'

'And tell them what?'

Claire simply shrugged, as if the question was redundant.

'Oh right,' Mickie snorted. 'So we're just gonna give 'em the same spiel Hazel just gave us, and they're just gonna pat us on our heads and say, "Thanks for bringing this to our attention, ladies; now on your bikes"? You wanna talk about non-starters? We both know the only way that one ends is with my big cousin banged up on a murder charge.'

Murder. The very sound of that word – so harsh, so final – made me want to throw up.

'You don't know that,' said Claire.

'Don't I? Well, let's just imagine how this is gonna play out. The cops show up, they see a deid boady laying on the floor—'

'It was an accident,' said Claire, as if no right-minded person could possibly think otherwise. 'No one was to blame.'

'And they're just gonna take our word for it, are they? Fancy placing a wager on that? Things don't turn out the way you want 'em to just cos you wish hard enough for it, Churchie.'

'I *know* that,' said Claire sharply. 'I'm just saying, coming clean as soon as possible will stand us in good stead later. It'll look less like we've got something to hide. Besides, it's only murder if it's premeditated and done with deliberate intent to kill. Otherwise it's culpable homicide.'

'Dancin' on the heid of a pin there, pal. Murder, culpable homicide – what's the difference?'

'The difference,' snapped Claire, 'is a few years versus a life sentence.'

I was struggling to process what I was hearing. Were we really sitting here contemplating how long I would or wouldn't be spending behind bars? It felt like they were discussing someone else – some other Hazel Knight to whom this had happened. This wasn't me. I wasn't a—

'Aren't you forgetting something?' Mickie's voice cut into my thoughts. 'The Es. First thing they're gonna do when they get the body back to the morgue is an autopsy. That shit stays in the bloodstream for days. They're gonna wanna know how he came to have it in his system. Where he got it from. And it's not gonna take 'em long to figure it out.' She turned to me. 'I mean, no offence, but your pupils are like bloody dinner plates.'

'It wasn't the drugs that killed him,' said Claire. 'Not directly, at any rate.' I think she was trying to be charitable towards Mickie, but she still couldn't resist adding that little dig.

'Might as well've been, way the filth'll see it. You know you can get seven years for supplying? You can get less for culpable whatsit.'

Claire sighed. 'It's not a competition.'

Mickie scowled and shook her head. 'I'm not going to jail. I wasn't built for it.' Her tone was defiant, but I could see from the look in her eyes that she was genuinely scared. 'It's all right for you,' she added, shooting a venomous look in Claire's direction. 'You're the only one here who's got nothing to lose.'

Claire didn't respond to that, but I could tell her sympathy wasn't exactly at an all-time high.

'Well, OK, then,' Mickie continued, lurching to her feet with her fists clenched, as if she was getting ready to give Claire a square go, 'take me out of the picture for a minute. Say, for talking's sake, Hazel's the only one with skin in the game. And say you're right and the cops are happy to accept the whole thing as one big, unhappy oopsie. It's still gonna come out it happened while she was having a drugged-up bed-time romp with a guy she just met. You know what the tabloids are like. Sell their granny for a juicy scoop. First sniff they get of it, it'll be all over the front pages. Next thing you know, her bosses are asking her to clear her desk. Can't handle the scandal, see. And Matthew? Well, all of a sudden that moral high ground she's had over the whole extrajudicial shagging thing's looking awfy shaky. Reckon he's gonna take her back after it all comes out in the wash?'

'A few hours ago you couldn't stop telling us how it was over and Hazel should move on as quickly as possible.'

With no comeback to that, Mickie merely sucked her teeth noisily and made a dismissive gesture with her arm.

'Well?' Claire turned to me expectantly. '*Is* it over?'

The pair of them had been busy discussing my fate amongst themselves for so long now that I wasn't at all prepared for being asked to contribute. My mind was an empty vessel. Thinking clearly – making a definitive statement of any kind – just wasn't on the agenda.

'I don't know,' I said unhappily.

Claire shook her head softly and shut her eyes. Mickie's shoulders slumped. She headed back to the sofa and sat down heavily. A leaden silence descended on the room, broken only by the ticking of the clock.

At length, I spoke again. 'Three.'

Claire stirred. 'Sorry?'

'You said we had three choices. What's the third?'

Claire said nothing.

'That's obvious,' said Mickie. 'We get rid of it.'

I looked to Claire for confirmation that this was indeed what she was thinking. Her silence told me all I needed to know.

'Think about it,' Mickie went on. 'No one knows he was ever here. We never ran into a soul on the way up the hill, or in all that time we were stood outside gassing in the pissing rain.'

'What about in the pub?' I said. 'There were dozens of people who could place us there – *and* him. The landlord knows he bought my drinks for me at the bar – and then there's the confrontation with those men over the table. Every man and his dog there's going to remember that – and that he was the one who stepped in on our behalf.'

'That's true,' said Claire, her jaw tight as she mulled the matter over. 'We can't pretend our paths never crossed. But Mickie's right – for all anyone knows, we left after the bust-up and came straight back here—'

'—and Aidan skipped off into the wide blue yonder and was never seen again,' Mickie finished.

'But . . . but what about his loved ones?' I blurted out, still desperately searching for a catch. 'His family, his friends . . . They've a right to know what happened to him. We can't just leave them wondering.'

Claire pursed her lips and said nothing.

With a sigh, Mickie got to her feet and moved to face me. Dropping to her knees, she took my hands in hers and squeezed them hard, forcing me to look at her.

'Listen to me, wee hen,' she said softly. 'There's no good outcomes here. We cannae change what happened. This is just the least worst option. The one that hurts the fewest people. Think about it: his rellies are gonna be cut up whether he dropped off the face of the earth or died in a sordid sex game with some thirsty wench from the big city.' She held up her hands in a peace gesture as I opened my mouth to protest. 'Just saying how the papers are gonna spin it, honeybun. Either way, his folks willnae thank you for clearing up their misconceptions.'

I said nothing. I couldn't argue with a word of what she'd said, but that didn't make it any easier to stomach. I looked past her to Claire. Her silence told me she and Mickie were, once again, in agreement.

I took a deep breath. 'If we're going to do this . . . ' I began, then stopped, the bare reality of what we were actually discussing once more hitting me in the solar plexus. '*If* we're going to do this,' I said again, 'how do we . . . ? I mean,' I added, almost sheepishly, 'there's quite a lot *of* him.'

Mickie pondered this, chewing the inside of her cheek. 'Either of yous ever see *Rear Window*?'

That did it for me. I shot out of my seat and fled down the stairs, reaching the bathroom just in time for the contents of my stomach to fire into the waiting toilet bowl. As I knelt on the floor, retching and spitting and sobbing all at the same time, I felt a hand on my shoulder. And then Claire was crouching beside me, holding my hair out of the path of the vomit as she rubbed my back.

'There now,' she purred. 'Just you let it all out.'

Gradually, my retching subsided and I was able to breathe properly again, my insides purged clean. I spat a final mouthful of acid saliva into the pan and shimmied backwards until I was sitting on the floor with my back against the bathtub. As I sat there, wiping my mouth with the back of my hand, Claire got to her feet, flushed the toilet and poured me a glass of water from the sink.

'I'm so sorry you're in this situation,' she said as I gulped down water, trying to salve my burning throat and wash away the foul taste. 'I wish there was something I could do to make it all go away.'

In that moment, I felt so profoundly grateful I could have kissed her. The unqualified support, the lack of I-told-you-sos – it's why her friendship means everything to me; why I remain convinced that her decision to sidle up to me and introduce herself that night at the student union was one of the best things to ever happen to me. She'd made her concerns about the course of action I'd taken tonight clear from the offset, and yet there was no gloating from her, no rubbing it in, no *you've made your bed, now lie in it* style remonstrations. Instead, she was knuckling down, searching for practical solutions to get me out of the hole into which I'd dug myself. She, truly, was being the bigger person.

'I'll back you whatever you decide,' she went on as I swallowed another gulp of water. 'You know I will. But it has to be your choice. Neither of us can make it for you.'

I gazed up at her, saying nothing. I felt a sliver of water run down my chin.

'Mum's cancer's come back,' I said suddenly.

'What?' Claire blinked at me in disbelief and shock. 'No! When?'

'We found out a couple of months ago. She asked me not to tell anyone – not until . . . ' I trailed off. 'The doctors are going to do what they can, but they're talking in terms of buying her time.'

Claire's face crumpled. 'I'm so sorry, darling.'

'I know.'

She lowered herself onto the floor next to me and laid her head on my shoulder. For a while, we remained like that, side by side, saying nothing. Mum's condition was something that had been lingering at the back of my mind since the moment Mickie raised the prospect of a public scandal. Being traduced by the press, labelled as a scarlet woman who seduced an unsuspecting local boy and lured him to his death – I might be able to weather that storm, but not the effect it would have on my mother.

'I want—' I began, then stopped. Collected my thoughts. Began again, with more conviction. 'I can't let this get out. It would destroy her.'

Claire didn't respond. There was no need. I knew she understood. Knew what I was telling her. After a moment, she stirred, eased herself upright and gave my shoulder a squeeze.

'I'll give you some time to yourself,' she said softly, then turned and slipped out, leaving the door open a crack behind her.

It was at least another fifteen minutes – and probably longer – before I finally got to my feet. Feeling lightheaded and loose-limbed, I made my way gingerly up the stairs, returning to the living room to find Mickie and Claire sitting on opposite sofas, both still but clearly poised for action. They watched in silence as I crossed the floor and came to a halt facing them.

'If we're going to do this,' I said, 'I don't him to be cut up or disfigured in any way. He has to remain *whole*. I want us to afford him what little respect and dignity we still can.'

For a long, agonising moment, neither Mickie nor Claire moved or spoke. Then, almost in unison, they got to their feet and made their way over to join me.

9

'The way I see it,' Claire said, 'the only two options are burial on land or at sea. And if we bury him at sea, it would need to be some distance from the shore so he doesn't simply wash up when the tide next comes in.'

'Then we'd need a boat,' said Mickie. 'And I dunno about yous two, but I never was much of a seafarer at the best of times – 'specially not when it's pitch black and blowing a gale.'

Claire considered this, then nodded. 'Agreed. So, land burial it is. Where?'

Mickie shrugged. 'The woods? There's plenty of woods nearby.'

Claire shook her head. 'Nearby's no use. What we want is a decent-sized patch of woodland some way off – somewhere people aren't going to think to look when the alarm goes up that he's missing, and where it's not going to be obvious to the first dog walker passing through that the ground's been disturbed.'

'Where, then?'

Claire was silent for a moment, lips pursed in thought. Then, without a word, she turned and headed for the stairs. She returned a moment later, clutching the AA map we'd relied on when we lost our way on the road here. She spread it across the coffee table, running her finger over the page as she traced a line west from Port Catrin.

'There.' She tapped a large area shaded green. 'It's about a thirty-mile drive. That should be far enough.'

'Right, then,' said Mickie, with glum resignation. 'Lead on, Macduff.'

We headed back down to the bedroom, Claire and Mickie leading the way while I trailed behind them, my reluctance to even set foot in there again causing each step I took to drag more heavily than the last. I think a part of me was almost hoping we'd get there and find that Aidan's body had disappeared, like the shock twist at the end of a horror movie.

No such luck. He was still there, exactly as we'd left him. The blood from his ears and nose had ceased to flow, and his skin had begun to assume a sickly, greyish hue. His wide, bloodshot eyes stared up at me as I slowly shuffled into the room, hugging the wall to keep as far away from him as possible.

'Can we not do something about his eyes?' I said.

For a moment, Claire didn't move. I could tell she saw my request as pointless – an unnecessary distraction from the task at hand. But then, after a moment, she bent down and closed Aidan's eyes with a single, deft movement.

I watched as, between them, Claire and Mickie stripped the bed and, using the sheet as a shroud, proceeded to wrap Aidan from head to toe. No words were exchanged as they worked, giving the impression that they were either communicating telepathically or had already agreed on a plan of attack – presumably while I was busy feeling sorry for myself in the bathroom. They were like a well-oiled machine, each seeming to sense implicitly what the other required at any given moment. It gave me a strange, almost comforting feeling to watch them working so seamlessly together. How grotesque, I thought, that it had taken something like this to bring them together.

As they beavered away, something lying on the nightstand next to the bed glinted in the light, catching my eye. Something round and metallic.

Aidan's pendant.

I chanced a glance at Claire and Mickie. Satisfied that they were thoroughly preoccupied, I stole over to the nightstand and slipped the pendant into the pocket of my jeans, then returned to my original spot while they were none the wiser. I can't for the life of me think what possessed me, but once it was done, I was hardly in a position to put it back – not without running the risk of being caught red-handed and having a whole lot of explaining to do.

Once Mickie and Claire were done, they lifted Aidan off the floor, Mickie taking the head while Claire grabbed his legs. I watched, a part of me feeling I should offer to help, though I was sure I'd just be getting in the way if I did. Worse still, I had a horrible mental image of myself fumbling and dropping him; of the back of his skull crashing down onto the floor for a second time. Instead, I followed them out into the corridor, trailing behind them like a twisted parody of a grieving relative walking behind the pallbearers in a funeral procession.

Mickie and Claire were both panting heavily by the time they finally reached the top of the stairs. They carried Aidan outside, briefly depositing him on the gravel-clad ground next to the Land Rover while Claire unrolled a tarpaulin sheet and laid it across the floor of the boot. It was well after midnight by now, and though it had stopped raining, the clouds remained thick and heavy above us, the moon hidden behind them. The village below us lay in darkness, barring a handful of windows that were still lit up.

'We should leave our phones behind,' Mickie said. 'GPS and whatnot.'

I was about to say I seriously doubted anyone would be able to trace our whereabouts given the ongoing difficulty in getting a signal in this neck of the woods, but I restrained myself. 'Mine's still downstairs,' I said instead. 'I never picked it up after—' I stopped, my breath catching in my throat.

Mickie hurried back into the house with hers and Claire's phones while Claire shut the door to the boot. The sound of it slamming seemed to reverberate all around us in the still air. She got into the driver's seat while I slipped into the back. A moment later, Mickie returned with a couple of shovels, having evidently swung by the tool shed on the way. She deposited them on the parcel shelf behind me before heading round to the front passenger seat. Claire fired the ignition and we were off.

She drove slowly, keeping the lights off as we crawled through the village. No one spoke, but I knew each one of us was praying – no doubt literally, in Claire's case – that we wouldn't encounter anyone on the road. We didn't, and, as we cleared the village and Claire began to ease a few more miles per hour out of the speedometer, Mickie let out an audible sigh of relief. I realised I'd been holding my own breath and let it out too. Our pace continued to quicken as Port Catrin dwindled behind us, though Claire didn't engage the headlights for a while yet – not till Mickie hissed at her to put them on or we'd go crashing into someone on one of those sharp bends. We sailed on past an isolated bungalow, and, for a moment, the glare of the headlights illuminated a gargoyle statue in its front garden. It seemed to leer mockingly at me, as if it knew exactly what I'd done.

We must have driven for over an hour, though, looking back on it, I was pretty out of it and barely paying any attention. We stuck to the lanes and backroads, steering clear of the smattering of small villages that dotted the countryside. We only met three other cars on the road, though each time, my heart leapt into my throat and continued to pound long after the other vehicle had sailed on by. I was acutely conscious, every step of the way, of Aidan's body in the boot behind me. On more than one occasion, I became convinced I could hear a rasping sound coming from back there, like laboured breathing, though neither Mickie nor Claire seemed to notice. I told myself it was just the purr of the car's engine.

Shortly after one a.m., the open fields on either side of us gave way to dense woodland. We continued following the same road for a while, the trees growing heavier and thicker. After another four or five miles, we came to a turn-off onto a narrow dirt track that wound off into an expanse of pine trees. Claire took the turn, and we followed the track until it ran out and the trees became too dense for us to take the car any further.

'This'll do,' said Claire.

The silence of the wood enveloped us like a thick blanket as we stepped out of the car. Claire and Mickie collected a shovel each and we set off, Claire leading the way with the torch that, sensible soul that she is, she always keeps handy in the glove compartment. I brought up the rear. An overwhelming sense of despair bore down on me, as if I was carrying an intensely heavy load on my shoulders. My throat felt swollen and achy. My chest seemed to be contracting. I desperately wanted to curl up into a ball, shut my eyes and not open them again till this had all gone away. But I knew that was impossible, no matter how much I might wish otherwise. So I plodded on, doggedly putting one foot in front of another until we came to a little clearing.

Claire tested the ground with her foot and turned to Mickie. 'What d'you reckon?'

Mickie prodded the ground with the tip of her Doc Marten. 'Never thought I'd say this, but thank fuck for Scottish rain.'

The pair of them started to dig. They worked in silence, gritting their teeth and getting on with it without complaint. Claire had to stop to take frequent breaks, either to get her breath back or to massage her aching hands, but Mickie proved to be made of sterner stuff. At five foot two, she may not look like much, but I've seen her with her top off and know she packs an impressive amount of muscle mass into a relatively small space – the result of a fondness for hitting the gym to burn off all the excess energy she carries around inside her. Occasionally, she paused to wipe sweat from her brow, but otherwise she soldiered on, clearly putting in the lion's share of the work.

I watched in silence, my feelings of guilt over the pair of them busting their asses for my benefit growing by the minute, even as I told myself I was being more use to them by keeping out of the way and leaving them to it. I was acutely conscious of my surroundings, my ears alert to every rustling leaf and snapping twig: all the normal nocturnal woodland noises, each one rendered ominous by virtue of what we were doing. My eyes strayed to a nearby tree – one of the few oaks amid a sea of pines. It was bent almost double, its aged branches sagging as if from exhaustion. *It looks like it's mourning,* I thought, and couldn't help but conclude that this was, somehow, an entirely appropriate place to stage a burial.

It took Mickie and Claire a little over two hours to finish their work. By the time they were done, they were both exhausted and clearly in varying degrees of pain, though neither of them uttered so much as a word of complaint. Claire had her pullover tied round her waist; Mickie had tossed her flannel overshirt on the ground. I was chilled to the bone in my hoodie, but the pair of them were so clearly overheated from their exertions that I could almost see the steam rising from their skin. But they didn't stand still for more than a few seconds. It wasn't even four a.m., but the woods were already getting lighter.

We headed back to the Land Rover, where Claire and Mickie hauled Aidan's body out of the back and set off, shuffling slowly back the way we'd come, weighed down by their cargo. They came to a stop next to the open grave and, bending at the knees, began to lower the body down.

The whole manoeuvre would have been perfectly choreographed if Claire hadn't lost her grip at the last minute. Mickie, unable to support the dead weight herself, was forced to let go as well. Aidan dropped into the pit and landed with a thud that echoed in the treetops and caused us all to freeze, ears pricked for any sounds of movement nearby. Hearing nothing, the other two relaxed.

'Sorry,' Claire whispered.

''Mention it,' muttered Mickie.

Slowly, reluctantly, I shuffled over to join them. Together, we gazed down at Aidan's body, lying peacefully in a grave that could hardly have been a better fit for him if it had been measured to size.

'We should get this over with,' said Claire.

Mickie looked at her in surprise. 'Aren't we gonna say anything? Like . . . I dunno, a prayer?'

Claire shot her a withering look and grabbed her shovel.

She'd already scooped up a load of dirt when I suddenly remembered.

'Oh shit – the picture!'

The others looked at me in confusion.

'The photo he took of me,' I said, looking at them beseechingly. 'It's still in his pocket. I put it there.'

I didn't need to spell it out. I knew they were both thinking exactly the same as me. *If anyone ever finds the body . . .*

'I'm not going down,' said Mickie, looking positively ill at the thought. 'Fuck that for a game of soldiers.'

I glanced at Claire. She hardly looked any more enthused by the idea than Mickie.

I made my decision.

'I'll do it.'

I'm not sure what motivated me to volunteer – a desire to spare my friends this ugly task, perhaps, or some subconscious urge to look on Aidan's face one last time, or maybe even just a need to do *something* other than stand and watch. I just knew it was something I had to do.

With the others' help, I scrambled down into the pit. Lit from above by the beam of Claire's torch, I gingerly unwrapped the shroud, exposing Aidan's face, his cheeks greyish and streaked with dried blood from his nostrils. Swallowing the wave of nausea that threatened to overwhelm me, I slid my hand into the shroud, reaching down to his breast pocket. I felt the outline of the little square of photo paper. Slowly, carefully, I drew it out. As I did so, my hand brushed the side of his face and I felt the bristles of his beard pricking at my skin.

As I leaned in to cover his face again, I once more thought I heard the sound of a faint breath escaping from between his lips, but when I placed the back of my hand near his mouth, I felt nothing. It was just nightly noises, I told myself. Claire was certain he was dead, and she was the one with a string of letters after her name.

Helped by Mickie, I scrambled out of the pit. As soon as my feet touched the ground, and before I even had time to collect my thoughts, Claire snatched the picture from my hand and pocketed it. As she did so, I experienced a momentary flash of something akin to anger, as if she'd just seized some cherished personal artefact from me. As if she didn't trust me. It only lasted for an instant, but a sense of ill-feeling continued to linger inside me as she picked up her shovel once more.

It took the two of them considerably less time to fill in the grave than to dig it, and within the space of fifteen minutes, they were done. They made the ground look as undisturbed as possible, smoothing over the dirt and dragging fallen branches and other foliage over to cover it.

Somewhere, on some distant farm, a cock crowed. That seemed as appropriate a signal as any that it was time to leave. Collecting the shovels and Mickie's discarded shirt, we turned our backs on our handiwork and headed for the car.

10

It was almost six o'clock when we rounded the corner and Port Catrin once more swung into view. It was properly light now, though the village still looked to be sound asleep. The fishing boats at the dock lay moored and empty, which I figured was a good sign. I didn't suppose much got done first thing on a Sunday morning in a quiet little place like this, but if anyone was likely to be up bright and early, it would probably be the fishermen. If they were still in their beds, odds were the rest of the town was too. Nevertheless, my heart remained firmly lodged in my throat till we'd made it safely to the top of the hill without encountering another soul.

At the entrance, Claire stopped us. 'Shoes off at the door. There's no sense in tramping mud and muck through the house.' As I bent to untie my shoelaces, she turned to Mickie. 'You and I had better strip as well. There's work to be done and the last thing we want is to cross-contaminate the scene of—' Her eyes strayed to me and she stopped abruptly.

The uncomfortable silence was broken by Mickie, who kicked off a Doc Marten and gave a suggestive leer. 'Hey, if ya wanted to see me nekkid, Churchie, all's ya had to do was ask.' She gyrated her hips as if gearing up to perform a striptease.

Claire sighed. 'There are few things on this earth I'd rather see less. Your outer clothes will be sufficient. Let's leave *something* to the imagination.'

'Spoilsport,' said Mickie, and pulled her T-shirt over her head.

In short order, she and Claire had both stripped to their underwear, their mud-soiled clothes forming a heap at the door next to our shoes. I followed them inside, the only one still fully dressed. To an outside observer, the scene would have looked utterly absurd, like some farcical comedy – though none of us was laughing.

In the living room, Claire turned to face me. 'While we're busy downstairs, I want you to go into the kitchen, find a dishtowel or something, and wipe down anything *he* might have touched.'

The pair of them headed downstairs while I made my slow, shuffling way into the kitchen. I found a flannel dishcloth draped over the tap at the sink which looked as if it would suffice. For a while, I stood there, clutching it against my chest, my fingers tracing the texture of the fabric. None of what was happening seemed in any way real, and yet the dishcloth *felt* real enough. I slid my hand under my hoodie and pinched my hip, hard. *That* felt real too. The fantasy that this was all just a deeply unpleasant nightmare was impossible to sustain.

Slowly, methodically, I made my way round the living room, giving every surface I thought Aidan had touched a thorough wipe – and, for good measure, most of the ones he hadn't as well. From downstairs, I heard the sounds of industrious labour: the sloosh of water, the slap of bare feet marching to and fro between the bedroom and the bathroom. I pictured Mickie and Claire on their hands and knees, soaking up Aidan's blood with towels from the bathroom, attacking the floor with scrubbing brushes. I continued my own clean-up operation, coming last to the sofa where we'd taken the Es and drunk ourselves silly. Aidan's windcheater was draped across the back of it, and our glasses were still sitting on the coffee table, alongside the pile of photos he'd lavished with such praise. My camera was there too, the picture I'd taken of him still in the ejection slot. I plucked it out and turned it over, revealing his smiling, still slightly bemused face, mouth half-open as he spoke the words I'd told him to repeat.

'Smile and say, "smelly feet".'

I smiled briefly at the memory – at our innocence, our obliviousness as to what was to follow – before swiftly pocketing both it and the rest of the snaps.

At that moment, I heard the slap of bare feet on the stairs. I hastily rearranged my face into an expression of neutrality and turned as Claire came into view. She was still dressed in her vest and pants, both of which now bore what looked like severely diluted bloodstains. There was a streak of blood on her cheek, too, which she either hadn't noticed or didn't care about. She gave me a brief nod but otherwise didn't acknowledge me as she tramped across the floor towards the fireplace.

'Is . . . is it done?' I asked, my voice momentarily catching in my throat.

'Nearly.' Her tone was curt and distracted-sounding.

'Where's Mickie?'

'Showering.'

I watched as she lit a fire in the hearth, poking and prodding the logs with a long poker until she was satisfied that the flames were ticking away nicely.

'I'll be back shortly,' she said, turning to me. 'While I'm gone, you should call Matthew.'

She pressed something cool and hard into my hand – my phone.

'But . . . what will I say?' I stammered.

For a brief moment, I caught a flash of annoyance in her eyes, as if she was thinking, *Do I have to do* everything *around here?* 'Whatever you'd normally say to him,' she said, a definite edge to her voice. 'We need to make it seem like nothing untoward has happened.'

I watched as she headed back downstairs, her footsteps receding into silence. I stood in the centre of the living room, toying with my phone. What the hell was I going to say? How could I possibly make it sound natural? My brain was so mussed up by everything that had happened that I couldn't even remember how I normally was with Matthew.

I was still dithering when Mickie materialised. She'd changed into clean clothes, the spikes of her hair still damp and glistening.

'Her Madge not here?' she said, looking around.

'I think she's still clearing up downstairs. Why?'

Mickie held up a plastic bag which, until now, I hadn't noticed her carrying. 'Said I was to bag my grundies an' all. Prob'ly so she can smell 'em – who knows what sorta kink she's hiding behind that schoolmarm act?'

She gave an expectant little smile, inviting me to laugh, but the joke fell flat in the heaviness that permeated the air. She gave a dismissive *gah!* and dropped the bag on the floor. 'Point her to these when she graces us with her presence. I'll be outside filling my lungs with healthy, clean air.'

She produced her lighter and a pack of cigarettes from her pocket and headed out, leaving me to grapple with my daunting task once more. I opened my Contacts list and scrolled down to Matthew's name, only to once more conclude that there was no way I could have an actual in-person conversation with him. Instead, I dashed off a quick text:

> Everything fine here. Signal still lousy – no point trying to call. Hope weekend going well. See you tomorrow. XOX.

I hit Send, then almost immediately regretted it. Wasn't I still meant to be pissed off with him? And surely there should have been some acknowledgement of his meandering, teary-eyed voicemail from last night – the one that had kickstarted the whole chain of events that had brought me to this juncture? I supposed I could just about get away with claiming not to have received his message due to the poor reception, but surely, after weeks of barely talking to one another, he'd see straight through this half-baked *love ya babes* crap? I told myself I was overthinking it. Matthew never was the most observant person to begin with when it came to other people's moods.

Once more, I heard footsteps on the stairs. This time it was Claire – like Mickie, now showered and dressed, her face pink and scrubbed with no trace remaining of the blood streak from earlier. She acknowledged me with a brief glance before heading over to the fire and inspecting it. Seemingly satisfied, she crossed to the sofa, grabbed Aidan's windcheater and, before I'd even properly processed what was happening, had tossed it onto the flaming pyre. I watched, wanting to object but unable to form the appropriate words, as she pushed it in deeper with the poker. The jacket curled and crackled, and a nauseatingly sweet, chemical smell filled the room.

Claire turned towards the coffee table, then frowned. 'What happened to those pictures?'

'Pictures?'

'The ones you took last night. They were here earlier when we came in.'

'Oh, those. I . . . I've got them.'

Claire's eyes narrowed. 'Why?'

'I . . . I don't know. I just . . . ' I trailed off with a helpless shrug, unable to articulate why I'd pocketed them and not sure I even properly understood it myself.

Claire held out her hand. 'Give them to me.'

With no small amount of reluctance, I handed them over. Claire flicked through them, inspecting each in turn, then lifted her head again.

'Is this all of them?'

I nodded, secretly wishing it wasn't. There was something about her penchant for destroying every last trace of Aidan that I found genuinely unsettling. I watched as she turned her back on me and crossed over to the fire, then tossed one of the pictures into the flames. A moment later, she turned to face me again, holding out the remaining bundle.

'Here.'

I took them from her and pocketed them quickly, for fear that she might belatedly decide my snaps of the local flora also constituted material evidence requiring immediate destruction.

'Is there anything else of his we need to get rid of?' said Claire.

'No,' I replied – then, as soon as I'd spoken, was suddenly aware of the round contours of the pendant, nestled against my right buttock in the back pocket of my jeans.

'Are you sure?'

'Yes,' I said, considerably more firmly this time. *You're not getting this,* I thought. *SOME part of him needs to survive.*

Claire gave me an odd look, and for a moment I wondered if she was going to order me to turn out my pockets. But just then, the front door crashed open and Mickie came striding in, the reek of nicotine accompanying her like a noxious cloud.

'All right, guys and dolls? What next?'

Claire held my eye for just a fraction of a second longer – then, to my considerable relief, broke it. 'Get your things together,' she told the pair of us. 'We're heading out.'

'Why?' I asked.

'Because we're going for a walk, that's why. Go on – I want us ready to leave in five minutes.'

11

There were few things I would have liked to do more than just curl up on the sofa and drift away into oblivion, but Claire was determined that we should keep up appearances. So we put on our coats and set off, tramping down through the village towards the coast.

I'm not sure how it was for Mickie and Claire, but for me it was like being inside a waking nightmare. I was utterly exhausted and felt dirty all over, even though I'd done nothing but stand and watch while they dealt with everything. I wished I could have had a shower or at least a change of clothes – but neither of these, it seemed, featured in Claire's master plan.

We tramped along the beach, the sand hard and crunchy underfoot, the wind whipping at our hair. There was barely another soul as far as the eye could see, save for a solitary dog-walker some way off. If, as Claire had presumably intended, the aim was to be seen by as many people as possible, we weren't off to an especially strong start.

I blinked heavily, trying to force my bleary eyes to focus. Everything – the sky, the sea, the sand, the shapes of my friends as they drifted increasingly further ahead of me – was merging together into the same colourless, miserable grey. None of it felt real. None of it seemed to matter. What was to stop me just sitting down where I was and not moving another step?

So that's exactly what I did.

The ground was harsh, the sharp stones and pebbles protruding from the sand cutting through the fabric of my jeans, but I barely felt it. I merely registered it on some abstract, theoretical level, as if it was happening to someone else. As I sat wondering what would happen if I never got up again, I was aware of Mickie and Claire, having realised I was no longer with them, stopping and turning to look back. I saw Claire say something to Mickie; Mickie nodding. Then Claire came striding towards me, clenched fists swinging by her sides.

'What are you doing?' she demanded, looking down at me from on high.

'I can't, Claire,' I said miserably. 'I can't do this.'

Claire sighed. 'Come on – get up.'

'I *can't*.'

For a moment, Claire didn't move. Then, abruptly, she dropped to her haunches and took my face in both hands, forcing me to look at her. 'You need to stop behaving like this, Hazel,' she snapped, her fingers digging into my cheekbones. 'What happened last night happened. You're going to have to find a way to deal with it.'

I felt the tears pricking at my eyes and knew what was coming next. I hated myself for it, but there was nothing I could do as they began to roll down my cheeks.

Claire sighed and lowered her head. 'I'm sorry – I didn't mean to bite your head off.' She squeezed my knee gently. 'Hey, come on. It's not for much longer, OK? I just need you to hold it together for a few more hours.'

I tried – I honestly tried. But it was no use. The tears were flowing unchecked now, accompanied by the sort of ugly, guttural sobbing that always makes people turn away in embarrassment. I couldn't help myself. It was as if all the anguish of the last few hours was finally pouring out of me in the only way it knew how.

I was aware of Claire glancing over her shoulder at Mickie and shaking her head. Mickie made her way over, though she stopped a couple of feet away and hung back, as if she was afraid to get too close to me. Claire got to her feet and, abandoning me, headed over to join her. I heard Mickie saying something, though her words were drowned out by the wind and my own choked sobs as I struggled to catch my breath.

'We're going to have to,' I heard Claire say. 'We can't just *leave* her here.'

They exchanged a few more words I couldn't make out, though I made no real effort to try. Then Claire handed Mickie her car keys and Mickie took off, jogging across the sand towards town. I remained on the ground, knees drawn into my chest, while Claire stood guard over me like a lone, silent sentinel.

After some time – I have no idea how long – I heard the sound of an approaching vehicle. Claire glanced in its direction, then got down on her hunkers and faced me again.

'Right,' she said, 'here's how it's going to be. You've got a poorly tummy. Yes?'

I nodded. I didn't understand, but I knew I had no choice but to go along with whatever this was.

'Say it.'

'I've got a poorly tummy,' I said, the words flat and hollow.

'And you're going back to the cabin for a lie down.'

'Yes.'

Claire extended a hand. 'Come on, then.'

As I struggled to my feet, I realised Mickie had brought the Land Rover to the edge of the beach. She was hanging out of the driver's door, wind whipping at her hair, eyeing me with concern. I allowed Claire to take me by the arm and lead me up the beach. They settled me in the back and we set off, trundling uphill through the town until we reached the foot of the gravel track leading to the house.

Claire nodded expectantly at the house. 'Out you get.'

I looked at her in surprise. 'What about you?'

'Your cousin and I are going for a drive,' Claire explained in a wearied tone, as if having to explain everything to me was taking its toll on her. 'Somewhere with plenty of people to see us. We'll be back by early evening. Stay inside, out of sight, and if anyone comes to the door, don't answer it.'

I got out and tramped up the path alone, feeling every inch the useless, pathetic failure that I was. It wasn't as if Claire had asked much of me – especially not after everything she and Mickie had done for my benefit – and yet even something as straightforward as not bawling like a silly baby appeared to be beyond me. Behind me, I heard the Land Rover performing a sharp U-turn and setting off back down the hill.

The cabin was monastically quiet as I stepped over the threshold, belying the violence that had occurred within its walls just a few short hours earlier. I craved sleep and oblivion's welcome embrace, but more than that I wanted a shower, and the feeling of clean water on my skin. I headed downstairs, opened the bathroom door and instantly choked back a scream.

The sight before me was, somehow, even more horrifying than that of Aidan lying lifeless on the floor with blood pooling around his head. It was like something out of a splatter movie. The bath was filled with bloody water, an assortment of towels and other linen floating in a thick, red soup. I felt a wave of nausea engulfing me, but there was no way I was going to make it to the toilet bowl – not without having to pass that monstrosity in the bathtub. Instead, I turned tail and ran, slamming the door behind me. I scrambled up the stairs on my hands and knees, forcing down the bile that had risen to my throat.

When my eyes and nose had stopped streaming, I dragged myself unsteadily to my feet and made my way over to the sofa, where I lay down, pulling the hood of my top up over my head and curling into a foetal position, wishing I could just shut my eyes and go to sleep and forget everything – for a few hours, at any rate.

But sleep wouldn't come. My brain refused to switch off, and the more tired I became, the more futile it was. And I was cold – so cold. It was a coldness the like of which I'd never experienced before. It penetrated my clothes and skin and the muscle underneath, cutting right to the bone. At one point, I got up and rekindled the fire Claire had lit, trying desperately to inject a little warmth into the house. But even that failed to offset the bone-numbing chill, even when I forced myself to stand so close to the flames I could feel my eyebrows beginning to curl. So I returned to the sofa and remained there for the next several hours, staring at the far wall till my eyes blurred.

Shortly after five, I heard the purr of an engine and the crunch of gravel as the Land Rover pulled up outside. I forced myself to get up off the sofa before Claire and Mickie came in, somehow feeling that I needed to look like I hadn't spent the better part of the day lying around feeling sorry for myself, even though I couldn't for the life of me think what else I was supposed to have been doing.

We exchanged relatively few words. Claire and Mickie seemed almost as subdued as I was. I wasn't sure whether the lack of sleep was catching up with them too, or if the full ramifications of what the three of us had done had only now started to sink in for them. The two of them set about getting dinner ready in the kitchen, continuing to present a convincing impression of a well-oiled machine working in perfect harmony.

Once the food was ready, they made me come and join them at the table, Claire loading my plate with a generous portion of beef casserole.

'Eat,' she said, her tone encouraging but intractable. 'You've got to keep your strength up. Especially after you've been poorly.'

'Yeah,' Mickie chimed in, 'it'll put hair on yer chest.'

It had been nearly twenty-four hours since food had last passed my lips, and by rights I should have been famished, but the thought of swallowing the rich, juicy stew immediately made me think of the downstairs bathroom and the horrific mess floating in the tub. But to show willing, I forced myself to down a couple of mouthfuls, then contented myself with listlessly pushing bits of meat and carrot around my plate while Mickie and Claire loudly and cheerfully reminisced about their visit to Dunnottar Castle and the drive along the coast. I had no idea for whose benefit this performance was being enacted, because I sure as hell wasn't buying it, but I was hardly in a position to say so.

Within twenty minutes, my eyelids began to droop and I found it increasingly difficult to keep my head from lolling onto my chest. I excused myself and dragged myself back over to the sofa, where I lay down and listened to the ebb and flow of Claire and Mickie's conversation, their voices mingling with the wind as it eddied around the cabin outside.

12

I only intended to rest my eyes for a moment or two, utterly convinced that sleep was impossible, but the next thing I knew, sunlight and birdsong were streaming into the living room and I was struggling into an upright position, blinking bleary, crusty eyes. Mickie and Claire were bustling to and fro, our luggage already piled high at the open front door.

'Welcome back, sleepyhead,' said Claire, with a kindness that I instantly felt I didn't deserve.

'How long was I asleep for?' I asked, arching my stiff shoulders.

'Pure ages,' said Mickie with a laugh. 'Soon as yer heid hit the deck, you were out like a light. Ya snoozed the whole night long, wee hen.'

'What time is it?'

'Just coming on for ten,' said Claire, returning from the kitchen with the bag from the bin containing our rubbish. 'It's almost time to go. We already packed your things.'

I blinked again, more forcefully this time, trying to shake off the cloud of confusion that hung over me. 'But how . . . ? When . . . ?'

Mickie flashed me a wink. 'Better shake a leg if ye dinna fancy getting left behind.'

I struggled to my feet and made my way downstairs. Despite having apparently slept for well over twelve hours, I still felt utterly drained, my head and limbs like heavy lumps of lead. As I gripped the bathroom door handle, I felt a momentary pang of dread, but when I opened it, the bath was spotless, with no sign of yesterday's horror show left behind. Once more, I wondered if it was possible the whole thing had simply been a horribly vivid nightmare – but then I slid my hand into my pocket and felt the contours of Aidan's pendant, and swiftly disabused myself of that notion.

I ran the tap, rinsed my face and slurped a handful of water, then headed back upstairs to join the others. They were waiting at the door, Claire clutching a bulging supermarket bag that I guessed contained hers and Mickie's soiled clothes.

'C'mon, slowpoke,' said Mickie. 'We've got nae hope of beating the mid-morning traffic at this rate.'

They were both, it seemed, intent on continuing the same light-hearted, fancy-free routine as the previous evening, but I could see in their eyes the strain of keeping up this façade. Behind all their exaggerated geniality, they were both dead on their feet.

'Hey, don't be forgetting this,' said Mickie, as I made for the door.

I turned to find her holding my camera out to me. I hesitated, then took it reluctantly. The thing had assumed such an accursed quality in my mind – the catalyst for everything that had unfolded since Saturday night – that a part of me didn't care if I never saw the thing again.

We trooped outside. Claire shut and locked the door, returned the key to its hiding place under the stone slab, tossed the bag of clothes into the boot, and then we were off. As we rolled through the village, the locals were out in force, the narrow streets positively teeming with people heading this way and that, at the sort of pace that suggested none of them had anything in the way of pressing business to attend to. As an elderly couple paused at the kerb to let us pass, Claire, clearly still determined to keep up appearances, gave them a farewell toot of her horn while Mickie waved jovially from the passenger seat. I sat in the back behind Mickie, eyes downcast, convinced that if anyone made eye contact with me, they'd instantly see right through me and my guilt would be laid bare.

We left the village behind us, cruising along the stretch of road overlooking the bay. The fishing boats were out at sea, bobbing gently on the horizon. The day was clear and bright, the surface of the water glittering like a thousand tiny emeralds – as if the sun itself had come out to speed us on our way.

There was little in the way of conversation during the journey south, with both Claire and I retreating into a brooding silence, shared but separate. I could tell Mickie found the atmosphere in the car stifling, and every now and then she made clumsy and obvious attempts to liven up the mood – patting out the rhythm of some song or other on the dashboard and eyeballing us expectantly in an effort to cajole us into singing along, or pointing elatedly at the fields and entreating us to 'look at the wee Highland coos', as if they were the most exciting sight she'd seen all weekend. When it became clear neither of us was going to bite, she turned on the radio and hunched low in her seat with her arms folded, stewing in her own juices.

The roads were considerably quieter than they had been on Saturday afternoon, and we made good time, hitting the outskirts of Edinburgh by twelve-thirty and rolling into the suburbs of Leith shortly thereafter. We were within a few hundred yards of Hermitage Place when, without warning, Claire pulled over, killed the engine and swung around in her seat to face us both.

'The police are bound to come looking for us,' she said, in the sort of tone that suggested she's spent the last few hours rehearsing this speech in her head. 'Probably not today or tomorrow, maybe not even this week – but sooner or later, they're going to track us down. There were enough witnesses in that pub that one of them's bound to tell them the man who disappeared without a trace was involved in breaking up an altercation involving three women from out of town on the same night when he was last seen. With any luck, they'll be less interested in us than in those mouth-breathers he left high and dry after promising to buy them all drinks – but even so, when they come, we have to be ready.'

Neither Mickie nor I said anything. We just sat and looked at her, awaiting further instruction.

'This is what we're going to tell them. We arrived in Port Catrin late on Saturday afternoon and went to the pub for our evening meal. There, Hazel exchanged a few words with a local man who bought us a round of drinks. He subsequently intervened when some other locals turned nasty after they discovered us sitting in their spot. At that point, we left the pub, went straight back to the cabin and never saw him again. Make sense?'

'With you so far,' said Mickie.

'It's important we stick to the truth as far as possible. The bigger the lie, the easier it'll be for them to poke holes in it.'

'That's not what Goebbels said.'

Claire continued as if she hadn't spoken. 'On Sunday morning, we went down to the beach, and in the afternoon you and I drove up to Dunnottar Castle while Hazel stayed behind with a bad stomach. There should be plenty of witnesses to corroborate our movements that day. We spent a final night at the cabin, then in the morning we packed our bags and hit the road just after ten.' She looked at each of us in turn. 'Agreed?'

Mickie raised her shoulders by the absolute minimum amount necessary to qualify as a shrug.

'What about when his disappearance hits the news?' I asked. 'Shouldn't we get in touch with the police ourselves? Won't it look less like we have something to hide?'

'No.' Claire's response was sharp and emphatic, as if viscerally resented the suggestion of any deviation from the plan she'd hatched. 'We wait for them to come to us. It makes no sense to draw any more attention to ourselves than we absolutely have to. Think about it: as far as we're concerned, the sum total of our involvement with him is that we rubbed shoulders with him briefly in a busy pub. Why should we recognise him, or his name mean anything to us?

'Plus,' she went on, as Mickie shot me a sceptical look, 'think how many young men go missing every day. Is every one of them the leading story on the national news? Of course not. At best, he'll probably get a thirty-second bulletin sandwiched between an item on the Prime Minister's latest gaffe and another on the football results. It would be perfectly plausible for the whole thing to have passed us by completely.'

'Right enough,' said Mickie, albeit without much conviction. 'Hardly ever watch it myself. S'all just lies and tittle-tattle.'

Claire flexed her jaw, saying nothing. I could tell she had something else on her mind – something she was debating whether or not to mention. At length, she spoke again.

'I think,' she said carefully, 'it would be a good idea if we never mentioned this again.'

'Aw, boo!' said Mickie. 'See, there was me planning on gabbing to my work pals about all the juicy shit I got up to on spring break.'

'I mean to each other,' said Claire tersely. 'It's less messy all round that way. We have to be totally disciplined about this. If we all stick to the story – if we live it, if we *believe* it – there'll be less chance of someone slipping up.'

'Meaning one of us two, I'm betting,' said Mickie, gesturing to herself and me. 'What about you, Churchie? Sure there's no chance of you shooting your mouth off in the name of *your* beliefs?'

'What's that supposed to mean?'

'Well, nae offence, but how do we know you won't blab it all to the vicar next time you're in the confession booth?'

Claire gave Mickie a withering look. 'I'm Episcopalian.'

'So?'

'Our lot don't tend to go in for confession.'

Mickie scoffed dismissively, as if she'd known that all along. 'Right. Well, just don't be clyping to the man upstairs either.'

'I'd hazard a guess he already knows.'

She spoke so coldly, and with such certainty, that her words pricked at even my stubbornly atheistic heart. They hung in the air like a vacuum sucking all the oxygen out of the car.

Eventually, Claire turned the key in the ignition again. We drove on till we rounded the corner onto Hermitage Place and the house Matthew and I shared crept into view. She pulled up at the gate, then placed both hands on the steering wheel and sat there, not moving.

A heavy silence descended. For almost a full minute, we sat there, not speaking. Even Mickie kept schtum, though I could tell from the way she was looking at the pair of us, brows arched in incredulity, that she regarded this behaviour as a manifestation of latent madness.

At length, I decided it was time to make a move. Unclipping my seatbelt, I grabbed my holdall and swung open the door. I took a deep breath and plastered a big fake smile on my lips.

'Thanks for a fabulous weekend, ladies,' I said. 'It's been truly unforgettable.'

Not stopping to wait to see how my attempt at 'living the story' had been received, I scrambled out and headed towards the house.

A rap on the window stopped me in my tracks. I turned to find Mickie winding down the passenger window. She beckoned me over. As I drew alongside her, she leant out and handed me a small, rectangular parcel covered in wrapping paper, no larger than a small notebook.

'Here. It's from both of us.'

I took it, momentarily confused. 'What's . . . ?'

'Uh . . . we were gonna give you it yesterday, but it kinda didn't seem appropriate. Happy B-day, cuz.'

With everything that had happened in the last thirty-six hours, I'd managed to overlook the fact that I'd turned thirty yesterday – at the moment when we were tramping across the sand and I did my sitting-down act, to be precise. In the grand scheme of things, it now seemed so arbitrary, so unimportant, that I almost laughed.

Mickie stretched her whole body out of the window and planted a kiss on my cheek, grinned, then withdrew back into the car and patted the dashboard, indicating to Claire that they should go. I remained at the kerb, watching until they rounded the corner and disappeared from view, before heading up the garden path.

13

It was eerily quiet inside the house, and there was no response when I called Matthew's name from the hallway. His coat was missing from the rack by the door, so I concluded he must be out. I'd clocked his car parked in the street, so it was a reasonably safe bet he hadn't gone far.

I dumped my holdall in the hallway, then paused to unwrap Mickie and Claire's present. Beneath the paper was a plain black velvet box, inside which I discovered a small, round locket on a chain. The locket, a gold disc with a blue gemstone inset in the centre, opened to reveal three separate compartments, each containing a tiny individual portrait photograph of Mickie, Claire and myself. The back was unadorned but for three lines of engraved text, each consisting of two letters: *HK, MS, CB.*

Hazel Knight, Mickie Shaye, Claire Bissell.

An involuntary sob caught in my throat. Despite all they'd done for me in the last couple of days, selflessly risking their own necks on my account, this small, unostentatious gesture was what really hammered home just how much their friendship meant to me, and how much I didn't deserve it.

Doing my best to clear my mind of such thoughts, I fastened the locket around my neck. It felt surprisingly heavy, but the presence of it, nestled against my sternum, comforted me in some indefinable way. Then I headed upstairs for the one thing I'd longed for more than anything else over the last twenty-four hours: a shower.

After more than forty-eight hours without a wash, it's difficult to convey just what a relief it was to step out of my grubby clothes and experience the sensation of clean, hot water on my body. It was almost enough to make the events of the last couple of days feel like a distant nightmare.

Almost.

Twenty minutes later, I stepped out of the shower, towelled myself dry and put on the thick, fluffy bathrobe I always wear when I'm having a rough day. My dirty, crusty clothes were still strewn across the bathroom floor where I'd abandoned them, and I began to gather them up, pausing to turn my jeans, which had turned inside-out in the process of peeling them off, the right way round. As I did so, something fell out of the back pocket and landed on the linoleum with a thud. A small, round disc on a rough string necklace.

Aidan's pendant.

I bent down and scooped it up, racking my brains as to where I could put it. Somewhere safe and secure, obviously, where no one was likely to go looking. But where? Then it came to me.

I stuffed my clothes into the laundry basket; then, still clutching the pendant, I crossed the landing to the bedroom, opened the bottom drawer of the dresser by the window and took out the memory box where I keep my grandmother's wedding ring, my first baby tooth and various other odds and ends of sentimental value. I unlocked it with its little gold key, stowed the pendant inside, locked it, shut the drawer, then got to my feet and cast around, looking for a separate hiding place for the key.

There was nowhere obvious in the bedroom, or at least nowhere that I could trust Matthew wouldn't inadvertently stumble across it. Not that I imagined he'd go raking through the contents of the box if he did – it's not as if he makes a habit of snooping through my things – but I wasn't prepared to leave it to chance. Still clutching the tiny key, I strode through the doorway into the landing—

And walked slap-bang into Matthew.

'Whoa, whoa, easy!' he exclaimed, as I let out a shriek of fright. 'It's only me.'

'I didn't hear you come in,' I managed to say, willing my thundering heart to settle.

'I heard movement upstairs and thought you might be a burglar. I crept up to investigate. I wasn't expecting you till later this afternoon.'

Was this remotely credible? Even if he *had* managed to avoid tripping over my holdall in the hallway, it seemed a bit of a stretch that his thoughts had immediately turned to 'burglar'. I found myself swiftly reassessing my earlier conviction as to him being unlikely to go snooping through my things.

'We figured we'd make an early start,' I shrugged. 'Before the roads got clogged with holidaymakers heading for home.'

As I spoke, I lowered the clenched fist containing the key to my memory box, trying to make the movement appear natural and unconscious as I slid it behind my hip.

'Nice drive?' said Matthew, apparently satisfied by my explanation.

'We made good time, yes.'

Could I *sound* any more tense? I reminded myself I had good reason to be off with him – that strained, awkward conversations of this sort weren't something that had only started today.

'You've been in the shower?' He nodded at my bathrobe.

'Um, yeah,' I nodded, then, feeling the need to explain myself, added, 'The facilities where we were staying were . . . well, they were a bit temperamental.'

'Bit like the reception, then?'

'Huh?' It took me a moment to cotton on. 'Yeah, exactly.'

We stood there, facing one another – both, it seemed, struggling to alight on any fresh material to keep the conversation flowing.

'Where were you off to?' It was Matthew who finally broke the silence.

'Sorry?'

'Just now, when you ran into me. Where were you going in such a hurry?'

'Um . . . nowhere?' I knew the rising inflection in my voice made me sound guilty as sin. 'Why?' I said, deciding to turn it around onto him. 'Where were *you*?'

'Newsagent.' He held up a copy of the *Caledonian* as proof. 'Thought I'd find out what's going on in the wider world.' He regarded me with a puzzled frown. 'Is everything OK?'

'I'm great,' I said, far too quickly and insistently. 'You just surprised me is all.'

'Well, I'm sorry I startled you.' He gave me a faintly patronising smile and moved to put his arm round me, then decided against it. 'Never mind. We'll put the kettle on and you can tell me all about what you and your friends got up to over the weekend.'

I followed him downstairs, tugging my bathrobe tighter about myself. I parked myself at the kitchen table while Matthew fussed around with the fancy machine he insists produces the best coffee in the Northern Hemisphere.

'I always say,' he declared, as he spooned grounds into the basket, 'that there's nothing like a properly brewed cup of coffee to perk you up after a long trip. So what's Port Catrin like? Is it nice?'

'It's very . . . ' I struggled to find the right word. 'Sedate. Very quiet, very picturesque. It's the sort of place you can imagine barely changing from one century to the next.'

Matthew laughed. 'I'm not sure I'd have coped, that far removed from civilisation. With *my* job, you can't exactly afford to be cut off from all contact with the outside world, even for a weekend.'

It seemed like there was a put-down in there somewhere – a suggestion, however unintentional, that my work was less pressing than his, or at the very least that my absence left less of a hole for my employers to fill – but I chose not to pull him up on it. An idea had just come to me. As he continued to press buttons on the coffee machine, his back to me, I slid the locket Claire and Mickie had given me out of my bathrobe, opened it and stowed the key in one of the compartments. Just as I slipped the locket out of sight again, Matthew turned.

'What's that?'

'Oh, that?' I felt my cheeks beginning to flush. 'It's just something Claire and Mickie gave me for my birthday.'

Matthew smiled pleasantly. 'That was nice of them.'

'It was,' I agreed.

Another awkward silence descended. I had no doubt we were both thinking the same thing: that the trip to Marbella, swiftly jettisoned after I caught him in the act, was supposed to have been *his* present to me.

'I, um . . . ' Matthew scratched the skin behind his ear awkwardly. 'I tried to call you the other night, but it went to voicemail. I don't know if you've checked your messages yet . . . '

'I have,' I said, waiting patiently for what was coming next.

'I . . . ' He sighed and ran a hand roughly over his face, embarrassed and, I thought, more than a little frustrated. 'Look, I wasn't myself when I made that call. I'd had a little too much to drink, was feeling a bit sorry for myself, so I might not have expressed myself all that well, but . . . ' He hesitated. 'Did you listen to it? All of it?'

I nodded.

'I meant what I said, you know – all that stuff about you and me, even if it came out a bit . . . garbled.'

He made his way over to the table and sat down opposite me,

while behind him the coffee machine continued to bubble and hum. Reaching across the table, he took my hand in his. I was briefly tempted to pull away, but instead I let my hand remain there, limp and unresponsive, as he caressed the skin between my thumb and forefinger.

'I want us to make this work, Haze,' he said, his voice low and earnest. 'You're the most important thing in my life, and I'm not just saying that. There's no one else I want to spend it with . . . if you'll still have me.'

I swallowed heavily. Forty-eight hours ago, I'd been seriously considering kicking him to the kerb in favour of a one-night stand with the man who now lay buried beneath the soil in a patch of woodland thirty miles west of Port Catrin. I'd genuinely been ready to take that leap into the unknown – to jettison everything that was safe and predictable and start again from scratch. Now, though? Now, I didn't know *what* I should do.

'I ended it with Vanessa,' Matthew went on, continuing to caress my hand as he spoke. 'Before I called you, I went to see her – to tell her it was over; that what I had with you was worth far more to me than whatever short-lived gratification I got from her. And she . . . well, it doesn't matter how she responded. *She* doesn't matter. What matters is you.'

He lifted my hand and pressed it to his lips, his eyes boring into me entreatingly.

For almost a full minute, I said nothing. I was trying to gather my thoughts – to put into words what I was feeling right then. Eventually, I drew in a heavy breath and spoke.

'I want,' I said, choosing my words carefully, 'I want, more than anything, to be able to wind back the clock to before it happened – before everything changed.'

I was referring to Matthew's affair, but as I spoke, I realised I could just as easily have been talking about what happened at Port

Catrin. In fact, perhaps that was what I'd really been thinking about all along.

'We *can*,' Matthew insisted, his eyes wide and eager. 'There's nothing stopping us.'

I pulled my hand away. He let it go without a fight. I sat there, contemplative, elbows on the table, chin resting on my steepled fingers. As I gazed into the pattern of the knotted pine tabletop, I remembered Claire's words in the car shortly before we'd parted company.

If we all stick to the story – if we live it, if we believe *it – there'll be less chance of someone slipping up.*

If I act like it didn't happen, I told myself, if I can *convince* myself it didn't happen, then maybe it didn't happen.

Live the story. BELIEVE it.

I lifted my head and met his eyes.

'OK,' I said.

'OK?' he echoed, eyes wide and filled with a desperate hope.

'Let's wind back the clock and start again. Let's go back to before – to how things used to be, when we were both happy and content and actually excited about being together. Let's . . . ' In a flash, an idea came to me. 'Let's get married!'

'*What?*' he spluttered.

I was scarcely able to believe it myself. I had no idea where it had come from or what had prompted me to blurt it out, but I made up my mind to run with it.

'Why not? We've been together all this time. It's crazy we've never properly tied the knot. We should have done it way sooner.'

'You're asking me to marry you?' said Matthew, a part of him still refusing to believe this wasn't either a dream or some sort of ruse.

'For the thousandth time, *yes*!' I half-laughed, half-shouted. 'Let's do the whole works. We'll rent out a massive venue, invite loads of guests – all your friends and mine. Then, afterwards, the two of us'll go on a big fuck-off honeymoon – somewhere hot, with reliable wi-fi and working showers.'

The smile on Matthew's face spread from ear to ear. 'Come here, you.'

Then, without warning, he swept me off my feet and, holding me in his arms like a groom carrying his bride, he pranced around the kitchen, laughing with joy and relief. For a brief instant, I saw him at ten years younger: the bold, spirited, impetuous boy I'd fallen for at uni, given to grand, spontaneous gestures just like this.

As he spun me around, my head back and my hair flying out behind me, I experienced a profound sense of both serenity and clarity. The more I thought about it, the more my spur-of-the-moment idea made perfect sense. We'd be renewing the foundations of our relationship, strengthening the ties that had once bound us together so tightly. Plus, I knew I'd be making my mum happy. She'd be over the moon for me, and it would mean the world to her to be able to watch her only daughter walk down the aisle while she was still around to see it. It would be a fresh beginning, a clean slate, and all the sins of the past, big and small, would be washed away.

Yes, I told myself, everything was going to be all right from now on.

14

One week later

Bright lights. A rank of video cameras on tripods. Behind them, a sea of expectant faces – notebooks, phones and Dictaphones at the ready. They watch as a side door opens and a cortège of three makes its way into the conference room in single file. Flashbulbs go off as they ascend the podium, taking their seats at a long table, microphones and a jug of water set out in readiness. Behind them, the banners bearing the Police Scotland insignia and 'Semper Vigilo' are a brilliant blue in the glare of the high-powered studio lights, which only accentuates the pallor of the dark-haired woman in her early thirties with the handsome, square-jawed features who sits between two stolid, grim-faced male police officers. You can sense the frisson of excitement that sweeps through the room, but no one barks out a question. No one shouts, 'Here, Shonagh! Look this way!' or 'D'you reckon your brother's dead, Shonagh?' There'll be time enough for all that later. For now, they sit and they wait, like a pack of hungry hounds at feeding time.

One of the officers pours water from the jug into three polystyrene cups and distributes them to himself and the others. The other takes his spectacles out of his pocket, places them on the bridge of his nose, adjusts the angle of the microphone closest to him and speaks into it in a clear voice with an Aberdonian twang.

'Good morning, ladies and gentlemen. My thanks to you all for coming out here today. I'll keep the introductions brief. I'm Chief Inspector George Gartland; this is Inspector Jim Ferguson, who is leading this inquiry. We are here this morning to appeal directly to the public for assistance in finding a missing local man, Aidan Cranston. With us today is Mr Cranston's sister, Shonagh.' He motions briefly to the woman by his side. 'Before I or my colleague say anything further, Ms Cranston has prepared a brief statement she wishes to read.'

Shonagh takes a small, crumpled piece of paper from her pocket. She unfolds it and examines it for a brief moment, her eyes darting back and forth as she skims the words written on it, before placing it face-down on the table and lifting her head. Her dark, clear eyes catch the glare of the studio lights and exploding flashbulbs as she gazes directly at the cameras.

'Aidan is twenty-eight years old,' she says. 'He is five foot eleven, has curly brown hair and a beard and is of a stocky build. He has three moles in the shape of an upside-down triangle on his upper left shoulder-blade and a small scar on the inside of his right thigh from a climbing accident when he was younger. He has a friendly, outgoing disposition and always goes out of his way to help others.'

Her voice is a flat monotone, long rehearsal and a determination not to allow grief to overwhelm her robbing it of any trace of emotion. As she speaks, the photographers continue to snap relentlessly, the flashing bulbs and clicking shutters filling the void as she pauses to take a sip of water and briefly consult her notes before continuing.

'Aidan has lived in Port Catrin all his life. He has a strong connection to the local area, and it is inconceivable that he would leave of his own volition. The papers—'

She stops mid-sentence – a momentary flutter as a trace of

emotion bubbles up to the surface. She pauses, swallows it, then takes a deep breath and continues.

'The papers all say that he is low-risk – that the police should forget about him and concentrate their resources on more pressing matters. Well, maybe to some there are matters that are more pressing, but not to me. Aidan is my only surviving relative. To me he is everything. And I implore you, if you know anything, please come forward.'

She stares into the cameras, holding their attention with her piercing, unblinking gaze.

'I would like to thank everyone who has sent flowers or kind words or offered their assistance to the search effort. I have set up a Facebook group, "Find Aidan". I would ask everyone to please join the group and share it as widely as possible. The average Facebook user has over three hundred friends. If every person who sees this broadcast posts the link on their feed, we can reach hundreds of thousands more. Please – help spread the word. Help bring my little brother home.'

She falls silent with her head bowed, as if she's too drained to hold it up any longer. As the cameras continue to click and flash – the press evidently sensing blood, or at least the possibility of a public breakdown – the less senior of the two police officers, Inspector Ferguson, picks up the slack.

'Aidan was last seen in the evening of Saturday the fifth of May at around nine-thirty p.m. in The Anchorage pub in Port Catrin,' he says. 'At the time, he was wearing a light brown waist-length windcheater, a red-and-black chequered shirt, a white T-shirt, blue jeans and brown Caterpillar boots. It is likely he was also wearing a round silver pendant around his neck with a triple spiral or triskelion design.'

He holds up a sheet of A4 paper showing a photograph of a pendant with the described markings. He continues to hold it for a few seconds longer, allowing time for the cameras to capture it and the journalists to scribble in their notebooks, before continuing.

'Aidan's absence was first noticed on the morning of Tuesday the eighth of May, when he failed to turn up for a pre-arranged painting and decorating job at nine a.m. He has no underlying mental or physical health conditions; nor does he have any debts. That said, while it is our assessment that he remains at minimal risk of harm, his disappearance is nonetheless significantly out of character. As such, we wish to give the public our assurance that we are taking his unexplained and prolonged absence extremely seriously.'

He gestures to Shonagh. 'Ms Cranston has already mentioned the Facebook group she set up, and I echo her encouragement to you to like, follow and share it as widely as possible. I would also ask anyone who believes they have information pertaining to Aidan's disappearance or possible whereabouts, no matter how unimportant it might seem, to call the local hotline without delay on 0163 296 0922 or to contact the Scottish National Missing Person Unit on 0131 496 1555.'

'Thanks, Jim,' Chief Inspector Gartland says as Ferguson falls silent. 'We'll now turn to questions from the media.'

A cacophony immediately begins in the audience stalls. While the two officers do their best to field the questions being shouted at them in as orderly a fashion as possible, Shonagh gulps back the rest of the water and sits in silence, slowly crushing the cup into nothing.

NOW

15

Three years later

The following is a transcript of a 999 call made at 22:36 on Sunday 25 September from the public telephone outside Urban Outfitters on Princes Street, Edinburgh EH2.

EMERGENCY OPERATOR (E.O.) — Emergency, which service do you require?

No response.

E.O. — Which service do you require? Fire, police or ambulance?

No response. A slight rustling sound, as if the mouthpiece is being covered.

E.O. — Hello? Is anyone there?

More rustling.

CALLER — Yes.

E.O. — Did you intend to call 999?

CALLER — Yes.

E.O. — And which service do you require?

Another pause.

CALLER — Police.

E.O. — Connecting you now. Please hold.

(NOTE: as noted in incident report, E.O. suspects, given distorted and artificial quality of caller's voice, use of some form of electronic device to disguise identity. Technicians at the Forensic Services Laboratory, who have been unable to ascertain caller's age or gender, concur with this assessment.)

POLICE CALL HANDLER (C.H.) — Police. What is your emergency?

No response.

C.H. — Hello, police. Do you require assistance?

Sounds of rustling.

C.H. — I said, do you require—

CALLER — *(Indistinct)* ... the woods.

C.H. — I'm sorry, can you repeat that, please?

Rustling.

C.H. — Can you repeat what you just said?

CALLER — Aidan Cranston's body is buried in the woods.

C.H. — Whose body? Can you tell me your name, caller?

Rustling.

C.H. — Hello? Caller, are you still there?

More rustling, growing increasingly frenzied, followed by sounds of fumbling.

Caller hangs up.

END OF TRANSCRIPT.

16

Two days later

'The new secondary school in Prestonfield will be our most ambitious undertaking to date,' Fraser declares, as if he's telling us something we don't know already. 'We've got a lot riding on this project, a lot of eyes are going to be on us, so we can't afford to fuck it up.'

A couple of the newer employees assembled in the large conference room on the third floor of the glass-fronted city centre building where Menzies, Sharp & Creadie's offices are located shift uneasily at the colourful language, but the rest of us don't bat an eyelid. I'm never quite sure whether it stems from an attempt to appear edgy or down with the kids, or a belief that chucking in the odd F-bomb will impress upon us the seriousness of the message. Either way, the effect is incongruous, but one I've grown used to. Middle-aged, rotund, with a penchant for pinstripe and a complexion that might best be described as porcine, Fraser Creadie looks like he'd be more at home holding court at the local country club, golf club in hand, than as one of the senior partners of the most in-demand architecture firm in Edinburgh. But then, looks can be – and, in my experience, frequently are – deceiving.

'I *had* thought,' he continues, pausing to slip his thumbs under the herringbone-patterned braces holding up his trousers, 'to hand overall responsibility to Gordon Allen, with his wealth of experience and expertise in the field, but at present he's tied up with the new wing at the Royal. So, after much deliberation, I've decided to put young Hazel in charge – provided she feels up to the challenge.'

I've been half-expecting this. Fraser and I discussed the project informally on a handful of occasions over the last few weeks, and he's thrown me enough nudge-nudge wink-wink bones for me to be reasonably confident of being in with a shot. But hearing it made official, in a room full of my peers and superiors, still causes my heart rate to ratchet up, my breathing to intensify, my palms to become slick. I swallow heavily, attempting to moisten a suddenly dry mouth, and will myself not to say or do anything to immediately make Fraser regret his decision.

'I'm absolutely up to the challenge,' I say, somehow managing to make myself sound calm and collected. 'I'm honoured you'd entrust me with a project of this scope.'

'It'll be the first major project over which you have complete control from beginning to end,' Fraser says. 'A big step up for you, but one the partners and I have every confidence you're ready for.'

I realise every pair of eyes in the room is fixed on me and that they're all waiting for me to say something. I gabble a little more, reiterating my gratitude and readiness to get stuck into what will undoubtedly be the biggest challenge of my career to date. I think I even promise not to let the firm down, just in case I haven't already been obsequious *enough*.

'Well, that's that, then,' says Fraser, beaming down at me from the head of the table like a proud patriarch. 'We'll schedule a meeting for later in the week to discuss the particulars, you and I. Shall we say four-thirty on Friday, my office?'

'Sounds good,' I nod, already making a mental list of all the prep I'm going to have to find time to fit in beforehand – brushing up on the latest government regulations covering building standards for school premises, for a start.

With this part of the agenda evidently having been concluded, Fraser turns to the next page in the binder in front of him. 'Next item of business: the long-delayed refurb of the City Chambers looks to be finally getting the green light, pending a vote tomorrow afternoon on our revised budgetary proposal. There's an old joke somewhere, I think, about how many politicians it takes to screw in a lightbulb . . . '

As he speaks, my phone emits what I recognise as the notification sound for a new WhatsApp message. There aren't many people who use WhatsApp to communicate with me and, when I surreptitiously slip the phone out of my pocket and check the screen under the table, I see that it's from Mickie, sent in the private, encrypted chat she created for herself, Claire and me – 'The Three Amigos'.

Mickie Shaye
SEEN THIS?????

I feel a tightening in my chest; a light-headedness creeping over me as my surroundings, and Fraser's voice, recede into the distance. Somehow, I already know this isn't going to be a funny cat video.

'Sorry, Fraser,' I say, cutting him off mid-flow as I stumble awkwardly to my feet, 'I need to take this. It's a . . . personal matter.'

He looks momentarily put out, then gives a silent nod of understanding and dismisses me with a gentle little wave. As he once more resumes his oratory, I shoulder my handbag and hurry out of the conference room, my legs feeling even longer and more uncoordinated than usual.

I find a quiet, out-of-the-way corridor – no small feat, given the open-plan nature of the floor the firm occupies, with no actual walls to speak of and glass pods in lieu of proper offices – and open WhatsApp. There's a link below Mickie's initial message, pointing to an item on the STV News website, and I can tell from the URL – a contraction of the headline – that it's not going to make for comfortable reading.

I tap the link with a clammy finger and the page fills my screen. '**Missing Aberdeenshire man: 999 call re-ignites three-year-old case**', the headline screams in large, bold type. Below it is a video, followed by the article itself. Unable to make my eyes focus properly on the tiny text, I fumble in my bag for my AirPods, pop them in and play the video instead.

It's a recording of an earlier news broadcast, the stiff-backed presenter sitting at his desk in a predominantly CGI studio, serious face on as he addresses the camera.

'Police are continuing to investigate an anonymous 999 call made on Sunday night regarding the whereabouts of a missing Aberdeenshire man. Aidan Cranston, a twenty-eight-year-old native of Port Catrin who has been missing since the May Bank Holiday weekend three years ago, is "buried in the woods", according to the caller, who is yet to be identified.'

The news feed cuts from the studio to what I instantly recognise as the payphone outside Urban Outfitters up on Princes Street. I know it really isn't the point I should be focusing on, but right now the thought at the forefront of my mind is that there are hardly any public phone boxes these days and that whoever made the call must have had to go out of their way to find one.

'The call, placed at a quarter to eleven on the night of the twenty-fifth of September, has been traced to a public telephone on Edinburgh's Princes Street,' says the newsman's voice. Then the camera cuts to a gaggle of police officers in a wood somewhere, all walking side by side in a long line, poking the ground with sticks as they go. 'Police, who say they are treating it as a credible lead until they discover proof to the contrary, have begun a comprehensive search of the various wooded areas near Port Catrin.'

The view changes again, this time to a large, still photograph of Aidan's face, grinning up at the cameraman from a corner seat in what I'm willing to bet is The Anchorage. He looks younger than when we met him, his hair a bit shorter, less tousled, but he exudes that same good-natured wholesomeness, his eyes as deep and brown as they were when I gazed into them during our long talk on the sofa in the cabin above Port Catrin all those years ago.

The newsreader is still talking, giving a bit of background on the case: last seen in the pub on Saturday night, no evidence suggesting anyone would have had it in for him, et cetera. I don't properly pay attention until the screen changes again – this time to a clip of a woman with long, dark, curly hair standing on a street corner in a city centre somewhere, trying her best to hand out flyers to a bunch of passing pedestrians who clearly couldn't care less. Again, I know her face, though I've never seen it in person. In the immediate aftermath of Aidan's disappearance, and for some considerable time after that, it was hardly ever off the TV or out of the newspapers. I'll never forget the sight of her, face ghostly white, sitting at that desk between those two policemen, reciting her pre-written plea for people to join that bloody Facebook group of hers . . .

'Over the last three and a half years,' says the newsreader, 'Aidan's sister, Shonagh, has worked tirelessly to keep her brother's case in the public eye, campaigning for the investigation to remain open long after the police ceased to treat it as an active concern. She issued a statement, saying, "This news vindicates my longstanding conviction that my brother was a victim of deliberate foul play. I urge the caller to come forward with what they know so Aidan may finally get the justice that has been denied to him for so long." '

The video ends. I stare at my phone's screen, at the 'Play Again' button overlaid on top of the photo of Aidan from earlier, those brown eyes seeming to bore into me with an intensity I can't look away from.

I'm aware my breathing is quickening again, and I know I'm on the verge of hyperventilating. One of my colleagues, whose face I recognise but whose name I can't manage to dredge up, shoots me a friendly smile as she passes. With an effort, I manage to return it, waiting till she's out of sight before slowly sinking to my knees as dread and the awful, gnawing sickness in the pit of my stomach completely overwhelm me.

In the years since that night at Port Catrin, I'd genuinely allowed myself to believe the three of us had got away with what we did; that it was possible for us to simply carry on with our lives as if nothing had happened. Now, it's all beginning again, and I can't help but wonder how long it will be before the truth finally catches up with me.

17

It's dark when I arrive at the large two-storey detached house in the Grange that the Bissells – Claire, Rob and their thirteen-year-old daughter, Eleanor – call home. Warm light streams from the large bay windows facing the street, and in spite of myself, my heart briefly lifts at the sight of its welcoming glow. Then, as the doorbell chimes melodically in the hallway, the reality of why I'm actually here comes flooding back and the familiar deep ache returns to the pit of my stomach. In the hours since Mickie sent her WhatsApp message, I've re-watched the bulletin on Aidan twice and read five or six other articles on various new sites, including the *Port Catrin Gazette*, which, incredibly, is an actual thing that actually exists. None of them contained any new information, but, like a scab I feel compelled to keep picking at, I can't stop myself from going back for more – again, and again, and again.

Claire opens the door, all smiles, moving to embrace me and kiss me on the cheek. 'Come in, come in,' she says, as if I'm here for a nice catch-up between old friends. 'Mickie isn't here yet, but I've put the fire on, so go on through and make yourself comfortable. I'll be through with the tea in half a tick.'

I head into the living room and take off my coat but remain standing as I drink in my surroundings. The Bissells have done well for themselves – Claire with her GP practice and Rob with some high-flying job with the City Council that I've never really tried to understand – and it shows in the décor. Everything is impeccably tasteful and just on the right side of expensive without tripping over into ostentatiousness. The mantelpiece is lined with photos of the happy family in various settings and combinations. There's even one of their overweight and now positively geriatric chocolate Lab, Coco, sporting the broadest grin of them all. All this blissful domesticity simply hammers home the profound mismatch between the setting and the subject I've come here to discuss.

Behind me, the door opens and Claire bustles in with a laden tea tray. She smiles briefly at me, almost as if we're sharing some sort of private joke, sets the tray down on the table by the sofa, then goes to the window, puts her hands on her hips and sighs loudly.

'Where *has* that girl got to? So typical of her to be the last to arrive.'

'I'm sure she'll be here any minute,' I say mechanically. It's true, Mickie and punctuality don't exactly make for easy bedfellows, but I've no doubt that she's well aware of the gravity of our present situation.

'How's Matthew?' Claire asks, as she begins to pour tea into matching mugs.

'Oh, he's fine,' I say, quickly and without really thinking about it. 'Listen, Claire, this business with the . . . you know, the phone call. Before Mickie WhatsApped us, did you have any inkling . . . ?'

Claire turns to me with a frown. 'Of course not – why would I? What, you think I wouldn't have told you?'

'No,' I say, immediately feeling foolish and more than a tad guilty for having besmirched her in some indefinable way. 'It's just, it's clearly been all over the news, and—'

'To be honest,' Claire says airily, 'lately I've been making a point to avoid the news altogether. There's always some new crisis or tragedy unfolding, and it's so easy to take these things to heart. I've actually deleted all the apps from my phone. I found I was spending all evening scrolling through the feeds, even when I was watching a movie or trying to read a book. That's the trouble with constantly being plugged into the internet – never truly being able to switch off. Don't you find that?'

She's talking both too loudly and a little too fast, her explanation far more elaborate than strictly necessary. But, as I'm still trying to figure out a tactful way of telling her she doesn't have to pretend not to be worried, not with me, she turns to the window again and gives a sigh that somehow manages to seem even more exasperated than the previous one.

'At *last*! Better late than never, I suppose.'

I follow her gaze and watch as a familiar small, spiky-haired figure in ripped jeans and a pleather bomber jacket tramps up the path, head down, shoulders drawn in. She pauses at the doorstep to take a final suck on the cigarette she's smoking, tosses the butt in the direction of the rhododendron bush – a move which provokes an angry intake of breath from Claire – then climbs the step and foregoes the bell in favour of a vigorous rap on the door. This is followed by footsteps in the hallway, the creak of the front door opening, then voices – Rob's strained, slightly constipated modulation and Mickie's languourous drawl, a touch too loud for an indoor setting. I hear Rob saying, 'They're through there,' followed by the clomp of approaching Doc Martens. Then the door swings open and Mickie is standing before us, looking us up and down like she's eyeing up a couple of exhibits in a shop window.

'Well, howdy-ho, girlies,' she says, slightly breathlessly and forcing the words out through teeth clenched into a tight and rather unconvincing grin. 'Fancy running into yous two here!'

As Claire serves the tea, it occurs to me that I can't actually remember the last time the three of us were gathered together like this. I've seen them both individually, and there've been communal gatherings of one variety or another where we've all been present – birthdays, the odd wedding, and, of course, Mum's funeral – but, now that I think about it, I reckon this could well be the first time it's just been us since . . . well, since *then*. Without any of us giving it conscious thought, we drifted apart, as if all three of us were, on some level, determined to avoid dredging up any associations with what happened that night in Port Catrin. Which I guess makes this a reunion of sorts, if not strictly speaking an actual anniversary.

'Well, this is all very nice,' says Mickie all of a sudden, 'but are we gonna just sit here all evening playing house, pretending none of us can see the whopping great Heffalump in the room?' Her hands are folded between her knees; her left leg jiggles up and down uncontrollably.

Claire doesn't say anything. She just stands there, lips pursed, still holding the jug of semi-skimmed she was in the middle of pouring.

'I mean, you know what this means, right?' Mickie goes on, looking at us imploringly. 'It means someone saw us. It's gotta.'

'That's one explanation,' Claire says quietly.

'Why? What's the other?'

'Well, you have to admit, it's a *remarkable* coincidence the call just happened to come from a phone box in the city the three of us call home.'

It takes Mickie a moment to cotton on, but when she does, she stares at Claire for a long, hard moment, then lets out a sharp, contemptuous cackle.

'What, you think someone *here* made that call? That's crackers. Actual, honest-to-God Christmas crackers. Why would one of us do anything as moronic as that?'

'I'm not saying they actually picked up the phone and made the call,' Claire says levelly. 'It could have come from a third party. What I'm suggesting is that someone might have been a little – shall we say incautious? Loose of the tongue, if you like. It may not even have been a conscious act. For some people, a relaxed environment is all it takes for them to let their guard down – especially if the right libations are involved.'

Mickie is on her feet now. 'If you've got something to say, Churchie,' she snarls, 'why don't you flaming well come out and say it?'

'Will you keep your voice down?' Claire hisses. 'I'm merely raising it as a possibility. I'm not accusing anyone of anything.'

'Didn't have to,' mutters Mickie. She slams back down into her seat, glowering. ''Case you're forgetting,' she adds pointedly, '*I* was the one who brought this whole thing to *yous*' attention in the first place. If I'd been the one shooting my mooth aff, d'you really think I'd've come running to *you*?'

'An attempt to divert suspicion?' suggests Claire, that one raised eyebrow doing an awful lot of heavy lifting.

'He who smelt it dealt it, y'mean? That's some primary school playground level shite there.'

'Besides,' Claire goes on, as if Mickie hadn't spoken, 'if someone *did* see us, why—'

At that moment, the door abruptly slams open and Eleanor comes stomping in, all baggy dungarees and heavy, sullen footsteps. She doesn't seem to notice us, or at any rate doesn't deem us worthy of acknowledgement. Claire clams up instantly, and the three of us sit there in silence, watching as Eleanor heads over to the power outlet at the far wall, bends down and unplugs a phone charging cable. She stands up and turns to find us all staring at her. For a couple of seconds, no one says anything.

'Forgot my charger,' she says, holding up the cable.

Again, no one speaks. Eleanor remains stationary for a moment longer. Then, with a curl of her lip and a shake of her head, she crosses the room and heads out, clearly having decided we're a right bunch of freaks. As the door slams behind her and her footsteps recede up the stairs, there's a palpable sensation of a release of tension, as if we've all been holding our breath and let it out in a single, collective gasp.

Mickie turns to Claire expectantly. 'You were saying?'

It takes Claire a moment to regain her train of thought. 'Hmm. Yes, as I was about to point out, if someone else *had* seen us, why wait more than three years to do anything about it? Why now? It doesn't make sense. And why the vagueness? Why "Aidan Cranston is buried in the woods"? Why not say *which* woods and who did the burying? If someone genuinely knows something, we'd have heard about it before now.'

Mickie, rubbing her chin pensively, says nothing, but I can tell from the look on her face that she's not buying it. I'm not sure I do either.

'If you ask me,' Claire goes on, 'a far more likely explanation is that someone simply made a lucky guess. Some do-gooder or attention-seeker who felt things had grown a bit too quiet on the investigation front and decided the best way to get things moving was to make an anonymous tip-off to the police, claiming to have information – and that "information" just happened to come within touching distance of the truth.'

Mickie continues to sit, brows pursed, chewing on the inside of her cheek. 'Or maybe,' she says suddenly, 'maybe it was a medium.'

'A *what*?' Claire all but splutters.

'Yeah!' Mickie sounds positively taken by the idea, as if the act of articulating it to the rest of us has helped cement it in her mind. 'If none of us lot blabbed and no one seen us doing it, then maybe it was a psychic who had some sort of vision.'

I wonder if I've somehow been transported into a parallel dimension where proclamations like this make any sort of rational sense.

'Think about it.' Mickie's on her feet again, holding court like some mad street preacher, all wavy arms and shouty voice. 'Whenever someone goes missing or a little kiddie gets abducted or what have you, you always hear about mediums getting involved – saying they've had visions of where they're being held or whatever. Supposedly the police even use 'em themselves sometimes, though they dinna like to make it public. So I'm thinking that's what's happened here. Some clairvoyant's had a vision of us, but you know what visions are like – they're vague, imprecise. That's how come they just said "the woods". And it'd explain how come they never came forward or said who they were – cos they were worried no one would take them seriously if they said they seen it in their dreams or whatever.'

Claire shakes her head, laughing incredulously. 'For crying out loud, would you listen to yourself? You don't honestly expect us to believe you buy into all that nonsense.'

'How no?' Mickie gives her a belligerent look. 'You believe in all sorts of hocus-pocus mumbo-jumbo about curing lepers and turning water into wine. Same difference frae where I'm standing.'

Now Claire's on her feet too, roused to action by this assault on her beliefs. 'Are you *seriously* trying to equate the two? Even by your standards, that's beyond objectionable.'

'Oh, right – your wacky superstitions are just fine and dandy but everyone else's are a load of old bollocks. You wanna check yourself in the mirror, Bissell. Pretty sure you'll find the word "hypocrite" written in big letters all the way across your giant forehead.'

With lightning speed, Claire moves towards Mickie, index finger outstretched. '*Listen*, you insolent little—'

'Does anyone want to know what *I* think?'

I blurt the words out before I'm even fully conscious of having spoken. I say it so loudly, so abruptly, and the sound of my voice is so alien after having sat in silence for the entirety of this conversation, that the two of them instantly stop going at it hammer and tongs and turn to face me, as if they'd forgotten I was even here. Confronted with the pair of them staring at me, my resolve wavers and I find myself wishing I hadn't said anything.

'I think,' I begin again, then almost immediately find my voice faltering. 'I mean, I wonder if maybe we should think about . . . well, coming clean.'

I say the last part almost in a whisper, already knowing they're not going to like it. I'm not sure I like it myself, but the idea's been rattling around inside my head since the news first broke this afternoon and I know I need to get it out into the open, even just to put it to bed.

'I just feel,' I carry on, as the other two continue to stare at me, saying nothing, 'that maybe, if we go to the police now and explain everything – that it was an accident, that we were scared, that we didn't know what else to do . . . ' I trail off unhappily.

'You think they'll go easy on us if, after all this time, we hold up our hands and confess to everything?' There's an ugly note in Claire's voice – akin, almost, to disgust.

I shrug helplessly. 'It's just an idea.'

'And you don't think that perhaps, just perhaps, the time to come clean was immediately after it happened, rather than after you roped Mickie and I into participating in your cover-up?'

That's definitely not my memory of how it played out. I don't recall myself doing much roping of *anyone*. But then, so much of that night – both the events leading up to Aidan's death and the aftermath – have a hazy, dreamlike quality in my mind – no doubt brought about, at least in part, by the E I took. I wait for Mickie to jump in, to set the record straight, but she's saying nothing. She just stands there, uncharacteristically taciturn, her lips a thin, pinched line.

'It's not just about you, you know.' Claire moves towards me, continuing to speak in that same low, withering tone. 'You might be perfectly willing to throw away the life and career you've built for yourself, but you don't get to make that decision on behalf of the rest of us. I have my practice, and Mickie has' – she glances briefly in Mickie's direction – 'whatever it is you do these days.' Eyes fixed on me again, now. 'Plus, I'm a wife and a mother – or had you forgotten that? Have you stopped to think about just what it is you're asking us to give up?'

I say nothing. I feel ashamed, ungrateful, self-absorbed – a nasty, self-centred excuse for a human being, unable to see beyond my own selfish plight.

'You can't claim innocence now, Hazel,' Claire says, her tone a touch more conciliatory. 'Innocent people don't hide evidence of serious wrongdoing, then lie about it for three and a half years.'

I lower my head, unable to withstand her gaze. I sit there, wishing the floor would open up and swallow me whole.

'I just want it all to be over,' I say in a small voice.

'It will be,' Claire says. 'Soon. Look at me.'

I don't move.

'Hazel. *Look* at me.'

Reluctantly, I lift my head and meet her eyes. She gazes down at me from on high – a patient, benevolent sage extending an olive branch to a wretched penitent.

'Here's how it's going to be,' she says. 'The police will no doubt be in touch with us before long. They'll want to re-interview all the old witnesses in case there's anything they've missed. It's standard procedure. And the fact the call originated from Edinburgh means it's almost inevitable connections are going to be drawn. But we got through this before and we'll get through it again. We just need to stick to our original story.'

I manage a small, half-hearted smile. 'Simple as that?'

'Couldn't be simpler. Just remember, they know nothing specific about the body's whereabouts, and they certainly don't have any concrete evidence as to our involvement. Think about it – if they had even a sliver of a case against us, do you really think we'd be having this conversation here rather than inside a police interview room?'

I don't answer. Claire sits down next to me; lays a gentle hand on my forearm.

'It's all going to be all right,' she insists. 'But I need you to be strong again.'

'Strong?' The word sounds as alien coming from my mouth as it does hers.

'Yes, strong like a warrior queen. We just need to get through the next few days. Perhaps the next week.' Her grip on my arm intensifies. 'If we stick to the plan – if we stick *together* – we'll all come out on the other side of this. I promise.'

18

Mickie and I leave together. We're going in opposite directions – I'm heading north to Leith, while Mickie stays out at Tollcross, about a twenty-five minute walk in a westerly direction – but my bus stop is on her route home, so we tramp up to Grange Road side by side, having seemingly come to the decision by silent mutual agreement.

Neither of us speaks. I suspect that, like me, Mickie's still processing the day's events. Me, I can't stop rerunning the words of Claire's 'it's not just about you' speech in my head. In all the years we've been friends, I've never known her to speak to me like that before, and it's thrown into sharp relief my distinct lack of gratitude in the face of her seemingly unlimited reserves of selflessness – in relation to this and all the other things she's done for me over the years. It's hard not to see myself as one of those bad friends who constantly takes and never gives anything back. And she's right: I never *did* stop to think about what Mickie and Claire had to lose – what they willingly put on the line that night when they agreed to pervert the course of justice to protect me.

We reach the bus shelter and I sink down onto the bench, my back bowed, feeling completely drained by the day's drama. Mickie remains standing, fiddling with a cigarette but making no move to light it. She smokes a lot more these days. It used to be just the odd one now and then, on special occasions or to combat stress, but lately, without me having been aware of it happening, she's morphed into a twenty-a-day girl. I consider telling her she needs to cut back but then realise that, under the circumstances, I have no right whatsoever to criticise.

'Is it just me,' Mickie says, breaking the silence, 'or is her nibs getting a touch too big for her booties these days?'

'She's just trying to make sure we all get through this,' I say weakly.

'She wasn't always this . . . *dictatorial*, though, right? I mean, she always did have a ten-foot rod up her jacksie, but this . . . ' She makes a hand-wavy gesture. '*This* is something else. That way she spoke to you back there? Guilt-tripping you, making out you owe her a debt? Seriously non-groovy.'

'It's not like that,' I say automatically – though, even as I speak, I wonder if I really believe what I'm saying.

'Looked that way to me,' says Mickie. 'Know what I reckon? I reckon this is all just one big power trip for her. A chance for her to throw her weight around. To lay down the law on us mere mortals. I bet she's loving this.'

'You don't know what you're talking about, all right?'

It comes out sounding way harsher than I intended, and earns me a surprised, quizzical look from Mickie.

'Look,' I say, forcing myself to adopt a more level tone, 'Claire and I go back a long way, OK? We were friends for years before you came on the scene.'

'I know that,' Mickie begins. 'I just—'

'Would you let me finish? My point is, I *know* her. I know what she's like. She's always been there for me. And I know, whatever happens, she'll always have my best interests at heart.'

'She tell you that, did she?'

I don't dignify that with a response. Having reached an impasse, the pair of us lapse into silence, me sitting hunched forward on the bench, Mickie leaning against the frame of the shelter, tapping her cigarette against her palm.

At length, I become aware of her eyes on me once more. I turn to find her looking at me strangely, frowning, as if there's something about me she can't work out. I straighten up.

'What?'

'If you lose any more weight, wee hen,' she says, 'we'll be able to see straight through you.'

I tug my coat tighter about myself, avoiding her eye. I know, from the looseness of my trousers and the increased prominence of my clavicles, that I *have* lost weight recently, and it's not as if I had a whole lot of spare meat on my bones to begin with. My appetite's not been great of late and, what with the busy spell we've been going through at work, it's been all too easy to get caught up in some task or other, only to glance up at the clock and discover it's already late afternoon and too late to bother with lunch, what with dinner only a couple of hours away. But I hadn't realised it was this obvious. Has everyone else noticed? Are all my colleagues discussing me behind my back, speculating as to what's wrong with me?

'I'm just after getting over the flu,' I say. 'It's nothing.'

The lie is out of my mouth even before I'm aware of having formulated it in my head. Mickie looks unconvinced, but she doesn't press it. She's silent for a minute or so, then pipes up again.

'Um, look. That . . . stuff you said back there . . . about coming clean, yeah? Were you serious about that?'

What does she expect me to say? *No, I was only kidding*? *I just said it to get a rise out of you both*?

She joins me on the bench, her thigh touching mine. 'Cos, uh, if you were . . . if you wanted to go to the cops together – me and you, I mean, without telling Charlie Church – it's not . . . I mean, it might naw be the worst idea in the world.'

I turn to look at her, drinking in the magnitude of what she's saying. What she's offering me. And, for a moment, I'm genuinely tempted to take her up on it. But then I feel the familiar presence, against my breastbone, of the locket the two of them gave me for my thirtieth birthday. The one with our initials and pictures of each of us. The one I've worn around my neck every day, only taking it off to shower and sleep. I think of Claire, with her job and her family and her wheezing, obese Labrador, and I know I can't do that to her. Not after everything she's done and continues to do for me.

I shake my head softly. Reach over and pat Mickie's hand. 'I wasn't, no. Not really. I mean, it was just a thought I had. I'm not ready to give up on everything – not yet. Besides, we swore an oath, remember? All for one and one for all.'

'Right enough, aye,' Mickie agrees, and I swear there's just the slightest sag in her shoulders as she says it, as if at least a part of her was hoping for a different answer.

'Why – *you* weren't thinking it was something we should do, were you?' I say.

'Course not,' Mickie says immediately, with a determined shake of her head. 'Totally mental idea. Forget I ever said anything.'

It's nearly ten when I get back home to Hermitage Place, and I'm profoundly relieved to shut out the damp, dark night. I get inside to find Matthew coming down the stairs, carrying a wheeled travel case. He falters momentarily as he catches sight of me, then continues to the bottom and deposits his case on the floor.

'You've been gone a while,' he says, somehow managing to make it sound like a criticism.

'Have I?' I respond. 'Defensive' seems to be my default mode tonight.

'Did you have a nice time with your friend from school?'

'It was great to catch up, yeah,' I say, hanging my coat on the peg by the door.

'Who was it you were seeing again? Kelly?'

'Sarah.'

I briefly wonder whether this was a deliberate attempt on his part to catch me in a lie. Not that he has any reason to think I'm being untruthful. Nor, for that matter, was there any particular need for me to make up a story in the first place. After all, I'm as entitled to catch up with Mickie and Claire as I am with anyone else. I'm probably just being paranoid on both fronts.

I wait for Matthew to probe me further about the evening's events, but after a moment he gives a curt nod and passes on by with barely a cursory glance at me. I remain in the hallway, listening as he bustles about in the living room, clearly on the hunt for something.

'Well' – his voice carries through from next door – 'it's always nice when you're able to make time to socialise.' His tone is benign, but I can read between the lines as well as the next person and instantly recognise the passive-aggressive put-down.

I remain standing in the hallway, picking restlessly at the strap of my handbag. What I really want is to go upstairs and run a hot bath with plenty of bubbles and have a nice, long soak before I get ready for bed, but I know I won't be able to settle with him going to and fro, charging up and down the stairs like a bloody rhino.

A moment later, he emerges from the living room, the passport in his hand proof that his hunting expedition has been successful.

'I should be back by next weekend at the latest,' he says, slipping it into the pocket of his coat, hanging on the peg next to mine, 'but there's an outside chance things could run on longer than that. It's anyone's guess what we'll find when we get there. By all accounts, the company did a piss-poor job of keeping their books in order.'

As he heads back up the stairs again, I find myself wondering – not for the first time – what it must be like to make a living swooping in to liquidate other people's failing businesses. Does shutting firms down and telling folk they're now unemployed provide good job satisfaction? I tell myself it's more complicated than that; that companies like the ones he's tasked with dissolving are already past the point of no return anyway, and that if the likes of him didn't go in and wind them up in an orderly fashion, the entire process would be a whole lot messier. Still, I can't help thinking there's an off-colour joke to be made about the pair of us. *The architect and the administrator – she builds things up while he knocks them down.*

I hear footsteps on the stairs again, and Matthew comes into view with a pillow and a rolled-up duvet tucked under his arm.

'What time's the flight tomorrow?' I ask, more for something to say than because I care overly much.

'*Early*,' he says emphatically. 'I've got a taxi coming at five-thirty sharp. I'll sleep on the sofa so you're not disturbed by me going. I know what a light sleeper you are.'

Again, he makes it sound as if I'm the one at fault, rather than him being the one who couldn't move around quietly if his life depended on it. In any event, this seems excessive – an over-the-top gesture designed to place me in a position of gratitude. It's not as if we normally share a bed these days anyway.

He fishes in his pocket and hands me a crumpled printout. 'I'm staying at the Waldorf in Covent Garden. If you need to get hold of me for whatever reason, it's probably best if you leave a message with reception. I'll be in and out of meetings all the time, and there are likely to be a whole lot of late nights, so there's no point trying to get me on my mobile.'

'I'm sure I won't need to,' I say blandly.

As it happens, I strongly suspect the real reason he doesn't want me trying to get hold of him is in case I call while he's busy screwing Charlotte, the junior colleague who's travelling down with him and with whom I'm almost certain he's having an affair. I idly wonder why it is that the women he goes for are always my polar opposite in every respect – petite blondes with ample bosoms and vivacious personalities. Though I suppose that makes *me* the odd one out – so, if you think about it, I should really be asking myself why he ended up with me when I'm so obviously not his type.

An awkward silence descends. This is the sum total of our interactions these days: passing one another in the corridor like tenants in shared accommodation, desperately searching for something to say to one another.

'Well, I should head to bed myself,' I say at length, trying not to make myself sound *too* eager to see the back of him. 'It's been a long day and I've been on the trot non-stop. Have a safe trip.'

'Try not to get into any trouble while I'm gone,' he says, and I immediately begin to wonder if he somehow knows something.

No, of course he doesn't. Don't be an imbecile, Hazel.

I keep my cool and lean in to give him the tiniest, most chaste kiss imaginable, our lips scarcely grazing one another. Then I turn and head upstairs, telling myself it's probably just as well he's heading down to London just now, because it means he won't be around when the police inevitably come knocking.

Upstairs, I lie on my back, listening as Matthew gets ready for bed, brushing his teeth in the pokey toilet under the stairs before heading through to the living room directly below me. For a while, I hear the creaking of the sofa springs as he tries to get comfortable, accompanied by the occasional sigh of frustration or muttered expletive. Then, at last, silence.

I wait till I haven't heard a sound from below for at least ten minutes. Then I switch on the bedside lamp, slide my laptop out from under the bed and lever myself up into a sitting position, perching it on my knees. I open the browser's incognito mode, navigate to Facebook and enter my login details, then move the cursor over to the 'Your Shortcuts' menu and select the option at the top of the list: the 'Find Aidan' group, three and a half years old and still going strong.

My Facebook presence is nothing to write home about. My profile picture is a random photo of a woman I found on Google Images, I have a grand total of five friends (all random requests which I accepted so my account didn't look quite so much like a sock puppet), and my name isn't Hazel Ellis but 'Colette Harper' – a combination of my middle name and my late mum's maiden name. Colette hasn't posted any status updates since she created her account a little over three years ago, but she likes Audrey Hepburn, the film *Amélie* and the band CHVRCHES, and the tourist attractions she's visited include York Castle and the Hofburg Palace in Vienna. All other information – her birthday, her location, her marital status – are set to private. 'Find Aidan' is the only group of which she's a member.

Find Aidan has only a single admin – one Shonagh Cranston, her profile pic as severe and unsmiling as a prison mugshot. Tonight, as is the case more often than not, the lack of a little green dot next to it indicates that she's not currently online. She seems to only come on when she has something specific to say, be it marking important milestones in Aidan's life such as his birthday and the date of his disappearance, or occasionally setting down her thoughts about some aspect of Aidan's case, or the handling of missing persons cases in general, in longer-form posts that almost verge on being full-blown essays. These are always well thought out and highly articulate; she's a good writer, clear-headed and able to make her points succinctly and effectively. She has very definite views on how things could be improved – more joined-up communication between the various national police forces, for instance, and challenging the prevailing faith in 'the right to disappear' for adults of sound mind. There can be no doubting she's a powerful advocate for her cause, or that anyone who stands in her way would be doing so at their own peril.

What's she doing right now, I wonder? What thoughts are currently going through her head? What's her state of mind? I wish I had more of a window into her psyche than her sporadic updates, which I suspect are carefully composed to present a particular face to the wider public.

I hover over Shonagh's profile pic, and a menu appears with various buttons, including the options to add her as a friend and send her a private message. Over the years, I've often been tempted to do one or both, but I've always refrained from doing so. Tonight, Colette's cursor remains floating over the Add Friend button, her finger resting on the button, knowing that if she applies even the smallest amount of additional pressure, it will register as a click. She continues to hold it there for almost a full minute, aware that the longer she waits, the greater the likelihood that her finger will slip or involuntarily twitch. If it does, she can tell herself she didn't mean to click Add Friend – it just inadvertently happened. If not... well, there's always tomorrow night – and if not, the night after that.

A sudden thud causes me to jump. I look up from the screen to the window on the other side of the room, curtains still open, to the sight of a bird flying away in the opposite direction, a little discombobulated but otherwise none the worse for its collision.

I look down at the screen again, and see that my sudden movement has caused the cursor to shift a couple of inches to the right, the resulting click harmlessly targeting the empty space next to Shonagh's portrait. I release the breath I belatedly realise I've been holding in. *Saved by the bell* – or, in this case, the blackbird. I close the laptop's lid, slide it back under the bed, switch off the light, turn over onto my side and try to sleep.

19

As it turns out, the police don't actually come looking for me at home. Instead, they drop in unannounced at eleven o'clock on Friday morning, right when I'm in the middle of giving a presentation about my vision for the secondary school to Fraser, the other senior partners and a handful of other semi-important types. I'm mid-sentence when there's a knock on the conference room door and Danielle, the fourth-year university student currently interning with us, pokes her head in and says a couple of detectives are here to see me. The timing could scarcely have been worse from my point of view, and, as I follow Danielle down the corridor to the vacant meeting room where they've been parked, I wonder if that wasn't their intention all along.

Danielle opens the door for me and steps aside. As I enter the small, airless cubicle – one of the few windowless rooms on the entire floor – a woman slightly younger than me, in a trouser suit and a blonde pageboy hairdo, rises from the chair she's commandeered. Her companion – in his fifties, schlubby, dressed in a scruffy trench coat and baggy trousers – is already on his feet but seems to be using the far wall to keep himself vertical.

'Mrs Ellis?'

'Hazel, please,' I manage to say, feeling my bowels clench as the departing Danielle closes the door behind me.

'DI Rosa Palmer,' says the woman, opening her wallet to show me her ID. 'This is my colleague, DI Angus Moir. Mr Moir's come all the way down from Aberdeen to see you.'

She makes it sound as if he's doing me a massive favour by being here, but all she achieves is to make my urge to defecate even more intense. If he's from Aberdeen, no prizes for guessing what this is about.

'Have a seat,' Palmer says, gesturing to the one she just vacated.

I do as I'm told, lowering myself into the chair without taking my eyes off either of them. Palmer perches on the end of the table facing me, while Moir remains standing, hands in his coat pockets. He puts me in mind of the hired muscle from a hundred and one gangster flicks: the one the mob boss keeps lurking in the shadows, a constant threat waiting in the wings to be let loose if the poor narc they've got tied up in the basement doesn't give them what they want.

'Have you any notion as to why we might be here?' says Palmer. Her tone is clipped, officious – the sort of pushy, ultra-confident woman that always causes me to retreat into myself. She's got one of those intense sorts of stares that makes you feel like she's seeing straight through you, and, as her pale blue eyes drill into me, I know I'm going to have to be at the top of my game.

I give what I hope passes for an innocent shrug.

'Been watching the news much lately?' she says.

I open my mouth to respond, only to stop dead, realising I have no idea what I'm supposed to say at this point. I experience a sudden, vivid memory of one of the most excruciating moments in my entire life: the Primary 5 Christmas play. The play was a major event in our school's calendar, and every year we devoted countless hours in the run-up to Christmas to preparing for it. That year, I'd been given a speaking part – only a single line, but one of the most important in the entire play. Over and over we rehearsed it, until I was practically saying it in my sleep – and yet, on the night itself, when it came to my turn to step up and deliver, I couldn't remember my line. I just stood there on the stage, the spotlight on me, wide-eyed and slack-jawed, an entire hall full of fellow pupils and their parents gazing back at me. A ripple of awkward laughter spread through the room, and, as I turned tail and fled in shame and mortification, it developed into full-blown gales of derisory guffaws that echoed in the rafters and in my burning ears.

As far as I was concerned, there was nothing funny about the situation then, and there's *definitely* nothing funny about the situation now. Realising I'm in very serious danger of fucking this up, I opt to play for time.

'Um . . . any news in particular?'

This time, I'm convinced Palmer's lip actually curls. 'Unless you've been living under a rock, I can't see how you could have failed to notice that there's been a fresh development in the Aidan Cranston case. All the media outlets have covered it extensively.'

'Oh, *that*,' I say, then immediately realise how flippant I sound. 'I mean, yes,' I add hastily, not having to work too hard at sounding suitably chastened. 'Yes, I saw that. It's . . . well, it's very sad, isn't it?'

Palmer makes a noise at the back of her throat that leaves me no clearer as to her views on the matter. She consults a small, wire-bound notebook, then looks up, fixing me with her cobalt stare again.

'You and your two friends, Claire Bissell and Mikaela Shaye, were in Port Catrin at the time of the disappearance. Back then, you told our colleagues – and this is confirmed by several eyewitness accounts – that you spent some time in Mr Cranston's company on the night he was last seen.'

'Only for about five minutes,' I say, then immediately want to kick myself. I'm being way too defensive, too obviously seeking to downplay my involvement.

Palmer manages the thinnest of smiles. 'Still, I'm surprised, when you realised there'd been a fresh development in the case, that you didn't feel compelled to get in touch with *us*.'

'To say what? That I'd seen it on the news?'

Oh God, Hazel, just stop. *Being a wise-ass might be Mickie's forte, but it sure as hell isn't yours.*

'Ach now, to be fair, the lassie leads a busy existence,' says Moir, levering himself away from the wall as Palmer swaps her smile for a scowl. 'A high-flying young professional working for a top architectural firm. Odds are she had other things on her mind.'

I'm too bamboozled to say anything. I thought Moir was meant to be Bad Cop, and yet here he is coming to my defence. I wonder if they chose their roles to discombobulate me, or if perhaps Moir's just a tad more sly than Palmer – going out of his way to put me at my ease, lulling me into a false sense of security so he can trip me up later.

'It's true,' I say, taking his line and running with it, 'I *do* have a busy life. Actually, I was in the middle of giving a presentation, and I've got a room full of folk waiting for me, so if you don't have anything specific to ask me, maybe I could just—'

'Sit *down*, Mrs Ellis,' Palmer barks as I begin to pre-emptively rise from my chair. 'We aren't through here.'

I park myself immediately, feeling every inch the disobedient schoolgirl ordered back into my seat after attempting to flee before my bollocking is complete. Not that I was ever disobedient at school. Or at home. I've been a good girl all my life. Well, apart from—

'We've got some questions we'd like to run through,' says Palmer, glowering at me with the look of someone who feels she's got my number. 'And the quicker you answer them, the sooner you can get back to your big important presentation.'

All told, I'm with them for about twenty minutes, though it feels like far longer. For the most part, they ask me the same questions a different set of detectives asked me three and a half years ago when, approximately two weeks after the events at Port Catrin, they showed up unbidden at my door. I'm on firmer footing now, all my rehearsed answers coming back to me as I repeat the same story I told the detectives back then. As I regurgitate the by now well-worn tale, it becomes increasingly apparent that Claire was right – this pair aren't here because they know something but because they're clutching at straws, chasing up every old lead in the off-chance that they'll somehow alight on something that was previously missed. If they had anything on me at all, any inkling whatsoever that I might have had anything to do with Aidan's disappearance, they'd have read me my rights long before now.

Moir's a bit more active now – almost as if, now that he's got started, he can't stop – though I note he keeps trying to steer things towards their logical conclusion, and for that I can't help but feel just a little grateful. In fact, if I didn't know better, I'd say he's in as much of a hurry to get out here as I am. Perhaps he misses Aberdeen. I wonder if the reason he's here at all is that he's the one who drew the short straw – the old duffer who's pushing retirement, sent down south on a wild goose chase because none of his younger, fitter colleagues fancied spending the week going door-to-door, raking over old ground. In a way, I almost feel sorry for him.

'This message,' Palmer muses, snapping me out of my thoughts. ' "Aidan Cranston's body is buried in the woods".' She recites the words slowly, ponderously, trilling the Rs and elongating the vowels. 'What do you suppose that means?'

I'm thrown. What does it *mean*? It's in plain enough English, isn't it? I can only conclude that she's inviting me to speculate, providing me with the rope with which to hang myself, and I realise I'm going to have to tread carefully. I think hard for a moment, before deciding to fall back on the theory Claire espoused the other night.

'If you ask me,' I say, 'it was probably just someone looking for attention – either out of sheer malice, or perhaps because, in their own weird, warped way, they thought they were being helpful.'

Palmer folds her arms. 'So you don't happen to think Mr Cranston is buried in the woods?'

'I don't think *anything*.' I give a wide, expansive shrug, clinging to the belief that the more baffled I appear, the more likely these two will be to buy my innocence. 'I honestly have no idea what happened to him. I hope he's alive and well somewhere – that he just took off for some reason and never came back. But I really don't know.'

Palmer continues to stare at me, long and hard. It takes all my willpower not to look away.

'Been to Princes Street lately, Mrs Ellis?'

'No,' I say, perfectly truthfully, though my jaw is like a clenched fist and my shoulders are braced as if for impact.

Palmer continues to hold my gaze, just long enough for it to become seriously uncomfortable. Then, abruptly, she breaks it, turning away from me to face Moir.

'OK,' she says, sounding mildly irritated, 'I think we're done here.' She turns back to me, proffering a business card. 'If, at any point, you happen to remember anything you've neglected to tell us, here's my number.'

As I dutifully take the card, Moir shuffles over to the table, where a stray notepad lies, presumably left behind by whoever last had use of the room. He tears a strip off the top page and scribbles his own number on it.

'I'll be sticking around for a few days,' he says. 'You can reach me anytime.'

As he hands me his number, our eyes meet and a look passes between us. For a moment, I feel naked, exposed, and once again I'm left with the unnerving sense that he knows more than he's letting on. This, I'm sure, is a man who is not really as he chooses to appear. There's a shrewdness behind his scruffy, genial façade, as if he's content to wait and play the long game.

I wish the detectives luck with their enquiries and head back to the conference room, just in case there's anyone still waiting for me to finish my presentation. Of course, the room has long since been vacated, the only semblance of life the swirling patterns of the screensaver on my laptop, still plugged into the projector. I gather my things and return to the relative privacy of my office, where I open WhatsApp on my phone and send Mickie and Claire the pre-agreed signal: a cat emoji. It joins their own matching emojis, both of which came through yesterday, within an hour of each other. I briefly wonder whether there's any significance in the fact that they left me till last.

I put my phone away and log into my computer. I know I should knuckle down and put the business with Moir and Palmer behind me – and God knows, there's enough work piling up for me to be getting on with – but, however good my intentions might be, rather than turn my mind to the sixty-three emails currently awaiting my attention, I instead open a new tab, click the YouTube icon and key *'Aidan Cranston'* into the searchbar.

I've already seen most of the videos that show up in the search results, but a new one, posted just yesterday, catches my eye. It was posted by an account with twenty-seven followers – some amateur videographer whose uploads normally consist of five-second clips of his dog. The video's title is *'Aidan Cranston Police Manhunt – Firhill Wood – EXCLUSIVE FOOTAGE'*.

I click Play. The screen changes to show a view of a small patch of woodland at the top of a low hill with a conical top. Police officers are combing it methodically with sticks and sniffer dogs. Enough of my seriously rusty photography knowledge remains intact for me to recognise, from the extreme foreshortening of the subject matter and the fact that the slightest movement of the camera causes the view to veer radically off course, that it was shot handheld from a considerable distance with a telephoto lens – though the fact that none of the officers have noticed the cameraman and told him to beat it is also a pretty good indicator. There's audio, but I don't dare to turn up the volume to more than a couple of bars: sound carries through these glass walls like no one's business. Even if I dialled it up full, though, I suspect I wouldn't be able to hear anything of any value: the howl of the wind completely overpowers the camera's cheap, built-in microphone.

The view pans sideways to reveal a figure standing a little way off, watching the officers like a troop master directing her charges. A woman in an anorak, her long, dark, wavy hair slick with dew. My tongue cleaves to the roof of my mouth. I'd recognise her anywhere.

Shonagh.

At that moment, and without warning, she turns towards the camera. For a second or so, she seems to stare directly at me through the screen, holding my gaze, and I find myself unable to look away. Then, as she opens her mouth to utter some expletive-laden verbal assault on the cameraman, the footage turns into a pixelated blur as, realising he's been rumbled, he hastily lowers his device. A moment later, the video ends.

I gaze at the now silent screen and the array of thumbnails telling me what to watch next. I know from the video's title that the footage is of a copse about ten miles from Port Catrin. The search has been moving further and further west over the last few days. If they keep going in the same direction, they'll eventually come to the woods where Aidan lies buried – assuming they *do* keep going, of course. I know Claire's convinced they'll call the whole thing off before long and that we just need to ride it out, but, try as I might, I can't bring myself to share her certainty.

My mind goes back to the last few seconds of the video. Shonagh's face, and the look in her eyes – wounded, accusatory – continue to haunt me. That potent combination of hurt and anger that's always present in her expression whenever she's caught on camera. Hurt, anger and a determination never to give up – to scour the earth, if need be, till she finds out what happened to her brother. In a way, it's always been her strength that's spoken to me more than her grief. There's something truly admirable about the stoicism, the steely dignity, with which she's faced her brother's disappearance, and I can't help but wish I had even a fraction of the inner strength she wears like a second skin. Was she always this way, I wonder, or did the circumstances in which she found herself force her to rise to the occasion? I'm strongly inclined to suspect the former. That sort of spirit doesn't just come from nowhere.

And on some level, I think that's ultimately what truly scares me: the knowledge that, long after the police have abandoned their search, Shonagh will still be out there pounding the streets, refusing to rest till she gets the answers she seeks.

20

On a cold, damp Saturday morning, Claire and I stand side by side among a sea of parents, grandparents and assorted family friends at the edge of the playing field at the back of Marchmont Secondary School, watching Eleanor and the rest of her team as they do fearsome battle with their arch-rivals from Bruntsfield Academy. 'You'll enjoy it,' Claire told me when she phoned the previous night and strong-armed me into coming. 'Eleanor will be delighted to have you there, and it'll be company for you while Matthew's away.'

Frankly I don't see what's to enjoy. I've never been able to get my head round football. Penalties, fouls, free kicks and all the other assorted rules and regulations mean nothing to me, and I haven't felt a burning desire to educate myself. Still, I'm able to follow enough of the proceedings to get the gist of what's going on – mostly on account of Claire, who issues a constant stream of loud encouragement to her daughter, punctuated by occasional, indignant calls for the referee to intervene – such as just now, when a much larger member of the opposing team, who I'm convinced is too old to be playing with a gaggle of thirteen-year-olds, slams headlong into Eleanor and knocks her to the ground.

'You can't allow that! *Surely* you can't allow that?' Claire shouts at the ref, who merely shrugs and turns his back on her. Eleanor, meanwhile, picks herself up off the ground with mud on her face and all down her jersey, and shoots her mother such a venomous look I half-expect Claire to turn to dust right there and then. I can't help but think that whoever said men have the greater capacity for violence never watched teenage girls playing competitive sport. At least this is only football. If it was hockey, they'd have been given sticks to hit each other with.

'You should have brought your camera,' Claire says to me, her tone bright and perky once again. 'You'd have got some amazing shots.'

I pretend not to hear her. Since the day we returned from Port Catrin three and a half years ago, my camera has lain on the top shelf of the cupboard on the upstairs landing, gathering dust. In my mind, it's become so tied up with you-know-what that I haven't been able to bring myself to touch it.

A gust of wind curls around me, and I shiver and draw my coat tighter about myself, tugging the sleeves down over my hands. I've been feeling inexplicably cold and lightheaded all morning – the past few mornings, in fact. Tired too – though, given my lack of sleep over the last week or so, that's hardly surprising. It's an all-encompassing, numbing sort of weariness that seeps into my bones, making me feel stiff and sluggish all over – like jet lag, only ten times worse.

The match ends, much to my relief. Marchmont win 3–2. Amid much jubilation from the home team and some gnashing of teeth from their away counterparts, Eleanor comes loping over to us, beaming, her skin – what little of it remains visible beneath the mud, that is – flushed pink.

'Did you see me?' she gabbles at Claire. 'Did you see my dummy run?'

'You were magnificent, darling, absolutely *magnificent*,' says Claire. 'Wasn't she, Hazel?'

I'm too busy trying to work out what a dummy run is, and

whether I should care, to come up with a meaningful response. 'Hi, Eleanor,' I eventually say.

'Um, it's "El" now?' she says, her intonation making it sound like a question. I contemplate asking her whether she spells it like the 'El' in 'El Chapo', or 'Elle' like the magazine, or even just the letter 'L', then decide nobody likes a smart-arse and that she's already serving up enough sass for both of us.

'Your Auntie Hazel was desperate to come and see you play,' says Claire, a reproachful note in her voice as she utters what my late granny would have referred to as a damn lie.

El gives me a flicker of a smile, then drops her eyes to the ground. She's at that truculent stage I'm told all teenagers go through but which I'm not convinced I ever did: determined to be treated like a grown-up but equally determined to make it clear to all and sundry that *actual* grown-ups are totally uncool weirdos with whom she wouldn't be caught dead conversing in public. Personally I've always found her – and people that age in general – a little intimidating, as pathetic as that must sound. I never know what sort of tone to shoot for with her, and invariably end up misjudging it and feeling like a clueless idiot. I can think of few things worse than being stuck in a room alone with her, which makes me exceedingly glad Claire's here to act as go-between.

'We'll wait for you in the car,' Claire says. 'Hurry up and go get washed and changed.'

'Actually,' El lifts her head fractionally, though eye contact remains conspicuous by its absence, 'a few of us are going to Sandrino's for milkshakes.'

'Oh.' Claire sounds genuinely put out. 'And how are you proposing to get home, then?'

El doesn't miss a beat. 'Isla's mum's picking her up after,' she says, glancing over her shoulder at a gaggle of her teammates as they beckon to her from the other end of the pitch. 'Isla said she'll run me back.'

'I see. And is Isla's mum on board with this plan?'

El sighs and tuts, as if having to explain herself is a huge and unreasonable imposition. 'It's *fine*,' she says.

'And your blood sugar level? Is *it* fine? I don't want to get a phone call in a couple of hours telling me you've had a hyper and been carted off to A&E. Have you got your insulin pen?'

'Yes, *Mum*,' says El, doing the exasperated eye-roll that seems to be an integral component of modern teenage girl vocabulary.

Claire thinks for a moment. 'On you go, then,' she says eventually. 'But don't stay out all day. There's still a driveway to be swept if you're expecting any pocket money this week.'

El says something under her breath which I'm pretty sure is sacrilegious, but she's already turning away from us, so I can't read her lips. I watch as she jogs over to join her friends and, together, they set off towards the showers at the back of the school.

'Come on.' Claire's voice cuts through the fog in my head. 'Let's take the scenic route.'

We set off, circling the perimeter of the fields that form the southern flank of the school's grounds.

'I swear she's becoming more and more obstinate,' Claire says. 'She won't do anything these days unless I bribe her.'

I make what I hope is a sympathetic noise. The perils and pitfalls of raising teenagers is an alien concept to me, and not one with which I'm ever likely to become familiar.

As we reach the gate at the bottom of the field, my eye is drawn to the solitary figure seated inside the bus shelter across the road, slumped forward, head almost touching its knees. From their size, build and awful posture, I conclude that they're a teenager, and that they're experiencing the unpleasant after-effects of a night of which they probably have little memory.

'Well, at any rate,' Claire says, following my gaze, 'at least she's not staying out till all hours and staggering home in the wee hours, doing her best impression of one of the walking dead.'

I don't respond. As I continue to stare at the figure, a glimmer of recognition stirs in me.

'Is . . . is that *Mickie*?' I say.

'Surely not,' Claire scoffs.

But even as she speaks, it all slots into place. I note the distinctive hairstyle, closely shaven at the sides, long spikes on top, and the familiar pair of Doc Martens tucked under the bench. And then, even as Claire takes my arm in an attempt to hurry me along, the figure lifts its head, instantly putting its identity beyond any conceivable doubt.

Even by Mickie's admittedly dubious standards, hers isn't a good look. Slack-jawed, bleary-eyed and with most of last night's eyeliner smeared halfway down her cheeks, it's clear she didn't spend last night in her own bed – or, I suspect, in anyone else's.

'It *is* her,' I say. I'm not sure whether to feel surprised, alarmed, pleased, or all three at once.

Claire, on the other hand, faces no such dilemma. Her displeasure radiates from every pore, and not for the first time I find myself wondering why I had to have the misfortune to end up with two best friends who are as different as oil and water. I can tell Claire would like nothing better than to pretend not to have seen Mickie and for us to continue on our way without a backward glance, but I'm not having it. I humoured her by coming along to El's football game; now she can jolly well humour *me*.

Quickening my pace, I cross the road to Mickie, Claire reluctantly tagging along behind me. As we come to a halt in front of the shelter, Mickie gazes up at us with a sort of furrow-browed look that tells me she's either in considerable pain or trying to remember who we are.

'Fancy running into *you* here,' I say, managing to sound bright and airy.

'Yes, fancy that,' Claire agrees, without enthusiasm.

'Well, well,' says Mickie, screwing up her features against the sun, 'if it ain't Tweedledum and Tweedledee. What's shakin', bacon?'

Now that we're up close and personal, I can see her pink-tinged eyes and smell the twin odours of stale smoke and alcohol on her clothes and hair. In fact, I wouldn't be overly surprised if she spent much of the previous night under the influence of more than just booze.

'What are you doing all the way out here?' I ask, trying to pretend I haven't noticed the state she's in. 'This isn't your usual patch.'

'Been out tripping the light fantastic. Woke up this morning miles fae hame wi a heid like a maraca and a mooth like sandpaper.'

I'm trying to work out how to convey to her that I wish she'd take more care of herself in a way that won't put her nose out of joint when Claire – who's never let Mickie's feelings stand in the way of saying what she thinks before and evidently doesn't intend to start now – beats me to it.

'I'm surprised you managed to remain upright long enough to drag yourself to the bus stop,' she sniffs. 'Or did your so-called friends carry you here, then leave you to your own devices?'

Mickie ponders this question for a moment, then gives an airy shrug. 'Honestly couldnae say one way or t'other. I was so out of it, they could've dressed me in a tutu and cuffed me to a lamppost and I'd've been none the wiser.'

She collapses into a fit of the giggles. Claire just stands there and watches her, stony-faced, until her laughter finally dies out. Seeing that her mirth at her plight isn't being shared, Mickie scoffs irritably and makes a clumsy swiping motion with her hand.

'Ah, don't you be fretting your wee head about me, Clarabelle. A slug of Irn-Bru and some co-codamol and I'll be right as rain.'

'Yes, because the obvious solution to the effects of one drug-and-alcohol-induced bender is to pump your system with *more* medication.'

Mickie scoffs. 'Like *you* care.'

'I care,' says Claire, slowly and deliberately, 'about the impact of your actions on those around you. About what seeing you in this state does to them.'

As she speaks, she glances momentarily in my direction. For some inexplicable reason, this fills me with shame and I quickly avert my eyes, pretending not to have heard her.

Mickie, on the other hand, shows no such reticence. Only too aware of what Claire's getting at, she scoffs loudly and contemptuously. 'Nice! Use her to justify yourself, why don't you?' With some effort, she hauls herself to her feet and takes a few tottering steps towards Claire. 'Listen, Churchie,' she says, squaring up to her, 'don't you be sitting there on yer high horse passing judgement on us mere mortals. The week I've had, I fancy you'd've been hitting the turps yourself f'you were in my shoes.'

They continue to argue, their voices rising and falling in turn as they trade and parry insults, but my mind has begun to drift again. The lightheadedness I was experiencing earlier has come back with a vengeance, and their voices sound distant and muffled. My eyes shift skyward, to the pale autumn sun, blindingly bright against the clear blue sky. I experience a sensation of levitating, of weightlessness, as if this existence is of little importance and that all I need to do is to let go and I'll float away to some place where all my mortal concerns will cease to matter.

I blink hard, my vision refusing to focus. My eyes drift from Claire and Mickie to the various pedestrians passing in either direction, many of those on our side of the road giving us the widest possible berth. On the opposite pavement, a man is approaching – tall, dark-haired, wearing a brown windcheater. He glances in our direction, no doubt drawn to Mickie and Claire's raised voices. As he gets closer, his pace slows, and, as he draws level with us, for a brief moment his face resolves into perfect HD clarity, and I see the unmistakable face of Aidan gazing back at me.

And then I'm falling – falling into a black, visionless pit with no bottom. And, as the darkness wraps me in its comforting embrace, I feel a strange sense of contentedness, as if this empty nothingness is where I've been meant to be all along.

21

When I come to, the first thing I see is the twin faces of Mickie and Claire peering down at me, and for a brief moment I wonder if I'm still in the pit; if I've fallen so far that I'm beyond their reach. Then a third face enters the picture – a man's, balding, careworn, framed by wire-rimmed spectacles.

'So you're back with us,' he says, smiling kindly. 'Gave us all quite a fright, so you did.'

I become aware of the rest of my surroundings and realise I'm lying in a bed in what appears to be a hospital side room, wearing one of those horrible paper gowns – the kind that don't close properly at the back. I realise, too, that there are electrodes attached to various parts of my anatomy, and a cannula in my inner elbow hooked up to a stand next to the bed with a bag of clear fluid hanging from it. It's always disconcerting to come to and find yourself somewhere other than where you expected to be, and doubly so when it turns out someone's stripped you naked and is pumping who knows what into your bloodstream into the bargain.

'What happened . . . ?' I manage to say.

'You blacked out,' Claire says, managing to sound both concerned and reproachful at the same time. 'You hit the pavement right in front of us. We couldn't rouse you for love nor money.'

'So we phoned for an ambo,' Mickie puts in almost gleefully. 'It was wild. Flashing blue lights and screaming sirens and big hunky men in uniform. You shoulda been there.'

I become aware of a tenderness in my lower jaw, and when I gingerly prod the area in question, the skin feels rough and sandpapery and a bolt of pain shoots up from it to my skull. It all comes back to me: Mickie and Claire's argument, the lightheadedness, the blurred vision – and then, just before I fainted, the brief glimpse of Aidan. I tell myself that's impossible – that Aidan's dead; that he's lying buried in the woods over a hundred miles from here. It can't have been him. It must just have been someone who looked like him – or else I really *am* starting to lose it. And yet I was so sure . . .

'But how . . . ? Why . . . ?' I say.

The bespectacled man – who I now surmise, from his faded green scrubs, is a doctor of some description – winces slightly before responding. 'Mrs Ellis, how would you say your appetite's been of late?'

The question comes at me out of nowhere. 'Um . . . all right, I think?' I say, slowly manoeuvring myself into a sitting position.

'And your fluid intake? Been drinking plenty of water?'

'I think so . . . '

'And what about food? Would you say you have a normal, healthy appetite?'

I shrug, trying hard to make sense, through the haze that still clouds my mind, of this procession of apparent non-sequiturs. 'Well, I mean, what even *is* normal at the end of the day?' I offer him a weak smile, which he doesn't reciprocate.

'How much do you reckon you weigh? A rough estimate is fine.'

'About sixty-five kilos, I think.' It's a wild stab in the dark: I can't remember the last time I set foot on the scales.

The doctor's expression remains grave. 'When you were brought in, we found that you were dangerously dehydrated. In the course of determining the quantity of fluids to give you, we had to calculate your weight.' He gives me a long, hard look over the tops of his spectacles. 'Our own estimate places you at just under sixty kilos, which would classify you as medically underweight.'

I say nothing, because there *is* nothing to say. What am I going to do? Tell him he's wrong? That he made a mistake in his calculations? Or that less than sixty kilos is a perfectly healthy weight for a woman of six foot one?

'Have you been feeling tired at all lately?' the doctor asks. 'Light-headed, lethargic, that sort of thing?'

'I—' I begin, then stop. It's true – all of it. And what's more, I realise that, on some level, I've been aware for some time that things haven't been right. Until now, I'd simply put it down to nerves and stress – a combination of the pressures at work and . . . well, let's just say the recent headlines. I try to remember whether I ate breakfast this morning. I have no memory of it one way or the other. And last night? What did I have for dinner? Does the fact I can't remember mean I didn't eat anything then either?

'It would be remiss of me to either overstate or understate the gravity of the situation,' says the doctor, 'so for now, what I'll say is that we're not at panic stations just yet, but at the same time it would be prudent to treat what happened today as something of a wake-up call. We'll continue to monitor you for the next few hours, but before we discharge you I'm going to arrange for you to have a chat with one of our dieticians.'

'I haven't got an eating disorder,' I say, instantly on the defensive.

'Doctor . . . Mathieson, is it?' Claire cuts in, elbowing her way past him to position herself between him and me. 'Can I just say, I'm a medical professional myself?' She extends her arm, trapping him in a businesslike handshake. 'Dr Claire Bissell – I'm a partner at the Braeburn surgery. My friend is registered at my practice with Dr Saughton. Far be it from me to interfere with your treatment plan, but surely it would make more sense for her to discuss her condition with someone who knows her and her medical history? I mean' – she gives a conspiratorial little laugh, as if they're a couple of peers discussing insider knowledge – 'we both know hospital dieticians are horrifically overstretched and only ever cover the basics: five fruit and veg a day, drink plenty of water, et cetera. I'll ensure she makes an appointment.'

Dr Mathieson looks decidedly unconvinced. He takes a step backwards, and I'm left with the impression that he finds Claire a rather intimidating presence, standing inches from him with her legs apart and her hands on her hips. I can't say I blame him – in this mode, she intimidates *me*.

He looks over her shoulder to me. 'Would you be happy with that arrangement?'

If I absolutely have to go through the ignominy of talking to someone about my ability to adequately feed myself, it's honestly six and half a dozen to me whether it's Dr Saughton or some unnamed hospital dietician. But I sense things will be a lot easier for everyone concerned if I go along with what Claire wants.

'Sure,' I say, trying my best to sound like it's no big deal. 'I'll make an appointment with Dr Saughton.'

The doctor casts another brief, uncertain glance in Claire's direction, then nods, the decision seemingly made. 'Very well. I'll leave the matter in your hands. But I'll be writing to Dr Saughton, recommending that you be signed off work for a period of recuperation.'

A surge of panic rises up inside me. 'But . . . but I can't! Things are really intense at the moment. I've just taken on this really important project, and—'

Claire shoots me a reproachful look. 'And don't you think that might be part of the problem? Prioritising work ahead of your health?'

I open my mouth to object again, then stop, realising it's hopeless. I let my shoulders slump in defeat.

'I quite agree,' says Dr Mathieson, whose attitude towards Claire seems to have thawed remarkably quickly now that he realises they're singing from the same hymn sheet. He turns to me again. 'I'll let you get some rest. I'll be back later to see how you're getting on. In the meantime, I'm going to arrange for a nurse to bring you a high-calorie drink.'

Claire waits till he's left the room, then immediately strides over to the door and shuts it behind him. She turns to me, eyes wide with outraged disbelief.

'What a busybody! What is it about hospital doctors and God complexes?' Her expression turns reproachful. 'You should have told me you were having problems. No – that's unfair. *I* should have realised something was off.'

'*I* told her she was looking too thin last week,' Mickie says. She's lying upside down in a wingback chair by the window with her feet in the air.

'And you didn't think it might be worth sharing your concerns with me?' Claire says, eyes flaring as she turns to her.

Mickie shrugs, her upper lip an upside-down 'W' as she smirks superciliously. 'Shouldn't've thought I *had* to. I'm not the doctor here, am I?'

Claire jabs a warning finger in Mickie's direction. 'If you've nothing helpful to say—'

'Oh, for crying out *loud*!'

At the sound of my voice, Claire stops in her tracks. She and Mickie both turn to face me as I drag myself into as upright a position as possible, the very act of shouting having taken more out of me than I anticipated.

'Can the two of you not go five minutes without getting in each other's faces? Here I am, lying in a hospital bed, invalided out, while the two of you do your best to re-enact the Battle of Five Armies.'

They both instantly look contrite. Mickie even manoeuvres herself into an upright position, such is the seriousness of the situation.

'I mean it,' I say, treating them both to the sternest expression I can muster. 'Any more of your nonsense and I'll be ringing the buzzer for the nurse to come and chuck you both out.'

Mickie gives a lopsided smile. 'Ah, you know we're only joshing. Sure we're not actually gonna brain one another.' She launches herself onto her feet. 'Tell yous what – I never did manage to get that pick-me-up I was after. I'll go see if there's a drinks machine somewhere – leave the two of yous to chat grown-up stuff while I'm gone.' She heads towards the door. 'Anything I can get you, wee hen? Mags? Fags? Sex toys?'

I manage a tight smile. 'I'll be fine.'

Mickie points an index finger at me, clicks her tongue and winks, then ducks out.

As soon as she's gone, Claire turns to me with a sigh and an exaggerated roll of her eyes. 'That *girl*! How are you supposed to get fit and healthy again with her driving your stress levels up to eleven?'

'Claire . . . ' I begin wearily.

'Actually, it's no wonder you're in this state to begin with, the nonsense she's been putting into your head . . . '

'It's honestly not like that—'

'You know she has mental health issues?'

'That's as may be, but I didn't break up a fight between the two of you just so you could slag her off behind her—' I stop mid-stream as what Claire's just told me belatedly registers. 'Mental health issues? What sort of mental health issues?'

'Borderline personality disorder, to be precise. As in emotional instability, a propensity for reckless behaviour, disturbed patterns of perception, the whole nine yards. She's been receiving treatment at the Alderwood for the last year or so.' She clocks my shocked expression. 'You didn't know?'

Her surprise seems genuine, and yet the fact she lobbed it out as a 'gotcha' just moments earlier does give me pause to wonder.

'I didn't,' I manage to say eventually. 'How did *you* . . . ?'

Claire shrugs. 'I accessed her medical records.'

'You *what*?' My voice drops to a shocked whisper. 'Claire, you can't *do* that.'

'It's no big deal,' Claire says airily. 'We doctors do it all the time.'

Do they? I'm not sure that's actually the case. If it is, then I'm pretty sure this is a trade secret Claire really shouldn't be passing on to me.

'Honestly,' she continues, seemingly oblivious to the thoughts running through my head, 'I'm slightly shocked she didn't tell you – you being her cousin. That's why I didn't say anything before. I figured it was none of my business.'

'But still enough of your business for you to access her records without her permission.' I give her a beseeching look. 'Claire, I can't believe you *did* that.'

Claire makes an impatient noise at the back of her throat. 'I don't know why you're getting so hung up on that. It really isn't the point.'

'So what *is* the point, then?'

With unexpected speed, Claire crosses the floor and perches on the end of my bed. She leans towards me, eyes boring into mine. 'Just this,' she says, her voice dropping to an urgent whisper. 'We already know she consumes dangerous quantities of alcohol, and that she's not averse to supplementing it with substances of a less legal variety. If she's doing all that on top of a condition that causes mood swings and impulsive behaviour . . . well, I'd say we're in uncharted territory, wouldn't you?'

'I suppose,' I say, more because it seems safer and easier to agree with her than because I'm genuinely convinced.

'You have to admit the fact she hasn't shared her diagnosis with you is cause for concern,' Claire continues, phrasing it as a statement rather than a question. She pauses, momentarily breaking off eye contact, before renewing it with even greater intensity. 'It certainly adds a fresh dimension to the whole question of the source of that phone call, wouldn't you say?'

I say nothing. Loath as I am to admit it, she has a point. Prior to this revelation, I hadn't seriously bought into the whole notion of Mickie either making the phone call herself or else blabbing about what we did in the woods to someone else and having no memory of having done so. Now, though – now I'm not sure *what* to think.

I become aware of a presence in the doorway. Almost as one, Claire and I turn to see Mickie standing there, a bottle of Irn-Bru in one hand and a bag of grapes in the other. She looks at each of us in turn, then raises an eyebrow.

'O-*kay*,' she says, drawing out the second syllable. 'Hope I'm not interrupting anything heavy. Two of yous looked like yous were about to lock lips or something.'

Claire instantly gets to her feet and backs off, evidently mortified – though whether at Mickie's insinuation or the actual subject of our conversation, I can't say. Looking for something to distract from her question, my eyes fall on the bag of grapes she's holding.

'Where'd you get those?' I manage to say.

Mickie follows my gaze and grins. 'Half-inched 'em from an old boy's bedside down the corridor. Old geezer willnae miss 'em – so busy staring at the ceiling he didnae even notice me.' Her expression turns pensive. 'Mind you, I never did check he was actually breathing . . .'

'*Oh* good lord,' Claire groans, deftly picking up the baton from me. 'You shouldn't *say* these things!'

'Circle of life, my friend, circle of life. We all exit stage left eventually. Can't afford to be squeamish about it.'

As they continue their back and forth, infinitely more good-natured than the last time they traded verbal barbs, I settle back against the pillow behind me, their words blurring into background noise as my mind drifts to its own thoughts. For the umpteenth time, I try to tell myself there's nothing for me to worry about. Everything's fine. *We're* fine. We're all going to *be* fine.

And yet I can't rid my mind of that vision of Aidan just before I fainted. Of the look he gave me, and of what it conveyed.

I know what you did, it said, *and so do you.*

22

I'm discharged a few hours later. Claire runs me home, accompanying me inside and clucking around like an overattentive grown-up child caring for an infirm elderly relative, settling me in my favourite chair, turning up the central heating, making me a mug of strong, sugary tea. To keep my strength up, she tells me.

'You know,' she says, as I gingerly take a sip of the oversweetened brew, 'there's really no need for you to see Dr Saughton about this – not if you don't want to. I can take care of everything. Honestly, it's crazy you're still seeing that pompous old duffer when my consulting room is right next door to his. We should have transferred you over to my list years ago.'

The tea I've just swallowed goes down the wrong way and I have to struggle to stifle a choke.

'We'll get you on a proper, balanced diet,' Claire goes on, seemingly none the wiser. 'I'll cook your meals and deliver them to you; you'll only have to heat them up in the microwave. In fact, why not come and stay at ours? Just till you're back on your feet – or at least until Matthew gets back from London. You know Rob and Eleanor would love to have you.'

I doubt that very much indeed, but I sense diplomacy is required here.

'It's really kind of you,' I say, 'but if it's all the same, I'd rather be in my own space. And about Dr Saughton – I'd prefer to talk to him if it's all the same. He knows my history.'

'*I* know your history, sweetie,' says Claire, squeezing my hand. 'I know you better than anyone. There's no one more equipped to take care of your needs.'

'I know,' I say, retracting my hand as firmly as I can without actually snatching it away. 'And I'm grateful for everything you're doing. But I can't be living out of your pocket. I have to have *some* independence.'

I can tell Claire's not happy, but she ultimately relents – though she does insist on personally calling Dr Saughton at home on my behalf. In the strident, high-handed tone she always uses while addressing her peers, she insists that he make space in his diary to see me first thing on Monday morning. Afterwards, she hands me the phone and I make the far more difficult call to Fraser, explaining the situation and letting him know it'll be some time before I'm able to return to work. I can tell from the tone of his voice that he's disappointed, though he makes a decent fist of sounding concerned for my wellbeing. He tells me not to worry, assuring me that the design of the secondary school will be safe in the reliable hands of Gordon Allen, and that there might even be scope for me assuming a junior role on the project once I'm fully recovered. It hurts, handing it over – removed from the first major project I've ever led and replaced by someone more experienced and less prone to flakiness. But I'm forced to admit it's for the best. If I'm being honest with myself, my eye's been off the ball for some time now. It's probably just as well I'm not responsible for any important decisions while all this is hanging over me.

'What about Matthew?' Claire says when I hang up. 'You should call him too – or I could do it for you if you like?'

I shake my head. 'Best not to worry him. He's got enough on his plate without adding me to his list of things to fret about.'

In truth, the pair of us haven't actually exchanged any direct words since he left for London, though he did text me the previous evening to tell me he'd be staying there for the weekend and would likely be gone for most of next week as well, if not longer. I'd be lying if I claimed I felt anything upon receiving that news – even the smallest twinge of disappointment.

'That's probably wise,' Claire says. 'And look, it would probably also be a good idea for you to steer clear of Mickie – at least for the time being. You know how she is. The last thing we need right now is for her to get you worked up needlessly – like when you collapsed this morning.'

I try to work out whether she's implying that Mickie was somehow responsible for my having fainted – and, if so, whether she sees herself as being without blame in the matter. That said, I don't feel particularly inclined to argue with her – for the time being, at any rate. As much as I hate to admit it, from the moment Claire dropped that bombshell about Mickie's mental health problems in my lap, something indefinable but profound shifted in my relationship with my cousin. All my interactions with her until we left the hospital and went our separate ways felt forced and unnatural, as if I was talking to a stranger. As if, whenever I looked at her, I no longer saw her – only the 'condition' that, until today, I didn't even know she had. It's as if she's been lying to me all this time. What else has she lied about, I wonder? What else has she failed to divulge? I've always liked to think I'm someone who's open-minded and progressive when it comes to mental health issues, but until now I've always perceived them as something that affects other people – not my close friends, and certainly not my immediate family. Now, when I imagine myself in proximity to her, my overriding emotion is one of intense personal discomfort – a fear that she might have some sort of crazy meltdown or act in some unpredictable way that I won't know how to deal with.

I know what that says about me, and if it's any consolation, I'm as far from proud of myself as it's possible to be. But it's one thing to recognise that your own feelings are self-serving, even reprehensible, and another thing entirely to knuckle down and do the legwork to actually confront and change them. And, right now, my own life is in enough of a mess without me trying to find the space to worry about someone else's problems as well.

I give Claire a tight smile. 'I reckon that's probably for the best.'

It's late evening by now and long past my normal dinnertime. If I'd been on my own and hadn't just collapsed from malnutrition, I'd have been tempted to just skip it, but Claire insists on cooking me a hearty meal, 'loaded with all the energy and nutrients your body needs', then stands over me and watches me eat it. I dutifully shovel forkful after forkful of the meaty stew into my mouth, approaching it like the endurance test it is, and she seems satisfied with my progress, though I manage to clear less than half my plate.

The following day, she's back again at first light, armed with all the necessary ingredients to make a rich and filling breakfast. Once again, I force myself to knuckle down and eat, as much for her benefit as mine, even though I typically can't face anything more substantial than cornflakes at this time of day. Claire remains with me throughout the day, keeping me preoccupied with constant conversation, short walks, a seemingly endless cavalcade of snacks and meals and even, at one point, a game of Connect Four when all the other possibilities have been exhausted.

On Monday, Claire has to work, but my appointment with Dr Saughton is at 9.15, so she gives me a lift to the practice and leaves me in the waiting room with an ancient edition of *House & Garden* to keep me occupied while I wait. Dr Saughton is, for once, running to time, and shortly thereafter I'm in his consulting room, stripping down to my underwear to be weighed, measured, poked and prodded. Afterwards, my blouse still only half-buttoned and one of my socks on back to front, I sit down with him to discuss the plan going forward. Much to my relief, he agrees, in his usual ponderous, paternalistic way, that I can be trusted to manage my own recovery. Prior to now, my single greatest fear was that he would propose booking me into one of those clinics you see on the TV where they make you talk about your feelings and measure your food intake down to the last calorie. At least I've been spared *that* ignominy . . . for now, at any rate. He wants to see me once a fortnight to keep track of my progress and, if deemed necessary, revisit the arrangement.

As I'm leaving the surgery, my phone blings an alert. I stop to examine the screen. It's a text from Mickie.

> Aloha chickadee, hope ur feeling more like urself 2day. Since ur all laid up at home with nowt 2 do, howsabout u & me get 2gether & do something? Day trip, go see a movie, whatevs. I'll pay LOL XOX

I stare at the message for several moments, unsure how to respond. If this was just Mickie – the old Mickie, the one I thought I knew – asking, I'd have been tempted to throw caution to the wind and take her up on her offer, Claire's reservations be damned. But this new Mickie – this unknowable Mickie, with her hitherto unrevealed personality disorder and umpteen unanswered questions as to just what she's been getting up to over the last couple of weeks – frightens me, much as I hate to admit it. I have no idea what's really going through her mind; have no idea what she's truly capable of at any given moment. When it comes down to a choice between the unknown and splendid isolation, the latter wins every time.

I text her back, telling her now's not a good time – that I just want to be by myself right now. Almost immediately, she sends me another message – a string of '??????' symbols and a 'confused' emoji. The message has barely appeared on the screen when the phone rings, Mickie's name on the caller ID. I reject the call, set my phone to silent and tap out a single short, curt message:

Leave me alone, Mickie.

And then, burning with shame, I pocket my phone and continue on my way.

For the next couple of days, I try my best to follow orders and put my feet up, relax and focus on building up my strength. It quickly proves to be easier said than done. Growing up, I watched enough medical dramas with my mum to know that it was highly unusual for a week to go by on any of those programmes without some pious doctor or nurse instructing a patient to 'just concentrate on getting better'. It always made me roll my eyes – this notion that you could mend a broken limb or cure a serious illness through sheer willpower. It's up there with 'try not to worry' and 'don't think about X'. It should be basic common sense that, the moment you tell someone not to think about something, that's precisely where their mind is immediately going to go – and yet still we persist. In my case, all my efforts to divest myself of thoughts pertaining to Aidan, Mickie or my present situation are singularly counterproductive, and none of the distraction strategies I attempt to employ have any effect. Even my normal go-to when I'm anxious or stressed – losing myself in a really good film – proves impossible. I hear the words and see the pictures on the screen, but I don't engage with them. In a final, desperate attempt to prevent myself from spending all day doomscrolling, I even lock my phone in a drawer in another room, but that only seems to make matters worse as it just leads to me fretting about all the possible explosive developments that could be occurring while I'm closeted away, cut off from the outside world. In the end, I admit defeat, retrieve my phone from quarantine and sit curled up on the sofa with the screen's glow illuminating my face while the shadows lengthen outside.

I don't see a whole lot of Claire during this time – not, of course, that I see a whole lot of *anyone*. With her at work during the day and occupied by various motherly and wifely duties in the evenings – running El to football practice, attending a charity do as Rob's plus-one – she has far less time on her hands to devote to little old me, though she still checks in with me when she can. On Monday night, she calls round with another batch of pre-cooked meals, takes one look at Dr Saughton's meal plan and orders me to disregard it completely, proclaiming him to be an out-of-touch old fossil who should have been put out to pasture years ago. 'Don't you worry,' she says, giving my arm a reassuring squeeze, 'I'll see you right. Just you leave everything to me.'

On Tuesday night, during a lull between refreshing the *Port Catrin Gazette* page and keeping an eye on the evening news on the TV, I head over to the Find Aidan Facebook group. I immediately see that Shonagh has posted one of her intermittent updates – a two-paragraph missive timestamped just over an hour ago, written in her usual terse, ungarnished prose.

> To be honest, lately I've been wondering why I bother doing any of this. Engagements are down month on month, members are slowly abandoning the group, and I have little if anything to show for three and a half years of blood, sweat and tears. It certainly hasn't brought Aidan home, or me any closer to knowing what happened to him. Would any of you honestly shed a tear if I shut up shop permanently?

No doubt those who walk the corridors of power, and who hate being held to account, will breathe a sigh of relief when I'm no longer on their case, and no doubt some of you will secretly be glad I'm no longer cluttering up your timelines with all these inconvenient negative vibes. I know, too, that others will see this an admission of defeat. A sign that I've let the bastards grind me down. That I've given up. Think what you like. I don't give a shit. Everything I've done, I've done for Aidan, but we all have a finite amount that we can give, and there comes a time when everyone reaches their limit. Well, I've about reached mine.

S.

There are a paltry twelve 'likes' below the post, and half a dozen love hearts. I'm strongly tempted to add to that total – to register my support, to offer my encouragement. *Don't give up,* I want to say. *Keep fighting. Stay strong.* The sheer absurdity of me willing on the very person from whom, after the police, I have the most to fear is not lost on me. Common sense dictates that it's strongly in my interests for her to give up. If anything, I should be thinking of ways to encourage her to throw in the towel. And yet the sight of this formidable woman on the verge of surrendering, of all the energy she's expended counting for nothing, feels like a punch in the gut. Until this moment, I don't think I realised just how much I'd actually been willing her on – drawing strength, in some strange, inexplicable way, from her relentless quest for the truth.

I hold down on the 'Like' icon below her post, and the various options appear. Which should I choose? The default, the 'thumbs up' symbol, would make it look like I was agreeing with the sentiments of her post – telling her she's right to call it quits. On the other hand, the love heart seems too cloying, too presumptive, and I doubt someone as tough and no-nonsense as Shonagh would appreciate it. Ditto the widely derided 'care' symbol – the little fellow face hugging a heart, which I don't think even I would consider using in a non-ironic context.

I continue to prevaricate for another minute or so, then scroll back up to the top of her post and click on her profile pic. Her profile loads, with the 'Add Friend' and 'Message' buttons below it. I hesitate for another moment, then quickly tap 'Add Friend' before tossing the phone aside as if it's scalded me. It lands on the floor a few feet away from me and lies there, face-down, the deed done. What I've just set in motion, and what good – or bad – will come of it, I've no idea, but Shonagh strikes me as someone who could do with a friend right about now.

Hell, *I* could do with a friend right now.

23

With a certain plodding inevitability, time continues to turn, every passing day much of a muchness with the one preceding it. Claire continues her sporadic visits and slightly less sporadic phone calls and texts, checking in with me, making sure I'm eating properly, getting plenty of rest and relaxation and – *sigh* – concentrating on getting better. And believe me, I know it comes from a good place. It's just that, right now, I can't think of anything *less* likely to set my mind at ease.

During this time, there's been no response to the friend request I sent Shonagh. I'm not sure whether she's actively ignoring it or simply hasn't seen it. I've thought several times about quietly rescinding it, and once or twice have actually got as far as hovering over the button, but something always stops me. Partly it's about not wanting to withdraw my admittedly puny show of support, but it's not just that. I think a part of me is genuinely curious to see how she responds. *If* she responds.

I continue to keep a weather eye on the news websites and TV channels for any fresh developments in the hunt for Aidan. Each time I come away empty-handed, I find myself experiencing that by now familiar sensation in my gut that's somewhere between relief and a curious lack of fulfilment. It's the uncertainty of it all, I suppose – being stuck in this constant purgatory, not knowing whether it's safe to breathe or not. It's not that I *want* to be caught, but at the same time, I'm not sure how much more of this limbo I can actually take.

It happens in the wee hours of Thursday morning. I've spent the last several insomnia-plagued hours in front of the computer in the spare room that serves as my home office, clicking around aimlessly and watching videos about the migratory patterns of elephants in sub-Saharan Africa. I've just reached the point of finally feeling like I might be ready to drop off when a sudden jaunty, trilling 'ping' sound rings out, indicating that I have a private Facebook message. In an instant, I'm wide awake and alert. I fumble for the mouse, pausing the video and clicking back to the open Facebook tab. In the corner of the screen, Shonagh's stony face stares back at me inside a little circle, her name and the words 'Active now' next to it. Below it is a short, terse message:

Who is this?

I don't move. I sit there in silence, staring at the words, trying to still my pounding heart. I consider closing the browser window, turning off the computer, yanking out the plug, fleeing from the office and hiding under my bed till daylight comes. But I don't move. For a few seconds, my fingers continue to hover over the keyboard, poised and ready. Then, my decision made, I type out my response.

'*You don't know me,*' I tell her (true), '*but I've followed you for years*' (also true) '*and I saw your post a couple of days ago and felt I had to do something*' (absolutely true).

'*What post?*'

'*The one about giving up. Please don't.*'

There's a pause before she responds.

'*What do you care?*'

I gaze at the screen, fingers poised, unsure how to respond. What am I supposed to say? That she should carry on for the sake of her legion of loyal followers who've developed a personal investment in her cause? That following her crusade from afar allows me to live vicariously through her, drawing inspiration from the strength she exhibits and which I so obviously lack? That the thought of her losing hope and admitting defeat hollows me out inside, even though I should, by rights, be praying for just such a turn of events? As if she doesn't already have enough problems of her own without being made to feel responsible for other people's!

A solitary *'Well?'* appears on the screen below Shonagh's previous message. I bite the inside of my cheek, then throw caution to the wind and begin to type.

'Because I know what it is you're going through.'

Hard though it might be to believe, I didn't set out to deliberately deceive her. I didn't mean, *I've experienced the same thing you're experiencing.* I don't know what it's like to lose a sibling. What I meant, as preposterous as it sounds, is that I feel intimately connected to Shonagh by virtue of the fact that I'm as wound up in what happened to Aidan as she is. Her story is my story too, even if she has no inkling of my involvement.

A pulsing ellipsis symbol appears, showing that Shonagh is typing again. A moment later, her message comes through.

'Who did you lose?'

In retrospect, there was no other way in which she was going to interpret my words. Perhaps, deep down, I knew that even before I'd typed them. Perhaps I even *wanted* her to interpret it that way.

'My sister,' I type.

'Tell me about her,' says Shonagh.

And so I do.

They say admitting you have a problem is the first step to recovery. That may be true, but it greatly downplays the importance of all the other steps that come afterwards. I know what I'm doing is illogical and runs contrary to my self-preservation, but I can't help myself. If the analogy wasn't a little too close for comfort, I'd be tempted to liken myself to a killer haunting the funeral or the scene of the crime even though he knows it increases his odds of being caught. I'm sure, if you put me in a room with a bunch of highly qualified psychologists, they'd have an absolute field day analysing me, trying to diagnose my major malfunction. Whether they'd succeed or not is anyone's guess, but something tells me the workings of my mind would remain a mystery to them.

Before Aidan, I was, by nature, an honest sort of person. I didn't bunk off school or claim the dog ate my homework or tell my mum I'd been studying at a friend's when we'd actually been out clubbing. Deception just wasn't in my nature. And it's not as if I had a habit of doing things that would have got me into trouble, so I had no real need to pull the wool over people's eyes anyway. Covering up what happened to Aidan wasn't just the largest and most sustained act of deception in which I'd ever participated – it was practically the first time I'd ever had to lie full stop. And I knew, as soon as the dust settled and the reality of what we'd committed ourselves to sank in, that if I was to avoid slipping up, I was going to have to change my entire ethos.

And so I started to lie about other things too. At first, it was just to keep myself in practice; to get comfortable with the idea of inhabiting two separate realities – the one in my head and the one I presented to the world. I started off small, telling Matthew I'd had moussaka for lunch when I'd actually had couscous, or telling my work colleagues we'd been to Northumberland during the Easter weekend when we actually went to the Lake District. At first, I had to work really hard at it, setting myself a daily quota of little white lies to invent, all the while keeping careful track of which untruth I'd told to which person. After a while, though, it started to feel like second nature. Do anything for long enough and it becomes a habit. Spend enough time lying and the lies start to feel more real than reality itself. I even started to enjoy the act of weaving my tangled web of falsehoods – of creating an alternate existence for myself that differed in a myriad of tiny ways from the one I actually led.

Back when I was at school, my status as an only child was a constant source of disappointment for me. Most of my friends had at least one sibling. Some even had two. I used to always wonder what it would be like to have a brother or a sister – a peer, someone in whom I could confide, someone who would understand me as well as I understood them. My friends always used to moan about their siblings, especially those who had younger brothers or sisters, but I could never understand it. *Don't you realise how lucky you are?* I wanted to say. *How can you not see what you have?*

Lots of young children have an imaginary friend – a special soulmate only they can see and onto whom they project certain, often idealised, characteristics. Well, I had an imaginary sister – an identical twin called Judy who no one knew about except me. I never told anyone about her, partly because I was afraid of being ridiculed and partly because, at least on some level, I realised that would defeat the purpose – that Judy was someone I'd invented for *my* benefit, not anyone else's. Imaginary friends are a widely misunderstood phenomenon. Many adults assume that the child must genuinely believe the companion they've created actually exists, whereas studies show that the overwhelming majority of children who have imaginary friends are perfectly aware that they don't actually exist. I was never under any illusion that Judy was anything other than a figment of my imagination – a manifestation of all the qualities I wished I possessed but didn't.

Judy was me, but she was also not me. Where I was shy and retiring, Judy was the life and soul of the party. Where I was careful and risk-averse, she threw caution to the wind. Where I was a diligent but unremarkable student, she was an effortless over-achiever – a child prodigy destined for greatness. Over the years Judy and I spent together, I went back and forth a great many times as to the specific field in which she excelled, but eventually I settled on ballet. It's not something I ever aspired to myself, but whenever I saw a performance of *The Nutcracker* or *Swan Lake* on TV, the dancers, with their perfectly streamlined muscles and graceful economy of movement, always seemed to epitomise just the sort of single-mindedness and determination to excel I wished I possessed myself but knew I never would. In retrospect, I suppose Judy was my first big lie, albeit one I never shared with anyone else.

And so I tell Shonagh all about her, conjuring her into being, laying detail upon detail, making her as real as if she were sculpted out of flesh and blood. In the process, I dredge up details I haven't thought about for more than two decades but which nonetheless spring to mind as effortlessly as if it was yesterday – as if I'm simply picking up from where I left off twenty years ago. Into this expertly crafted mix, however, I add a fresh development. At the age of thirteen – around the time I put away childish things, including my imaginary sister – Judy disappeared.

I'm not sure where this new twist originates from, but the details spring into my mind so readily that I don't even have to think. I tell Shonagh about the day Judy went missing – how she was on her way home from dance practice in the city centre and failed to make her usual connection at Waverley Station. I tell of our parents' increasing unease – in this alternate timeline, my dad was still alive at this point – which, as the evening deepened, exploded into full-blown panic. Of the front doorbell ringing, heralding the arrival of two uniformed police officers, who my mum insisted on plying with endless offers of cups of tea, refusing to take no for an answer until they capitulated. Of the officers' questioning my parents, followed by my own time in the hot seat as they made me recount every detail of the last time I saw my sister. Of how the more senior of the two had flaky skin and dandruff on his collar while the other kept blowing his nose. I tell of the weeks and months that followed; of the lengths the whole family went to to keep Judy's disappearance in the spotlight; of the trips into town every weekend to hand out flyers plastered with her face; of how my dad took to spending almost every waking moment pounding the streets, walking the length and breadth of the city in the hope that he would somehow find her. And then of how, in our own individual ways, we slowly adjusted to life without Judy – until, without even being aware of it happening, it simply became the new normal, the hole she left in the family ever-present, destined never to be filled.

As I continue to weave my web of falsehoods, I realise at some point that, far from consoling Shonagh and talking her round from her defeatist mindset, this has become about me using her as a sounding board – a sponge to soak up all the fictitious angst I've created as an outlet for my *actual* pent-up fears and anxieties. I tell myself this isn't just for my benefit – that, by getting Shonagh to focus on something other than her own despair, I'm pulling her back from the brink, persuading her to postpone the point when she decides to nuke the Facebook group and shred all her flyers for at least another day. And that's good . . . right? At any rate, that's what I keep telling myself.

Throughout my account, Shonagh doesn't say much in response, other than the occasional *'go on'* or *'I'm still listening'* to prompt me. If I hadn't already been able to tell from her various media appearances, it would have quickly become apparent that she's not one for ostentatious displays of emotion or empty platitudes. And yet I don't mind. In fact, I think I'd find it a whole lot harder to keep going if she *did* say things like, *Oh, you poor thing* or *I'm so sorry you've had to go through this.* Somehow, it makes me feel like less of a fraud to have my sob story met with the online equivalent of stony silence.

When I finally stop typing, having produced several screens' worth of text, for a long time Shonagh makes no response. I'm beginning to wonder if I've scared her off, if she's come to the conclusion that she's made the mistake of pandering to a nutter – and really, who could blame her? – when I see the little ellipsis symbol once again.

'Thank you for sharing your truth with me.'

I almost want to laugh. My truth? If she had even the smallest inkling . . .

I become aware of the first fingers of daylight creeping into the room from over the tops of the trees of Leith Links; of the faint sound of birdsong outside. We must have been talking for far longer than I realised. Hours have passed since her pithy opening salvo, and the rest of the world will soon be emerging from its peaceful slumber.

'I'm sorry I burdened you with all that,' I say.

'That's OK. It's not like I was planning on getting any sleep anyway.'

I try to work out whether she's making a self-deprecating joke or simply being sarcastic. I'm half-tempted to respond with a laughing emoji, but she doesn't strike me as the sort of person who holds with packaging feelings into cutesy corporate pictograms.

'I'd better let you go,' I say instead.

'OK.'

I picture her about to switch off her screen or close her laptop lid or pocket her phone – whichever method she's been using to communicate with me.

'Wait,' I type quickly.

The animated ellipsis appears, followed by a '?'

I hesitate, unsure how what I'm about to say will be received. Nothing ventured, nothing gained, I suppose.

'I just want you to know that, any time you need to vent to someone, or you need anything at all, you can talk to me.'

I imagine her looking at her screen, one eyebrow raised, lip curled scornfully at this invitation to bare her soul to a complete stranger. For a moment, I think she isn't going to dignify my offer with a response, but then the ellipsis appears once more.

'We'll see,' she says.

I wait for almost a full minute before concluding that the conversation is at an end. I close the chat window and am about to switch off my screen when a notification message pops up in the corner of the window.

Shonagh Cranston accepted your friend request.

24

For the next few days, I hear nothing from Shonagh, and when I check Facebook, the absence of the little green dot next to her picture tells me that she's offline. To be honest, it comes as something of a relief. In the cold light of day, my decision to engage with her at all, let alone spin her a pack of lies that would be disproved with even the most cursory Google search for stories about a missing Edinburgh girl called Judy Harper, looks like the actions of a madwoman. A part of me hopes that, friend request acceptance or no, she's figured me for a flake and decided to have nothing further to do with me. I can't even *begin* to imagine what Claire would say if she knew what I've been getting up to.

Speaking of Claire, on Saturday she rings me to announce that we're having a girls' night in tonight at my place – just me, her, a takeaway and a movie. 'Just like old times,' she says, her voice tinkling with merriment, and by that I know she means the halcyon, pre-Mickie days, back when she still had a monopoly on my friendship. And, much as it pains me to admit it, I'm almost inclined to agree. It's certainly true that, one way or another, life was less complicated back when it was only the two of us.

Claire arrives in the early evening with a sheaf of menus for different local takeaways – 'So what's it to be? Chinese? Indian? Thai? My treat!' – and half a dozen Blu-rays still in their cellophane wrapping – 'Which shall we start with? Come on – you're the one who knows about films.' The common theme running through the selection is that they're almost all female buddy movies pitting two best friends against the world. I honestly couldn't care one way or the other, but to please Claire I pick at random, settling on the Thai Kitchen for dinner and that perennial classic, *Thelma & Louise*, for the evening's entertainment.

'Great choice!' says Claire, then adds, with a conspiratorial grin, 'So which of us d'you suppose is Thelma and which is Louise?'

Before long, we're both settled on the sofa, tucking into stir-fry while Geena Davis and Susan Sarandon go on the run across the American Southwest. I've seen it before, of course, but not for some time, and I'd forgotten that the incident which kicks everything off is Louise killing a stranger who hits it off with Thelma in a bar. A stranger who was in the process of trying to rape her at the time – but still, it hits just a little too close to home. I cast a sidelong glance at Claire, but if she's picked up on the unfortunate parallel, she's not letting on. She's in unnervingly high spirits, engaging with the events on screen to a level that I normally only associate with overly excitable American cinema-goers: whooping with laughter at the funny parts, gasping out loud at the shocking bits, then turning to check whether I too am responding appropriately. My heart's not really in it, but for the sake of an easy life, I force myself to play along. At least she's managing to refrain from tutting at the swearwords and sexual innuendos – a habit that normally makes watching anything rated more than PG with her something of an endurance test.

The evening wears on, and the film continues to unfold. The girls are on their way to Mexico now, racing south through the desert with half the state's law enforcement hot on their tail. Amid a cacophony of screeching tyres and wailing sirens, the front doorbell rings.

I'm immediately on my feet. 'I'll get it,' I say, hurrying towards the door before Claire can lodge an objection.

'Want me to stop it for you?'

'No, it's fine. Just let it run.'

'OK,' she says, 'but hurry back. I seem to remember there's a good bit coming up.'

As I head out into the hallway, I experience the immediate and palpable sensation of a great weight lifting from my shoulders. I hadn't taken on board just how stifling Claire's company was, and any respite, however brief, feels like a blessed relief.

That is, until I open the front door and see who's standing on the top step.

'Mickie!' The word escapes my lungs in an explosive gasp. 'What are you doing here?'

'What?' She shrugs belligerently. 'I can't come and pay my big cuz a visit just cos I feel like it?'

She looks terrible. Her eyes are bloodshot, her hair greasy and unwashed, and the reek of spirits coming off her is so strong it almost blows me backwards.

'I thought we agreed to play things cool for a bit,' I say, trying not to breathe in too deeply.

Mickie ponders this, frowning. 'Nope, don't remember agreeing to any such thing. Sounds like one of Charlie Church's high and mighty edicts.'

As if on cue, a blast of gunfire explodes from the living room. I glance over my shoulder involuntarily, and Mickie's eyes narrow.

'Is she in there?' She snorts disgustedly. 'Oh, very nice – give your cousin Mickie the cold shoulder but invite old sour-tits round for a knees-up, why don't ya?' She rises up on tiptoe and yells past me, 'Why'n't ya come out here and show yourself, ya skeevy old boot?'

I slip out onto the porch, shutting the door behind me. 'Keep your voice down! You'll upset the neighbours.'

'Well, we certainly can't have *that*,' Mickie says sarcastically, her voice still several notches too loud. 'Wouldnae wanna land you in the shitter with the Neighbourhood Watch.'

I don't dignify that with a response. I can already picture Mrs Marchbanks peering through her lace curtains, lips pinched in disapproval.

'Listen, listen.' Mickie succeeds in dialling down the volume a little, though the effort she has to put into modulating herself reminds me of a shaken can of fizzy juice just waiting to explode. 'I'm sorry, all right? I'm just a wee bitty on edge right now cos of all this craziness.'

I cast another reflexive glance over my shoulder. Claire must surely be wondering where I've got to by now.

'Anyways,' Mickie continues, 'what I actually came here for was to see if you wanted to clear out for a bit.'

'Clear out?' I repeat, wondering if I've heard her correctly.

'Aye!' She grins eagerly, mistaking my echoing of her words for encouragement. 'I've got a butt-load of time off owing at work – pulled a bunch of back-to-back double shifts while half the staff were off with lurgy – and you're out to pasture for the foreseeable, right?'

'Right,' I say, really not liking where this is going.

'So what's to stop us?' She spreads her arms wide. 'Think about it – you, me, the open road, the sun on our faces and the wind in our hair. What could be better? We can leave this drizzly backwater far behind us and jet off to someplace with year-round sun like, I dunno, Cape Verde, or – fuck it – maybe Phuket.' She mispronounces it the way you'd expect. 'Whaddaya say?'

She sounds so enamoured by the idea and is staring at me so expectantly that a part of me almost feels compelled to say 'yes' simply to avoid disappointing her. But this – the crazy ideas; the spontaneous, off-the-cuff schemes dreamt up on the spur of the moment without any thought given to the practicalities – this is *exactly* what Claire warned me about. Until this moment, a part of me had still struggled to square her revelations about Mickie having BPD with the Mickie I thought I knew. Now, though, it all makes perfect sense. These are not the thoughts of a rational mind, and I realise, to my horror, that I'm not merely unnerved by Mickie. I'm *afraid* of her.

I instinctively take a step back, reaching behind me so my hand rests pre-emptively on the door handle. I try to be subtle about it, but I can tell, from the flicker in Mickie's eyes, that she's noticed.

'What?' She spreads her arms again, a maniacal smile stretching her lips wide. 'It's me – your wee cousin Mickie. You know me.'

'Do I?' There's a flinty edge to my voice that I don't recognise.

Mickie frowns in confusion, then gives an awkward, disbelieving laugh, as if she too is unnerved by this situation.

'What's going on here, wee hen? You're acting like you've seen a tattie-bogle.'

I open my mouth to tell her she's wrong – that I'm not spooked, that her proposal just caught me off-guard. But then I think, *Why should I?* I shouldn't have to justify myself. After all, I'm not the one who showed up on her doorstep, drunk and disorderly, trying to sell her on some harebrained scheme I cooked up in a fit of delirium.

'Look,' I say, in as authoritative a tone as I can manage, 'I just don't think it's a good idea at the moment. We're *all* on edge – not just you. That's why, right now, we need to keep cool heads and avoid doing anything rash. What we need is stability, not this . . . ' – I gesture feebly, searching for the appropriate word – ' . . . this volatility.'

Mickie stares at me for a long, hard moment. 'Fuck's *that* supposed to mean?'

I say nothing.

'She's said something to you, hasn't she?'

'I—'

'She's been putting ideas in your head.'

'She hasn't!' I blurt out, my instinct to deny everything kicking in before my brain has time to catch up. 'She's just . . . I mean, *we're* just . . . ' I trail off, realising I have no idea what I'm trying to say.

My shoulders sag. I sigh. 'She told me, Mickie, all right? She told me you've been getting treatment for borderline personality disorder.'

For a few seconds, Mickie says nothing. She simply stares at me, opening and shutting her mouth like a beached whale. 'But what . . . ?' she splutters, when she finally finds her voice. 'When . . . ? How did she . . . ?'

I raise my shoulders in a helpless shrug, giving what I hope passes for a sympathetic grimace. Under the circumstances, and given what I imagine Mickie to be capable of while she's in this mood, telling her that Claire broke into her private medical records hardly seems like the smartest move.

Mickie's eyes are blazing now, surprise and confusion having given way to a righteous fury. 'How dare she?' she demands, and I wonder if she hasn't already guessed how Claire came into possession of that knowledge. 'How fucking dare she? She had no right.'

'She shouldn't have *had* to,' I say, cringing inwardly at how self-righteous I sound. '*You* should have told me. You let me think everything was OK when all this time you've been—'

'What?' Mickie's tone is one of withering contempt. 'A nutter? A fruitcake? An inconvenience to your precious fucking bougie lifestyle? Cos that's what all this is about, right? That's how you see me. That's how come you've been giving me the brush-off – isn't it?'

'You should have told me,' I say again, though more weakly this time. 'I could have helped you.'

It's too little, too late, I know, and on some level what makes this whole situation so painful is that I know she's right – or, at least, that she's in the right ballpark. My avoidance of her has, at least in part, been down to the fact that I've simply got too much going on in my own life to make room for someone else's problems – even if that someone else is my own cousin.

Mickie gazes at me, arms folded, weight balanced on one hip, shaking her head in disgust. 'So that's how it is, is it?' She snorts a contemptuous laugh. 'Nothing quite like a crisis to show you who your friends *really* are, huh? Y'know, I really thought you of all people would be on my side. But clearly blood doesnae count for shite with you – does it, *wee hen*?' Somehow, she succeeds in making the familiar term of endearment sound like the worst swearword imaginable.

'It's not about taking sides,' I begin weakly, conscious that she doesn't seem to have heard a single word I said. 'It's—'

'*BULLSHIT!*'

She screams it so loudly my entire body flinches. I stare at her, frozen to the spot, gripped by a sudden fear that she's going to hit me. She's all but unrecognisable, her face pale and hollowed out, her lips drawn back in a maniacal grin that puts me uncomfortably in mind of a ghoul.

'You know what?' She throws her hands up in the air. 'Forget it. I dunno why I bother. If you and that *bitch* wanna have your own wee clique and shut me out of it, that's your look-out. Dinna let me stop yous.' She turns to go, then, thinking of something else, swings round again. 'In fact, why don't the two of yous go and scissor each other? Cos it's dead obvious you're both totally gay for each other!'

And on that, she turns on her heel and storms off down the garden path. At the bottom, she stops to aim a savage kick at the gatepost, misses and almost ends up going arse over tit. She only just manages to right herself, and, robbed of the dramatic exit she so obviously craved, slinks off along the pavement with her head low. I wait till she disappears from sight before heading back inside and locking the door behind me.

'Was that Mickie?' Claire says cheerfully as I slip back into the living room. 'I thought I heard her voice. What did she want?'

'Oh!' I say, completely unprepared for the question. 'She was just passing and stopped to say hi.'

'And she didn't want to come in?' Her tone is neutral, but she can't quite hide the fact that she's far from unhappy about this state of affairs.

'Um . . . no, she had somewhere she needed to be.'

'Shame,' says Claire; then, almost without pausing to draw breath, 'I decided to pause the film, by the way. Figured you wouldn't want to miss the end.'

We settle in for the last fifteen minutes of the film, which unfold before my glazed, unseeing eyes as a kaleidoscope of incomprehensible shapes and colours. I keep rerunning my confrontation with Mickie, pondering all the ways I could have handled it that would have avoided things ending the way they did. I only really come to for the film's final moments, when Thelma and Louise, trapped by the police on one side and the Grand Canyon on the other, seal their pact to 'not get caught'. As they floor the accelerator and plunge into the canyon in glorious slow motion, I find myself wondering what I would do if I found myself in a similar position.

25

The remainder of the weekend passes without any fresh catastrophes. Mickie makes no attempt to contact me, either by phone or in person, and I assume she's either sobered up and is keeping a low profile because she's ashamed of her behaviour the previous night or is still stewing in her own juices, convinced that the forces of the entire world – and Claire and I in particular – are unfairly conspiring against her.

On Monday morning, I'm on my way back from picking up a few odds and ends at the convenience store a couple of blocks away when my phone rings. I don't recognise the number, and answer it with some trepidation.

'Hello?'

'Is this Hazel?' The voice is guarded, apprehensive, slightly husky.

'Yes?'

'Mickie's cousin?'

A sudden pang of apprehension. 'That's right.'

'This is Roxy.' Pause. 'Mickie's flatmate.'

Roxy. I vaguely remember meeting her once, fleetingly – a tall, thin transgender woman who communicated almost entirely in monosyllables and spent most of the time watching me warily from behind her improbably long, shiny hair. The fact I can't think of a single earthly reason why she would be calling me does nothing to allay my fears.

'What's wrong?' I ask. 'Is Mickie OK?'

'I'm sure it's nothing, but . . . ' There's an awkward pause. 'I mean, it's not like I'm her keeper, but . . . '

'What? Spit it out, Roxy.'

She gives a heavy sigh. 'Mickie didn't come home last night.' Pause. 'Or the night before.'

Meaning she hasn't been home since our doorstep confrontation on Saturday night. I suddenly feel very sick. The calorific breakfast I made myself eat earlier this morning sits precariously in my stomach. I shut my eyes and concentrate on breathing slowly and steadily through my nose.

'Have you rung around?' I say, once the feelings of nausea have subsided a little. 'To her other friends, I mean. She might be staying with—'

'Of course I have,' Roxy says testily.

'Right.' I rub my forehead with my free hand, trying to coax my mind into gear. 'Are you at the flat now?'

'Yes.'

'OK. Hold tight – I'll be right there.'

Claire's at work and not answering her mobile, so I ring the surgery's general enquiries number and demand that the receptionist put me through to her. When she picks up, something cautions me against giving her the whole story over an open line, so I simply tell her something's come up and that I need to see her straight away. My anxiety must be writ large in my voice, for she drops everything without asking for any further details and sets off immediately. I head down Easter Road on foot and we meet partway, her Land Rover roaring up to the kerb beside me not ten minutes later.

'What's happened?' she demands, as I slide into the passenger seat.

When I explain the situation to her, her look of apprehension swiftly changes to one of irritation. Clearly Mickie going missing doesn't rate highly on her list of priorities. However, when I make it clear I'm heading over to Mickie's place with or without her, she relents and agrees to drive me there, the morning's appointment list be damned.

Shortly afterwards, we pull up outside the discount pizzeria in Tollcross below Mickie and Roxy's flat. We head upstairs to find Roxy waiting for us in the hallway, munching agitatedly on a well-chewed strand of hair. We head into the flat and she leads us through to the living room, which vaguely resembles a bomb site, old pizza boxes vying with discarded socks for pride of place. There's even a pair of underpants – no doubt Mickie's, no doubt unwashed – draped over the back of the threadbare sofa.

I make Roxy repeat everything she told me for Claire's benefit – which she does, haltingly and with much hyperventilating.

'I don't like this at all,' she says, when her story reaches its conclusion. 'It doesn't seem like her. I mean, we've only been flat-sharing for a few months, so obviously I don't know her as well as you do . . . but this isn't normal – right?'

I open my mouth to speak, then stop. Until just over a week ago, I'd have agreed that this was indeed very much out of the ordinary for Mickie. For as long as I've known her, she's always been spontaneous and given to following whatever crazy scheme leaps into her head, but she doesn't just drop off the face of the earth without letting the people in her life know what's what. On the contrary, my call history and text messages are a testament to her need to provide an up-to-the-minute running commentary of her whereabouts and (mis)deeds. But that was before Claire told me about her BPD diagnosis. All of a sudden, 'normal' doesn't seem to be a particularly helpful term where Mickie is concerned. Add to that the fact that she appears to have gone missing immediately following our Saturday night bust-up and it's hardly surprising if Roxy's concerns are very much a mirror image of my own.

'I was going to ring the police,' Roxy continues, when neither of us says anything, 'but I thought I'd better wait till yous got here.'

'Oh, I'm sure that's not necessary,' Claire says quickly. 'She's always doing things like this.'

'Actually—' I begin, only to stop short when I feel Claire's foot surreptitiously pressing against the side of my leg.

'Are you sure?' Roxy says to Claire. She doesn't seem to have noticed my abortive attempt to interject.

'Absolutely,' Claire says, with total certainty. 'She gets these ideas into her head and acts on them without any regard for the practicalities or the impact on other people. None of this is remotely out of character.'

Roxy turns to me, silently seeking confirmation. I can tell that at least some part of her hopes I'll contradict Claire – that I'll say actually, no, this *is* completely out of character for Mickie and we should be sending up red flares without any further delay.

I give a reluctant shrug. 'I'm sure she'll be back soon,' I say, feeling myself deflating as I speak.

'Well, that's settled, then,' says Claire, sounding altogether too pleased about this state of affairs. 'No doubt she'll turn up in a week or so and regale us all with tales of her antics. In the meantime, if you hear anything, do let us know. We'll be sure to do likewise.'

We take our leave of Roxy – who, I sense, is little more convinced by Claire's reassurances than I am – and head back down to the street. I wait till we're safely back in the car and Claire is doing up her seatbelt before I speak.

'I need to tell you something,' I say. 'About Mickie's visit on Saturday night. She . . . didn't just stop to say hi.'

'Go on,' says Claire, in a tone that suggests she already guessed as much.

So I tell her the whole story, leaving nothing out: the madcap plan for us to go away, her losing it when I turned her down, the things she said about me and Claire. When I'm done, Claire sighs and shakes her head, as if none of this comes as any real surprise to her.

'She always has been a jealous little so-and-so,' she says. 'It riles her that you and I go back years while she's the new kid on the block.'

'You think?' I say uncertainly. It has, of course, occurred to me before now that my relationship with my two best friends is somewhat topsy-turvy, in that despite being related to Mickie by blood, I've known Claire for far longer and, in a lot of respects, still know her far better. But until now, I never considered that Mickie might feel threatened by this state of affairs.

'Oh, undoubtedly,' Claire says. 'She tried to drive a wedge between us – only you saw straight through her, and when you called her out on it she got the hump and stormed off in a huff.'

That's not quite how it played out, and it feels distinctly like Claire's rewriting an event she didn't witness – but I know she'll only take it badly if I point this out, so I let it drop.

'Anyway,' Claire continues, 'this just reinforces what I said back at the flat. Odds are the stroppy little madam's simply gone off on an extended sulk because she didn't get her way. In fact, she's probably gone on that foreign holiday she tried to rope you into. Mark my words – right this very minute, she'll be sunning herself on some beach somewhere on the other side of the world, having a right old cackle about the worry she's causing you.'

'So you don't . . . ' I begin, then stop, reluctant to continue my train of thought. I force myself to press on. 'You don't think we *should* call the police?' I say in a small voice, almost feeling like I'm tensing for a blow.

'Of course not!' Claire snorts. 'That's almost certainly just what she wants. When children act out, you don't indulge them – you starve them of attention. That's the approach I've always taken with Eleanor, and take it from me, it works a treat.' She shakes her head firmly. 'No, just leave her to get it out of her system and she'll soon come crawling back with her tail between her legs, no doubt trying to convince you *you* were the one at fault.'

'But her condition,' I say helplessly. 'The personality disorder. That changes things, surely? We don't know what sort of state she might be in – what she might do. *Especially* if she's not receiving any treatment for it.'

Claire gives me a long, hard look, and I feel myself wilting under her gaze. 'That may be so,' she says at last, an icy coolness in her voice, 'but given your relationship with the strong arm of the law, I'd say the last thing we should be doing right now is inviting the police to involve themselves in our affairs – wouldn't you?'

Her words are like a punch to the solar plexus. When did Claire become so casually cruel? Or was she always this way and I just didn't notice? The fact I know she's absolutely right doesn't make it any less painful.

And then, just like that, her expression softens. 'But don't worry,' she says, her tone magnanimous, 'I'm sure it'll all work out.' She smiles and, reaching across, gently runs a hand through my hair. 'And now, let's get you home. You've had quite enough excitement for one day.'

26

Over the next twenty-four hours, I try my best to force Mickie's disappearance from my mind, repeating to myself Claire's less than convincing mantra that there's no cause for concern. But it's no use. Nothing can distract me – not housework, not the inane chatter of the daytime talk shows on the radio, not even my by now habitual refreshing of the news sites for any updates on the hunt for Aidan. I try texting and calling her, but my texts go unread and her phone keeps going to voicemail. I ring Aye Choons, the record store where she's worked for the last couple of years, but the manager there hasn't heard from her and, despite confirming that she does indeed have an abundance of annual leave owing, tells me she didn't put in for any prior to swanning off without a word and leaving them in the lurch. Having exhausted every other possibility I can think of, I start ringing round any friends of hers for whom I have contact details, but, in what is by now an all too predictable refrain, none of them are able to shed any light on her whereabouts. Indeed, I sense, from their general lack of curiosity or concern, that they're not overly exercised by her absence, and I find myself wondering just how genuine their friendship actually is.

Mind you, my own track record in that department is hardly something to be proud of – to put it mildly. Ever since Mickie disappeared, I've been replaying my treatment of her in my head – both the confrontation on my doorstep on Saturday night and, more generally, the way I responded to Claire's revelation about her mental health. It's as if this fresh crisis has forced everything into perspective, allowing me to see my own actions for what they really are. Somehow, I managed to make it all about me. *My* sense of having been kept in the dark. *My* discomfort at discovering she had a mental health condition. At no point did I stop to consider what it must have been like for her, facing what would have been an incredibly scary and distressing situation on her own, without any support from her family and friends. What must it have been like to live inside her head throughout this ordeal? And what does it say about my observation skills that I failed to pick up on the fact that something was wrong?

All of this, of course, only makes me wish more fervently that I could do the one thing that, under normal circumstances, I'd have done without delay: pick up the phone, call the police and register her as a missing person. And yet I'm paralysed by my own desire for self-preservation. Perhaps it would be fine. Perhaps Claire's simply being over-cautious in her determination for us to avoid drawing attention to ourselves. But I daren't take that risk. I try to tell myself I'm not just thinking of myself – that all three of us have skin in this game. But it doesn't wash. Deep down, I know it all boils down to me needing to save myself at all costs from the consequences of my own actions.

On Tuesday evening, I get my first actual phone call from Matthew since he went away. Things are going well, he says. The firm's accounts turned out to be in an even worse state than they'd been led to believe, but they're slowly but surely getting on top of them and are looking to wrap things up in another week or so.

'We're going to press on now there's light at the end of the tunnel,' he says, 'which means I won't be back up for the weekend. But, all being well, we shouldn't be much longer than another week. If things go to plan, I should be home by next Wednesday or Thursday.'

'That's a shame,' I say automatically, then immediately wonder whether I meant, *That's a shame you won't be back for the weekend* or *That's a shame you're not going to be gone even longer*. I'd be lying if I said I've missed his presence. Yes, the house feels unbelievably quiet and empty at the moment – but then, it scarcely felt any less so before, with the two of us living together but effectively leading separate lives.

A lengthy silence unfolds. 'So what's happening back in good old Leith?' Matthew says eventually. 'Anything to report?'

'No, nothing much,' I say brightly, lying with the effortlessness that comes with long years of practice. 'You know how it is. Life goes on.'

We remain on the line for a few more minutes, trying to make small talk, but my heart isn't in it and I sense that his isn't either. I listen out for any telltale sound that points to him having company, but I hear nothing untoward. Either he waited till Charlotte was powdering her nose in the en suite before calling me or there's nothing going on at all and I'm simply letting my paranoia run away with me.

'Well,' he says, when it becomes clear we've exhausted every possible topic of conversation, 'I won't keep you up. You'll be wanting your bed.'

It's not until he's rung off and I've returned my phone to my pocket that I realise it's only just gone eight o'clock.

The evening continues its long, slow march towards midnight. I'm in the process of trying – unsuccessfully – to distract myself with some documentary on Netflix about a husband and wife eking out a living herding reindeer in the extreme north of Norway when my phone, lying on the sofa beside me, blings a Facebook Messenger notification. I snatch it up immediately, my mind immediately flooding with the hope that it's Mickie. It's not her, of course. It's someone else entirely, and the sight of her name instantly sets my heart racing and the sweat running cold on my skin.

'*Hi,*' says Shonagh.

In retrospect, I realise the fact I hadn't heard from her for so long had lulled me into a false sense of security, to the point that I'd genuinely allowed myself to believe I'd heard the last from her. But now, here she is, large as life, and I don't know whether to respond, to close the chat window or to chuck my phone down the nearest drain.

'*Hi,*' I tap back, once I've forced my hands to stop shaking.

'*Sorry it's been so long,*' she says. '*I've had stuff on.*'

'*Anything exciting?*' I ask, then immediately regret my choice of words.

Shonagh, however, doesn't seem to mind. '*Depends on your idea of "exciting",*' she types, and even adds a wink emoji for good measure. The gesture feels unexpectedly chummy – almost intimate.

I key in a quizzical '*?*'

'*Remember how you said, if I ever needed anything, I should get in touch with you?*'

I do, and I wish to God I'd kept my big yap shut. What can she possibly have in mind?

'*Of course,*' I say.

'*So I've been corresponding with my local MSP over the last couple of weeks. She's been highlighting the flaws in the law's approach to missing persons with the Justice Secretary for a while now, and he's convening a forum next week to discuss potential reforms. They've asked me to appear as an expert witness.*'

'*Wow,*' is all I manage to come up with.

'*Not gonna lie, I feel pretty vindicated. After all this time, I've finally succeeded in getting their attention.*'

I can almost hear the breathlessness in her voice; her wide-eyed, overawed expression, as if she still can't quite believe it herself.

'That's fantastic! I'm so pleased for you.' Smiley face emoji.

'I mean, I know it's probably too late to do any good for Aidan, but if it improves the outcomes for other young men like him, then it'll all have been worth it.'

'I admire what you're doing,' I tell her – truthfully. *'Not many people would have kept going the way you have.'*

'I've just done what anyone in my position would have,' she responds – which I somehow can't bring myself to believe.

'When's the forum?'

'That's the tricky part. It's Friday, first thing. I'm going to need to get the train down the night before. Is there any chance I could bunk at your place?'

I stare at the words on the little 5.5" screen, my heart hammering against my ribs. *Shit,* I think. *Fuck. Oh JESUS, fuck!*

'I realise it's last-minute,' Shonagh continues, *'but I'm having no luck finding a hotel. Not on my budget anyway. And I know you're in Edinburgh so . . . '*

For almost a full minute, I don't move. I just continue to stare at my phone while the voice-over on the TV continues to drone on in the background, the words incomprehensible.

The pulsating ellipsis symbol appears, indicating that Shonagh's typing another message. When it comes through, the hint of desperation that accompanies it is palpable.

'I can kip on your sofa or in a sleeping bag on the floor if need be. And I'll be out of your hair at first light. You'll hardly know I'm there.'

I want to say no. To tell her I've already made plans for that night or that I've moved to the other end of the country or that I'm not comfortable with the idea of opening up my house to a complete stranger. But I can't. I'm racked by enough guilt as it is already without turning her away in her hour of need. Surely, after all the heartache I've caused her, it's the least I can do.

I do a quick mental calculation. Matthew's not due back till next Wednesday at the earliest, and Claire volunteers at the soup kitchen her church runs on Thursday nights, so the odds of either of them showing up unannounced whilst I'm taking high tea with the sister of the man whose death I caused are relatively low. I might just be able to make this work.

'Of course,' I say. *'I'd be glad to have you.'*

'Are you sure?' Shonagh types. *'I don't want to impose.'*

'Honestly, it's no trouble,' I reply, already experiencing a queasy sensation in the pit of my stomach that, in a strange way, I almost relish. *'My husband's away on business right now,'* I add. *'It'd be great to have some company.'*

Did I tell her before that I was married? Already, the precise details of our previous conversation seem fuzzy and vague. I told so many lies and half-truths that night that I haven't a hope of remembering them all. But if what I'm saying now contradicts anything I said previously, Shonagh doesn't seem to notice – or, at any rate, she doesn't question it.

'If you're absolutely sure it's not going to be a problem . . . ' she says.

'Positive. I'll pick you up from the station. Just let me know when your train's due in.'

Long after Shonagh has logged off, having forwarded me details of her travel arrangements and thanked me again, I remain poised on the sofa, my phone clenched between my clammy hands, wondering just what I've set in motion. If I was playing with fire before, then I've surely just thrown a Molotov cocktail into the heart of my very existence. Is it seriously going to be possible for me to maintain the fiction of being Colette Harper while she's staying under my roof? Can I really continue to hide the truth about what happened to her brother while she's in the same room as me, looking directly into my eyes?

At length, a fresh thought begins to solidify out of all the doubt, uncertainty and stomach-churning terror. What if I don't *want* to maintain the fiction? What if I were to use this opportunity to come clean – to confess to Shonagh, in person, putting her out of her misery and freeing myself from the guilt that's been eating me up from inside? Would it not be a relief to both of us? An end to all the waiting, the doubt, the awful uncertainty?

The idea continues to percolate in my mind until, like the delayed reaction to a dose of medication, the magnitude of what I'm actually contemplating finally registers, at which point it becomes a race against time to reach the bathroom before this evening's meal leaves my stomach and ends up on the floor.

27

The next couple of days are like the final countdown to a long-dreaded job interview or medical appointment, only dialled up to eleven. Time passes both agonisingly slowly and far too quickly. Mentally, I'm all over the place – sometimes gripped by something approaching euphoria, other times with overwhelming dread. I'm beset by a sea of conflicting emotions, which steadily intensify as the day that could well determine the course of the rest of my life draws ever closer.

When Thursday morning dawns and I open my bleary, sleep-deprived eyes, the overpowering thought in my mind is that I can't go through with this. I need to message Shonagh, tell her I've come down with gastric flu and that she'll just need to make alternative arrangements. All through the last thirty-six hours, doubt about my plan has been steadily building, and it now explodes into a fit of barely contained terror. I find myself paralysed, unable to contemplate performing the basic functions of my morning routine, like getting washed and dressed, or even getting out of bed.

Stop it, I tell myself. *You don't need to commit to a particular course of action now. See how you feel once she's actually inside the house.*

In an attempt to keep my mind off my impending doom, I force myself to knuckle down, making sure the house is fit for receiving guests and beginning preparations for dinner. Against the odds, I succeed in losing myself in the drudgery of my allotted tasks, and the next thing I know, I'm looking up at the wall clock to discover that it's four-thirty and Shonagh's train is due in just over an hour.

As I hurriedly load the chicken I bought for our evening meal into the oven, it suddenly occurs to me that the first words out of Shonagh's mouth when we come face to face will probably be, *Why don't you look anything like your profile picture?* In a fit of panic, I hurry to the bathroom with my laptop on tow, where I spend the next half-hour in front of the mirror with my hairbrush and makeup kit, attempting to bring my appearance more in line with that of the random model whose likeness I appropriated. We're not *that* bad a match, I suppose. We both have dark hair and pale skin, and we appear to be roughly the same age – though that's basically where the similarities end. For one thing, she has the perfect skin and cheekbones of a professional model, whereas I . . . don't. I'll just have to hope Shonagh assumes I'm one of those people who goes crazy with the filters.

By the time I'm done transforming myself, I'm cutting it so fine I don't even have time for the loo. As I hurry down the steps to my car, it occurs to me that it's not too late to back out – that Shonagh doesn't actually know where I stay and it would be the easiest thing in the world to just not turn up to collect her. But then I picture her standing outside the station, lost and alone in an unfamiliar city, once more suffering as a result of my actions, and I know I can't do that to her.

As I crawl along Hermitage Place towards the junction with Duke Street and Easter Road, I briefly catch sight of a man heading along the pavement in the rear-view mirror. I clock his gait and trench coat and draw in a sharp breath. I swear to God it's Moir – same outfit, same overall build and bearing. Unless, of course, there are *two* schlubby, middle-aged men hanging around Edinburgh doing their best Harry Lime impersonation. And if it *is* him, why the hell is he still lurking around these parts? Surely he should've been safely back in Aberdeen yonks ago?

I steal another glance at the mirror. There's no longer any sign of him. Either he's turned into one of the houses or there never was a man to begin with and, just like my glimpse of Aidan before I fainted, I've imagined the whole thing. I'm not sure which possibility I find more unsettling.

Needless to say, I'm not in a great frame of mind when I pull up at Waverley Station fifteen minutes later. I was already on edge, but this sighting – imagined or otherwise – has tipped my paranoia into overdrive. The prospect of Moir prowling the very street where I live has reduced me to such a jelly-like wreck it's a wonder I've actually made it here in one piece.

I park nearby and head into the station, making for the food court – our pre-arranged rendezvous point. I spot her straight away – a solitary, straight-backed figure standing under the Caffè Nero sign with a large rucksack strapped to her back. She hasn't seen me yet, and once more it occurs to me that I could just walk away and she'd be none the wiser. Instead, I take a deep breath, swallow the nausea rising up in my throat, and head towards her.

'Shonagh.'

She turns to face me, a questioning and – it seems to me – borderline hostile look in her eyes.

My God, I think, *she looks like him.*

Having previously only seen her in grubby newsprint or through the haze of an LED screen, I hadn't, until now, appreciated just how stark the likeness is: the same almond-coloured eyes; the same dark, thick eyebrows; the same strong jawline. But, where Aidan was all good-natured smiles and deep, rich laughter, his sister doesn't look like she smiles or laughs much at anything. I suppose with good reason.

'Colette?' she says, her tone uncertain, almost as if she already suspects she's being played.

My heart is hammering, my mind racing at a hundred miles an hour, but I manage to force an easy smile. 'Welcome to Edinburgh.'

We both stand there awkwardly, within touching distance but neither of us making any sort of move. I resist my natural inclination to embrace her – she really doesn't look like a hugger – but a handshake feels too stiff and formal under the circumstances. Mind you, she doesn't look like much of a handshaker either.

In the end, she breaks the impasse with an expectant shrug. 'Are we going?'

I snap out of it. 'Of course. Sorry. I brought the car. It's this way.' I gesture to her rucksack. 'Shall I take your—?'

'I can manage,' she says curtly, and immediately takes off, striding towards the exit while I, allegedly the host welcoming her to my city, hurry to catch up with her.

For the duration of the journey home, Shonagh makes no attempt at conversation, and my own feeble efforts to make small talk – remarking on the heavy traffic or the fact that it looks like rain's coming in – fail to elicit anything more than monosyllabic, non-committal grunts. She sits there, staring straight ahead, clutching her rucksack to her chest like she's worried I'll try to steal if from her. Is this what it's going to be like all evening, I wonder? If so, the next few hours are going to be excruciating. I suppose I'll just have to hope she's one of those country people who goes to bed at sundown and rises at the crack of dawn. Or perhaps she'll want to go up to her room early to practice whatever barnstorming speech she's planning to give at tomorrow's forum.

It's not till we arrive back at Hermitage Place and step over the threshold that she utters more than a solitary word at a time. 'Bloody hell,' she breathes, gazing up at her surroundings, 'this is certainly a house.'

This instantly puts me in mind of Aidan's reaction to the cabin at Port Catrin, and I feel a surge of shame at the comfortable, middle-class existence I've so often taken for granted. I've no idea what Shonagh's own circumstances are, but given the amount of time she devotes to her cause, plus her comments about being unable to afford a hotel, I don't imagine she's able to hold down a high-paying job as well.

'Would you like to freshen up before dinner?' I say, trying to paper over my discomfort. 'The bathroom's upstairs. You can have a shower or . . . I mean, you don't have to,' I add hastily, worried she'll think I'm insinuating that she smells – which she doesn't, by the way. 'Only if you want.'

'I'll just dump my stuff,' she says, indicating to her bag.

She has a surprisingly deep voice – rich and husky, like a dark, smoky wine. Her Aberdeenshire accent is more muted than Aidan's, her inflections less obviously 'provincial', but the likeness is definitely there, as it is in everything else about her, from the line of her jaw to the way her eyes dart sideways at me when she's listening to me talking. It's profoundly unnerving.

'Of course. Uh . . . it's this way.'

I lead her up the stairs to the spare room, the bed already made up, ready to receive its unfamiliar occupant. I leave her to unpack and head downstairs to finish getting the evening meal ready. The chicken is almost done, which just leaves the veg. It belatedly occurs to me that I should probably have asked Shonagh beforehand if she has any dietary requirements. I have this idea in my head that country folk will eat anything, but that's probably just my prejudice talking again. She could be vegan for all I know.

As I'm draining the spuds, my eyes fall on a pile of unopened mail lying on the kitchen counter, every envelope bearing the name of either Matthew or Hazel Ellis. A momentary surge of panic courses through me. I'm no closer than I was before to deciding whether or not I'm actually going to tell her the truth, and until I've made up my mind, I'd rather not leave any evidence lying around that I'm not who I claim to be. Quickly, I gather them up and bundle them into the spice drawer – the best hiding place I can find at such short notice. At the same moment, I hear Shonagh's footsteps clumping on the stairs, and I force myself to adopt a relaxed, open expression and head out to meet her, praying I haven't left any more identifiers lying around to be found.

Throughout the evening meal, the dominant sounds are those of scraping cutlery and rhythmic chewing. Shonagh attacks her loaded plate like she's mounting a military campaign, shovelling forkful after forkful into her mouth, only pausing for long enough to swallow between each mouthful. The accompanying conversation, if you can call it that, is only marginally less one-sided than in the car. ('How was your journey?' Shrug. 'Got me here, didn't it?') Afterwards, however, when we head through to the living room with a bottle of Matthew's favourite Cognac and a couple of tumblers, the alcohol seems to have a loosening effect on her tongue and she starts to become more communicative.

'This is all dead impressive,' she says, making a vague gesture to our surroundings. 'What was it you said your husband did again?'

I try to recollect what, if anything, I've told her about Matthew. Nothing, as far as I can remember, though she certainly knows he's out of town on business. I decide keeping things vague is the best approach.

'He works in finance,' I say. 'The hours are long and he's away a lot, but the money's good.'

Shonagh raises an eyebrow. 'Sounds like you've bagged yourself a keeper.'

'It's not just him,' I say, unexpectedly defensive at the insinuation that I'm just some sort of lady of leisure who contributes nothing to the money pot herself. 'I work too.' *Just not right now.*

'You in finance as well, then?'

I almost laugh, picturing myself and Matthew sporting matching business suits and briefcases – the ultimate power couple.

'Actually, I'm a senior designer at an architectural firm.' I add the 'senior' bit for a touch of much-needed extra clout. 'What about you? Is there anything you do besides—'

'Besides spending my life bashing my heid against a brick wall?' There's an acidic bitterness to Shonagh's voice. 'Nothing so hifalutin as you and your man, that's for sure. I work part-time at a gym. Fitness instructor.'

I have a sudden mental image of this severe, hard-faced woman in a sports bra and leggings with her hair tied back, barking instructions into a headset mic.

'Is there a lot of demand for that sort of thing in Port Catrin?' I say. Given the average age of the town's inhabitants, I'm struggling to imagine there being a massive supply of bright young things looking to strengthen their core and tone up their glutes.

'Couldn't rightly say. I cleared out of that place soon as I was old enough to fend for myself. Aidan, he stuck it out, scraping a living, but I always wanted the buzz of the big city. Took myself up to Aberdeen at nineteen and never looked back. Course,' she adds, more quietly, 'if I'd known then . . . '

She doesn't need to say any more. If she'd known she only had a finite amount of time with Aidan, she wouldn't have been half as quick to leave him behind for the bright lights of the Granite City.

'But then,' she continues, 'it's like I always say: there's no point fretting over things you haven't the power to change. What's done is done. Maybe I could've been a better big sister to him, but . . . '

She makes a half-hearted gesture with her hand, as if to say, *it is what it is.*

A silence falls. As we sit there, nursing our respective drinks, I wonder, for the umpteenth time, whether I can actually go through with this. Whether I can bring myself to come clean and submit myself to her ensuing wrath. But before I've even had the chance to draw breath, Shonagh pipes up again.

'Did you know they're calling off the search?' she demands, lifting her head and looking at me with a wild, almost accusatory glint in her eyes.

'Surely not?' I say, aiming for supportive concern even as a not insubstantial part of me hopes she's right.

'They say they're not, but I can read the tea leaves as well as anyone. They think it's a waste of time. And they're probably right,' she sighs. 'Heaven knows I've given up any hope of him turning up in one piece after all this time.'

I eye her guardedly. 'So you're convinced he's . . . '

'Dead?' Shonagh's expression is devoid of any emotion. 'Let's call a spade a spade, shall we?'

She's silent for a moment, gazing down at her lap with her head bowed, as if she's drawing deep from the well of her inner strength. I shift uneasily in my seat, toying with my glass, not daring to take my eyes off her. I'm left with the uneasy sense that I'm sharing a room with a wildcat, liable at any moment to strike without warning.

Finally, she lifts her head and looks me dead in the eyes. 'Yes,' she says. 'Yes, I think he is.' She draws in a heavy breath, her entire body shuddering as she expels it. 'It's not as if there haven't been plenty of false alarms over the years: bodies of young men turning up in different places all over the country that I've been asked to go and identify. In the early days, I always used to pray it wouldn't be him, because that would mean there was still a chance he was out there somewhere. But at some point, it went from me praying it wouldn't be him to me praying it *would* be – because at least then I'd know.'

She continues to hold my gaze, her almond eyes boring into me with such intensity that it's all I can do to stop myself looking away. At length, she lowers her head once more.

'I've accepted he's dead,' she says, with aching finality. 'All I want now is something concrete I can grieve for. Something physical.'

When watching the various interviews Shonagh has given to the media – and believe me, I've watched them all – I always found it striking that she never once made a direct address to her brother; never gazed soulfully into the camera and beseeched him to come home. In a strange way, I found that admirable. It said something, I think, about her strength of character. No ignominious pleading from her – just calm, stoic, dignified determination. But it also told me something else. It told me that, whatever she might have said to the contrary, deep down she always believed Aidan was dead. Over the years, I've had plenty of time to think about the hole his disappearance must have left in her life. But somehow, sitting face to face with her – seeing her grief, her bone-weariness, the way it's hollowed out her entire existence – has thrown the magnitude of what I've done to her – what I've *taken* from her – into sharper relief than ever.

A deep sigh racks her. 'I know it's not healthy. This . . . all of it. Obsessing. Spending all this time and energy looking for answers I know I'm never going to get. But I feel I have to. I feel I owe it to him.'

This is it, I think. *If you don't say something now, you never will. Speak or forever hold your peace.*

I lick my dry lips. Swallow a heavy gulp. 'Shonagh . . . '

Her eyes flick up to meet mine. 'Aye?'

'I . . . ' I begin, and then, with a heavy heart, realise I can't do this.

I can't tell her what I did. I'm too afraid of what it will set in motion. Too much of a coward to face the consequences of my own actions. My trail of lies. I was stupid to have ever thought otherwise. But there's something else too. Something I now see with awful, aching clarity. After all my lies and deception, after allowing her to believe that I was on her side – that I was her *friend* – revealing the truth, tearing the whole edifice down before her eyes, would be infinitely crueller than any lie I could come up with.

'Yes?' Shonagh's eyes continue to bore into me.

'I think Aidan would understand if you moved on,' I say, my heart deflating as I speak. 'In fact, I reckon he'd want you to try to put it behind you, if you can.'

It's about as far removed from what I set out to say as I can imagine, and stands in complete contradiction to the reason I originally reached out to her on Facebook: to try to persuade her not to give up. But now I see that, under the circumstances, persuading her to let go is the kindest thing I can realistically do.

Shonagh sighs again. 'I know. It just . . . feels like a betrayal. Of his memory, y'know? If I throw in the towel, if I just give up . . . well, then what was the point of the last three and a half years?'

'You're doing good,' I say. 'You're using your platform to make a difference.'

Shonagh gives a wan smile. 'Sometimes I believe that. But most of the time, it feels like I'm just pissing in the wind.'

'What about tomorrow? The missing persons forum? You said it yourself: you've finally got their attention.'

'We'll see. Ah'll no haud ma braith.' For a moment, her speech drops into broad Aberdonian, which somehow has the effect of making her sound even more bitter and hopeless.

'What about you?' she says after a moment, once more fixing me with her steely gaze.

'Me?'

'Have *you* moved on? From your sister, I mean?'

For a moment, I don't know what to say. I wasn't prepared for this question; have no ready-made reserve of falsehoods from which to draw. As I sit there, mentally casting around for some narrative hook to latch onto, it occurs to me that, in the time that's passed since I told Shonagh about Judy, I *have* gained some real world experience of what it's like to have a loved one go missing. If, three or thirty years from now, Mickie still hasn't reappeared, what will my life look like? Will I still think about her each and every day, wondering if she's out there somewhere – and if she is, whether she's safe and happy? Or will she become like my parents, about whom I can go for days or even weeks at a time without thinking, and whose absence in my life only registers when a particular sight or sound or smell triggers a memory of some shared experience?

'Maybe it's not so much about moving on,' I say eventually. 'Maybe it's about compartmentalising the different parts of your life – finding a way to keep Aidan's memory alive while still finding room for other things.'

Shonagh says nothing. We sit in silence, the creaking of the central heating pipes the only sound in the whole house. Noticing that Shonagh's glass is empty, I reach for the bottle and pour her another finger of Cognac, then top up my own for good measure. Shonagh lifts her glass and contemplates the dark, liquid swirling inside before knocking it back.

'You know, I envy you,' she says. 'I probably shouldn't, but I do. I don't just mean the big house, the great job, the husband – though those are all nice things, obviously. No, it's the whole package.' She adjusts her position, setting down her glass so she can use both hands to make her point. 'You've got a life beyond Judy. Her disappearance isn't the only thing that defines you. I dunno, maybe it's because you were still young when it happened. You weren't done growing yet, so you were able to keep moving forward.' Her shoulders sag, and she sinks lower in her seat. 'For me, it's like life ended the day Aidan went missing. Since then, I've been stuck on pause, waiting for an answer a part of me knows I'm never going to get.'

I feel like saying she wouldn't envy me so much if she knew even a fraction of the truth behind the façade. But I know I can't. As overwhelming as my problems may seem to me, I know they pale into insignificance compared to what she's going through.

'Well, let's look at what you've got,' I say, propelling myself into a more upright position in an attempt to force myself into a more proactive frame of mind. 'You've already got your part-time job at the gym. I'm sure you could make a career of it if you wanted.'

'I guess,' says Shonagh, with little enthusiasm.

'What about relationships? Is there anyone special in your life?'

'Nuh.' Shonagh shakes her head firmly. 'I mean, don't get me wrong – I fuck, but I don't do long-term relationships. In my experience, they only ever disappoint. Men are all much of a muchness – they take and take and take from you; then, once they've wrung every last drop out of you, they leave you for the next poor sap.'

I laugh awkwardly. 'Bit extreme, isn't it?' I say – though, even as I do, I'm left with the uncomfortable sensation that she's just described Matthew to a T.

'Honestly,' Shonagh says, 'I sometimes think the world would be a much happier place if there was a rule everyone had to follow which said you weren't allowed to bang the same person more than once. Mind you,' she adds, her expression growing more pensive, 'early on, I used to wonder if that was what did for Aidan. There was this theory doing the rounds that he'd hooked up with some quine and gone off with her. It wasn't completely implausible. He always *was* led by his dick.'

And thus, inevitably, we once more circle back to Aidan, whose spectre haunts our every exchange; the element that, unbeknownst to Shonagh, binds the two of us irrevocably together. I swallow the last drops of my Cognac to cover my unease. What she's positing feels altogether too close to the truth for comfort.

'But then,' she continues, her tone once more shifting into one of weary fatalism, 'he wouldn't have stayed gone – or at least he wouldn't have broken off all contact forever. He'd have found a way to let me know he was out there somewhere.' She gives a limp smile and shrugs. 'So you see, that's how I know he's not.'

Neither of us says much more after that. Before long, Shonagh starts making noises about getting an early night, and we head upstairs to our separate rooms. I lie in bed, listening as she moves about in the room next door. She settles soon enough, but for a long time afterwards I remain awake and alert, and when I finally do get to sleep, my dreams are both vivid and deeply unsettling. In one, I'm burying Mickie in the woods. She's alive and wide awake and keeps asking me what I'm doing and telling me to stop, but I just keep shovelling earth on top of her until she finally falls silent.

In the morning, I get up to find Shonagh packed and ready to go. I offer to make her breakfast, but she doesn't want any. We head down to my car and set off for Holyrood – a mere ten-minute drive, even during rush hour. Before long, I'm pulling over next to the shallow pond outside the cluster of parliament buildings with their distinctive deconstructivist design. In front of them, the flags flutter in the breeze atop their posts, while various pedestrians stride by at a brisk clip, all no doubt with pressing business of their own to attend to.

'Well, good luck,' I say, as Shonagh unbuckles her seatbelt and prepares to make tracks. 'I mean, I'm sure you don't need it, but good luck all the same.'

'Thanks,' she says, a little stiffly. I sense that, for all her collectedness and steely resolve, inside she's a bundle of nerves. 'And thanks as well for . . . all this.'

'Don't mention it. You'll let me know how it goes?'

'I'll DM you later.' She hesitates. 'Unless you want to come with me?'

'Come *with* you?'

She shrugs. 'Why not? You've experienced a loved one go missing too. Your perspective's as valid as mine.'

The warning voice in my head is screaming at me that this is a monumentally terrible idea, and I hear it loud and clear. Standing up in a room full of people, most of them no doubt experts of one variety or another, attempting to maintain the fiction I've concocted, the odds of my being unmasked would go through the roof.

I shake my head. 'No – this is your moment. Go. Make your brother proud.'

Shonagh gives a tight little smile, then rummages in her pocket and produces a pen and a crumpled receipt. She scribbles something down.

'Here.' She hands me the receipt. 'That's my number. If there's ever anything I can do . . . just call me.'

'I will,' I say, slipping the receipt into my coat pocket, already knowing hers is positively the last number I'd ever consider calling.

'Thanks,' she says again. 'For humouring a mad lassie.'

Then, without a backward glance, she gets out of the car and strides across the concourse to the entrance. As I watch her go – a solitary, lonely figure ploughing her own furrow with her shoulders hunched and her head bowed – I know, beyond a shadow of a doubt, that the last window of opportunity to tell her the truth has now closed for good.

28

When I arrive back at Hermitage Place, the street is almost preternaturally quiet. Those who have jobs to go to will have left ages ago to beat the early morning traffic, while those past retirement age are unlikely to set foot outside for some time. As I stand on the doorstep, fumbling in my bag for my keys, I hear the crunch of feet on the gravel behind me. Assuming it's the postman, I turn to receive whatever combination of bills and mailshots he's bringing me today, only to let out an involuntary shriek. Standing before me is DI Angus Moir.

He smiles disarmingly. 'Did I give you a wee fright? Sorry about that.'

Somehow, he doesn't sound it. Rather than dignify his question with an answer, I turn my back on him and resume searching for my keys.

'What takes you out and about at such an hour?' he enquires conversationally, as I finally succeed in locating them.

'Shopping.' The lie passes my lips before I've had time to think it through.

'Got any bags I can help you with?' He looks around, as if he expects to see them sprouting from the hedgerow.

'I only went for paracetamol,' I mutter, holding up a pack from my bag and hoping he won't notice it's already half-empty.

Moir gives an 'ah' of understanding. 'Well, hope it clears up, whatever it is.'

I give a flicker of a smile and turn to unlock the door. It takes some effort – my hands are shaking and clammy – but eventually I manage.

'You'll be wanting to come in, I take it?'

Said more out of obligation than any actual desire to play host to this glorified doorstepper.

Moir beams. 'Don't mind if I do.'

He bounds up the steps behind me, surprisingly sprightly for someone of his girth. Inside, he stoops and picks up some mail lying on the mat, then makes a big show of wiping his feet, clearly keen to demonstrate his credentials as a mindful guest. I watch impassively, hoping my stone-faced silence and folded arms will encourage him to get to the point of his visit and then bugger off.

He inspects the envelope at the top of the pile. 'Ooh, urgent communication from the DVLA for Matthew. You'd better mind and give it to him right away. You know what that lot are like when you make them wait.'

'I'll make sure he gets it,' I say, snatching the bundle from him. I'm not sure what annoys me more – the over-familiarity of 'Matthew' or his presumptiveness in thinking he has the right to rifle through our mail.

'He's not at home, I take it?'

'No, he's down south on business.'

'Ah. Shame.'

He stands there, arms folded behind his back, rocking on the balls of his feet. I continue to face him, saying nothing, hoping I'm making this as uncomfortable for him as he is for me. He catches my eye, raises an expectant eyebrow.

Defeated, I gesture to the living room. 'Would you like to come through?'

'Oh!' he says, as if the thought hadn't even crossed his mind. 'Thank ye kindly.'

I lead him through, making a point of not offering him a seat. He doesn't seem to mind. In fact, he seems content to wander around, eyeing the place up like a prospective buyer inspecting a property on the market.

'Not working this morning, Mrs Ellis?'

'No, I'm . . . off sick.'

Moir glances briefly in my direction. 'Sorry to hear that. Nothing contagious, I hope?'

If I say yes, will you leave me alone?

I spot the empty Cognac bottle and glasses lying on the coffee table the same moment he does.

'Been entertaining?'

'Yes,' I say stiffly, 'I had a friend over to stay. An old classmate from . . . ' – I say the first thing that comes into my head – ' . . . Plymouth.'

'Must've taken off early, then.'

'Yes, it's quite a journey back to Plymouth.'

'Quite, quite.' He nods approvingly, picking up an ornament from the mantelpiece and turning it this way and that. An ornament that belonged to my late mother, thank you very much.

'Were you here yesterday?'

I blurt the question out before I can stop myself. My patience was already stretched close to breaking point, but the sight of him fondling my dead mother's property like a pervert rummaging through a knicker drawer has well and truly tipped me over the edge.

He turns in my direction with a bemused smile. 'Yesterday?'

'Yes, the day before today. Were you here?'

He pauses to consider the question, all the while weighing the ornament in his hand. 'I've been all over the place, as it happens. Very picturesque city, Edinburgh. Wee bit touristy for my liking, mind – a touch too "tartan and shortbread". That's why I like visiting the more out-of-the-way areas.'

There's no way this level of obfuscation isn't an act.

'Is there something I can help you with, Mr Moir?' I say. 'And would you mind putting that down, please?'

To give him his due, he complies immediately. However, he then proceeds to jettison all of the goodwill he's just clawed back by parking himself on the sofa uninvited – a move which suggests he doesn't intend to leave anytime soon. He sits there, rubbing his jowls with a slab-like hand while I wait for him to come to the point.

'Here's my problem,' he says. 'My conundrum, if you like. I have a pressing need to account for Aidan Cranston's movements beyond the point when his last known sighting took place. We've no idea whether whatever happened to him occurred on the Saturday night or at some point on Sunday or Monday – just that he failed to report for work on Tuesday, meaning we have a roughly sixty-hour period to account for. That's an awfully large window of time. I'd love to be able to narrow it.'

He's silent for a moment, then claps his hands together, so suddenly and unexpectedly that I can't keep myself from flinching involuntarily.

'Now, you and your friends left Port Catrin at around midmorning on the Monday?'

'That's right,' I say, wondering if he's really going to make me go through this again. Every man and his dog has heard the story of our movements at least a dozen times.

'And on the Sunday, you spent most of the day at the cabin while your friends went sightseeing. Remind me again why that was?'

'I had an upset stomach.'

'Ah, yes. And your current . . . ailment – the one that's keeping you from your work – would it happen to be of a similar nature?'

'I'm afraid I find that question rather intrusive.'

If I've learnt one thing about men over the years, it's that implying that any mystery ailment is down to 'women's troubles' is a surefire way to get them to stop asking about it.

Moir holds up his hands in a peace gesture. 'Of course. Forgive me, Mrs Ellis. I don't mean to pry. Now, while you were laid up, resting and recuperating, your friends drove up to Dunnottar Castle, didn't they?'

'If you know the answer, why are you asking me?'

I know it's probably unwise to antagonise him, but he's seriously starting to get on my nerves. I dearly wish he'd just come to the point of his visit instead of toying with me like a cat with a ball of string.

'And apart from Dunnottar Castle,' he says, ignoring my question, 'is it possible they went anywhere else?'

'You'd have to ask them.'

'I did,' Moir says, in a tone which suggests he fully anticipated me saying that. 'Or, at least, I asked your friend Dr Bissell. She was most cooperative. But I'm afraid, when the time came to put my questions to young Ms Shaye, she was unavailable – which is to say I was unable to locate her either at her home address or her place of work.' He steeples his plump fingers together and gazes up at me from the sofa, a shrewd look in his eyes. 'Would you, by any chance, be able to enlighten me as to her whereabouts?'

A trickle of sweat runs down my back. 'I think she's gone away on holiday,' I mumble, my eyes dropping to the floor.

'Any idea *where* she might have gone, or when we might expect her back?'

'I'm not her keeper, OK?' I snap, before catching myself. 'Sorry. I'm afraid I've really no idea. I'd tell you if I did.'

One of these statements, at least, is true.

'A pity. Well, when she does re-appear, I'd be grateful if you'd convey my eagerness to speak to her at her earliest convenience.'

I give a noncommittal grunt, privately thinking that if Moir's so determined to track Mickie down, the resources he has at his disposal are a hell of a lot more extensive than mine. I wonder what's going through his head. As far as I can make out, he's working on the assumption that whatever happened to Aidan occurred on the Sunday and that one or more of us was involved. If I had to guess, I'd say his suspicions point towards Mickie and Claire rather than myself, hence his questions about their whereabouts. If so, then on the one hand it's a relief to know he's so far off base, and it suggests he's working on a mere hunch rather than anything concrete. But on the other, the fact his hunch involves us at all is serious grounds for concern.

'What makes you so sure something happened to him?'

Moir glances up from whatever private thoughts he's been entertaining. 'What's that?'

I jerk my head up sharply, realising to my horror that I've spoken aloud.

'I . . . I mean . . . '

Deep breath, Hazel. Turn the tables on him. Put *him* on the spot for once.

'Aidan – I mean, Mr Cranston. Why are you suddenly so convinced something sinister happened to him – whether it was on the Saturday, or Sunday or Monday?' I manage a semi-belligerent shrug. 'I thought the prevailing belief was that he went off somewhere of his own accord. At least, I can't think of any other reason for the police's lack of action during the last three and a half years.'

Channelling a wee bit of my inner Shonagh, there. But it's not all play-acting on my part – as absurd as it probably sounds, I'm genuinely angry on her behalf. Somehow, the fact I'm criticising the police for having failed to successfully prosecute the crime *I* committed doesn't seem remotely hypocritical right at this moment.

'I think,' Moir says levelly, 'you're forgetting the small matter of the phone call claiming that his body was buried in the woods. I'd say that alters the landscape somewhat, wouldn't you? It would be remiss of us not to thoroughly investigate the caller's claims, however far-fetched they might seem.'

'Is that not likely to have just been some crank?' I'm aiming for 'unconcerned', but it just comes out sounding dismissive and flippant. 'Besides,' I add, hoping to strike a more constructive tone, 'if someone knows something, why would they wait till now to say anything? And why make it something as vague as, "he's buried in the woods"?'

Moir strokes his chin thoughtfully. 'Hmm, yes. Your friend Dr Bissell said something remarkably similar when I spoke to her.'

And that's what you get for lifting someone else's words wholesale.

'Anyway,' he continues, 'I'm not completely discounting the possibility that our man just upped and left off his own back. It would be mighty out of character, though. On that point, I happen to agree with his sister. He had strong ties to the local area, including longstanding commitments to his various employers. And he had no criminal record to speak of either, barring a minor caution for drunk and disorderly at seventeen.'

'Could it not have been a random attack? Some madman decided to take a pop at him, then got rid of the evidence?' I'm aware of the ring of desperation in my voice.

Moir looks up at me, squinting slightly as if he's trying to get a better angle on me. 'Are you familiar with the principle of homogamy?'

I shake my head.

'It's the theory that folk are more likely to be victims of crime if they tend to associate or share similar characteristics with the criminal classes. For obvious reasons, it's not something we like to draw attention to when making appeals to the public, but it's one of the first things we look at in any case where we suspect foul play.'

That comment riles me more than it should. 'So you're saying you think he brought this on himself?'

'Nothing of the sort,' says Moir smoothly. 'Mr Cranston didn't mix with any criminals or share any of their typical characteristics. And besides,' he adds, giving me a look that goes right through me, 'so-called "stranger danger" is a relatively rare phenomenon. Most victims of murder are killed by people they know. We investigated Mr Cranston's known associates and surviving family thoroughly and are confident none of them had anything to do with his disappearance.'

Murder. It's the first time any police officer that I know of has explicitly used that word in relation to this case. It tells me everything I need to know about Moir's current line of thinking.

'What about those men in the pub?' I say, scrambling for a bone to throw him off the scent. 'The ones who were noising us up before he stepped in. Calum MacKintry and his friends. They seemed like an unsavoury bunch. Could they not have had something to do with it?'

Moir chuckles drily. 'Between you and me, Mrs Ellis, Calum MacKintry's the sort of man who uses his fingers for counting. His ilk haven't the wherewithal to make a body disappear. And yes, before you ask, they were investigated thoroughly at the time. No,' he continues, leaning back in his seat and gazing up at the ceiling in contemplation, 'I fancy a cover-up of that sort would have required the faculties of a rather more . . . sophisticated mind.'

'Well, I wish you all the luck in the world finding them,' I say, crossing to the door and holding it open. 'Now, if there's nothing else I can do for you, I'd appreciate it if you'd leave me to get on with my day.'

'Of course.' Moir remains seated. 'I was forgetting you were under the weather.'

'It's not that. I just don't see why I should put up with this harassment when I've done nothing wrong.'

Moir rises to his feet. 'Now, now, Mrs Ellis. I can assure you, there's no call for throwing around terms like "harassment". Let's not lose our sense of perspective, shall we?'

I say nothing, partly because I don't trust myself. I just glower at him, continuing to hold the door at arm's length.

Moir gives a little smile, as if responding to some private joke to which I'm not party. He smooths down the creases in his trousers, straightens his coat collar and moves towards the door, pausing as he draws level with me.

'That'll be all for now,' he says, his tone languid even as his eyes drill into me. 'But, as the lead investigator to a potentially serious crime, I am well within my rights to ask any questions I deem pertinent of anyone connected with the case, however tangentially – and I'll thank you to remember that. Good day.'

I see him to the front door, determined to make sure he actually leaves. Even after he's stepped out onto the porch and I've slammed and locked the door behind him, I remain in the hallway, listening as, following a pause that lasts far too long for comfort, his footsteps descend the steps and make their shambling way down the path before finally being submerged beneath the other sounds from the street.

29

As soon as Moir is gone, I get out my phone, delete my 'Colette Harper' Facebook account and uninstall the app, before heading upstairs to purge my computer's browser history. I've made up my mind never to contact Shonagh again. What the hell possessed me to reach out to her in the first place, far less invite her into my bloody home on a pack of lies about us being kindred spirits?

I'm going to get on with my life – that's what I'm going to do. I'm going to act like none of this every happened; like it's got nothing to do with me. If I live it, maybe I can believe it. And if I believe it, maybe it can be so.

I ring Fraser, telling him I'm feeling much better and that I'd like to discuss coming back to work ahead of schedule. He's surprised to receive my call, and I can't tell, from the tone of his voice, whether he's pleased or disappointed at the prospect of having me back on the team. I think I sense a degree of reluctance from him, but that might just be my paranoia talking. Either way, he agrees to me coming in on Monday at four to chat through my options. It might, he says, be possible to ease me back in gently with what he calls a less performance-critical role – i.e., one with less responsibility. At least for the time being. *So, when the next nervous breakdown inevitably happens, we're not all left holding our dicks,* is the implicit subtext.

It's hard not to feel like I'm being banished to the backroom, but

I'll take it. Anything to get some degree of normality back in my life. Anything to keep busy.

During this time, I make no attempt to get in touch with Claire, and she doesn't try to contact me either. It comes as a considerable relief. Ever since Moir's visit, I've been waiting for her to ring me, demanding a blow-by-blow account of what I said to him. Somehow, I just know she'll blame me for his continued interest in us and our movements. I realise, with some dismay, that I've become . . . well, not afraid of *her*, per se, but definitely afraid of how she's going to react to certain things. I realise, too, that this is something that predates our recent troubles. It's become more pronounced lately, for sure, but in retrospect I can see that, for some time now, I've been modifying my behaviour around her, choosing my words to avoid putting her nose out of joint – like when a child accidentally breaks some treasured family heirloom and tries to conceal the fact from their parents for as long as possible, knowing that there will inevitably be hell to pay. Was I always such a doormat, or have I turned into one gradually?

The next few days pass uneventfully enough. I try my best to keep myself occupied, going for long walks and spending hours scrubbing the inside of the bath with bleach and emptying the kitchen cupboards only to re-fill them in exactly the same configuration as before. It's all straight out of the Coping Strategies 101 rulebook, designed to keep my mind off the important stuff, and it doesn't really work, but at least I have a spotlessly tidy home to show for it.

I awaken on Monday to what feels for all the world like a new beginning. The pale, late October sun is shining into the bedroom through the curtains, there's birdsong in the air, and for the first time in as long as I can remember, I feel a sense of hope. Where it comes from, I have no idea, but I make up my mind to embrace it.

Conscious of the fact that today's the day of my big sit-down with Fraser, I check my reflection in the bathroom mirror for imperfections. Fraser ranks image above virtually every other attribute, even competence, and expects his underlings to be well-groomed and presentable at all times (though I note he doesn't seem to apply this rule to himself). My hair hasn't been cut in ages and is in serious need of taming – and I even spot a handful of solitary grey ones that I could have sworn weren't there a week ago. The state of my nails is even more shocking: some bitten down to the quick, others long enough to take someone's eye out, all of them sporting ragged cuticles. I realise I'm going to need to do something about both before I walk through the doors of Menzies, Sharp & Creadie's offices, so, without further ado, I book an appointment with my usual salon and set off into town.

I emerge shortly after midday, looking and feeling altogether more presentable, ready to face the world – or at least Fraser Creadie. I'm feeling so much like a new woman that, while I'm waiting for the bus, I even ring Matthew for the first time since he went down to London. My call goes straight to voicemail (not altogether unsurprisingly), so I leave him a message entreating him to let me know once he knows for sure when he'll be coming home, and suggesting we go out for a slap-up meal to celebrate. I'm not sure if I genuinely believe dinner at a Michelin Star restaurant is enough to hit the reset button on our marriage, but I'm in such a buoyant frame of mind that, right now, anything seems possible.

As I round the corner onto Hermitage Place, the first thing I see are the two police cars parked at the kerb about two hundred yards ahead, directly outside my house. Instantly, my heart leaps into my mouth and I slow to a crawl. I see several figures milling about on the pavement – uniformed officers in their regulation black shirts and luminous hi-viz vests. I hear the blood rushing in my ears. My head is swimming. Every step I take becomes more leaden than the last, and yet still I force myself to keep moving forward, even as I think to myself, *This is it. I've been found out. They've come to take me away.*

One of the officers moves to one side, and I realise someone else is there – someone who, until now, has been hidden behind the cluster of uniformed men. Claire. Almost at the same moment I spot her, she turns and catches sight of me. Even from this distance, I can see that her face is ashen. For a moment, she doesn't move. She just stands there, staring at me, stricken. Then, pushing past the officers, she breaks into a run, heading towards me with her coat tails billowing out behind her. She clears the distance between us in seconds and, before I even know how to respond, pulls me into a forcible embrace, pressing me tight against her, crushing my face into her shoulder.

'Oh Hazel,' she says, her voice wrought with anguish, 'I'm afraid something dreadful has happened.'

30

Twelve hours earlier

It was well after midnight when Gregor Murray had finally been able to hang up his apron and call it a day. The Piri Piri Palace had been going like the clappers all evening, a seemingly endless supply of fresh punters streaming through the door in search of spicy sustenance. And even once the doors had finally closed, his travails still weren't over. No – the floor had to be mopped, the inside of the oven scrubbed spotless, the day's takings counted and bagged under the watchful eye of Mr Alonzo, who he knew from bitter experience would make him do it all over again if the final tally was off by so much as a penny.

Finally released from his labours, Gregor made his way south along Gardner's Crescent, making for Lochrin Basin, the small harbour that marked the start of the Union Canal and its thirty-mile journey west to Falkirk. If he followed the canal for its first mile or so, it would take him almost to the door of his parents' place in Shandon – all told, a forty-minute walk from the city centre, which only made the thought of the shower that awaited him all the sweeter. The hot water bills had skyrocketed since he'd started working at the Piri Piri Palace, but after six weeks on the job, the whole family could attest to the unfailing ability of the distinctive odour of piri piri sauce to seep into every crack and crevice.

He reached the canal and began to follow the footpath running along its north side, earbuds in, volume cranked up to max. Past the modern, cube-like flats with their cramped little balconies and the brightly painted boats of various shapes and sizes bobbing gently on the water's surface. On towards the Viewforth Bridge underpass, the new-build flats giving way to craggy tenements on one side and untamed scrubland on the other, the tall cranes looming beyond the weeds auguring the arrival of yet more identikit high-rises.

He was more than halfway home when he saw it. It was just an impression – a shadow on the periphery of his vision, glimpsed so fleetingly that it might just have been an eye floater or a trick of the light. But something told him this was no illusion. Something caused him to slow, then stop altogether. Gingerly, he made his way to the side of the path, stepping into the knee-high tangle of shrubs on the bank of the canal. This part of the path was unlit, but enough light seeped through from the nearby streets for him to make out the shape floating among the weeds at the water's edge.

Fishing out his phone, he silenced the dubstep that was playing and activated the torch mode. Holding the phone aloft and at arm's length, he leant forward towards the water's edge, trying to get a better look at whatever it was that had caught his eye. At first, he thought it was a large bag or sack of some description, left there by some clatty bastard who'd decided to make the city's waterways his own personal dumping ground. But once again, something gave him pause. He leaned forward further still, stretching as far as he dared lest he lose his balance and fall in himself. For an instant, the glare of his phone's torch illuminated the shape in full, giving him a brief but crystal clear view of it.

With a shriek of fright, he recoiled, lost his footing and went tumbling backwards, landing hard on his backside. Oblivious to the pain, he scrambled backwards up the bank, hands and feet scrabbling madly at the mud underneath him. He kept reversing till he collided with the wall on the northern side of the path, bringing him to an abrupt and decisive halt. He remained rooted there, a crumpled, panting heap, staring wide-eyed at the tangled undergrowth in front of him, which now mercifully shielded him from the sight that had caused him to react with such horror.

That was no sack of rubbish – or, at least, it was unlike any sack of rubbish he'd ever seen. This particular sack had arms, and legs, and a head, floating face-down in the gently lapping water.

31

The squat, anonymous brick building has a distinctly bunker-like quality, like the last outpost on the edge of an embattled frontier. Except we aren't in enemy territory – we're deep in the heart of Edinburgh city centre, just off Cowgate. Claire and I sit side by side in the back of the police car as it winds its way slowly up a narrow, cobblestoned slope flanked on either side by high brick walls. A wire fence surrounds the building, with an inset gate leading to a flight of stone steps, at the foot of which lies the unassuming-looking entrance – a small gatehouse with two glass-fronted doors. A gangly young man in grey scrubs stands waiting for us. As he greets us with a wave and a nervous half-smile, I can't help thinking he looks like a teenager on work experience – far too young to be doing this.

The police officer in the passenger seat gets out and opens the door for us. We slide out meekly and follow the man in scrubs into the building, the two officers bringing up the rear. He leads us down a narrow, cornflower-yellow-panelled corridor decorated with tasteful framed paintings of landscapes and 'no smoking' signs. A random bouquet of flowers perched on a stand is the only thing I've seen since crossing the threshold that looks vaguely alive. We come to a halt outside a door with a sign labelled 'VIEWING ROOM' and a tall, narrow window just above the door handle. I try to look through it, but the room beyond it is in darkness.

They explained it all to me on the way here. The body was found in the early hours of the morning by a kid walking along the canal on his way home from work. Judging by the state of decomposition, it had been in the water for some time – at least a week – and had probably only risen to the surface very recently, once the build-up of putrefying gases was sufficient to cause it to become buoyant.

Putrefying gases. State of decomposition. At the thought of what awaits me behind the door, my knees begin to buckle. It's only thanks to Claire, who's had her arm looped through mine ever since we got out of the car, that I don't collapse completely.

I turn to her in a state of breathless panic. 'I . . . I don't think I can . . .'

'It's OK.' Claire's voice is firm but gentle. 'I'll do it.' She turns to the man in scrubs. 'I'm medically trained. I've seen dead bodies before. It's better if it's me.'

The mortuary technician glances briefly at the two officers. They, in turn, look at one another, conferring in silence. At length, they seem to reach a mutual agreement, and the older and – I presume – more senior of the two turns to the technician with a nod.

Claire gives my arm a brief squeeze, then gently extricates herself from me, pausing to make sure I'm not going to collapse as soon as she lets go. She and the older officer follow the technician through the door, which shuts behind them with a gentle – but no less ominous – click. I drag myself over to a nearby chair and sink into it, as much to preclude the possibility of me face-planting as to take the weight off my feet. The remaining police officer – who barely looks any older than the technician – remains standing. He glances across at me and gives a wincing, sympathetic smile, which I feel compelled to return – at least partly because I feel genuinely sorry for him having been placed in this position.

We wait, and we wait. After what seems like an eternity, the door opens and Claire emerges, accompanied by her two minders.

Instinctively, I rise to my feet. Our eyes meet, and she gives a small, almost imperceptible nod.

A long, low moan escapes from somewhere inside me. I'm not aware of making it – I just hear it reverberating in the narrow, otherwise silent corridor. It sounds inhuman, like a wild beast in its death throes. In an instant, Claire is by my side, taking hold of my arm and ushering me towards the exit.

'Come on,' she says. 'Let's get you some fresh air.'

I step out onto the cobblestones, a light drizzle stinging my cheeks, mingling with my tears. Claire, hot on my heels, draws alongside me and stands, rubbing my upper arm reassuringly.

'I'll need to make arrangements,' I say, my mind racing, focusing on the practicalities in an attempt to take some of the edge of the raw grief. 'For the funeral, I mean. And I have to contact her mum in Australia. Let her know what's happened. God, I don't think I even have a number for her.'

'I can take care of that,' says Claire. 'Just leave it all to me.'

I turn to face her. She seems blurry and indistinct, like a badly focused photograph. 'How?' I whisper beseechingly. 'How can this have happened?'

Claire gives a helpless shrug and a sigh. 'I don't suppose we'll ever know. It's just one of those awful things.'

I break away from her and pace up and down the pavement, trying to slow my pounding heart, but it's no use. If this isn't a bona fide panic attack, it's the next closest thing.

'It's all my fault,' I say, more to myself than to Claire. 'I did this.'

'*No*,' says Claire, with absolute certainty. 'Oh, love, don't say that. None of this is down to you.'

I swing round to face her. 'But it is! I treated her like shit on my heel. Everything she was going through, suffering alone . . . and she reached out to me and I turned her away. And now—'

Whatever I intend to say next is lost amid an outpouring of uncontrollable sobs. The tears are flowing unchecked now, running down my cheeks in rivulets, causing my vision to swim. I'm aware of Claire moving towards me, folding me into her arms.

'We don't know that,' she says. 'You know what sort of state she was in that night. She was as drunk as anything. We've no reason to assume she did this deliberately. It's possible she just missed her footing and fell in.'

I blink tears from my eyes, shaking my head as she continues to hold me close. To my mind, it makes little difference whether Mickie threw herself into the canal with the express intention of taking her own life or simply ended up in such a state that she lost all control of her basic motor functions and fell to her death. Either way, if I hadn't rejected her that night – if I hadn't treated her like a leper because I couldn't handle her having mental health problems – she'd almost certainly still be alive today.

'Shh,' says Claire, and I realise I must have voiced at least some of these thoughts out loud, though I had no awareness of doing so. 'Don't try to speak.'

She continues to hold me, stroking my hair and whispering reassurances into my ear. Gradually, and yet far more quickly than I would have anticipated, my sobs subside, and my breathing becomes easier. It's as if my body senses the futility of it all – knows that crying won't accomplish anything and that its energy will be better put to other uses.

'You know,' says Claire, in that slightly distant tone she always adopts whenever she's working something out in her head, 'what's happened is awful – truly awful – but perhaps there's a silver lining to all of this. We might be able to turn this to our advantage.'

I straighten up, breaking free of her grasp and staring at her, wondering if I've misheard. 'What do you mean?'

'Just this,' says Claire, in her *don't say no till you've heard everything I have to say* voice. She glances over my shoulder, then, taking me by the arm, shepherds me to the other side of the road, moving us out of earshot of a gaggle of students heading up the pavement towards the university hub up the hill.

'Odds are the police will knock this whole "body in the woods" business on the head before long,' she carries on, her voice barely above a whisper. 'But supposing they don't – supposing they continue to sniff around us, asking questions . . . Well, wouldn't it be nice to be able to give them what they're looking for on a plate?'

A feeling of cold, nauseating dread begins to creep over me. I think I know where she's going with this, though I can scarcely bring myself to believe it.

'What they're looking for?' I manage to say.

'A signed confession, perhaps?' Claire shrugs, as if this is a perfectly reasonable suggestion. 'Something in writing, admitting sole responsibility for Aidan's death? We'll need to figure out the specifics, of course – make sure the whole thing is airtight, logistically speaking – but, in principle, it could work.'

I just stare at her in horror, unable to believe what I'm hearing.

'Think how much you and I have to lose,' she continues, her eyes shining with the conviction of a zealot. 'Oh, Hazel, I know it seems distasteful, and I wouldn't suggest it under any other circumstances. But why not let at least *some* good come of Mickie's death?' She shrugs, almost carelessly. 'I mean, it's not as if she's in a position to offer a contradictory account.'

I can't believe how cavalier she sounds, just tossing it off like it's nothing. She stands there, smiling expectantly at me, as if she sees nothing remotely unreasonable about the course of action she's just proposed.

'I don't know you,' I manage to whisper.

The smile fades from Claire's lips, replaced by a look of impatience, as if she can't believe I'm being so difficult. She opens her mouth to say something, but before she gets the chance, I turn my back on her and begin to walk, moving quickly to put as much distance between us as possible. She calls after me, but I keep going. I hurry down the slope and across the road, playing chicken with the mid-morning traffic, then set off up Blackfriars Street without looking back.

32

When I've covered a quarter of a mile or so and am reasonably sure I'm not being followed, I stop and catch my breath. Over the past days and weeks, Claire has said and done many things that have surprised me – frightened me, even – but this latest example eclipses all the others. Even as a kite-flying exercise, it's utterly unconscionable. And if she's actually serious about framing Mickie for murder – Mickie, whose body is barely even cold – then I can only conclude she's not the woman I thought I knew.

I wander aimlessly for a while, stalking the alleyways and side streets of the city centre. To what end, I'm not sure – to clear my head, perhaps, or to try to numb my feelings of guilt and grief through sheer force of attrition. It's late afternoon when I finally find my way back to Leith. As I turn onto Hermitage Place, I notice Matthew's Porsche at the kerb outside our house. There are no driveways on our street, so bagging a spot for your car operates on a strictly first come, first served basis. Sometimes you end up getting a spot next to your own house, but most of the time, you have to just park wherever you can. At the time Matthew went off to London, his car was parked a couple of hundred yards further up on the other side of the road. Now, it's right at our front gate, occupying the spot recently vacated by the two police cars that greeted me the last time I returned from my travels.

As I near the house, the front door opens and Matthew emerges, a large cardboard box wedged under his chin. As he sets off down the garden path, I quicken my pace. Noticing me, he stops in his tracks. For a moment, he just stands there, as if he's unsure what to do. Then, seeming to have found his resolve, he continues towards the street with a renewed sense of purpose.

'What's going on?' I demand breathlessly, coming to a halt at the gate.

'What are you doing here?' he says. 'You weren't supposed to be here.'

I watch as he opens the back door of his Porsche and shoves the box inside. The entire back seat is packed with boxes, bags, a couple of suitcases . . . His golf clubs are lying on the rear shelf, and the monitor for his home computer occupies the front passenger seat, its cable coiled round it and knotted at the top, like a ribbon on a birthday present.

And, in an instant, I understand.

'You weren't supposed to be here,' he says again in empty self-justification, and slams the door shut. 'I thought you'd be at work. I just came back to collect my things. I . . . ' He turns to face me with a helpless shrug. 'I thought it would mean less drama.'

They say it never rains but it pours, but even so, I can't quite believe the Fates have conspired to drop this bombshell on me now of all times.

'But . . . but why?' I eventually manage to say – because it's the only thing I can think of *to* say.

Matthew gives me a look that somehow manages to mix contempt with pity. 'Oh, come on. We both know why.'

And it's true. Of course it's true. I know exactly why he's doing this – and, more to the point, I've known for a long time that it was coming. But just like the night at Port Catrin, when Matthew's drunken, tear-soaked call stopped Aidan and me in the act, he's once again brought things to a head before I'm ready, forcing me to confront the inevitable *now* instead of endlessly deferring the moment of truth.

'Look.' Matthew's expression softens somewhat. 'It's driving us both mad, living under the same roof. You know it, I know it, so why carry on denying it? Why not spend some time apart, get a bit of distance, a bit of perspective, and then . . . then maybe we'll see how the land lies.'

'But where will you live?'

And, just like clockwork, there I go, fixating on the practicalities to avoid facing up to the bigger picture.

'I've got a small flat lined up in the city centre,' Matthew says – and I can tell, from the way he lowers his eyes, that he's ashamed to be admitting this. Because it must mean he's been planning his escape for some time now, all the while concealing the fact from me. 'It's closer to the office,' he adds, as a halfhearted afterthought. 'To be honest, I've thought for a while now that I ought to have somewhere in town for those late finishes and early starts.'

'And is Charlotte going to be joining you?'

I'm not sure what spurs me to articulate the subtext out loud. After all, she's been the unspoken elephant in the room for a long time now – ever present, never acknowledged. Perhaps it's his dishonesty – his cowardly attempt to cushion the blow by presenting his change in living arrangements as partially a matter of convenience. Or perhaps it's because I realise I have nothing left to lose.

For a couple of seconds, Matthew just stares at me, seemingly lost for words. Then he scoffs and shakes his head. 'Don't be *ridiculous*,' he says – but I know, from his delayed response, and his inability to meet my eye, that I've hit the nail on the head.

I say nothing. He says nothing. He stands there, one arm resting on the hood of his car, watching me. I belatedly realise he's waiting for something. For me to plead with him to stay, perhaps – for me to make one last, desperate bid to convince him we can make this work. It occurs to me that, if I tell him about Mickie, it would probably at least result in him delaying his departure. It's there, right in front of me: an open goal, a free kick, a temporary stay of execution. But I'm not going to do that. I'm not going to use my cousin's death as a ploy to blackmail someone who self-evidently doesn't want to be with me into staying. I've done more than my fair share of awful things in the name of my own self-interest, but even I have my limits.

I lower my eyes. 'Just go,' I tell him.

I feel his gaze continuing to rest on me for a moment longer, and I sense that a part of him genuinely hoped I'd try to talk him out of this – and maybe even hoped that whatever I said to him would work.

The moment passes. 'I'll see you, Hazel,' he mutters, then drops into the car, revs the engine and pulls off.

I wait till I can no longer hear the car's engine before lifting my head. As I stand there, shoulders sagging, eyes downcast, I sense, rather than see, that I'm being watched. I turn towards the house next door, just in time to see Mrs Marchbanks' lace curtains fluttering to a standstill. I glare back at them, knowing beyond a shadow of a doubt that she's still lurking behind them, watching me through the sheer fabric, enjoying every moment of my humiliation.

The house is cold and achingly empty when I enter it. There is, I realise, a degree of irony in the fact that, for the first time in as long as I can remember, I find myself missing Matthew and wishing dearly that he was here with me. Well, not missing *him* as such – more missing any sort of a human connection.

With companionship in painfully short supply, I settle instead for company of another sort: a bottle of red and an appropriately large glass, both of which I carry through to the living room. There,

I compound my sense of despair by digging out and putting on the DVD of my wedding video. One of Matthew's mates took it upon himself to record the whole thing, flitting around the function room we'd hired for the reception and asking the guests to record messages of congratulations for the happy couple. He took the raw footage to some guy he found on Fiverr, who cut the whole thing together, interspersing monologues to the camera with B-roll footage taken throughout the day.

There's me, sandwiched between Claire and Mickie, my two chalk-and-cheese bridesmaids, my arms wrapped round their waists, all three of us beaming while Mickie – still wearing her combat boots under her dress – makes rabbit ears behind Claire's head, to her utter obliviousness. It was only three months since Port Catrin – a testament to the spur-of-the-moment nature of the whole enterprise – but already the events of that night felt like a lifetime ago ... or a distant nightmare. In retrospect, I can see that all three of us were acting slightly larger than life – but that, in itself, was hardly a crime. Was this not my big day – in theory, the happiest moment in any woman's life? It was only natural that we were all a little giddy, a little overly effusive, like caricatures of our normal selves.

There's me and Matthew sharing out first post-nuptial kiss, the humanist minister who officiated the ceremony smiling beatifically, having furnished us with plenty of well-considered words of advice on the recipe for a successful, lasting marriage – words I can't for the life of me now remember. It almost choked me, repeating my vows – especially the bit about being loyal, faithful and truthful and keeping no secrets from each other. We wrote them ourselves to give them more of a personal touch, but the night before, I was sorely tempted to score that part out, and only the knowledge that Matthew would notice and want to know why stopped me from doing so.

There's Mickie – who got over her reservations about my giving Matthew another chance once she learned there was a big, fuck-off wedding in the offing – getting off with Greg, the best man, behind the wedding cake, their tongues so far down each other's throats that they fail to notice they have an audience – and one armed with a recording device at that. Thankfully, what happened next remained on the cutting room floor: Greg's girlfriend Amy discovering them in the act, calling Mickie a filthy slag and dumping Greg on the spot. Mickie, of course, had no regrets – 'A piece of ass waiting to be tapped,' as she put it – but poor Greg was forced to make his own way home to the apartment he and Amy shared, to find all his worldly possessions littering the street.

And there's Mum, by then already in a severely weakened state but determined to soak up every last second of her daughter's big day. The camera tracks in on her as she watches the proceedings from the chair where she spent the entire evening, monarch of all she surveyed, a strained but contented smile extending from ear to ear. She might have cut a lonely figure at times, parked in a corner far from the main action, but a steady succession of friends and well-wishers stopped by at regular intervals to make sure she had everything she needed and to tell her she must be so proud – a sentiment which she was only too happy to confirm. Right now, I'd give just about anything to be able to have just one more conversation with her – to open up to her about everything that's happened and ask her what I should do. It's a pipe dream, of course, and just as well. The thought of what finding out what I did would do to her is too dreadful to even contemplate. As awful as it is to say, I suspect it's ultimately better that she's not around to see how things have turned out. Better that I can no longer be tempted to come clean to her, thus shattering her illusions as to the sort of person her daughter actually is.

* * *

For a time, everything was great. Vow flutters aside, my big day was all I could ever have hoped for. The venue was perfect, the ceremony itself went off without a hitch, and I had all my favourite people in the world gathered together in one room. And then there was the honeymoon in Sorrento – two weeks of sun, sea and copious amounts of the other 'S', during which I managed to not even think once about Port Catrin and the web of lies I'd spun. And even the return to grey, windswept Edinburgh couldn't put a damper on my spirits. I felt as if I'd been reborn, buoyed up on a wave of boundless optimism, attuned to all the little delights in life that I hadn't previously appreciated. Even the rain felt like something fresh and new, washing away everything that was old and bad like manna from heaven, making way for this fresh new chapter in my life.

All this unfolded against the backdrop of Mum's final months. I've often thought of her passing as the point when it all began to go seriously wrong – the first sign that things weren't going to be OK; that I wasn't going to get my happily ever after. A couple of months after the wedding, her health went downhill with a speed that was as dizzying as it was terrifying. I watched her declining before my eyes as she submitted to a series of experimental treatments, each one more invasive and with lower odds of success than the last, until she was little more than a hollowed-out husk – a shell of her former self. By the year's end, she was gone. Mickie – who had a non-existent relationship with her own mother but always got on like a house on fire with her 'wee Scottish mammy' – howled herself hoarse at the funeral, while I just sat in numb silence, too overwhelmed to articulate any sort of external emotional response.

It took a little longer for the cracks in my marriage to Matthew to become apparent, but, by the end of the first year, all the old irritations and contradictions I'd somehow allowed myself to believe would be solved by the simple act of making our relationship legally binding had returned with a vengeance. There were his nakedly right-wing views, which he continues to insist aren't actually right-wing, just 'common sense'; his frequent trips away, usually with a glamorous younger female colleague in tow; his lack of interest in, or understanding of, the work I did, which I repaid in kind tenfold; his flashy friends from the world of finance, with whom I couldn't even pretend to have anything in common. All things that, individually, it might have been possible to work around on the basis that all relationships involve a degree of compromise and putting up with each other's idiosyncrasies. Taken together, though, the effect was akin to death by a thousand cuts.

I've often wondered whether my pathetically low self-esteem caused me to settle for the first man who showed me even a passing interest, accepting all his flaws and foibles because I'd managed to convince myself I could never hope to do any better. Because I was grateful to him for even deigning to acknowledge I existed. To this day, I honestly don't have an answer to that.

For nearly a year after the wedding, Matthew and I tried without success for a baby. By mutual agreement, we never made any serious attempt to investigate the causes of our failure – so that neither of us could ever blame the other for being the one at 'fault'. But I've long harboured an unspoken fear that, regardless of whichever of us it is that has the wonky biology, this is my punishment for Aidan. I know, I know – it goes against all the fundamental tenets of my supposedly clear-headed, atheistic worldview, but I can't help it. We're nothing if not a tangled web of contradictions, we humans. Let me have this one.

As I sit there, drinking my wine and watching my wedding continuing to unspool, I find myself wondering – and not for the first time – whether a baby would have stopped our relationship from hitting the rocks. And there can be no denying that it well and truly *has* hit them, and that we're simply delaying the inevitable divorce proceedings, accompanied by lengthy discussions with a succession of lawyers, hashing out who gets what and how much of it, while they gleefully feather their own nests with the proceeds of their exorbitant rates. I suppose it's possible a child might have proved to be the missing vital ingredient that would have made us complete. More likely, though, it would simply have been the latest in a long line of futile attempts to fix something fundamentally broken – condemned to be caught in the crossfire of our dysfunctional relationship, made every bit as unhappy by our inability to see eye to eye as we made each other.

And therein lies the rub. When you build a house on a lie, sooner or later the foundations are bound to crumble. And bit by bit, what Mickie, Claire and I did chipped away at me and at our marriage – unnoticed at first, but growing slowly and silently from within, just like the tumour that took my mum from me, until every moment spent in each other's company was a shouting match waiting to happen and we could no longer stand to even sleep in the same bed together.

The DVD ends. The screen goes blank. I remain motionless for another minute or so, my back propped against the sofa, empty glass heavy in my hand. At length, I reach for my phone and check the screen. I have about a hundred texts and missed calls from Claire, the content of which I can well imagine without needing to open them. There are half a dozen from Fraser too, and I belatedly remember that, right about now, I should have been sitting in the conference room with him, discussing my imminent return to work. It's too late for that now – not that I give a damn anymore. Right now, I couldn't care less if I never see the place again.

I can't stay here. Leaving my glass and the bottle on the floor, I drag myself to my feet and head out into the hallway, where my coat lies abandoned on the bannister. As I pull it on, my hand instinctively slips into the pocket and I feel something inside: a dog-eared scrap of paper, its once crisp corners blunted by repeated friction. I take it out and unfold it. It's an old receipt, the ink faded and largely obscured by a phone number written on top, followed by a name: 'SHONAGH'.

Without even giving it conscious thought, I take out my phone and key in the number. The call is answered almost immediately.

'Shonagh Cranston.'

Curt, officious, no-nonsense. *Speak now or forever hold your peace.*

'It's me,' I say.

'Colette?'

I choke down a breath. 'Can you come?' Then, tearfully, 'I need you.'

33

Claire pulls into the driveway of the Bissell family home and kills the engine. For a couple of minutes, she remains seated behind the wheel, her breathing slow and deliberate as she composes herself. She can't remember a time when she was as exhausted as she is now. Exhausted, and beyond exasperated. On one level, she knows she shouldn't have expected any reaction from Hazel other than the one she got. On another, though, she desperately wishes Hazel wouldn't insist on being so infuriatingly *emotional* all the time. There are practicalities to consider as well, and it strikes Claire that this bull-headed refusal to countenance the unsayable is partly why they're in this mess in the first place.

As Claire crosses the threshold, brushing Coco away as she comes wheezing through from the kitchen to have her ears scratched, Eleanor comes pounding down the stairs, breathless and seemingly on the verge of hysteria.

'How's Auntie Hazel?' she demands. 'Is she all right?'

'Why aren't you at school?' says Claire, more focused on the incongruity of her daughter's presence in the house on a weekday afternoon than on the question.

'I told them I had a tummy bug and they sent me home,' El replies impatiently, as if it's the sort of thing she does all the time – and, for all Claire knows, perhaps it is. 'Is Auntie Hazel OK?'

'She's coping about as well as you'd expect,' Claire says, choosing her words for the degree of interpretation they invite, before turning towards the stairs.

'Did she leave a note?'

El's voice stops Claire in her tracks. She turns to face her. 'Who?'

'Mickie. That's what people do when they . . . y'know . . . isn't it?'

Claire hesitates. She was relatively circumspect when she texted both El and Rob to tell them what had happened, saying only that Mickie had been found in the canal following 'a tragic accident'. That her daughter's mind has already gone straight to the possibility of suicide touches her somewhere deep and intimate.

'I'm not sure,' she says – aware, even as she speaks, that she's deliberately hedging her bets, leaving the door open in case Hazel can be made to see sense.

She begins to climb the stairs, hoping to leave it at that – at least till she's had a little time to herself to set her thoughts in order. No such luck. Eleanor gives chase almost immediately, pounding up the steps behind her.

'But why?' she demands, her voice shrill and incessant. 'Why would she do this?'

'I've no idea, darling,' Claire says distractedly. She reaches the top of the stairs and makes for the bathroom, where she'll at least have the advantage of a locked door between herself and her daughter.

'Mum,' El insists, still hot on her heels. 'I really need to talk to you. Mum. *Mum!*'

Claire turns to face her wearily. 'I'm really sorry, sweetheart,' she says, in as patient a tone as she can muster, 'but it's going to have to wait till later.' Until she's had a shower and a change of clothes – and, more importantly, a chance to think – she knows she'll be in no fit state to field a barrage of questions from an anxious thirteen-year-old.

She sets off again, noting to her relief the lack of pursuing footsteps this time. However, as she reaches the bathroom door, El's voice pipes up once more from the far end of the corridor.

'Do you think . . . do you think it could have had anything to do with that phone call?'

Claire stops dead, her hand on the doorknob. On some level, she recognises that a connection has just been made that should not have been, though her mind can't quite connect the dots. Slowly, she turns to face El.

'What do you mean?'

'I mean,' El says, 'it's just that . . . well, since the police came and spoke to you, you've been so weird and edgy.' She's hedging, one foot curled round her other leg, unable to meet her mother's eye. 'You, Mickie, Auntie Hazel . . . there was that night when you all got together here, and when I came into the room you all clammed up like a bunch of guilty kiddos talking about sex.'

Claire's eyes narrow. 'El,' she says, advancing towards her, 'is there something you're not telling me?'

'No!' says El immediately, her voice rising to a panicked squeak. 'I mean, I just . . . ' She trails off.

'Eleanor,' says Claire, slowly and firmly, 'what are you trying to say?'

The fight seems to leave El. Her shoulders slump. Her head sinks.

'It was me,' she says in a quiet voice. 'I made the 999 call.'

For several long, uncomprehending seconds, Claire finds herself incapable of doing anything other than stare at her daughter in silent disbelief.

'*You?*' she eventually manages to splutter. 'But . . . but how . . . ? What . . . ? When did you . . . ?'

Somehow, El manages to make sense of this string of non-starters. She gives her mother a small, sad smile, the look in her eyes almost pitying.

'I didn't know,' she says softly. 'Not for sure. Not till now.'

Claire finds herself unable to speak or even form a coherent thought. She just stands and gawps, wide-eyed and tongue-tied until, eyes downcast, El begins to speak again.

'It wasn't just one thing, really. It was a whole bunch of things all adding up over time. Like the bag of muddy clothes you brought back after your trip to Port Catrin. You took it straight into the kitchen, but I saw you loading them into the washing machine. And, in the early days, you were totally fixated on the investigation. I mean, you tried to hide it from me and Dad, but I saw you when you thought I wasn't looking – scrolling through articles on your iPad, watching videos on your phone. And you were always dead funny whenever I tried to ask you what the police questioned you about. Like you'd get really short with me, like when I was little and I'd ask where babies came from and that sort of thing.'

As she speaks, Claire feels her stomach contracting; her legs growing increasingly rubbery. Now, she slowly slides down the wall till she's sitting on the floor, gazing up in a mixture of disbelief and horror as El looms over her, in a reversal of the normal mother–daughter dynamic.

'There were other things too,' El goes on. 'Things that just seemed . . . I dunno, seemed *off*. I don't remember what all of them were. But those were the main ones. And then, a couple of months back, you and me and Dad were all watching that film on the telly where the guy gets buried alive and has to claw his way out, and you said something like, "That wouldn't happen like that. A couple of blokes can't just dig a grave in the woods in five minutes flat." And then Dad asked you how you knew that and you went really quiet and told him to shush and watch the film. And that's when I remembered the bag of dirty clothes, and the articles, and all the other things, and I started to wonder.

'I wanted to be wrong,' she puts in quickly, her tone defensive – as if, even now, she regards it as a black mark against her character to have suspected her own mother. 'I wanted so *badly* to be wrong. That's why I snuck out and made the call – that night you and Dad were out to dinner with the Bickertons. Cos I thought, "They can investigate it, and when they find there's no one there, it'll mean Mum's innocent". And if there *was* a body . . . ' She trails off, uncomfortable with where this thought leads.

'I didn't *want* you to go to jail,' she says after a moment, her voice small and childlike, achingly earnest in her desperation for her mum to believe her. 'I just thought, if they found him, it'd give his sister some closure, and no one would ever need to know who made the call or who buried him in the first place.'

Claire shuts her eyes and leans the back of her head against the wall. She's had it all wrong – so dreadfully, dreadfully wrong. In her eagerness to keep the show on the road, she cast around all manner of wild accusations, blaming Mickie and Hazel for the leak, when all this time she should have been looking closer to home.

She becomes aware of a new sound. She opens her eyes and sees that El is crying. Tears stream down her face, accompanied by ugly, choking sobs. Immediately, Claire hauls herself to her feet and takes her daughter in her arms, guiding El's head to her shoulder.

'I'm so sorry, Mum,' El manages to say between sobs. 'I never thought any of this would happen. I never wanted to get you or anyone else into trouble.' She snorts back a noseful of snot. 'It's just . . . you always told me to do what's right – to tell the truth, to speak up if I saw someone doing something wrong.'

'Shh,' Claire whispers, stroking the back of El's head with her free hand. 'You've nothing to be sorry for.'

'But it's my *fault*!' El wails plaintively. 'She's dead cos of me.'

'It *isn't*,' Claire says with conviction. 'None of this is down to you. You hear me? None of it.'

El lifts her head from Claire's shoulder. She sniffs, wipes her nose on her sleeve, and gazes up at her mother with glistening eyes. 'What's going to happen now, Mum?' she whispers.

And suddenly, she's no longer the sullen, truculent teenager that Claire barely even recognises half the time. She's her little girl, wide-eyed and innocent, desperately seeking her reassurance that, against all evidence to the contrary, everything's going to be all right.

'I don't know,' says Claire quietly, and it feels like the most genuinely truthful moment she's experienced in ages.

34

I find a quiet alcove in The Coach & Horse, a dingy free house on the Royal Mile with a distinct 'old man pub' whiff about it, order myself a pint of whatever's on tap and settle in for the long haul. It's the sort of place I'd normally avoid like the plague, but it's quiet and suitably anonymous, and I also reckon it's the last place anyone would think to look for me.

As the afternoon wears on, giving way to evening, I munch my way through a couple of packets of crisps, driven more by the knowledge that I need to eat *something* than by genuine hunger, but for the most part I stick to liquids. Mercifully, the staff leave me to my own devices, other than to offer me periodic refills, which I gladly accept. The other drinkers steer clear of me too. Normally, in a place like this, I'd expect to have been propositioned at least once or twice, but the decrepit, mostly older men who make up the bulk of the pub's clientele give me a wide berth. They probably recognise a head-case when they see one, concluding that I'm likely to be more trouble than I'm worth. And they're probably right. That's two people dead now because of me – hardly the most auspicious of track records.

It's after eight when Shonagh finally arrives, sinking into the bay seat next to me, flushed and a tad breathless. For a moment, she looks as if she might be thinking about folding me into a hug, but if she is, she decides against it.

'I got here as quickly as I could,' she says, 'but you know what the trains are like. Are you OK? You sounded awful on the phone. What's happened?'

I can't speak. I find myself overwhelmed with gratitude towards her for dropping everything to be with me, without even knowing why. The fact that I can't tell her the truth – or, at least, can only give her a heavily fictionalised version of it – only renders the injustice of it all the more stark.

'Is this . . . is this about Judy?' Shonagh's eyes bore into me. 'Have you had news?'

I say nothing. I haven't the strength left to lie, let alone to begin to explain that, actually, this isn't about my twin sister who went missing when I was thirteen but my cousin who went missing a week ago and somehow make it sound halfway credible.

'Shit,' Shonagh says, drawing her own conclusions from my silence. She bites her bottom lip, shakes her head ruefully. 'I was worried something had happened. I tried messaging you after the forum and it said your account had been deleted. I figured you had your reasons, but I should've—' She stops abruptly, lifts her head to look at me once more. 'Is she . . . ?'

'She's dead.'

It comes out as a low, piteous moan, all my anguish distilled into a single exhalation of breath. I don't even think about what I'm saying – I'm beyond that – but reality and fiction have dovetailed to such an extent that somehow, within context, my words make sense.

'Christ.' Shonagh shakes her head slowly. 'That's . . . I dunno what to say. Just . . . sorry.'

I want to tell her I don't deserve her pity; that I'm a disgusting liar who, right now, is only experiencing a small fraction of what she deserves. But I can't. Instead, I manage a small smile. 'Thanks.'

'What happened?' Shonagh asks. 'Did they find . . . ' – she lowers her voice to a tactful whisper – ' . . . a body?'

'I'd rather not . . . '

'Of course,' she says quickly. 'You don't have to tell me anything if you don't want to.'

She gets it completely – or at least she thinks she does. That, in part, is why I reached out to her of all people. That and the fact I seem to have managed to burn every other bridge in my life.

At length, Shonagh stirs. 'You're empty,' she says, indicating to my glass. 'I'll get you another. Reckon we could both use a couple of stiff ones.'

I dutifully force a smile at the obvious innuendo. As Shonagh gets to her feet and heads to the bar, I can't help noting the parallels to that fateful night in Port Catrin all those years ago. It too began in a pub, with a Cranston buying me drinks. It's as if, somehow, I've come full circle.

For the next few hours, we remain in our little alcove, exchanging the odd word now and then but mostly just drinking in silence. Shonagh insists on buying every round, telling me it's her pleasure after the trouble I went to, putting her up at my place, and I have neither the strength nor the will to argue. At some point, I become aware that I'm drinking far more than is sensible; that I'm starting to feel decidedly woozy, my surroundings slipping in and out of focus and a warm, not altogether unpleasant sleepiness creeping over me. And yet still Shonagh continues to buy me drink after drink, as far as I can tell matching my intake shot for shot. I can only assume I must not appear as drunk as I actually feel. I've always thought of myself as a lightweight when it comes to alcohol, but I'm starting to wonder if I actually put on a better show of being able to hold my liquor than I previously realised. Either that, or Shonagh is willingly plying me with booze despite knowing I'm past the point of being able to see straight – and I somehow can't picture her doing anything so irresponsible.

I become aware of a change in the atmosphere around me; feel the bite of cold wind on my cheek and realise we're outside. And then we're in the back of a taxi, Shonagh's telling the driver my address and we're setting off, purring our way through neon-lit streets as we head north towards Leith. My head feels unconscionably heavy, so I lay it on her shoulder. She doesn't shift or push me away but simply allows it to rest there, as if she hasn't noticed – for which I feel almost pathetically grateful.

And then I feel the cold air again, and Shonagh's helping me up the steps and leaning me against the door and asking me for my key. I presume I manage to find it, or else she does, for the next thing I know, we're inside, and she's easing me into the recliner in the living room, and she's leaning over me, her brows pursed together in concern as she asks me if I'm all right. In the dim half-light, the only illumination coming from a small table-lamp, she looks more like her brother than ever, with her deep brown eyes and dark hair and strong, almost masculine jawline. On a sudden impulse, I lift my head and kiss her on the lips.

She doesn't exactly try to stop me, but she doesn't reciprocate either. She just remains there, unmoving, almost marblesque, until I've tasted my fill and sink back into the recliner, exhausted from the effort. Shonagh raises an eyebrow and gives a small, slightly incredulous smile.

'Oooo-*kay*, not quite what I was expecting. I don't think that's a very good idea, do you?'

It seems to me I've made so many bad choices of late that I'm not even sure what a good one looks like anymore. Before I can put this rather confused sentiment into words, however, Shonagh speaks again, her tone unexpectedly gentle.

'Look, it's not that I'm not flattered. I just don't think it's wise under the circumstances. Besides, I don't swing that way.'

I don't either, but for some reason, right now that seems beside the point. Perhaps it's because she reminds me so much of Aidan, or perhaps it's because I'm so lonely, so ground down by grief and fear and exhaustion, that I'd have responded in this manner to any act of kindness and compassion, regardless of who it came from.

'I think we should probably get you to bed,' says Shonagh, who seems to have belatedly realised just how out of it I actually am. 'That's not supposed to be a come-on, by the way.'

I allow her to help me up the stairs, directing her to the main bedroom, where she draws back the duvet and lays me out on the bed, then proceeds to remove my shoes and trousers. As she slides a pillow under my head, the golden locket round my neck catches her eye.

'Better let me take this,' she says. 'Last thing we want is you choking in the night.'

I want to tell her to leave it – that it's the last little piece of Mickie I have left to cling onto – but it requires too much effort, so I say and do nothing other than to dutifully raise my head so she can unfasten the chain. The last thing I remember seeing before my eyelids close is Shonagh standing in the doorway, leaning against the frame and watching me, the light from the landing behind her rendering her in silhouette.

I awaken with a sudden jolt, my entire body tensed and alert. At first, I'm not sure where I am or how I got here. Then, the familiar sights of my bedroom, dimly visible through the first light of dawn seeping through the curtains, come into focus and I relax. Then I hear it – the same sound that, in all likelihood, woke me. The sound of someone saying my name.

'Hazel?'

'Yes?' I say, wondering who could be speaking to me and why their voice sounds at once familiar and completely alien.

'So your name isn't Colette, then,' says the voice, and I'm suddenly aware of Shonagh standing at the foot of the bed, the light from the window falling on one side of her face while the other remains in shadow. She holds up an envelope and reads from it.

'"Hazel Ellis, 15 Hermitage Place, Leith".'

For a moment, she's silent, unmoving. Then, without warning, she scrunches the envelope into a ball and hurls it at me with such ferocity that my hands instinctually shoot up to protect my face. The projectile glances harmlessly off my knee and I lower my hands and gaze up at Shonagh. She hasn't moved from the foot of the bed. There's a cold, steely resolve in her eyes that chills me to the marrow. Slowly, she raises her hand – the one from the side that, until now, has been shrouded in darkness – and holds up something small and round on a rough string chain.

'What are you doing with this?' she says, her voice as harsh as knives.

I don't speak – I physically can't. And in any event, I know there's nothing I can say that will satisfy her. My mind is racing, the events of the previous night coming back to me in a deluge of fragmented snapshots. I remember her helping me to bed, partially undressing me, removing the locket from around my neck – the locket containing the key to the keepsake box where Aidan's pendant has lain hidden for the last three and a half years.

'He's dead, isn't he?'

I lick dry lips, still struggling to process what's happening. I know I'm wide awake, but it still feels like I'm trapped inside a dream, and I still can't get my tongue to do my bidding. I just nod.

'You killed him.'

It's a statement. Not a question.

'No,' I say, finding my voice at least. 'I mean, I didn't— It was . . . it was an accident,' I finish feebly.

Shonagh seems uninterested in the distinction. Her expression doesn't bear a flicker of any emotion beyond cold, calculated rage.

'And what did you do with him?'

'I . . . we . . . we buried him.'

'Where?'

'In the woods.'

Her eyes suddenly flare. 'Don't act fuckin' glaikit!' she roars. '*Which* woods? Where?'

I hesitate – only for long enough to draw breath, but for Shonagh, it's one procrastination too many. She strides towards me, bringing her face so close to mine I can see the bloodshot redness in her eyes and the glint of her small, sharp teeth.

'You answer me now,' she snarls, 'or so help me God, I'll beat the truth out of you.'

She means it – of that I'm in absolutely no doubt. I also know that, right now, there's no impediment, moral or physical, to her doing to me whatever she sees fit. She's both far stronger and far more ruthless than I could ever hope to be. There's no way she wouldn't take me in a straight fight.

I draw myself up against the wall behind me, trying to make myself as small as possible. 'I don't know what the woods are called,' I say, doing my best to force my teeth to stop chattering. 'All I know is they're about thirty miles west of Port Catrin.'

'Can you find the spot again?'

'I'm not sure. Maybe.'

'You'd better start being a whole lot surer,' Shonagh snaps, 'because believe me, I am *not* in a patient frame of mind.'

'Yes,' I say, though I know the panic coursing through me is hardly conducive to anything approaching certainty. 'I can find it.'

Shonagh grabs my trousers from the floor and hurls them at me.

'Then fucking move.'

35

The street is silent and deserted as we step out into the grey dawn. Shonagh brings up the rear, frogmarching me down the steps to my car and indicating for me to get into the driver's seat before heading round to the passenger side herself.

'We need to go to Port Catrin first,' I say as she shuts the door. 'Otherwise I won't be able to retrace the route we took.'

Shonagh shoots me a look that verges on contemptuous, then gives a slight nod. 'Fine.'

We head north through Leith, following the same route Mickie, Claire and I took more than three years ago – except this time we drive in total silence and the roads are virtually empty. As we cross the Queensferry Bridge and continue north up the M90, I finally risk breaking the silence.

'How long have you known?'

For several seconds, Shonagh says nothing. When she finally speaks, her tone is sullen and terse, as if she resents having to explain herself.

'I didn't know anything for certain – not till I found his pendant. But I suspected from the off that you weren't all you claimed to be. After our first conversation, I went and did some digging. I couldn't turn up anything about a promising young dancer called Judy Harper who went missing in Edinburgh twenty years ago – and a case like that would have been headline news in every corner of the land. I couldn't figure you out at all. I thought perhaps you might be some sort of weirdo stalker type – I've run into those before. But there was something about you that intrigued me. Something . . . different. So I decided to play along for a while to see where things went.'

She falls silent. We drive on for a while, past Inverkeithing and the Dunfermline Crematorium. We've just passed the turn-off for Glenrothes and Kirkaldy when she stirs again.

'My turn. When did it happen?'

I glance up from the road momentarily. 'Sorry?'

She turns to look at me. She's got that raging I'll-rip-your-head-off-and-shit-down-your-neck look in her eyes again.

'You. Murdering my brother. When did it happen? Sunday?'

'No – Saturday night,' I say – aware that, in answering her question, I've effectively conceded that I *did* murder him. 'He came back to the cabin with us for drinks after the pub. Things . . . things got heavy between us. We ended up in the bedroom. There was a . . . ' Deep breath. 'There was a struggle. He fell, and . . . ' I trail off into silence.

Shonagh says nothing. I continue to drive, the low hum of the car's engine the only thing between us and total silence as we race up the smooth trunk road.

'You have to believe me,' I say, trying my best to multitask between paying attention to the road and making eye contact with her in an attempt to appeal to her better nature. 'I never meant for this to happen. It was just an awful, terrible accident. I'm so sorry.'

Shonagh's expression doesn't change. She shakes her head. Makes a contemptuous noise at the back of her throat.

'You people,' she says quietly. 'You think you can do whatever you want. You come into our communities and build your holiday homes and weekend bungalows, totally oblivious to the folk you're displacing. The roots you're ripping up. You treat the land like it's your own personal theme park – your convenient little bolthole for whenever you fancy a break from your city life – and to hell with those of us who were here before you. Who worked the land for generations. Who survived the Famine and the Clearances. And then, when you've had your fun, got your nature fix or whatever, you swan off back down south, without a second thought to the mess you've left behind. You've been doing it for centuries.'

As I listen to her low, husky voice, each syllable bristling with barely controlled loathing, I realise she's no longer talking about Aidan. At any rate, not *just* about him. She's speaking to resentments that are far older and run far deeper. Resentments born out of growing up in a part of the world where the scars of colonisation and depopulation are still riven into the landscape and the memories of its people.

She turns to look at me, eyes simmering. 'Aidan never harmed a soul in his life. All he wanted was to live his life, to give back to his community and earn a wage to support himself – just like our parents, and their parents, and their parents before them. You took all that from him.'

After that, I don't dare speak again. We make good time over the next couple of hours, the roads considerably quieter than they were the last time I made this trip. Port Catrin comes into view far sooner than I expected, the hill rising up in front of us against the peat-grey sky as the road curves around the coastline. I'm all set to continue along it, but as we approach the turn-off for the village, Shonagh stirs and points.

'Take a left. We're making a pitstop.'

I do as I'm told, continuing to follow her directions as we head into Port Catrin and make our way partway up the hill before turning off onto a side street with a handful of houses – more of a scraggly, desultory dirt track than a proper road. She instructs me to pull over outside a low, dilapidated cottage with a small wooden hut at the bottom of its overgrown garden. Somehow, I just know this is Aidan's former abode.

'Out,' says Shonagh.

We both get out of the car and pick our way through the weeds and brambles to the hut. Shonagh tries the door. It's locked, but it takes her only a single sharp shove to smash the ancient latch. As she roots around inside, I briefly contemplate making a run for it, but before I have time to give thought to where I'd even go, she's back, clutching a rusty shovel.

'Move,' she says.

We set off again, returning to the main road as it continues north past Port Catrin before curving west, heading inland. To my surprise, I have little difficulty recalling the route. I seem to have taken in a whole lot more of the previous journey than I realised at the time, to the extent that every landmark along the way is etched into my memory, from the bungalow with the gargoyle statue in its garden to the final turn-off onto the narrow dirt track leading into the woods.

I bring the car to a halt at the same spot where Claire parked her Land Rover all those years ago. Shonagh motions for me to get out, then leans into the back seat to retrieve the shovel. As she turns her back to me, I grab the keys on impulse and slide them into my coat pocket. Shonagh doesn't notice.

We set off into the woods on foot, me walking in front like a condemned prisoner while Shonagh brings up the rear, shovel slung over her shoulder. I wonder what she plans to do with me once we've located Aidan's body – that is, assuming she even knows. I get the sense she hasn't thought about much beyond simply finding him.

On and on I tramp, and with each fresh step, my anxiety deepens. The process of osmosis through which I seemed to absorb the car journey has failed me, and I have no idea how to find the clearing where we buried Aidan. The forest looks so different in the daylight. Perhaps, if we'd come under cover of dark...

Behind me, I sense Shonagh's growing impatience. She's surely noticed by now that we haven't been heading in anything resembling an actual direction for some time. The tension builds and builds, until finally she breaks the silence.

'Where the fuck is it?'

Fuck. Whenever she says that word, she instils it with a harshness that I experience on an almost physical level. In part it's her accent, the 'uh' sound created at the back of her throat and released in a short, sharp burst, but mostly it's the absolute venom with which she spits it out. And I know she's a hair-trigger away from doing me some very serious harm if I don't come up with the goods pronto.

'Not far now,' I assure her, managing to sound a good deal more confident than I actually feel.

I press on with renewed urgency, though I avoid quickening my pace, lest I give her the impression that I'm trying to get away from her. I keep moving, breathing in short, sharp gasps – a combination of the exertion of trudging over the rugged terrain in shoes that really weren't made for it and the anxiety ballooning inside me. And then I see it: the mourning oak tree, if anything even more stooped and wearied than when we buried Aidan under its shadows.

'We're here,' I say, with a sense of relief that I know is misplaced.

I press on into the clearing, Shonagh hot on my heels. It takes me a moment to orient myself, but, based on the position of the oak tree, I soon locate the spot where Claire and Mickie dug the grave. The ground, as overgrown with moss and other vegetation as the rest of the clearing, appears undisturbed, the passage of time having eradicated any trace that humans ever interfered with it.

'There,' I point. 'That's where . . . '

For a moment, Shonagh neither moves nor speaks. She simply looks where I'm pointing, her chest rising as she inhales a heavy breath. Then, abruptly, she stirs and wordlessly tosses the shovel to me. I fumble but manage to catch it. As I stand there, clutching it with both hands, she utters a single word.

'Dig.'

All through my life, I've done everything I can to avoid unnecessary physical exertion. I'm not built for it. The work I'm now forced to do would have been challenging for someone in peak physical fitness, but for me – a skinny, certifiably underweight office worker with zero muscle tone – it's the most gruelling activity I've ever undertaken. Shonagh shows me neither sympathy nor willingness to help. She just stands there, feet parted, arms folded, watching as I toil away in the pale light of the mid-morning sun.

An hour, two hours, three . . . I've no idea how much time passes as I continue to dig, teeth clenched as I try to power through both the ache in my arms and shoulders and the far more acute pain in my hands, chafed raw by the rough wood of the shovel's handle. On and on I dig, my mind having long since ceased to function in any meaningful sense. I have no room in my head for anything now beyond somehow willing my body to perform just one more thrust with the shovel. If I focus on them one at a time, treating each one as its own mini-victory, then maybe, just maybe, I can keep going . . .

And then, all of a sudden, the shovel's blade connects with something hard and solid.

Instantly, I snap back into consciousness. I'm not sure if Shonagh actually hears the sound of the metal striking whatever immovable force has halted its trajectory or if she simply senses, from the fact that I've stopped digging, that I've found something. Either way, she springs forward, shoving me roughly aside as she drops to her knees and begins to scrabble at the soil with her bare hands. I back off, panting, dripping with sweat and caked in mud, as she digs on and on, blind to all else. Once again, the thought of escape enters my mind, and it occurs to me that now might well be the optimal time to slip away.

But just then, Shonagh's scrabbling comes to a halt. For a moment, she kneels there, a look of confusion frozen on her pallid features. Then she resumes digging with a renewed frenzy. Sensing that whatever Shonagh has discovered is unlikely to be good news for me, I begin to shuffle backwards – not far enough to attract her attention, but enough to remove myself from arm's reach.

Shonagh stops again. She lifts her head, staring up at me with a look I can't read.

'What the fuck is this?' she whispers.

Shaking with trepidation, I move towards her and peer over the edge into the freshly excavated grave. For a moment, my brain can't make sense of what it's seeing. Then, in a flash, it clicks together. There below me, still partially submerged beneath the soil, is the skeleton of some poor woodland creature – a fox, I think, though I can't be one hundred percent sure. One thing's for certain: it's not Aidan.

Slowly, I turn to look at Shonagh with wide, uncomprehending eyes. She stares back at me with a simmering fury that makes every previous expression of animosity from her seem like a warm-up act.

'Is this a joke to you?' she says, her voice a strangled hiss. 'Is this some sort of game?'

'I . . . '

'Did you bring me here just to torture me, you sick, perverted little cunt?'

I open my mouth, intent on telling her I have no idea how this could have happened, but even as I draw in a breath, I realise she has no intention of listening to anything I say. With a roar of pure, animalistic rage, she lunges at me. I scramble backwards, and Shonagh, missing her footing, trips and tumbles headlong into the mound of earth from the grave we just excavated. I struggle to my feet, turn on my heel and run.

I stumble through the trees, low-hanging branches slapping at my face, heading in what I can only hope is the way we came. Behind me, I hear Shonagh, already back on her feet, crashing through the foliage towards me. I come to my car and dive into the driver's seat, scrambling to retrieve the key from my pocket and fit it into the ignition. As I turn it, Shonagh emerges from the trees in front of me, barrelling towards me, caked in mud, her lips drawn back, revealing bared teeth. I rev the engine, frantically spinning the wheel as I perform an ungainly one-eighty-degree turn, then floor the accelerator and take off up the dirt track, the car bouncing violently on the uneven ground as I wrestle frantically with the wheel to avoid colliding with the trees.

I reach the road and slam on the brakes. I make a hard right-hand turn and roar off up the tarmac, foot on the accelerator pedal. I risk a glance in the rear-view mirror just as Shonagh comes crashing out of the woods. She turns, sees the car and takes off after it, pelting up the road with a speed and determination that would put an Olympic sprinter to shame. But she's not fast enough. I keep one eye on the mirror as I press down on the accelerator, the needle on the speedometer steadily climbing – fifty, sixty, seventy . . .

Eventually, Shonagh disappears from view, outpaced and outmatched as I continue to roar towards the horizon.

36

I drive in a blind panic, with zero sense of where I'm actually going. I just keep hoping that, if I take any road that seems to lead in a vaguely southerly direction, I'll eventually find my way home. I force myself to keep to the speed limit, balancing the need to put as much distance as possible between myself and Shonagh with the equally pressing need to avoid getting stopped by the first police car I encounter.

As I drive, my mind keeps flashing back to the sight of that forlorn little skeleton in the grave. I can't even begin to understand what it means. All I know is I'll never be able to forget the look of primordial hatred in Shonagh's eyes. It's as if I dangled the promise of closure in front of her, only to yank it away at the last minute. Somehow, the fact that for once – just for once – I didn't set out to deceive her only makes the cruelty of it feel all the more savage.

I've been driving for twenty minutes or so when a bleep sounds in my pocket as my phone's signal – which must have cut out at some point prior to our approach to Port Catrin – is restored. I pull it out and call up the Sat Nav app, which finally allows me to work out where I am and in which direction I need to head to get back to Edinburgh. As my breathing gradually slows to something approaching a normal rhythm, something occurs to me. Shonagh no doubt has her own phone with her, but, given how far the blackspot extends, it's likely to be as much use to her as my own was until moments ago. Which means her only hope of raising the alarm is going to be to make her way to the nearest village on foot – which is almost certainly several miles away – or hope to strike lucky and flag down one of the few cars on the road in that neck of the woods. If *I'm* lucky, I might have a few hours. Equally well, though, I might have considerably less. However much time I have, I've got to make the most of it.

As I race along the Old Military Road towards the Bridge of Dye, I fumble with my phone, selecting Claire's name from the contacts list.

She picks up after a couple of rings.

'Hazel? Where have you been? I've been worried sick. I've been trying—'

'I'm in trouble,' I say, cutting her off. 'I need your help.'

A beat, then:

'Where are you?'

Brisk. No-nonsense. She's clearly picked up on the urgency in my voice.

'I can't explain right now, but I'm in deep shit. *Seriously* deep shit. I'm on my way back to Edinburgh.'

'All right,' says Claire after a moment, during which I expect she's managed to imagine every possibility except the one that actually transpired. 'I'm at work right now. Come to the surgery. We'll—'

'No, not there!' My voice rings shrill in my desperation. 'It has to be somewhere quiet. Somewhere out of the way.'

Another pause.

'OK,' says Claire, her tone guarded. 'What about the Kyoto Friendship Garden? That's out of the way, and there shouldn't be too many people at this time on a—'

'I'll see you there,' I say, and end the call before she can get out another word.

* * *

The Kyoto Friendship Garden, in the rear grounds of Laurieston Castle on the north-western outskirts of Edinburgh, was a favourite haunt of ours during our student days. On sunny days we'd often head up there if we both had a free afternoon and spend a few hours wandering around the traditional Japanese rock garden and lounging on the grass on the banks of the koi pond, pouring over our respective revision notes.

Today, though, the sky is overcast and the sun conspicuous by its absence. I arrive a little after one-thirty and head for the Doric column in the centre of the garden, brushing self-consciously at the mud stains on my coat. Claire is waiting for me in the pillar's shadow, her back to me. Hearing my approach, she turns, her features taut.

'What's going on?' she demands, as I draw to a halt facing her. 'What's happened to you? Where have you been?'

She grows increasingly horrified as I recount the events of the last few hours, along with the all-important context of my illicit correspondence with Shonagh. She shakes her head, her expression somewhere between disbelief and dismay. I deliberately keep talking, scarcely drawing breath in my effort to avoid giving her a chance to say anything. When I finally get to the bit about digging up Aidan's grave and finding his body gone, the colour drains from her face almost entirely.

'Why?' I say, posing the question as much to the empty garden as to Claire. 'Who would *do* something like that?'

Claire says nothing. It takes me a moment to notice that she's avoiding meeting my gaze. My own eyes narrow.

'Claire?'

'It's better if you don't know,' she says quietly.

I realise this revelation hasn't come as a surprise to her.

'What?' I demand. 'What aren't you telling me?'

Claire's silence continues for another agonising moment. Then, at length, her shoulders sag, a great sigh escaping from her lungs.

'Right from the beginning,' she says, in a voice so low it's almost a murmur, 'my single greatest fear was that one of us would be so overwhelmed by guilt that they'd feel the need to tell someone what we did.' She raises her head, forcing herself to finally meet my eye. 'And I always knew . . . ' – she corrects herself – ' . . . *we* always knew – Mickie and I, that is – that if anyone was going to break, you were the most likely candidate.'

To see yourself as others see you . . . Given everything else that's happened, it really shouldn't get to me so much, but the thought of Claire and Mickie – two people who couldn't see eye to eye on anything if their lives depended on it – discussing me behind my back and agreeing that I was a weak-willed flake, liable to betray my friends at the drop of a hat, still manages to sting.

'That afternoon,' Claire continues, 'when the two of us drove up to Dunnottar Castle, we put together a plan. We would go back that night and move the body under cover of dark. In the evening, when I made dinner, I mixed enough sleeping medication into your portion to knock out a horse. You were out like a light in twenty minutes flat. We waited until after nightfall before setting off. We went back to the grave, dug up the body and replaced it with the carcass of a dead fox Mickie found nearby. That was her idea,' she adds, in a tone that suggests she thinks she's being charitable in according Mickie posthumous credit. 'She thought, if the police ever searched the area and sniffer dogs picked up some trace of Aidan, with any luck their handlers would think it was the dead animal they'd smelt.'

'The body. Where is it now?'

I'm struggling to process what I'm hearing, struggling with the very notion of the pair of them carrying out what Claire claims they did, but it strikes me that this is the single most pertinent question to be resolved.

'We scoped out a site during our travels in the afternoon,' says

Claire, her ability to meet my eye once more taking a nosedive. 'Don't worry – there's no chance anyone will find it. Not if they search for a thousand years.'

'Claire.'

'Like I said,' she retorts tersely, 'the whole point was that you were never supposed to know. If there's no body, there's no evidence – or at least there wouldn't be any if you hadn't hung onto that damned pendant.'

'Just tell me. What difference does it make now?'

Claire sighs noisily. 'You know,' she snaps, 'everything we did, we did to protect you. That's all I've ever tried to do. And if you think, after everything we've been through, that I'm going to hand you the rope to hang yourself, you've got another thing coming.'

I once read a quote which said that we always assume people who commit acts of violence are suffering from a deficit of morality, when in reality what they actually have is an *excess* of it, at least in their own minds. Until now, I've never given them much thought, but those words now resonate with me as if they were written with this very situation in mind. Claire might not have committed any violence herself, but it amounts to the same thing: she's so convinced of her own virtuousness that she's managed to persuade herself that her actions – *our* actions – were beyond reproach. That we're the good guys and the ones who would hold us to account for our crimes are the ones at fault. And the scary thing is, I can see exactly where that mindset comes from. Don't we always see ourselves as the hero in our own story? No one ever thinks of themselves as the villain.

'What difference does it make?' I say, lowering my voice to an urgent whisper as a solitary tourist in a poncho passes us on the stone path, camera in hand. 'It's all going to come out now. It's only a matter of time before Shonagh raises the alarm, if she hasn't already. We *have* to go to the police and plead mitigating circumstances. It's our only option.'

For over a minute, Claire says nothing. She stands there, jaw tensed, wind whipping at her hair as the gears of her mind slowly turn. The tourist's footsteps recede into the distance.

'Not the *only* option,' she says eventually, speaking slowly and carefully, as if she's still mulling the matter over. 'After today, you can never go back to your normal life – that much isn't up for debate. But I'm not ready to throw in the towel yet – not after we've come this far.'

I raise my shoulders in a helpless shrug. 'I don't understand.'

'Mickie,' says Claire. 'She of all people was on to something, I think. That night, when she showed up at your door and tried to persuade you to go away with her – well, it might not have been such a bad idea after all.'

The ramifications of what she's saying hit me like a lead weight. So many times during the last three and a half years, and in the last few weeks especially, I've found myself thinking that the situation in which I've found myself is impossible – that what I'm experiencing only ever happens in books and movies. Or at the very least, doesn't happen to people like me – safe, boring Hazel Ellis with her job and mortgage. And yet here we are, actively discussing me fleeing to some far-flung corner of the globe where the law enforcement back home can't touch me.

'But . . . but what about you?' I manage to say. 'Your neck's on the chopping block as much as mine. You'd need to come too.'

The thought of her remaining behind to carry the can – once more putting her life on the line for me – makes my stomach roil. But then, try as I might, I simply can't picture her abandoning Rob and Eleanor to join me in exile.

'Don't worry about that,' Claire says.

She looks around, then, without warning, seizes my arm and begins to walk me back up the path towards the car park.

'Look,' she says, her voice an urgent whisper, 'I need to get back to work to avoid arousing suspicion. Then I'll need a few hours to make the necessary preparations. You're going to have to keep out of sight for the next few hours. We'll meet up again after nightfall.'

'Where?' I say, trying to keep up with her brisk stride. 'Here again?'

Claire comes to a halt. She chews her bottom lip. 'No,' she says, after a moment, 'I don't think so. It probably isn't wise for us to use the same place twice.' She thinks for a moment. 'The top of Arthur's Seat. We'll meet there. It's not far from the surgery, and there shouldn't be anyone there after dark.'

'Arthur's Seat,' I repeat, nodding slowly, trying to make it seem like I'm taking all this in my stride – that we're not seriously planning a clandestine meet-up under cover of dark to arrange for me to skip the country to avoid a murder charge.

'You'd better get going.' Claire's voice cuts into my thoughts. 'I'll stick around here for a bit before heading back. It's best we don't leave together.'

She's silent for a moment, then reaches out and gives my arm a squeeze, her eyes boring into mine with a frightening intensity.

'I'm going to sort this, Hazel,' she insists. 'Don't worry.'

37

As soon as she gets back to the surgery, Claire informs Amna, the receptionist, that she is under no circumstances to be disturbed for the next hour, then locks herself in her office with the slider on the door set to 'DO NOT DISTURB'. Inside, she buries her face in her chair cushion and lets out a roar of desperation that comes from some deep, primal place and lasts for well over a minute.

Once she's finished screaming, she paces; she sits, head in her hands; she claws at her hair, coming away with great long strands of it trapped between her fingers. The cold tendrils of fear course through her veins – a deep, suffocating terror at the thought that this whole house of cards is about to come crashing down around her. Equally potent, however, is the burning fury that consumes her. She rages against everyone and everything – mankind, God, the universe. Most of all, though, she rages against Hazel. Hazel, who, after everything she's done for her, has conspired to completely fuck her over.

From the moment she first laid eyes on her that night at the freshers' party at the Lounge Bar, she knew Hazel was someone in desperate need of saving from herself. Indeed, if Claire hadn't come along when she did, chances are Hazel would still be exactly the same person she'd spotted standing alone in the corner, clutching her drink and wearing an expression akin to that of a child separated from her parents at the supermarket: lost, alone, on the verge of crumbling into a pile of dust. No one else would have taken her on if Claire hasn't stepped in that night; if she hadn't resolved to offer some Christian charity to a hopeless case.

At the time, she thought she was doing the right thing. Now, though – now she's slowly coming to the conclusion that you can't help those who refuse to help themselves. For the last fifteen-odd years, she's given, given, given, asking for nothing in return – and now? Now the stupid little cow has thoughtlessly lobbed a hand grenade into both their lives and has the gall to act like she's surprised it went off. And, as a direct result, the very survival of the ordered, upstanding life Claire has spent the last three and a half decades carefully building for herself hangs in the balance – to say nothing of Mickie, lying cold in a drawer in the City Mortuary.

The night Mickie turned up on Hazel's doorstep, pissed as a newt and shouting the odds, Claire, despite her claims to the contrary, heard everything. Every last one of Mickie's wild accusations; her pathetic attempts to persuade Hazel to run away with her. She resolved then to confront her – to tell her, in no uncertain terms, to butt out of Hazel's life, for all their sakes. After leaving Hazel's house that night, she called Mickie and suggested they meet to resolve their differences once and for all. She suggested the Union Canal – neutral ground, somewhere out in the open where they could have it out without being disturbed.

It was dark when Mickie finally arrived, by which point she'd been drinking for several hours and was so wasted she could barely walk in a straight line. Right from the get-go, she refused to listen to reason. She just kept shouting the odds, accusing Claire of poisoning Hazel against her, calling her a control freak and a holier-than-thou pearl-clutcher, telling her that if anyone should fuck off out of Hazel's life, it was her. She kept getting more and more agitated, until, without warning, she swung for Claire. Claire managed to sidestep just in time, but Mickie's reflexes, blunted considerably by her alcohol intake, failed her and she ended up careering headlong into the canal. After a moment, she surfaced, splashing about and hollering every curse word under the sun.

Up until the moment Claire scrambled down the bank to the water's edge, she genuinely had intended to reach out and pull Mickie to safety. But as she gazed down at the spiky-haired little goblin, scowling up at her with heartfelt loathing in her eyes, something else took over. Something instinctual, primal. Before she knew it, she was pushing down with both hands, holding Mickie's head under the water, bearing down on her with all her strength. Mickie fought like a mad thing, of course. She thrashed and she squirmed. Once or twice, she managed to force her head above the surface long enough to gulp down a lungful of air, but Claire kept pushing and pushing until, eventually, Mickie stopped struggling and sank like a stone. Within moments, the water was still and peaceful once again, as if it had never happened. As if Mickie was never there.

After that, it was simply a case of waiting. She knew that multiple factors could affect the timeframe, including the weight of the body and the temperature of the water, but that, unless prevented by some sort of physical obstruction, all victims of drowning rise to the surface eventually. In Mickie's case, it took a little longer than she'd anticipated, but the inevitable duly happened, and, to coin a famous phrase, things would never be the same again. At least she was able to spare Hazel the trauma of having to identify the body, bloated and discoloured, parts of the face eaten away by the fishes. Even then, she was still putting her friend's comfort ahead of her own.

Claire rubs her eyes and lets out a heavy sigh. If she could name a single, overriding emotion to describe how she currently feels, it would be *tired*. Tired of being the one who has to do everything – the one who has to hold it together, to put out the fires started by other people. Why should it always be her role to be the responsible one; to rescue others from their own mistakes? And it's not as if she ever gets a word of thanks for it – from Hazel or from anyone else. Even her own daughter has got in on the act of late with her idiotic call to the police. Just for once, she'd like to be the irresponsible one. The one who goes around spreading her legs for every man who looks her way. Who leaves wet towels and dirty undies on the bathroom floor for someone else to pick up. Who can kill a man through sheer carelessness, then sit back and watch as her friends move heaven and earth to save her from the consequences of her own actions.

But of course, she knows she can't. This is her lot in life; her cross to bear. And now, if she intends to cling onto even a vestige of the life she's built for herself, she's going to have to do something that, just a few short hours ago, would have been virtually unthinkable. The plan began to take shape in her mind in the Friendship Garden, though in truth the foundations for it had been laid years ago. That Saturday night at the cabin in Port Catrin, even as she and Mickie were discussing how best to help Hazel, her mind was already turning, secretly plotting her own escape route – to be deployed only under the direst of circumstances. Well, those circumstances are well and truly upon her now.

She settles herself at her desk. Composes herself. Picks up the phone and calls reception.

'Amna,' she says, 'I'm feeling a might poorly. I'm going to have to knock off early. What? No, I don't think it's anything serious, but if I *am* coming down with something, I'd rather not pass it on to the patients. Reschedule the rest of my consultations this afternoon, will you? You're a star. Thanks.'

She grabs her coat and heads for home. It's still only early afternoon, so Rob will be at work and El will be at school; Claire put her foot down this morning and made her go, to keep up appearances.

She pulls up outside the house just before quarter to three. Before heading inside, she makes a brief detour to the garage, where she opens Rob's tool chest and selects a large, flat-bladed screwdriver. She enters the house, pausing in the hallway to ruffle Coco's ears before heading up to the first-floor landing and lowering the hatch to the attic. With the screwdriver in one hand and her phone in the other, torch activated to light the way, she climbs the steps, then shuffles on her hands and knees through the crawlspace until she finds the spot she's looking for. There, she uses the blade of the screwdriver to jimmy the loose floorboard up, then reaches into the space below and pulls out the thing she stowed there three and a half years ago, ready to be retrieved should it ever become necessary.

A photograph of Aidan, sitting on the sofa in the living room of the cabin at Port Catrin, facing the camera with a guileless smile.

The photograph she covertly slipped into her waistband in that selfsame living room the following morning, before tossing a random picture from the pile she'd confiscated from Hazel into the roaring fire.

The photograph that has always been her insurance policy.

She pockets the photo, climbs back down to the landing and closes the loft, then heads along the corridor to El's room. She takes it slowly, making sure only to open the door the bare minimum amount required for her to slip through the gap, and treading carefully across the floor lest she disturb the organised chaos that is the array of clothes, shoes, books and other odds and ends strewn across the carpet. She heads round to the nightstand on the far side of the bed, opens the drawer and carefully sifts through the various items El keeps in it – the football magazines, the old iPod and earbuds, the DVD of *Pulp Fiction* she thinks her mum doesn't know about – until she finds what she's looking for: the spare insulin pen, loaded and primed for overnight emergencies. She makes sure it's full, then pre-emptively turns the dial up to the maximum dosage, before pocketing it and making good her exit, leaving everything exactly as she found it.

She checks her watch. Just gone three o'clock. She still has hours to kill before it gets dark, but she knows she can't spend them here. Slipping out without arousing suspicions will be that much harder once the rest of the family are home. She heads downstairs, fixes herself a sandwich and eats a late lunch (or is it an early dinner?) at the kitchen table, Coco gazing up at her with doleful, expectant eyes. Then she gets out her phone and composes a text to Rob and El, telling them that, owing to a couple of appointments having seriously overrun, she's going to have to stay late at work to get through the admin that's piled up.

Then, feeling an unexpected sense of serenity, she drops her crusts into Coco's bowl, bids the great lumbering brute farewell, pulls on her coat and sets off.

38

From Laurieston Castle, I drive east along Ferry Road and then south down the B901, heading in the direction of the city centre. I'm about halfway there when it occurs to me that, if Shonagh *has* made contact with the police, there'll probably be an alert out for my licence plate, so I abandon my car in an empty side street and continue on foot. I decide it would be advisable to change my appearance while I'm at it, so I head into the first charity shop I come to, where I exchange my mud-stained coat for a clean one, and add a beanie hat and a pair of oversized sunglasses for good measure. I've walked for all of five minutes before I catch sight of my reflection in a shop window, realise I look like a pantomime spy in some World War 2 B-movie thriller and promptly ditch the glasses, though I hang onto the beanie.

I've got hours to kill before it gets dark, and, disguise or no disguise, I figure the less time I spend in the public eye the better. In the end, I head into the rundown little cinema on Collier's Lane and hole up in the back row of the single screening room, watching a matinee of Buster Keaton films with half a dozen other patrons who pay me as little heed as I pay them. I try hard to concentrate on the screen to take my mind off my plight, but it's no use. The characters' problems pale into insignificance compared to my own, and the pictures and words dissolve into meaningless noise. I doze in fits and starts, nodding off only to jolt awake a few minutes later, convinced I've just felt the firm grip of the local law enforcement on my shoulder.

As the sun sinks lower, I emerge from the cinema and make my way south towards Holyrood Park, keeping my head down and my coat buttoned up to my chin. I pass the Parliament and Holyrood Abbey, entering the park from its northern edge on Queen's Drive. From there, I follow the footpath as it winds around the contours of the hill, the setting sun casting the rugged scrubland in a warm, reddish glow. As I climb, I pass various sightseers coming downhill, heading back into town for their evening meal or home to their warm houses, their contented expressions confirming that a grand day out was had by all. A few call to me in greeting, and I force myself to nod and smile, all the while studiously staring ahead, determined not to be drawn into conversation with them.

I'm puffing and panting by the time Arthur's Seat comes into view – a rocky outcrop partially surrounded by a chain-link fence, the dirt path becoming a sturdier stone-paved affair for the final stretch. I reach the summit and, worn out from the climb, sink down onto a relatively flat, smooth piece of rock and sit gazing out at the majestic view before me. Further downhill, I see the shapes of the last few stragglers – little more than black specks now – making their way to the bottom of the hill. The various undulating peaks and troughs of the hillside stretch out before me, and beyond them, the city itself, a thousand and one lights twinkling in the distance as darkness sets in. I draw my coat tighter about myself and settle in to wait.

Time passes. How long? An hour? Two? More? I can't say; I've turned off my phone – which hasn't been charged since Sunday night, nearly forty-eight hours ago – both to conserve the tiny sliver of battery life that remains and in case the police are able to use it to trace my location. Still Claire doesn't show. The park must surely be empty by now, though it's so dark it's impossible to say. The whole place could be crawling with fellow travellers for all I know, each waiting to make a secret rendezvous of their own. The air has turned distinctly chilly, with not even a light breeze to rustle the heather. I blow on my hands and rub them together, then tuck them into my sweaty pits, which I reckon constitute the warmest area of my body right now.

My thoughts turn to what lies ahead. In just a few short hours, I'll have left behind everything I ever knew: my home, my job, my friends, the city where I've spent my whole life. I'll be fleeing with little more than the clothes on my back to some undetermined destination where I'll have to start again from scratch. Where will I stay? What will I do for work? What language will they speak there? Will I even be able to make myself understood? Is it really possible for Claire to have squared all these circles for me in the space of just a few short hours?

Where *is* Claire? My mind is working overtime, imagining all the reasons why she could have been delayed. Perhaps she wasn't able to slip out of the house without Rob and Eleanor noticing. Or could the police have caught up with her? Is she currently sitting in a cell somewhere, being sweated in an effort to force her to divulge my whereabouts? Or has she simply concluded that I'm more trouble than I'm worth and abandoned me to my own devices? I could hardly blame her. I still can't quite believe everything she's done for me, never once asking for anything in return.

I'm on the verge of turning on my phone and using some of its precious juice to check to see if she's sent me any sort of message when I hear a noise behind me: the sound of rocks skittering across stone, dislodged by careless feet stumbling in the dark.

I swing around, my heart pounding with fear and adrenaline. 'Who's there?' I call. 'Claire?'

An agonisingly long silence, then:

'It's me.'

A moment later, Claire draws alongside me, only just visible in the light of the pale half-moon. She doesn't turn to look at me so much as cast a sidelong glance in my direction, as if she's trying not to let on that she's noticed me. Then, gingerly, she lowers herself down into a sitting position next to me. For a brief while, we neither speak nor directly acknowledge each other, sitting together in something approaching companionable silence. And yet, for reasons I can't quite quantify, something seems *off* about her, as if the person who's come here to meet me is an impressive but imperfect facsimile of the real Claire.

'I thought you'd be here sooner,' I say, breaking the silence before it becomes unbearable.

'Sorry about that,' she says. 'It's been crazy. I had a nightmare getting away.'

She *sounds* like Claire, and yet once again I feel like I've detected something I can't put my finger on – like a performance of a favourite song that's played perfectly but for that one note that's ever so slightly off-key.

She exhales heavily and shakes her head with a dry laugh. 'We're quite the pair, aren't we, you and I? Who would have thought, when we first met all those years ago, that it would end with us sitting here, facing this quandary?'

'Yeah,' is all I can say, partly because I can't think of anything more profound and partly because something about her demeanour, her tone of voice, her entire *vibe*, continues to unsettle me in some undefinable way.

'I wish there could have been another way,' Claire says. 'I wish it hadn't come to this.' A philosophical shrug. 'But there's no use crying over spilt milk. We just have to play the cards that are dealt us.'

As perverse as it is, it occurs to me that Claire and Shonagh would probably get on like gangbusters if they met. In so many respects, their outlook on the world is exactly the same. But then, that's been Claire's philosophy for as long as I've known her: practical, level-headed, sensible, taking action to deal with situations as they arise instead of wasting time wallowing in self-pity or playing the *what if?* game. I reflect, for the umpteenth time, on how I don't deserve a friend like her; how I have no right to ask anything of her after the coach and horses I've driven through her life – to say nothing of Aidan and Mickie, and all the other people that, one way or another, I've let down.

'What happens now?' I ask.

'Now?' Claire sounds surprised by the question. 'Now we're going to do what has to be done to make this right.'

And yet still she waits. I wonder why she's prevaricating. Why doesn't she reveal her master plan – whip out the phoney passport and plane ticket she's acquired for me, or whatever else she has in mind? I remind myself that this is, in all likelihood, the last time we'll see each other, and that it's possible Claire is simply savouring this moment: two old friends who've stuck together through thick and thin, the last remaining soldiers left on the battlefield. And who am I to deny that to her? If she wants to sit in silence, delaying the moment of parting for a few minutes longer, she can do just that. I draw my knees up to my chin, hugging my legs against my chest as I gaze out at the city lights twinkling below us.

The moment is shattered by the sudden eruption of a jaunty, tinny tune from Claire's pocket, which I instantly recognise as the one that plays when Rob calls her. Instinctively, I turn towards her, and as I do so I catch sight of the thin, cylindrical object she's holding in one hand, even as she fumbles to silence her treacherous phone with the other.

'What's that?' I say, even though I already know the answer. Mum had one for years, and I saw Claire use one just like it on

Eleanor umpteen times in the years before she was old enough to do it for herself.

Claire turns towards me, the glow from her phone momentarily illuminating the panicked expression on her face before the light fades.

'It's nothing,' she says, her voice shrill and artificially light-hearted. 'Just a little something to calm your nerves. Trust me – I'm a doctor.' She gives a forced little laugh, which I don't share.

'What the fuck?' I manage to whisper.

Claire sighs, her earlier apprehension giving way to a businesslike impatience, as if I'm being unreasonably difficult. 'Look – we can either do this the easy way or the hard way. If you try to fight it, you'll only make things worse.' She gives a philosophical shrug. 'I'm told it's not unlike dropping off to sleep.'

She's barely finished speaking when, without warning, she lunges at me, the insulin pen primed and ready for action. I manage to dodge out of the way just in time, sliding across the smooth rock surface as she stumbles and drops to her knees. Instantly, she's on her feet again, swinging round to face me as I too scramble upright, staring at her in horror and disbelief.

'What are you *doing*?' I cry, even though, once again, the answer is obvious.

'It's quite simple, really,' Claire says in an offhanded tone as she paces sideways like a jungle cat encircling its prey, her eyes not leaving me for an instant. 'When the authorities discover your body, they'll also find a photograph of Aidan, taken on the night of his murder, alongside a note confessing to having killed him and enlisted Mickie to help you get rid of the evidence.'

'You're insane!' I splutter, unable to believe what I'm hearing or the matter-of-fact manner in which she's stating her intentions. 'Totally insane.'

Claire doesn't seem to hear me. 'Pinning it all on Mickie was never going to work.' She shakes her head and scoffs softly, as if I was the one who suggested it, not her. 'You need two people, minimum, to pull off a stunt like that.'

She lunges again, and once more I manage to swerve out of the way at the last possible second. This time, I manage to remain upright, though only just; my feet slide on the smooth rock and I have to stick my arms out to maintain my balance, like a skater on an ice rink.

'It's all right for you,' Claire says, once more encircling me from a few feet away. 'You've thrown away everything you had through your own sheer carelessness. I've got a husband, a daughter, a job, a home. I can't lose those things.'

She hurls herself at me once more, and this time I'm not quick enough. She manages to get hold of me, her grip vicelike as her fingers dig mercilessly into my upper arms. I struggle and squirm, desperately trying to break free, but it's hopeless. She's stronger than me, and driven by desperation and a ruthlessness I can never hope to match.

And then, before I'm even properly aware of what's happening, she's behind me, looping one arm round my neck as she raises the insulin pen in her free hand. I scrabble with both hands, trying to dislodge her arm, but it's no use. I feel the breath being crushed from my lungs, my vision starting to swim, my will to fight fading . . .

In a last, desperate effort, I bring my head up in a sudden, sharp movement, catching Claire's chin in a vicious backwards head-butt. I hear Claire grunting in pain and surprise, hear the pen skittering across the rock as it falls from her hand. Her grip on me loosens and I break free.

I flee blindly in the dark, my sense of direction completely askew, no thought in my mind other than that I must get away. Too late, I become aware of Claire pelting after me. Before I can dodge her or even turn to face her, she throws herself at me in a rugby tackle that brings us both to the ground. Her entire weight bears down on me, crushing the air from my lungs. Then, before I have time to react, she grabs my head in both hands and slams it hard against the rock.

Again she slams, and again, and again. My vision swims. I feel myself go limp, too concussed to put up any further resistance. I'm aware of her clambering off me, of her footsteps receding as she strides back the way she came, of the sounds of scraping and shuffling and muttered cursing, and I guess that she's searching in the dark for the pen. Out of the corner of a half-closed eye, I see the light of her phone illuminating the ground, and for a brief instant, I make out her silhouette as she stoops and lifts something. I think to myself, *It can't end like this*, and with a great effort I force myself to move. I can't manage anything more than an ungainly sideways roll, only to stop short as I feel the ground giving way sharply. I'm right at the precipice. Another foot or so and I'll be over the edge.

Footsteps approach as Claire heads back towards me. I don't move. I don't try to fight her. I know there's no point.

'I hate having to do this,' she says, her voice devoid of all emotion as she kneels beside me, pen in hand. 'I wish there could have been another way – but at the end of the day, family comes first.'

She unbuttons my coat and tugs up my pullover, exposing the pale flesh of my belly, and leans in, pen poised between thumb and middle finger. I feel her pinching a fold of flesh just beside my navel, followed by a sharp jab as the needle pierces the skin. Momentarily, she lifts her index finger from the plunger, ready to press down on it.

'You know,' she says, 'if it counts for anything, your cousin didn't put up half as much of a fight as you.'

Her words, and the implication behind them, hit me like a bucket of ice water. The only words that, at this stage, could possibly galvanise me into action. Summoning all my remaining willpower,

I bring up my right knee in a sudden, sharp movement. It connects with her chest, winding her and causing her to double over as the pen once more slips from her hand. At the same instant, I hurl my entire body towards her, colliding with her lower legs and knocking them from under her. She stumbles forward, hands flying out to break her fall, but they close on thin air. With a bloodcurdling scream, she goes over the cliff edge and plunges into darkness. Even in the still night air, the soft thud as her body hits the ground several feet below is barely audible.

For several long, agonising moments, I remain lying on the hard rocky ground, swallowing ragged little gasps of breath, my ears straining for sounds of life. I hear none. Eventually, I succeed in summoning the energy to roll over onto my stomach. On hands and knees, I crawl towards the precipice and peer over the edge.

Through the unyielding darkness, I can just make out the shape of Claire, lying on her back on a rocky outcrop about fifteen feet below, limbs splayed like a starfish. I lean forward as far as I dare, straining my ears for any sounds of life. Then, just when I'm on the verge of abandoning all hope, I hear a faint groan.

My heart in my throat, I scramble down the cliff-face, all the while fearing that, any second now, I'll lose my hold and find myself plunging into oblivion myself, either to join Claire on the ledge or to continue plummeting past her until some other ridge or outcrop breaks my fall. But somehow, I manage to make it down without mishap, alighting on the ledge and crawling over to Claire on all fours.

She's breathing heavily, great racking sobs as she struggles to fill her lungs with air. When I lay my hand on the ground next to her head, it feels damp, and I realise it's her blood.

'Claire,' I say uselessly.

'H . . . Hazel.' She forces the word out between ragged breaths. 'I'm . . . I'm . . . '

I squeeze her shoulder gently. 'It's OK,' I say, as if we've just had a minor tiff and she didn't just confess to murdering Mickie and try to inject me with a lethal dose of insulin. 'Don't worry about it. Listen, I'm going to go and get help. You just need to sit tight till—'

'No!' Her hand shoots out, grabbing my arm. 'No point.'

I take her hand in mine, squeezing it tightly as I feel tears beginning to well in my eyes. 'Don't say that. You're going to be fine. I'll be back before you know it and . . . ' I choke back a sob. 'I can't lose you as well.'

Claire manages a strained smile – more a grimace, really. 'You'll be fine,' she says through gritted teeth. 'You'll figure it out. Listen.' Her cold, limp hand suddenly hardens, gripping mine. 'About twenty miles north of the woods where we . . . you know . . . there's a little loch. The one with the island in the middle with the old stone tower. About half a mile out from the shore . . . ' She gives another tight smile. 'Well, you know what to do.'

It takes a moment for me to realise what she's telling me. I force it to the back of my mind. I don't need this information right now. I don't *want* it. All I want is for her to be OK – for her to scramble to her feet, a little bashed and bruised but otherwise none the worse for her fall, and for us to head down the hill together to find Mickie waiting for us at the bottom.

'Claire,' I say again, the tears flowing unchecked this time.

Claire sucks in another racking breath. 'Hey,' she manages to say, her smile faint but tender. 'It's time for you to be strong.'

I try to laugh, but it comes out as a choked sob. 'Strong like a warrior queen?'

'Exactly.' With considerable effort, she raises her arm, the tips of her fingers lightly tracing the contour of my jaw. 'Give my love to Rob and El,' she says. Then her arm falls to her side; her mouth goes slack; her eyes stare up at the night sky, unseeing.

'Claire,' I whisper. 'Claire. *Claire!*'

I pat her cheeks, I shake her by the shoulders, I call her name over and over, but she doesn't hear me. She just lies there, limp, broken, lifeless, dashed to pieces on the rocks.

39

All through the night, I remain by Claire's side. I know I should move – get myself off this treacherous precipice and onto firmer ground – but I can't bring myself to leave her on her own. So I sit, legs curled under me, Claire's limp body nestled against my thigh, gazing out at the view before me. In the distance, the three Forth Bridges – monuments to three different centuries of Scottish engineering – are illuminated in an array of colours. Closer but still far off, the city lights glitter below, as bright as ever but fewer in number now that most people have gone to their beds. I'm left with the feeling of being the only person in the entire world who's awake, fated to keep up my silent, lonely vigil.

As the night draws on and the cold light of dawn begins to break in the east, I return to the question of what I'm going to do. Flight is still an option, though I've no idea where I would go or how I'd survive. Besides, if the events of the past few weeks have taught me anything, it's that the sins of the past have a habit of catching up with you, no matter how deep you bury them or how far from them you run. Even if I travelled to the ends of the earth, left Hazel Ellis far behind me, reinvented myself completely, something tells me I'd still spend the rest of my life looking over my shoulder. And then there's the small matter of my conscience. I think about Mickie and Claire, and what our secret, of which I'm now the last surviving keeper, did to them, and what it will do to me if I have to live with it for the rest of my days.

And this, ultimately, is the rub: even if I evade justice until the day I die, I'll still have to live with the knowledge of what I did; of the lives I ruined through my actions. Regardless of whether the incident that sparked all this off was an accident, and regardless of how many of the events that followed were outwith my control, the ultimate responsibility for the trail of destruction at whose end I now sit lies with me and me alone. I did this. No one else. Me. And it's time I stopped pretending otherwise. I have it in my power to end all this – now.

I look towards the east. It's growing lighter by the minute, the sun an angry red orb rising over the Fifth of Forth. I take out my phone. For several minutes, I weigh it in my hand, contemplating all the different ways this could go. Then I switch it on, open my call history and dial the last number but one.

The person at the other end picks up after only a couple of rings.

'Yes?' says Shonagh, in a voice that could cut through stone.

'It's me,' I say.

There's no response, but I sense Shonagh's silent fury, more than likely accompanied by disbelief at my audacity in calling her.

'Please don't hang up,' I say, aware I have only a limited window in which to convince her to listen to me. 'Just hear what I have to say.'

The silence continues, though at least the line doesn't go dead.

'I want you to know,' I say, 'that I'm going to accept complete responsibility for Aidan's death. As soon as this call ends, I'm going to hand myself in to the police. I know nothing I say or do can bring him back, but there's one thing I *can* give you.'

No response, but I can tell, from her slow, steady breathing, that Shonagh is still listening, waiting to hear what comes next.

'The spot we dug up yesterday morning . . . about twenty miles north, there's a loch with an island in its centre. You'll find his body about half a mile out from the shore.' I hesitate, then add, 'It's the best I can do.'

A long, agonising silence unfolds, during which I can no longer hear Shonagh breathing. I begin to wonder if she's even still there. Then, at last, I hear it – quiet, almost imperceptible.

'Thank you.'

With a click, the line goes dead.

I remain still for a minute or two, phone resting in my hand. Then, steeling myself for the task ahead, I put it away and proceed to go through Claire's pockets, searching each one in turn until I find what I'm looking for: the photo of Aidan on the sofa. For a second or so, I gaze down at it, at his naïve, unsuspecting smile. Then I pocket it, get to my feet, and begin my descent.

By the time I reach the bottom of the hill, it's fully light – though, as I make my way through the housing area on the south-western flank of the park, the streets are still deserted, barring the occasional passing car or early-morning dog-walker.

I arrive outside the police station on St Leonard's Street and gaze up at the forbidding-looking V-shaped façade. I take a deep breath – possibly, now that it occurs to me, the last I'll ever inhale as a free woman – and head through the revolving door.

At the enquiries desk, a portly, middle-aged officer with a Captain Ahab beard is tapping away at a keyboard. He continues typing as I come to a standstill facing him. I wonder if he's even noticed me.

'Excuse me . . . '

'With you in a second,' he says, raising an index finger to forestall me but still not looking up from his keyboard.

I continue to wait, feeling oddly chastened. I wonder how he's going to respond when he realises he has a wanted felon standing in front of him. I could turn around and walk straight back out the door if I had a mind to.

Eventually, he finishes his typing and lifts his head, fixing me with a most hospitable smile. 'Yes, madam, how may I help?'

'Um . . . ' I find my throat unexpectedly thick. I cough to clear it and swallow a mouthful of saliva. 'My name is Hazel Ellis. I'd like to speak to someone in charge, please.'

'That might be a bit difficult,' he says, still smiling jovially. 'It's a bit early for anyone "in charge" to be in. Could *I*, perhaps, be of assistance?'

'If it's all the same,' I say, in as firm and unyielding a tone as I can muster, 'I'd prefer it was someone in charge.'

If he's at all put out by this slight to his authority, he doesn't let it show. Rising to his feet, he gestures towards the empty waiting area.

'Why don't you take a seat over there? As soon as someone senior comes in, I'll let them know you're here.'

As I head over and take a seat, I can't help thinking that this is all a bit anticlimactic. I'm not sure exactly what I was expecting. Immediately being surrounded by a SWAT team and ordered to lie face-down on the ground does seem a bit far-fetched. But it certainly wasn't *this*. I could, I suppose, have given him more of an explanation as to the nature of my visit – but then, I'd assumed my name would be sufficient.

I continue to sit, listening to the desk officer clacking away at his keyboard and whistling periodic snatches of some tune I half-remember. What will prison be like, I wonder? Will I have to wear a uniform, or will they let me keep my own clothes? Will I get my own room, or will I have to share it with someone else – some imposing, eight-foot-high gorilla called Svetlana with a shaved head and tattoos up the wazoo? What will happen to the house? Will one of the neighbours hold my mail for me? Do I need to tell the gas and electricity companies to shut off the supply?

I'm focusing, of course, on the trivialities – the small, practical steps that allow me to avoid thinking about just how much my life is about to change. And I feel surprisingly OK about that. My decision has been made, and, soon enough, the matter will be out of my hands. For the first time in as long as I can remember, I feel at peace. I could probably sleep right now, were it not for the fact that this plastic seat is so damned uncomfortable.

I hear footsteps approaching. A shadow falls on me. I look up to see DI Angus Moir standing over me. His expression is devoid of any judgement. In fact, it appears almost sympathetic.

'Well, then, Mrs Ellis,' he says, 'I gather you have something important to tell me.'

40

One year later

So that's my story – more or less. I gave Moir a complete account of everything that had happened, leaving nothing out, and providing the photo of Aidan as the *pièce de résistance*. Separate teams were dispatched to retrieve Claire's body from the ledge on Arthur's Seat and to locate and search the loch north of the original burial site in the woods. It didn't take them long to locate Aidan's body. I don't know what sort of a state it was in after three and a half years submerged underwater, and I don't want to, but I do know Shonagh made a positive ID.

In the end, I was charged with two counts of involuntary culpable homicide and multiple other counts of perverting the course of justice. I plead guilty to each and every charge levelled against me, which the judge told me counted in my favour when he was sentencing me. Fun fact: it's possible to be convicted of culpable homicide but serve no time for it. In the case of Claire's death, I was deemed to have acted in self-defence, while what happened to Aidan was ruled to be a tragic but unforeseen accident with no premeditation on my part. What ultimately did for me was the 'perverting the course of justice' stuff, for which, in the most severe instances, the maximum penalty is life imprisonment. In my case, however, the judge handed down a sentence of five years behind bars, of which I must serve a minimum of thirty months before I'll be considered for parole.

So, ultimately, the original act was judged less severely than the ensuing cover-up. If I'd just come clean from the off, if the three of us hadn't done what we went on to do, chances are we'd all be alive and well today, and I would have had to endure nothing worse than the ignominy of my infidelity becoming public knowledge – which, in the long run, might actually have been for the best. It would probably have spared me three years of loveless marriage, at any rate. As it is, in all likelihood I'll be out in under three years for good behaviour, at which point I'll have to figure out how I'm going to reassemble the pieces of my old life – or, perhaps more likely, start again from scratch.

In the meantime, prison's not so bad – or, at least, not as bad as you might think. Yes, the days are long and monotonous, and there are some right head-cases amongst the other inmates that you need to avoid if you know what's good for you, but I've actually found the day-to-day existence surprisingly straightforward to adjust to. It may be dull and repetitive, but I'll take that over scary and unpredictable any day of the week. Every aspect of the day is divided into manageable, regimented chunks, from our allotted shower times to the periods when we can use the yard for exercise to the three meals that are served up, like clockwork, at the same times each day. I'll say one thing for the penal system: since they locked me up, I haven't skipped a single meal.

It's probably stating the obvious, but I've come to the conclusion that I'm at my happiest when I don't have to make difficult decisions. I don't really mind being told what to do, especially if it's by someone who I feel has my best interests at heart. I suppose that's ultimately why Claire and I were so drawn to one another, and what ultimately made me such a perfect target for her. We were ideal foils for one another – me in need of someone to take me under her wing and her in need of someone to mould as she saw fit. I'm not sure how conscious a course of action it was on her part – and I prefer to believe she did it unknowingly, to begin with at any rate – but, in retrospect, I can see that she was manipulating me from the very beginning, preying on my self-doubt and lack of self-esteem, carving out a role for me as her dependent.

In all the time I've been incarcerated, Matthew has been to visit me just once, and then only to serve me with divorce papers. I gladly signed them just so I could see the back of him. If the last few years have taught me anything, it's that life's too short to waste on self-absorbed, narcissistic men for whom you're only ever a convenient fallback for when the latest piece of skirt fails to work out. I'm far more saddened by the fact that neither Rob nor Eleanor have been to see me, though I can't say I'm unduly surprised. I just hope El is coping, and that one day I'll have the opportunity to explain to her in person what happened to her mum and why I did what I did.

The visiting room is in its own wing, adjoined to the main building but separate, designed to keep the outside world at arm's length from the drudgery of daily prison life. This ethos extends to the décor of the small, bright room – the walls decorated with children's drawings, charts of food groups and animals that wouldn't look out of place in a nursery classroom. Indeed, 'classroom' is very much the defining aesthetic, down to the low, round tables and multi-coloured plastic seats. A guard stands in the corner, arms folded behind her back as she keeps an eagle eye on her charges, but otherwise a light touch is very much the name of the game when it comes to keeping law and order here. Several of the tables are already occupied by inmates and their visitors, a handful of the women perching children of varying sizes on their knees. The one furthest from the door, however, is occupied by a single individual – rigid, straight-backed, her jaw fixed, her thick eyebrows furrowed in their familiar perpetual frown. This is the table I now make for.

'All right?' Shonagh says gruffly as I sit down opposite her.

'Uh-huh,' I say, folding my legs under the chair. 'How was your journey?'

She pulls a face. 'Nightmare as usual. Railworks at Arbroath. Train got held up for ages. Couldnae run a menodge.'

I glance past her shoulder at the view through the window of the garden outside, lush yellow leaves littering the neatly cut grass. 'Still, nice day.'

She sucks in a breath and nods philosophically, as if, all things considered, that balances it out. 'Aye,' she says. 'It is that.'

It would be fair to say I was somewhat taken aback when I first received Shonagh's visitation request, a few weeks after I arrived at Cornton Vale. I was expecting her to spit in my face or hurl herself at me and tear my hair out at the roots and have to be dragged off by an army of prison guards. But instead, she sat there on the other side of the table, arms folded, and asked me how I was doing; if the screws were treating me all right; if I was getting any hassle off the other inmates. After that, we mostly sat in silence, facing one another and saying nothing, or making idle chit-chat about the weather and our respective daily routines. At the end of the hour, she left with barely a nod. I assumed I'd never see her again, but a month later, another request came in, and the month after that, yet another. It wasn't until her third or fourth visit that I realised this wasn't part of some elaborate revenge scheme she was cooking up; that her trips down from Aberdeen really didn't have any ulterior motive.

Her visits aren't frequent, but they *are* regular – a distinction I never truly appreciated until I found myself in a situation where my only contact with the outside world came in the form of these rigidly timetabled, hour-long appointments with the woman whose life I ruined. I tend to do most of the talking, asking the most extensive questions and giving the most comprehensive answers. Shonagh's not much of a conversationalist at the best of times. Her answers tend to be fairly monosyllabic, her own questions of the generic *How was your day?* variety. Mostly, she just sits and listens, arms folded, legs apart, face impassive. Sometimes, if neither of us feels like talking, we just sit, facing one another and waiting for the hour to pass.

I still don't fully understand why she came here in the first place, or why she continues to come. Not out of love for me – that much I can guarantee. At any rate, I'm not Pollyannaish enough to think she's forgiven me; that we're going to bond over our shared experience and become bestest buddies – though I do get the impression, now that the whole truth has come out, that she at least has some understanding of my reasons for doing what I did. In time, perhaps, forgiveness will come. For now, though, it's enough that we both seem to be able to understand what the other has been through and take some measure of comfort from that shared knowledge. We've never discussed Aidan: his name hasn't come up during these visits once, and yet he's always there – the perennial invisible guest at the table.

'So what's been happening?' I ask, as the silence between us grows increasingly onerous. 'Have you seen whatshisname again?'

'Aye,' she says, eyes flitting to her lap. 'We've been out for drinks a couple more times, and . . . ah, I dunno. No firm plans for anything else, but I guess we'll see where it goes.'

Occasionally, when we touch on a subject that's close to her heart, I see the inklings of a smile on her face and she softens ever so perceptibly, her sharp angles appearing a little less harsh. These moments rarely last for long, but somehow, they always manage to rejuvenate me. The thought that, after putting her life on hold for so many years, dedicating nearly every waking moment to her brother's cause, she's finally managing to find pleasure in the things life has to offer, gives me more succour than anything else I can imagine.

Shonagh lets out a heavy breath, as if she's expelling such trifling thoughts from her body. 'What about you?' she says, folding her hands in her lap, all business-like. 'How have you been filling your days?'

I tell her about the Open University courses I'm doing, and the photography class I've taken up. A woman comes into the prison once a week to teach the inmates the ins and outs of using a camera. I signed up for it on a whim – anything to make the days pass more quickly – and have found it unexpectedly therapeutic. Until now, I hadn't realised just how much I'd missed the simple act of choosing a subject, lining up my shot and clicking the shutter. I don't have access to my old Instax, obviously, but I make do with the tools at my disposal. And besides, there's something to be said for moving forward instead of remaining irrevocably beholden to the past.

My account having reached its natural conclusion, I fall silent. I've run out of questions to ask Shonagh, and she doesn't offer me a fresh prompt either. All around us, the conversation continues – a rough tapestry of different pitches and timbres, all with their own lives, their own problems and hopes and fears. I shift my weight, trying to get more comfortable on the hard plastic chair. Shonagh tucks a ringlet of hair behind her ear absentmindedly. On the wall beyond her head, the big hand of the clock continues its slow, inevitable march towards '12'. Throughout the room, I sense an upping of the ante, a renewed sense of urgency taking hold as people, increasingly aware that they have only a finite amount of time left, trip over themselves in an attempt to say everything that needs to be said before the hour is up.

Shonagh and I meet each other's eyes, and something passes between us – some inarticulable sense of shared knowledge to which only we are party. The others might feel like the clock is ticking, but the two of us are in no hurry. Anything pressing can always be said another day. I'll still be here next time she makes the journey down. And the next time. And the next time after that.

Around us, life goes on.

Acknowledgements

The origins of the novel that would ultimately become *Bury Your Secrets* go back more than a decade, when I came up with the idea for a feature film script focusing on three women who head to the north-east of Scotland for a long weekend and return having buried a man in the woods. Since then, virtually everything about it has changed beyond recognition – including the medium – and yet that core concept has remained intact throughout its journey to the page. Some ideas just beg to be written, and for me, this was very much one of them.

I've lost track of the number of people with whom I've discussed the project over the last ten years – either to get advice on an especially tricky plot dilemma or just to test out my 'elevator pitch' on fresh, unsuspecting ears. Many of them are my former colleagues from Glasgow Libraries. I also owe a debt of gratitude to Betsy Reavley – both for publishing my first novel and for providing some extremely useful feedback on an early draft of this one. More recently, my mum, who has been my first reader on every book since *Cruel Summer*, helped me resolve a number of thorny plot holes and ensured that the manuscript went off to my editor with considerably fewer typos than would have been the case if I'd been relying solely on my own tunnel vision-afflicted eyes.

Massive, massive thanks go to Suze Clarke-Morris for taking on the job of editing this book at short notice and doing an absolutely sterling job of helping me knock it into shape. I met Suze when I appeared on a crime fiction panel at Aye Write! 2019 (my first ever public event as an author), and, since then, we've gone on to become firm friends. This book's final brainstorming session took place during our first ever 'business lunch' (non-expensable, alas) at The Lion & Star in Kirkintilloch – which, thankfully, afforded us a far warmer welcome than Hazel, Claire and Mickie received from the staff and clientele of The Anchorage. We managed to conclude the trip without burying anyone in the woods either, so all in all I reckon we did pretty well.

Much thanks must also go to Tim Barber, who, as always, did a stellar job designing a cover that managed to subvert my expectations while still perfectly capturing the story's tone and subject matter, and to Kelly Lacey, for organising the blog tour. Somewhat inevitably, these are among the final components to come together on a project like this, and, as such, it isn't always possible to afford them the credit they deserve in the acknowledgements, but both are an utterly essential part of the process and key to any book's success.

Muchas gracias, too, to the Proofreading Posse: Luiz Asp, Pam Fox, Sarah Kelley, Vivien Martin, Daniel Sardella and Caroline Whitson. Your eagle eyes are much appreciated!

And finally, a huge, heartfelt thank you to everyone who continues to read my books and helps keep me in spending money. Until next time, stay safe, and watch out for tattie-bogles.

The quote Hazel references in Chapter 36 about acts of violence stemming from a surfeit rather than a deficit of morality is from Steven Pinker, *The Better Angels of Our Nature* (2011).

Printed in Great Britain
by Amazon